BOOKS BY REBECCA FORSTER

Eyewitness

Rebecca Forster

Silent C Entertainment

For My Son, Eric
Thanks for Sharing the Adventure

ACKNOWLEDEGEMENTS

Writing is not a lonely profession when you have excellent friends to cheer you on. Many thanks to Hamilton C. Burger, fabulous author of children's books, Jay Freed, fabulous keeper of the emoticons, Bruce Raterink most fabulous bookseller and buddy ever, Judy Kane fabulous eagle eye, and Jenny Jensen who is just plain fabulous. Steve, I couldn't do it without you and to my eldest son, Alex, thanks for your unshakeable faith.

Author's Note:

    This book was inspired by my trip to a remote village in Albania where my son served as a Peace Corps Volunteer. I learned about ancient Albanian laws and modern crime. I also learned about the legend of Rosafa. Rosafa, a national heroine, was predestined to be encased in a castle's stones so that the walls would stand strong. Worried about her infant son, she accepted her fate on the condition that her right breast be exposed to feed her newborn son, her right eye to see him, her right hand to caress him, and her right foot to rock his cradle. The Albanian peoples' history, resilience, sacrifice for family, and adherence to a code of honor are a reality. Their hospitality to a visitor was humbling.
Eyewitness is a story about the collision of two cultures, two sets of rules, and two visions of justice, and the battleground is Hermosa Beach.

CHAPTER I

1966

Yilli had been left to guard the border, a chore he thought to be a useless exercise. No one wanted to come into his country, which meant he was guarding against his countrymen who wanted to get out. But even if those who were running away got by him (which more than likely they would), the government had mined the perimeter. It would take an act of God (if God were allowed to exist) guiding your feet to step lightly enough so that you didn't blow yourself up. Yes, it would take quite a light step and a ridiculous will and he, Yilli, didn't think there was anything outside his country that was any better than what was inside. So, he reasoned, there was no need for him to be sitting in the cold on this very night with a gun in his hand.

That was as far as Yilli's thoughts went. He was a simple man: wanting for little, satisfied with what he had. Which was as it should be. All of these other things — politics and such — only served to make life complicated and very miserable. In his father's age and his father's before that, a man knew what was wrong and what was right because the Kunan said it was so. A man protected family above all else, not a border that no one could see.

Yilli shifted, thinking about his mother, his father's time, but mostly about his comrades who believed they had tricked him. His mother had named him Yilli and that meant star. His comrades reasoned he was the best to watch through the night, shining his celestial light on any coward who tried to breach the border. Then they laughed and went off to have some raki, and talk some, and then fall asleep sure that they had fooled Yilli into thinking he was special.

Yilli smiled. Simple he may be, stupid he was not. Star, indeed. Shine bright. Hah! They knew he was a good boy, and he knew that they made fun with him. That was fine. His comrades were all good boys, too. None of them liked to be in the army or to carry arms against their countrymen, but that was the way of the world and they took their fun when they could.

Yilli picked up a stone and tossed it just to have something to do. He heard the click and clack as it hit rock, ricocheted off more stone, and rolled away. Rocks were everywhere: mountains grew from them, the ground was pocked with them, the houses were hewn from them. He threw another stone and then tired of doing that. His back ached with his rifle slung across it, so he slipped it off, leaned it against his leg, and sighed again. He sat down on a rock, spread his legs, and let the rifle rest upon his thigh.

He, Yilli, was twenty years old, married, and he would soon have a child. He should not be sitting on a rock, afraid to walk out to pee in case he should be blown to pieces. He should not be sitting in front of a bunker made of rock, throwing rocks at rocks. He had a herd of goats to tend in his village. Or at least he thought he still had a herd of goats. Sometimes the government took your things and gave them to others who needed them more. He didn't need much, but no one needed his goats more than he did.

Yilli's mind and body shifted once more.

He wished he had a letter from his wife. That would pass the time. But he was told not to worry. The state would see that he got his letters when he deserved to get them. But how could he not worry? He loved his young wife. She was slight and pretty, and he had heard things about childbirth. It could tear a woman up and she could bleed to death. Then who would take care of the child? If the child survived, of course. And, if the little thing did survive, milk was hard to come by. Not for the generals, but for him and his family it was. If he didn't have his goats and his wife died, he would be screwed.

Yilli picked up another stone. He held it between his fingers, raised his arm, and flung it away. The sound of rock hitting rock echoed back at him. He reached for one more stone only to pause before he picked it up. Yilli raised his head and peered into the dark, looking toward the sound that had caught his attention.

Fear ran cold up his spine and froze his feet and made his fingers brittle. His big ears grew bigger. There was a scraping sound and then a cascade of displaced stones. Slowly, he sat up straighter and listened even harder. Someone or something had slipped. But how could that be? Everyone in these mountains took their first steps on stone and walked their journey to the grave on it. Yilli knew what every footfall sounded like and out there was someone stepping cautiously, nervously, hoping not to be found out. They were frightened. That was why they slipped.

Yilli raised his eyes heavenward just in case the government was wrong and there was a God. He thought to call out for his comrades, but that would only alert the enemy. That person might cut him down before his cry was heard. It was up to him, Yilli the goat herder, to protect his country and this border he could not see.

He rose, lifting his rifle as he did so. The gun was heavy in his hands. His breath was a white cloud in the freezing air. Above him the moon shined bright and still he could not see clearly. He narrowed his eyes, looking to see who or what was coming his way. He comforted himself with the thought that it might be a wandering goat, or a dog, or a sheep, but he knew that could not be right. The hour was too late and livestock would not be out. Also, animals were more sure-footed than humans. Yilli swallowed and his narrow chest shuddered with the beating of his heart.

"Who is there?" He called out, all the while wishing he were in bed with his pregnant wife, the fire still hot in the hearth, the goats bedded down for the night. "Who is there? Show yourself."

He raised his rifle. The butt rested against his shoulder. One hand was placed just as he had been shown so that his finger could squeeze the trigger and kill whoever dared approach. His other hand was on the smooth wood of the stock. He saw the world only through the rifle sight: a pinpoint of reality that showed him nothing.

The sound came again, this time from his right. He swung his weapon. There was sweat on his brow and on his body that was covered by the coarse wool of his uniform. His fingers twitched, yet there was nothing but the mountain in the little circle through which he looked.

Sure he now heard the sound coming from the left, Yilli swung the rifle that way only to snap it right again because the sound was closer there. That was when he, Yilli, began to cry. Tears seeped from his eyes and rolled down his smooth cheeks, but he was afraid to lower the rifle to wipe them away. The tears stopped as quickly as they had begun because now he saw his enemy. It was only a shadow, but this was no goat or dog. This was the shadow of a man and he was coming toward Yilli.

"Ndalimi! Do not come closer. I will shoot. Ndalimi!" Shamed that his voice trembled like a woman, he stepped back and took a deep breath.

"Ndalimi!" Yilli shouted his order again, but the man didn't stop. He didn't even hesitate. It appeared he either had not heard Yilli, or was not afraid of him or, was simply desperate to be away.

Yilli lowered the muzzle of the rifle and raised his head to see more clearly. He blinked, thinking he only knew one person so big. But it could not be Konstadin coming up the mountain, moving from boulder to boulder, sneaking from behind the rock. Still, it was someone as big as Konstadin. Yilli snapped the rifle back to firing position. If it had been Konstadin, the man would have called out to him in greeting or to let him know that he had news from home. But if it were Konstadin bringing news of Yilli's wife, how did he know to come to this place? He had told no one of his orders. Yilli became more afraid now that there were all these questions. He had also become more determined because he, Yilli, was not just a good boy, he was a man in the service of his country.

"Ndalimi!" Yilli barked, surprising himself, sounding as if he should be obeyed. His grip on his rifle was so tight his arms and fingers ached.

"Yilli."

He heard the hoarse whisper that was filled with both hope and threat, but all Yilli heard was an enemy's voice. He saw now that there were two of them. Perhaps there were more men coming, rebels ready to kill him in order to take over the government. These men could be desperate farmers wanting Yilli's rifle so that they could protect their families. One of them might hit him or stab him and the other would take the rifle. They might shoot him with his own gun.

Tears streamed down Yilli's face now. His entire body shook, not with cold but with a vision of himself bleeding to death without ever seeing his wife, or his child, or his goats.

With that thought two things happened: the giant shadow loomed up from behind a boulder and the rifle in Yilli's hands exploded. His ears rang with the crack of the retort; the flash from the muzzle seared his eyes. Near deaf as he was the scream he heard was undeniable.

From the right a smaller man ran toward the little clearing and threw himself to the ground. He landed on his knees just as the moon moved and brightened the mountain. Yilli, who had been blinded, now saw clearly. It was not a man at all who had run fast and sure over the rocks but a boy. It was Gjergy.

It was Gjergy who cried out to the man lying on the ground. The boy pulled at him and wailed and held his arms to the sky. Yilli could see the bottoms of the other man's boots and the length of his legs. He saw that man was not moving.

As if in a dream, Yilli moved forward until he was standing beside them, the smoking rifle still in his hand. It was Konstadin, Gjergy's brother, man of Yilli's clan, lying on the ground, his arms thrown out, and his eyes wide open as if in surprise. His shirt was dark with the blood that poured out of his broad chest. Then Yilli realized that this was not Kostandin at all, it was only his body. Eighteen years of age and he was dead by Yilli's hand.

"What have I done?"

He had no idea if he screamed or spoke softly. It didn't matter. What was there to say? That he was a reluctant soldier? That he didn't know how this had happened? That he was sorry to have taken a precious life? How could he make Gjergy, this boy of no more than twelve years, understand what he, Yilli, did not?

The rifle almost fell from Yilli's hands. His heart slammed against his chest as if trying to tear itself from his body and throw itself into the hole in Konstandin's. He, Yilli, wanted to make Konstandin live again, but the cold froze his legs, his arms, his very soul. His breath came short and iced in front of his eyes. His head spun. He blinked, suddenly aware that Gjergy was rising, unfolding his wiry young body. Yilli thought for a minute to comfort the boy, explain to him that this had been a tragic mistake, but Gjergy was enraged like an animal.

"Blood for blood," he screamed and lunged for Yilli.

Unencumbered by Gjergy's grief, Yilli moved just quickly enough to save himself. Gjergy missed his mark when he sprung forward and did not hit Yilli straight on. Still, Yilli fell back onto the ground with the breath knocked out of him. Instinctively he raised the rifle, grasping it in both hands, and holding it across his body to ward off the attack.

"Gjergy! It is me!" Yilli cried, but the boy was mindless with rage and would not listen.

"You murdered my brother." Gjergy yanked on the rifle, but Yilli was a man eight years older. He was strong and fear made him stronger still.

"No! No! It was an accident," Yilli cried.

Just as he did so, a bullet whizzed past them. Then another. And another. Yilli rolled away fearing his comrades would kill him and praying they did not kill Gjergy. He could not imagine bringing more sadness on the mother of those two good boys.

Gjergy bolted upright, scrambling off Yilli, running away faster than Yilli thought possible. He ran like the child he was, disappearing into the night, leaving only his words behind.

Blood for blood.

Gjergy had not listened that Yilli was only a soldier and that this was not killing in the way the Kunan meant. He had no time to remind the boy that the old ways were outlawed, and that he must forget that he had ever said such a thing. If he did not, there would be more trouble.

Suddenly, hands were on Yilli. His comrades had come running at the sound of the shot. Two of them ran after Gjergy even though they all knew they would not find him.

"Stop. He is gone." Yilli called this as those who remained pulled him to his feet.

"Who was it?" one of them asked.

"No one. A stranger," Yilli answered.

"This is Konstadin," another soldier called out.

"The one with him was a stranger." Yilli repeated this, unwilling to be responsible for a boy suffering the awful punishment that would be imposed should he be found out.

Then no one spoke as they stood looking at the body. All of them knew what this meant. It was Skender, captain of them all, who put his hand on Yilli's shoulder. It was Skender who said:

"It is a modern time. Do not worry, Yilli."

Yilli nodded. Of course, he did not believe what Skender told him any more than young Gjergy had believed him when Yilli tried to say that the killing had been an accident.

Though his comrades urged him to come to camp to rest, though all of them offered to take his watch now that this thing had happened, Yilli went back to sit on the rock where only a few minutes ago he had been thinking about his wife and his child. He put his rifle on the ground and his head in his hands.

He was a dead man.

2013

Josie slept alone the night the storm came up from Baja and crashed hard over Hermosa Beach. It was as if Neptune had surfaced, blown out his mighty breath, and wreaked godly havoc on Southern California with an all out assault of thunder, lightning, and hellacious wind. Yet, because she was curled under her duvet, because her bedroom was at the back of the house, it was no surprise that Josie wasn't the one to hear the frantic knocking on the door and the screaming that came with it.

It was Hannah who woke with a start. It was Hannah who was terrified by the darkness, the howling wind, the driving rain, and the racket made by a man pounding on the door as if he would break it down. It was Hannah who tumbled out of bed and ran for Josie, staying low in the shadows for fear that whoever was outside might see her through the bare picture window.

Hannah called out as she ran, but her shriek was braided into the sizzle of lightning and then flattened by a clap of thunder so loud it rattled the house. She threw herself into the hall. On all fours, she crawled forward, clutched the doorjamb, pulled herself into the bedroom, and felt her way in the dark until she touched Josie.

Once. . .

Twice.. . .

Five. . .

"Josie! Josie!"

Hannah kept her voice low. If she raised it she would get more than Josie's attention; she might get the attention of the man outside.

"What? Hannah. . .Don't. . ."

Ten. . .

Twelve. . .

Josie swiped at the girl's hand, annoyed in her half sleep. That changed when the wind blew one of the patio chairs into the side of the house. Josie clutched the girl's hand, rolled over, and put the other one on Hannah's shoulder.

"Sorry. Sorry. It's okay. Go back - "

"Josie, no. Get up. Someone's out there."

Hannah pulled hard. Clutch and pull and tap and shake and whisper. Hannah would have crawled in bed with Josie had she not sat up, reached over, and hit the light on the travel clock she preferred to the effervescent glow of a digital. Midnight. No one in their right mind would be out at a time like this, on a night like this. Josie released Hannah's hand and ran one of her own through her short hair.

"Hannah, you were dreaming," Josie mumbled.

Just then the small house shuddered, reverberating as it put its architectural shoulder into the huge wind that angled the drive of the rain. Beneath that, rolling in and out was something else that finally made Josie tense. Hannah pitched forward at the same time, throwing her arm over Josie's legs as her head snapped left. She looked toward the hall. Her hair flew over her face when she whipped back to look at Josie again. Her bright green eyes were splintered with fear; Josie's dark blue ones were flat with caution.

Josie put her hand on Hannah's shoulder and moved her away. She kicked off the covers and swung her long legs over the side of the bed as Hannah fell back onto her heels. Josie put her finger to her lips and nodded. She heard it now: the hammering and the unintelligible screams. Josie snatched up her cell and handed it to Hannah.

"Three minutes, then call 911."

Hannah nodded, her head bobbing with the time of her internal metronome. Josie pulled on the sweat pants she always kept at the end of the bed. She went for the drawer where she kept her father's gun, thought twice, and left the weapon where it was. This was no night for criminals. Even if it were, they wouldn't announce themselves.

Josie started for the living room just as lightning scratched out a pattern in the sky and sent shards of light slicing through the window and across the hardwood of the floors. The tumble of thunder was predictable. Josie cringed as she caught movement out of the corner of her eye. Hannah had followed her into the hall. Josie put her hand out and pushed hard at the air.

Enough. Stop.

Hannah fell back. Another lightning flash lit up her beautiful flawed body: the tattoos on the girl's shoulder, the scar running up her thigh where Fritz Rayburn had dripped hot wax on her just for the fun of it, the mottled skin on her hand where she had been burned trying to save her paintings. Coupled with the fear on her face, Hannah looked as if some cosmic artist had outlined her into the canvas of Josie's house. The man pummeled harder. Josie turned toward the sound just as his words were scooped up and tossed away before they could be understood. Behind Josie, Hannah moved. This time Josie commanded:

"Stay there, damn it!"

Instead, Hannah darted into the living room, defiant, unwilling to leave Josie alone if there were any possibility of danger. She would take Josie's back the way she had in the mountains, the way she always would. But Josie had no patience for good intentions. She twirled, put her hands on the girl's shoulder, and pushed her away.

"Hannah, I'm not kidding," she growled.

Hannah's eyes narrowed, her nostrils flared, but she fell back a step to satisfy her guardian. In measured strides, Josie crossed the living room and took the two stairs that led to the entry. She threw the porch light switch. Nothing. Another stutter of lightning gave Josie time to see Max curled up on his blanket, asleep and oblivious. Age had its blessings.

Above her, the tarp covering the place where she was installing the skylight snapped and whipped.

Behind her, Hannah paced and touched.

In front of her the man at the door continued to pound, but now Josie was close enough to understand that she was hearing cries for help. She threw the deadbolt and flung the door open. A man tumbled into her house along with the slanting rain. He was soaked to the skin, terrified to the soul, and high as a kite.

"Billy, man. . .gotta come. . ." He blabbered. He sputtered. He spit. He dripped. "Billy needs you . . .bad." He coughed. He snorted. He hacked. "At the pier. . .come. . ."

His eyes rolled, hooded, and then closed briefly. Struggling to his feet, he started to go inside but slipped on the wet floor. When he tried it again, Josie pushed him back.

"You can show me. Wait. Out there." Josie gave him one final shove, slammed the door shut, and dashed past Hannah who was running toward her room at the front of the house.

In her bedroom, Josie pulled on her running shoes and snatched up a flashlight. She was headed out again just as Hannah flew out of her bedroom, barely dressed, and struggling into a slicker. Josie raised her voice even though she and Hannah were facing each other in the entry.

"Stay put. Call Archer."

Josie elbowed past, but Hannah's terror was transferred to her like pollen. She turned to see that this was about more than the weather or even the man outside. *Left alone. Abandoned. Someone else more important.* Hannah was right about two out of three. Tonight, whatever was happening to Billy was more important than Hannah's fear of abandonment. Leaving her alone wasn't something Josie wanted, it was something she had to do.

Grabbing Hannah's shoulders, Josie peered through the dark at those green eyes and mink colored skin. She pushed back the mass of long, black, curling, kinking, luxurious hair. Josie let her hands slide down Hannah's arms, bumping along the spider web of hair thin scars that crisscrossed her forearms, grasped her wrists, and held up her hands. She looked at the phone.

"Tell Archer to get to the pier. I'll be back as soon as I can."

Josie pulled Hannah close and kissed the top of her head before ripping the door open again. The wind and rain rushed in, but the man was gone, running off to find a warm dry place. It occurred to her that he might have been hallucinating, imagining something had happened to Billy Zuni. In the next second Josie shut the door behind her. If there was any chance Billy needed her she had to go.

Tall and fast, she raced under the flash bang of the lightning and the bass beat of thunder. She didn't try to dodge the puddles because water was everywhere: pouring down on her head, stinging her face, weighing down her sweat pants, slogging in her running shoes. Her long t-shirt clung to her ripped body. She squinted against the rain, holding one hand to her brow to keep the water from her eyes. She steadied the broad beam of the huge flashlight in front of her on The Strand before veering off the pavement and onto the sand. Josie stumbled, tripped, and fell. The wet sand was like concrete and her knees jarred with the impact. She shouted out a curse though there was no one to hear. Then it didn't matter that she was alone on the beach in one mother of a storm. The scream she let out cut through the sound and the fury. Her heart stopped. She froze for an instant, and then she scrambled to her feet.

Josie sidestepped parallel to the pounding surf, trying to hold the beam of light on a spot near the pier pilings. Frantically she wiped the rain away from her eyes hoping she was mistaken and that what she thought she was seeing was an illusion. It wasn't. Under the yellow halo of light emanating from the massive fixtures on the pier Billy Zuni was caught in the raging, black ocean.

"Billy! Billy!"

Instinctively Josie went toward the water, unsure of what she was going to do once she got there. The waves were ugly. Riotous. Challenge them and they would swallow you up. If you were lucky, they might spit you out again. If you weren't. . .

She didn't want to think about that.

Knowing it was going to be tricky to get past them, Josie danced back and forth on the shore, taking her eyes off Billy for seconds at a time, searching for an opening in the surf as the waves rose and fell in a furious trilogy.

Bam! Bam! Bam!

Josie looked back toward the pier. She couldn't see Billy.

Bam! Bam! Bam!

She looked again and saw him. A swell broadsided him, throwing him out of the water like a rag doll.

"Oh God!"

Kicking off her shoes, peeling off her sweat pants, Josie buried the butt of the flashlight at an angle in the sand. She gauged the swell of the next wave.

Bam.

And the one after that.

Bam.

And after that.

Bam. Bam.

Just when she thought it was futile, Josie saw an opening. Half naked, she ran into the water. A wave crashed into her shins, spume erupting into a cloud of stinging froth that covered her to her chest and knocked her off balance. Before she could right herself the water pulled her feet out from under her. Josie fell hard on her butt. Twisting and turning, she fought against the suction of the backwash, dug her heels into the sand bed, righted herself, and put her open-palmed hands out like paddles to cut the pull of the surf.

The next wave smashed into her belly like a brick, but she was still standing. Before she lost her nerve, knowing she had no choice, Josie leaned forward, arms outstretched, and started to push off. She would have to slice through the surf and get deep, and stay submerged long enough to let the second wave roll over her. Surface too soon and she would be washed back to shore; too late and she was as good as dead. Muscles tensing, Josie was already in her arch when a strong hand grabbed her arm.

"No. No. Don't!"

Archer dragged her back to the shore, both of them buffeted by the waves, stumbling and clinging to one another just to stay ahead of the water.

"Billy's out there! Look!"

Josie whipped her head between the man who had hold of her and the boy she could no longer see. Her protests were lost in the howl of a new wind. Archer wasted no time on words she would never hear. Instead, he dug his fingers into her arms, shook her, and turned her away from the ocean.

Help was not only coming, it had arrived. Josie fell against Archer and watched the rescue vehicle bump over the sand, its red, rotating light looking eerie in the blackness. The night guard braked and simultaneously threw open the door of the truck. He left the headlights trained on the water. In the beam, the guard ran straight for the ocean, playing out the rope attached to the neon-orange can slung across his shoulder. Tossing it into the sea, it went over the waves and pulled him with it.

Josie broke away from Archer. She pulled her arms into her body, raised her hands and cupped them over her brow to keep the rain out of her eyes. Archer picked up the flashlight and her sweat pants. The pants were ruined. He tossed them aside and watched with her as the lifeguard fought to reach the boy.

Billy seemed velcroed to the pilings by the force of the water only to be torn away moments later and tossed around by an ocean that had no regard for an oh-so-breakable body. Josie cut her eyes toward the last place she had seen the lifeguard. She caught sight of him just as he went under. A second later he popped back up again. The bright orange rescue can marked his pitiful progress. Josie sidestepped, hoping to get a better view. Archer's free hand went around her shoulder to hold her steady and hold her back. She shook him off. She wouldn't do anything stupid. Archer knew she wouldn't. He was worried she would do something insane.

Suddenly the guard was thrown up high as he rode a gigantic swell. It was exactly that moment when fate intervened. A competing swell sent Billy within reach. Josie let out a yelp of relief only to swear when the man and the boy disappeared from view.

"Christ," Archer bellowed.

He held the flashlight above his head, but when Josie dashed into the surf again Archer tossed it aside and went with her. The water swirled around their feet as they craned their necks to see through the nickelodeon frames of lightning.

"There! There!"

Josie threw out her arm, pointing with her whole hand. The boy was struggling. For a minute Josie thought he was fighting to get to the guard, then she realized Billy was fighting to get away from him. She screamed more at Billy than Archer.

"What are you doing?"

Billy and the guard went under. When they surfaced the boy had given up. It seemed an eternity until they were close enough for Josie and Archer to help, but the guard was finally there, dragging a battered and bruised Billy Zuni to the shore.

Josie crumpled to the sand under Billy's dead weight. Cradling the teenager's head in her lap, she watched while the guard did a quick check of his vitals before running to call for an ambulance. Under the light Archer held, Billy's skin was blue-tinged and bloated. Suddenly his body spasmed; he coughed and wretched. Water poured out of his mouth along with whatever had been in his stomach. Josie held tight knowing all too well the pain he was in.

"It's okay. You're safe now," she said.

Billy's arms encircled her waist. He pushed his head into her belly. As the rain poured down on the world, and lightning crackled over their heads, Billy Zuni clutched Josie Bates tighter and cried:

"Mom."

Stunned, Josie looked up just as lightning illuminated the beach. She saw Archer's grim face and then she saw Hannah standing in the distance. Unable to remain alone in the house or stand by while Billy was in danger, Hannah had followed Josie. But the girl's eyes weren't on Billy Zuni, and she had not heard him cry for his mother. Hannah was looking toward The Strand, peering into the dark, not seeing anything really, but only feeling that there were eyes upon them all.

CHAPTER 2

1968

Yilli walked behind his goats, his head down, his eyes on the road beneath his feet. He had not wanted to come out that day, even to tend to the animals, but his wife said he must. He did not remember his wife telling him what he must and must not do when they were first married; he only remembered her being slight and pretty and liking to be taken to his bed. Now she was mother to a daughter and snapped often at him.

"Yilli, get up!"

"Yilli, see to the goats!"

"Yilli! Yilli!"

Always she had something for him to do, and always he did not want to do it. He did not want to walk out with his goats alone in the hills. He did it because his wife said he must. Now the sun was setting, and he was almost home. He saw that there was smoke coming out of the chimney of his house. In the yard he saw his little daughter, Teuta, sitting in the dirt and making her little piles of stones. He saw his wife hanging out a rug. He saw the mountains towering around his stone house that was far away from towns and people. Yilli was thinking that he should not walk with his eyes cast down, that life was good, and God had been kind when suddenly he heard a crack.

It was loud, and it was close, and Yilli's heart thudded in his chest with great fear. His feet were running before he even thought to make them move. His goats scattered as Yilli tripped, righted himself, and nearly tumbled down the rocky slope to his house.

"Teuta! Teuta!"

He called to his daughter as he ran. Teuta looked up. The little girl smiled at her father. She raised her hand to greet him. But when her father did not greet her, when he continued to yell, she knew something was wrong and began to cry.

"Nënë!"

Yilli's wife came to the door to see what horrible thing was happening. Yilli rushed past her.

"Close the door. Close the door!"

She did as her husband said after she gathered up her crying daughter. Then they all stayed in the house as Yilli told the story of tending his goats and hearing a shot and he fearing for his life — no, fearing for the life of his wife and child - and running home to save them.

Yilli's wife listened to all this as she bounced Teuta on her lap. Yilli told his story many times while he paced in the house and drank some raki. He paced for a very long while more as he looked out the windows. His wife looked, but all she saw were the mountains and the one road that came through them to their house.

When her husband was calm, and before it became night, Yilli's wife went out to collect the goats. She looked and looked, but she saw no person. She listened and listened, but she heard no gunshots. Still, it could have happened, what Yilli said. There were many soldiers about and many bad people these poor days. It could have been a robber. But what did Yilli have to rob?

She found the last goat near the road where Yilli said someone shot at him with a rifle. It was there she found a large rock that had tumbled down from the mountain. She looked at it. She put her hand on her hip and looked at it hard. Certainly, the falling of a big stone made a crack did it not? Yilli had been a soldier. He knew the sound of a gun but perhaps he mistook the sound of rock falling. Still, he was her husband and she knew that she must believe him in all things.

Taking the goats, she put them in their pen and then went to the house where Yilli sat with his raki as Teuta played at his feet. Night came. While she served the soup she had made and the fish she had fried, while Teuta chattered in her baby talk, Yilli's wife looked at him often and wondered if, perhaps, Yilli had been sent home from the border because he was mad.

2013

The young man clutched the steering wheel as he waited for the old man to give him a signal. It was getting late. Soon the sun would be up and people would be stirring. That concerned him, but the old man just sat there, staring at the dashboard, wrapped in his huge raincoat, still and silent.

"*Ja-Ja.* Let's go." The young man knew he sounded upset and impatient, but he couldn't help himself. If they didn't go soon his legs might not hold him up and he would be shamed. He touched the old man's arm. He softened his tone. "Uncle? *Ja-Ja?*"

The old man turned his head, not so much interrupted as returning himself to this time. He looked at the young man.

"I am sorry. I was thinking." He said this in the old language.

"Yes." The young man answered in the same way, proud that he had not forgotten how. "We should go inside. I need to be at work soon."

"Yes. It is important you go tomorrow," the old man said. "Like always."

"Like always." The younger man muttered.

He checked the rearview mirrors. Just to make sure he didn't miss any thing, he looked over his shoulder one way and then the other. The neighborhood was generally quiet, but one could never be too careful. Even with the storm, someone might be out. They were out after all.

Satisfied, he got out of the car, paused to open the trunk and retrieve the bag inside, and then he opened the passenger door. He stepped back to let the uncle out of the car while his eyes darted to the small houses hugging the sides of the wet street. The old man rested his big hand atop the car and the young man realized how shameful it was that he had been proud of a piece of metal. The car was nothing in the grand scheme. The old man had opened his eyes to so many things. He touched his uncle and they walked to the house.

The door was unlocked and a single light burned as they had expected. They went through the living room, and the kitchen, and to the place where the washer and dryer stood. The young man opened the lid of the washer, stripped, loaded his wet clothes inside, waited for the old man to do the same, and then he turned it on. The sound must have disturbed the young man's wife because she appeared, dressed in her thin robe, arms crossed, looking worried. Her lips parted, but before she could speak she made the mistake of looking at the old man. He did not acknowledge her. She looked at her husband, and a shiver ran down her spine. She glanced at the washer, and then disappeared into the back of the house.

She was just crawling into bed when she heard another cabinet in the washroom open and close, and she heard something fall. She hoped they weren't making a mess she would have to clean up later. When her husband came into their bedroom and dressed again, she kept her eyes shut even though she wanted ask what he had been doing. When she heard voices, though, her curiosity got the best of her.

Carefully, she got out of bed again. Hiding in her own house, she spied on her husband and the old man. They had dressed in fresh clothes and now her husband was welcoming other men into her home at an hour when no one should be awake. The last one to come in asked:

"Well?"

The old man shook his head and set his mouth. Some of the visitors shook their heads as they settled down to finish this night with coffee, talking quietly of places the young man's wife had never seen, in a language she could not understand. Her mother had been right. It was never good to marry someone from another place. She checked on their son who slept like a baby even though he was a big boy of five. Then she went back to bed wishing her husband was with her and the old man was gone.

***

"Jesus, Archer, what kind of mother is this woman? I could barely tolerate it when she left that kid out on the beach all night when the weather was good. Locking him out tonight was criminal. Billy could have died out there."

"Maybe that's what he wanted."

Josie considered her lover, her friend, her honest man for a minute before turning her head, resting her elbow near the window, and covering her mouth with her cupped palm. If Archer was right and Billy wanted to kill himself, then everyone in Hermosa Beach who said they cared about that kid were liars including her. Josie dropped her hand and tried to remember the last conversation she'd had with the boy. Was it a day ago? A week? Longer? As if reading her mind, Archer reached out and squeezed the hand that rested in her lap. She squeezed back.

"You should have to get a license to be a mother," Josie muttered.

Archer snorted. There was no arguing that. Both of them had run across a lot of women who never would have qualified. Linda Rayburn threw Hannah under the bus to save herself; she did it with style. Josie's own mother had abandoned her without a word of explanation; she had done it with surgical precision. And there was Archer's long dead wife and her son. Lexi had brutally betrayed every tenet of motherhood. But Billy's mom was something else entirely. If Archer were a betting man, he would lay odds they were about to meet a woman who didn't think about her son one way or the other.

"There it is." Josie sat up straighter. "One in from the corner."

Billy's house wasn't in the fanciest neighborhood in Hermosa Beach. It was sandwiched between an equally decrepit house on the right and one under construction on the left. The small patch of lawn in front of Billy's house was dead and dry despite the deluge of the last eighteen hours. Paint peeled off the gutters and around the windows. There was a hole in the downspout by the front door and the rain had poured through it to create a huge puddle on the painted porch. A rusting bicycle shared the space with the skeleton of a dead bush in a broken pot. The upstairs windows were covered with tin foil, and the downstairs window with a flag.

Archer pulled the Hummer into the driveway and stopped behind an old Toyota. The front end listed to the left where it was missing a wheel. No one had bothered to block the back wheels because the driveway was broken into shards by the roots of a ficus tree. The car wouldn't be rolling anywhere without divine intervention. Archer set the parking brake and cut the lights.

"You can wait here if you want." Josie reached for the door handle.

"I'll go with." Archer reached for his. "You might need a witness."

They opened their respective doors. It was two in the morning. The storm, furious though it had been, was passing on.

They walked through a light drizzle that would be gone by ten, and reached the front door at the same time. Since Archer was closer, he rang the bell. One light was on upstairs; downstairs was dark. Josie reached over Archer and rang the bell again.

Silence.

She moved him out of the way and laid on it as if she could push it through the stucco. Still no one came. She tried the knob. Locked tight. Josie fell back, looked up, and checked out the permanent security bars on the windows. Billy's mom wouldn't get past them sneaking out a window and if ripping them off was the only way to get in, Josie might do it.

"Hey! Open up!" Josie shouted but nothing happened. She called again. "Open up, Goddammit!"

"Good one, Jo. Swearing will get her attention."

Josie shot Archer a withering look.

"I'm going around back. Someone's up, and I'm not leaving until I talk to whoever it is. Then I'm going to call the cops and have that woman arrested for neglect. Child endangerment. Attempted murder. If Billy had drowned. . ."

Josie's litany feathered out to nothingness as she strode toward the back of the house. Whatever was going to happen, Archer would hear about it soon enough. She wasn't gone two minutes when he heard someone moving inside the house. Before Archer could call her back, the door opened.

"Come on in," Josie said.

"Don't you think we should wait to be invited?"

"Believe me, nobody is going to be upset."

Josie pushed the door open wider. It didn't escape Archer's notice that she used her elbow to do so. She flipped on the light the same way. It was an awkward but understandable gesture considering what he was looking at as soon as the room was illuminated.

"Guess we know why she didn't answer," he said.

"Think Billy saw her do this?" Josie asked.

"That would explain him freaking out," Archer muttered. "He may be luckier to be alive than we know."

They stood side by side, surveying the scene, each lost in thought as the seconds ticked by. Finally, Archer glanced at Josie.

"You okay, babe?"

She nodded. It was the guy on the couch, the one with a bullet through his skull, who didn't look so good.

CHAPTER 3

1985

The legislature was divided. Half of them argued for the status quo: isolationism, socialism, one party – no, one man – rule. The problem was, there was not a man with an iron hand to govern. Enver Hoxha, supreme leader for half a century, was dead. This definitively proved that he, the supreme leader, had been, after all, nothing more than any other man. The other half of the lawmakers found their voices and spoke what people had been afraid to say for decades: under Hoxha's rule the country had suffered.

Traditions had been destroyed-
National personality had been obliterated-
People feared one another-
The Cult of the Ugly had ruled –

Calls for freedom were rampant in the halls of government and drowned out those who did not want change. The echo was heard in the capitol and filtered to the towns and then to the villages. The people rose up. Once again they embraced their ancient culture with pride and looked to the future with hope.

People wept and danced with happiness - all except Yilli. Yilli, the good boy, the goat herder, spoke with his wife, told her what he had done, closed his doors and shuttered his house for good.

2013

The couch was pushed against the wall in the corner of the living room. To one side was a crate with a lamp on it. In front of the couch was a low coffee table that was nicked and scratched, its finish long since dulled. The dead man's legs were sprawled in front of him: left on the floor, right on top of the table. There was an armchair covered in floral fabric close to the table on one side and a lawn chair on the other.

Archer picked his way around the furniture and put two fingers to the man's neck. He shook his head even though neither of them needed confirmation that the guy was a goner. The gunshot had entered the left temple neatly and then blown blood and brains over the upholstery and wall when it exited. Josie maneuvered around the opposite end of the sofa, looked behind it, picked up the skirt and looked under it. She stood and slid her gaze over the floor. The gun wasn't in the guy's hand and it hadn't been ejected.

"No weapon. Not suicide." Josie whispered, but she wasn't telling Archer anything he didn't know.

If this were a suicide, the man would have stabilized himself with both heels on the coffee table or both feet on the ground. More than likely he would have put the gun in his mouth. The body was contorted in a way that indicated the victim had been reacting to something, and that something was probably a gun being pointed at him.

"Fed Ex." Josie noted the man's uniform.

"He was off the clock," Archer added.

The guy was holding a notebook, not an electronic tablet. There was no truck on the street and no evident delivery in the living room. The blood was too fresh for this to have happened during working hours. Archer looked at the notebook. There was a logo on the top, but he couldn't make it out. There were names written in it, and some of them were starred. Archer looked up to see Josie heading for the stairs.

"You wait for me, Jo," Archer cautioned.

Josie paused half way between the front door and the staircase. Before he could join her, something caught his attention and he veered off toward the kitchen.

"Got another one." Archer poked his head in for a better look at the woman spread-eagled face down on the linoleum.

"Is it her?" Josie asked as she worked her way back toward him.

"Nope. It's a guy. Took one in the back. The shot blew his wig off," Archer said as she joined him.

This man was at least six-four, his feet were huge, and his hands were the size of baseball mitts. Josie couldn't see his face, but she could see the tufts of black hair billowing around his back and shoulders in bizarre contrast to the orange and pink satin backless dress he wore. The skirt had bunched up around his ass. He was an old fashioned kind of guy, preferring a garter and stockings to panty hose. One of his pink pumps was still on, the other rested near the fridge. The kitchen was small, neat and clean. He had been making a dash for the back door, but he didn't have a chance. Not in those heels.

"Poor Billy. God only knows what went on in this place." Josie leaned into Archer. "Let's see if good old mom is still here."

"She's not," Archer said.

He was about to lecture her on disturbing a crime scene, but Josie was already on her way upstairs. He caught up with her and took her arm. He almost lost her a few months ago; he wasn't going to chance it again.

"Me first."

"I thought you were sure she was gone."

"There's sure and there's positive," he reminded her.

Josie fell back to make room for him. The stairs creaked under his weight. Josie tried to avoid the weak spots, but her efforts were futile. A spindle was missing and the railing was cracked. The carpet was threadbare and torn. Above them was a landing packed tight with boxes. The poster that had launched Farrah Fawcett's career hung on the wall above them. The blond bombshell smiled brilliantly, eagerly, innocently, as if she had no idea that the red maillot clinging to her small breast exposed her erect nipple. It was racy stuff for the time. Archer's first thought was that the poster was a collector's item. His second was that the poster was an antique. His third was that there was no room for anyone to hide on the landing, so he moved on, craning to see past the boxes. Josie stepped lightly and joined him.

Alert to the slightest movement, listening for any sound no matter how small, they swept the upstairs. Flanking the narrow hall were two bedrooms: one was dark, and the other was lit. Billy's mom had a thing for sixty-watt bulbs.

Archer motioned toward the closest bedroom, and Josie nodded. He approached the dark room, reached through the door, and found a switch. The light popped on. When he motioned again, Josie followed Archer into a woman's bedroom.

Pink, plastic-coated free weights were in one corner along with an ab exerciser. Clothes were everywhere: on the floor, the bed, on the little wicker table, spilling out of the tiny closet. There was a table that served as a desk. It was piled with magazines: Vogue, Cosmopolitan, and one in a foreign language that Josie didn't recognize. There was a flat screen television facing a waterbed. An unframed poster of a naked man and woman was thumbtacked into the wall like a headboard. The subjects were not professional models and the photo was grainy. The woman in the picture was very pretty and young; the man wasn't that good looking. Josie turned in a tight circle and then nudged the closet door open with her toe. It was packed with cheap clothes and shoes.

"Be back," Archer whispered.

Josie stepped back, squishing a stuffed toy underfoot. Josie picked it up, thinking it was an odd thing for a grown woman to have. She started to pitch it toward the bed, but changed her mind. She didn't want to disturb anything that might keep Billy's mom from getting what she deserved.

"There's not much in Billy's room," Archer was back, keeping the conversation going as if he never left. "His backpack is in there. Some surfing posters. The bed is made. At least his room is nice."

"Too bad he didn't get to use it much," Josie noted.

Archer shrugged as he took out his phone.

"I'll call it in."

Archer never dialed. Josie held up her hand and walked around the far side of the bed. He followed.

"Crap," she muttered.

Archer couldn't have said it better. Lying in an impressive pool of blood on the yellowed linoleum was a nearly naked woman. Long matted hair covered her face. One arm was thrown up and over her head as if she had been trying to crawl away, but the other was pulled behind her, the bone jutting through the skin where it had been broken. There was a wash of blood on the wall, rivulets of blood, pools of blood, streaks of blood. There was so much blood, so much violence, that Josie and Archer both reached the same conclusion at the same time.

"This one was personal." Josie turned away, touching Archer's hand as she did so. "Make the call. I'll go to the hospital to be with Billy. I want to know-"

Before Josie finished her thought, before Archer could remind her they had come in the same car, the woman on the floor moved.

CHAPTER 4

1987

Everyone danced at Teuta's wedding except her parents. It was not unusual for Yilli and his wife not to be at the wedding of their daughter. Tradition had it that the bride's family stayed home to weep for their lost daughter. They had followed tradition exactly. Yilli had even wrapped a bullet in a leaf, handing it to Teuta's husband as he stole her away. It was a symbol of his power over her. The bullet meant that Teuta's father had given her husband the right to kill her if she was not a dutiful wife. Of course, he wouldn't do that. He was a modern and handsome husband who delighted Teuta. The matchmaker had done an exceptional job. Now that there were elections and democracy, Teuta could only imagine what wonders the future held for them. Yet her father, Yilli, was distressed by the turn of fortune. He no longer seemed to care about anything: not his goats, not her mother, not their new world. Then again, he was old now and not much would change for those who lived so far from the towns and villages. Perhaps that was what ailed her father. She was married, and he was old. But Teuta did not think it was so simple.

Just as she was thinking all these things, Teuta's husband cried out with joy. She looked up to see him dancing: arms high in the air, feet moving, grinning as his friends clapped him on the back. He looked happy and when he caught her eye he looked happier still. Teuta left her chair and threw herself into the joyous crowd. Today, tonight, the next days, she would celebrate her marriage. Yilli could wait. They had all the time in the world.

2013

Archer raised the woman's head and held a towel to her throat while Josie went for the phone. It took seconds to give her urgent information to the dispatcher who simultaneously notified the cops and the paramedics. Josie wanted only one thing – to keep this woman alive long enough to find out what happened in this house. Archer was careful to note everything he touched, especially how he handled the woman. He spoke words she might hear but probably couldn't comprehend.

Wait. Hold on. Breathe.

He didn't take his eyes off her when the sirens sounded in the distance.

Here they come now. Here they are. Hold on. Hold on.

That was the last thing Josie heard because she was taking the stairs two at a time before running outside to flag down the responders. The first to arrive were Hermosa PD black and whites, then came an ambulance, and finally a sheriff's investigative unit. Josie advised them about the surviving victim and the dead men and then stood aside. Down the street she heard a door open. There was probably more than one person along the way who wakened to watch the police cars barrel by.

Archer was with her a second later, sent outside as the sheriff's investigators and cops secured the scene. Those were things he used to do and things he didn't miss. Neither Archer nor Josie speculated about the woman's survival, what Billy knew, or who the victims were. It would be the height of stupidity for an investigator or lawyer to do that, but that didn't stop them from thinking about it.

It was five minutes before Billy's mom was rushed past them to the waiting ambulance, an oxygen mask covering her nose and mouth, an IV started. Upstairs, Josie only had an impression of the woman. Cocooned under the sheet, strapped to the gurney, she looked to be the size of a child.

Archer and Josie were interviewed separately, gave their statements coherently, offered contact information, and were released before the bodies of the two men were removed. Archer took Josie home. They kissed one another. Josie grabbed her keys and headed for the hospital. Archer was off to the beach to wait for the town to wake-up, to watch for the man who had banged on Josie's door, to begin doing everything a cop would do but with more speed and greater latitude. Then he would try to piece together the mystery of Billy Zuni's close call with death in a raging ocean. It was eight in the morning when he and Josie parted and eight-thirty when she reached Torrance Memorial Hospital. She was thinking that it was ironic that it took a tragedy to get Billy and his mother under the same roof when she sidestepped an aid, passed the nurses' station, and found room 217.

* * *

The bed nearest the door was made up and empty; the one near the window was half-hidden behind a grey curtain strung on an elliptical rod. Josie assumed that the sheriff's investigator had arranged this. She couldn't remember his name, but she remembered him. The man had been efficient, unflappable and smart enough to cover his investigatory ass by isolating Billy until he could be interviewed. Thankfully, he hadn't isolated Billy completely. No one had stopped Josie from going in and no one had put Hannah out.

Hannah was curled up in the chair, knees to her chin, a thin blanket pulled up to her shoulders. Her head was turned and her riot of curls covered part of her face, fell over the back of the chair, and cascaded across her shoulders. Her shoes were tucked under the chair, and her bare feet peeked out from under the blanket. A gold toe-ring sparkled even in the flat, filtered light. Josie could just glimpse the black and red ink of the tattoo that snaked from one shoulder and tipped out on the curve of her neck. Of late Hannah had taken to wearing her gold nose ring again. She looked like a warrior woman, a Nubian princess, a fierce young fighter at rest.

Billy, on the other hand, was almost unrecognizable.

He lay still as death in the narrow bed, his face swollen, and his bruises spreading like the rainbow atop an oil slick. His skin was scraped and speckled with dried blood where the rough concrete of the pier pilings had flayed him. An IV dripped into his left arm and his right was in a cast. Machines monitored his heartbeat, his pulse, and his blood pressure. There was a bandage on one side of his head where his hair had been shaved and his head stitched.

Josie looked past the bed and out the window. A child hurt always hit her gut hard. A wounded child never truly healed, and she was living proof. Perhaps if she could see her mother once more, and ask why she had left her only child, Josie might stop hurting. Then again, she might not.

Her lips tipped. She almost laughed at the irony of this situation. All hurtful things began with a mother and all thoughts of mothers led back to her own. But this wasn't about Josie, so she hunkered down next to Hannah and touched her shoulder.

The girl's eyes opened: not lazily because her slumber had been disturbed, not gently because she was drawn out of a pleasant dream, but narrowly and warily. Josie could only imagine what Hannah saw in that millisecond before recognition: dark houses, Fritz Rayburn's sadistic face, her own mother's resentful one, Daniel Young's psychotic visage, a gun, a knife, the flame that would maim her, wound her, kill her. Then it didn't matter because in the next second she recognized a friend and those flint edged eyes softened.

"Hey," Josie whispered.

"Hi." Hannah pushed herself upright, pulling the blanket with her. It was always too cold in a hospital room. "You went home."

Josie looked down at her clothes. She forgot that the last time Hannah had seen her she was half-naked on the beach. So much had happened since then, clothes were the last things Josie noticed. Hannah, though, made noting change a high art. She knew a safe harbor when she saw it, and a corner when she was boxed into it. This room was neither.

Josie twisted a lock of the girl's hair, more to have something to do so she wouldn't stare at the blanket that was jumping rhythmically as Hannah fidgeted beneath it. The girl's eyes darted to the doorway.

"I'm alone," Josie assured her.

"I thought Archer would come at least."

"He had some things to take care of."

"You talked to Billy's mom, didn't you? Does she care at all?" Hannah's chin quivered. "He could have died out there."

"But he didn't." Josie wanted to choose the right time to tell her what they found in Billy's house, so she gestured toward the bed and dodged Hannah's question. "How's he doing?"

Hannah eyed Billy. "He seems okay. He stopped talking."

"What was he saying?"

"Nothing I could make out." Hannah took a deep breath, hesitated, and finally confessed: "I told them I was his sister. Otherwise they wouldn't let me in. Just so you know."

Josie bit her lip as she tried to decide whether to congratulate Hannah on her inventiveness or take her to task for lying. She decided congratulations were in order. Hannah's lie kept her close to Billy and a relationship wasn't that farfetched. There were markers for every other genetic helix in Hannah's DNA, so why not a little Viking or whatever Billy was.

"They can't wake him up, Josie."

"It's shock. It may be a few days before he comes to." Josie put her hand on Hannah's arm but her touch didn't stop the drumming of Hannah's fingers as her agitation grew.

One. . .two. . .three.

Obsessive. Compulsive. Poor Hannah. She had almost healed - until now.

"Please, say his mom is coming." The girl pleaded, keeping her eyes on the unconscious boy.

"No, she isn't."

Hannah unclasped her hands. One snaked from under the covers just long enough to flip her hair over her shoulder. Her jaw angled into a hard angry line and then relaxed. She was trying so hard to control her instincts.

"I knew she wouldn't, but we're here. So it's okay."

"It's not what you think, Hannah-"

Josie stopped talking. Her radar was up. They were not alone. Keeping her hand on the girl's shoulder, she stood and faced the person hovering in the doorway. He smiled. He said:

"I hope I'm not intruding."

CHAPTER 5

1991

Teuta smiled at her little girl who smiled back at her mother. Though she was but one year, she was old in her soul so it was nice to see her smile. She was a beautiful little thing with dark hair and full cheeks. But the man who was to take the picture of the little girl was not happy. No Shqiptare smiled for a picture, not even a little girl. This would be the first Teuta's parents had seen of their grandchild, so it must be perfect.

Teuta wagged a finger, and the little girl's lips closed, and her big serious eyes looked even more somber. Pleased, the photographer took the picture and the little girl raised her hands to her mother. Teuta swooped in to pick her up. She and her handsome young husband had made a good girl who would grow beautiful and she would marry well. She would have beautiful children to be Teuta's grandchildren. That is how life would go, Teuta was sure.

She paid the photographer but counted her lek carefully. Her husband had invested as everyone had and soon they would be rich. Until then, she must be cautious. That, the bankers and the government told them all, was how things worked when there was freedom.

2013

The detective walked into the room like a visiting relative reluctant to disturb the family but having no intention of leaving after making the effort to get there. He nodded to Josie and asked how she was holding up. She had barely answered when he turned his attention to Hannah. She was a beautiful and interesting girl, and it hadn't escaped his notice that she had tracked him as if he was a hunter and she his prey.

"I'm Detective Montoya. I'm here to help Billy."

Mike's introduction was accompanied by a smile so genuine it usually disarmed victims and criminals alike. Hannah was neither, and she was cautious. She looked him square in the eye, considered the hand he offered, and decided to take it. Then Mike Montoya made a mistake. He put his other hand on top of hers. She snatched hers back and drew the blanket over her arms.

"I'm surprised you're here." Josie caught his attention before he could say anything more. He turned smoothly.

"My team is still working." He looked over his shoulder at Billy. "I understand he dodged a bullet. No major internal injuries. A concussion, but so far no swelling on the brain."

"Then you know more than we do." Josie's eyes flicked to Hannah. "This is Hannah Sheraton, my ward. She goes to school with Billy. She came with him in the ambulance."

"And I assume you just got here?" Mike asked.

Josie picked up on the prompt. "I did. Hannah and I haven't had a chance to talk about what happened."

Mike nodded. He would let Josie Bates break the news of what happened in Billy's house to Hannah. There were other things he wanted to know, but Hannah had her own agenda.

"Billy didn't do anything. What happened was an accident." She was spoiling for a fight. She snapped those big, green eyes of hers at Mike and then Josie. "I know how this goes. You think Billy did something wrong or else you wouldn't be here. But sometimes shit just happens and it isn't against the law. It happens because -"

"Hannah, that's enough," Josie's warned.

"That's all right. I have three girls of my own." Mike's comment indicated that he could understand Hannah Sheraton because he had daughters, but his girls would never be as old as this one if they lived a hundred years. He tried again now that he had some idea of what he was up against. "I'm glad Billy has someone with him who cares. He must mean a lot for you to stay with him all this time."

"He's just my friend." Hannah muttered.

"May I?" Before Hannah could object, Mike pulled a chair up and sat down.

"It's been a very long night for all of us. Maybe this isn't the best time." Josie didn't want him to get too comfortable, but there seemed to be no stopping him.

"Just a few questions." He turned his face like a priest in the confessional and shut Josie out. This was between him and Hannah.

"Do you know what happened to Billy? Do you know why he was in the ocean last night?"

"None of us knows why," Josie responded.

Montoya smiled slightly. Josie Bates' concern for Hannah and what she might say was telling, indeed. Montoya knew that she was concerned about the girl, but he also knew Josie Bates, the lawyer, was trying to control the flow of information.

He had known who she was the minute she gave her name at the crime scene. She was a fearless advocate, a headline maker, a woman who might not seek the limelight but found herself in it nonetheless. Josie Bates could be a brick wall or a conduit to the people he needed to talk to. Mike had never been a fan of brick walls and was not fond of running headlong into one.

"Hannah was with him in the ambulance," he reminded her. "She's been with him since he got into this room. Isn't that right, Hannah?"

"He almost drowned. You shouldn't be coming here to harass him," Hannah objected.

If there had been a confession in that ambulance, Hannah Sheraton gave no indication she heard it. That meant there hadn't been one, or she was a darn good little actress. He said:

"I came because I want to help. The way I can do that is by understanding what kind of person Billy is."

"He's a good person. A happy person," Hannah answered.

"It's hard to be happy all the time. Was he happy at school?"

"He managed," Hannah mumbled.

"That doesn't sound good," Mike nudged.

Josie moved into his peripheral vision. Hannah paid no attention to her.

"Sometimes people made fun of him, but that happens. It doesn't mean anything."

"And at home? How was that?" Mike pressed on.

"We all know about his mother - " she began, but Josie interrupted.

"None of us ever met the woman, detective. Whatever Hannah might tell you would only be hearsay." The tone of Josie's voice told Mike this interview was going to be over sooner than later.

Mike swiveled toward Josie. "This isn't an interrogation."

"Billy and Hannah are minors," Josie reminded him. "And this is a sick room. If you'd like to talk to us somewhere else, we can do that after I've had a chance to speak with Hannah."

Mike's bottom lip pulled up, his chin crinkled as if he was thinking about her suggestion. The fingers on his right hand drummed once on his knee. He considered Hannah, let his gaze linger on Billy, and then he stood up.

"No one needs protecting from me," he assured them.

"Caution is ingrained," Josie answered.

"Curiosity is my handicap," he countered. "I find it more productive."

"I'll walk you out." Josie started for the door. Before Mike followed, he held out his card to Hannah.

"If you think of anything that might help, I hope you'll call."

Mike didn't wait for an answer. This girl would never call him if Josie Bates had anything to say about it, and she made that clear in the hall.

"If you need to question Hannah, call me and we'll make arrangements. She likes to think she's tough, but she's only sixteen."

"She's an old soul," Mike noted.

"Let's not dance around anything where these kids are concerned. You didn't ask, but I can tell you that Hannah was home with me last night. She woke me up when she heard the man at the front door. She saw what happened on the beach and rode to the hospital with Billy. That's it."

"So noted," Mike said.

"And set aside," Josie suggested.

"Can't do it, Ms. Bates. Those two young people might not even know what information would be helpful. You should encourage Hannah to talk to me now."

"Billy is the one with information. It might be days before you can talk to him and days more before he can piece things together. "

"Minutes concern me. Better that I rule out any involvement on his part."

"Isn't it a little early to finger Billy as your perp?" Josie scoffed.

Mike smiled. "Interesting that should be your first thought. I was thinking witness."

"Since this discussion is moot until he's coherent, let's not assume either," Josie answered, embarrassed by her amateur mistake.

"Agreed. I'd like to have your clothes made available to us so our lab can rule out any evidence you two left in the house. We already have what was left of Billy's."

"Sure. We'll get it to you."

"Thanks." Mike lingered. "By the way, why didn't you ride to the hospital with Billy? I would have thought you'd want to stay with him to make sure he was alright."

"I wanted to talk to his mother," Josie said.

"This was your own idea?" he pressed.

"Yes. Who else's would it be?"

"I'm curious about the urgency. You let a sixteen-year-old girl accompany Billy to the hospital when you weren't sure of his condition, when the hospital might have needed an adult to consult with. You could have talked to his mother after you knew more."

"But I didn't do that, did I?"

"No. I suppose the real question is, did Billy say anything on the beach that made you think you needed to go to that house immediately?" Mike asked.

"You mean like telling me he just killed two people and attempted to kill his mother?" Josie smiled. "No, detective. No seaside confession."

"It doesn't hurt to ask."

"Have you talked to anyone about Billy?" she asked. "I mean have you notified child services?"

"We informed the district attorney," Mike said.

"Who caught it?" Josie asked.

"Carl Newton." Josie nodded as Mike went on. "He'll confer with the county counsel regarding Billy's placement unless there's a clear alternative for the boy's care."

"Billy is seventeen," Josie said.

"The law says he's a child until he's eighteen," Mike reminded her.

"I'll see what I can do about finding his people," Josie answered.

"I think that would be best under the circumstances. No matter what happens, that boy is going to need a lot of support."

Mike didn't have to say more. The standard no matter what happens implication spoke volumes. Josie had known from the minute she saw the carnage in that house that Billy would be the investigator's top priority.

"True. Just remember, you only talk to him if I'm present," Josie reiterated.

"Unless a relative is located," Montoya responded.

"Or his mother is able to assign permissions," Josie went on. "Did the doctors say when you will you be able to talk with her?"

Josie turned back to look at Hannah who had not taken her eyes off Billy. Mike looked back at the teenagers, too.

"I doubt they would know, Ms. Bates." He turned his gaze on her. "We're not sure we've found Billy's mother yet."

CHAPTER 6

1996

Teuta pulled her shawl tighter and looked down at the little girl on one side of her and then the baby nestled in her arms. Her children had slept well given the cold and the bad roads and the hard seats of the wagon. Teuta hadn't slept soundly since she learned her father was ill. She loved him, and as the years went by she was sad that her marriage had taken her so far away. Perhaps if she lived closer things would have been different. Yilli had become so reclusive that it was all her mother could do to get him to the hospital. Teuta finally knew why. It seemed everyone had known except for her. Such an old sin. But now Yilli was a sick old man who would soon die. Who would care about him except those who loved him? Besides, there were other things to worry about in these changing days. She worried about why they all still lived like peasants.

The wagon jolted. She held her children tighter. Riches, she thought. She wished she had not listened to such talk. She had not believed what the government or her husband said. She wanted him to get his money back from the bankers now. He had promised to try. Meanwhile, she still traveled in a wagon drawn by a horse and what little money they had was sewn into the hem of her skirt.

The wagon jolted again. Again she clutched her daughter who clutched right back. Teuta glanced harshly at the old man but he didn't notice. He did not care if this was a hard road. If she complained he would have just told her to wait for a furgon, but the furgons did not run all the time and those that did often broke down. The cart was slow, but it was steady and it was what they could afford.

Teuta sighed and looked off to the countryside. On the horizon was the concrete skeleton of what would someday be a home for many families. The stairs reached up three floors, but only the bottom level was finished with a door and windows and walls. When each son married, another floor would be finished. Teuta's husband was a first son so they lived on the second floor of the family home. The second son, his brother, had died in prison before the government fell. Poor boy. At least she wouldn't have to worry so much about her children being imprisoned for no good reason. Still, there were things to be afraid of. Her father would die afraid. Poor father.

"Here is where you want to go"

The old man's voice startled her. Teuta was surprised to find that she had slept. Now she blinked as the cart stopped. She woke her older child. The old man lifted her down as if she were nothing more than air. He reached for Teuta and lifted her and the baby down, also.

"Faleminderit."

She thanked him but kept her eyes down. It was bad enough to travel alone with a man who was not her husband. She would not shame herself by looking him in the eye.

Teuta adjusted her skirts and gathered her children. She raised her eyes to the foreboding place that was her destination. Behind her the old man moved on. He had seen too much in his life to be worried about her one way or the other. If she needed courage, she would have to find it elsewhere.

He climbed back into his cart and took the reins in his hands. He was missing three fingers on the right one. Times had been hard for so many who were older. When the man and his cart were out of sight, Teuta went into the hospital hoping she had arrived in time to bring some comfort to Yilli, her father, who had once herded goats.

2013

In the ICU the walls were glass so that the nurses and doctors could easily monitor the sickest of the sick. Inside the room that interested Josie was the woman they had found at Billy's house, the one who had been attacked so ferociously that she hardly looked human, the one Josie and Archer assumed was Billy Zuni's neglectful, selfish mother.

Thanks to Mike Montoya's suggestion, Josie now had her own doubts.

The woman in the bed was all too human, petite, pale, and, above all, very young. It was her youth that had given Montoya pause and Josie had to agree it was a curious turn. Children gave birth to children all the time, but logic dictated that could not be so in this case.

This girl topped out at twenty-five. Even if she were twenty-seven or eight that would mean she would have had Billy when she was ten. She and Billy couldn't have survived without the help of family or friends. She couldn't have worked, rented a house, or driven a car. If she tried to do any of that, she would have come to the notice of social services at the very least. She hadn't. When pressed, Montoya offered no hard facts for his conclusion and that made Josie all the more curious.

She checked out her surroundings: one nurse worked at the desk, another conferred with a doctor at a patient's bedside, two rooms down a man slept in a chair next to a woman's bed. The nurse at the desk got up; Josie Bates made her move and walked into the room.

Up close the woman in the bed looked younger still. Her eyes were wide set, her nose short and round. Her cheeks were full, and her lips beautifully bowed and pitifully slack. There was a tube down her throat that attached her to a machine that breathed for her and IVs that fed her cocktails of nourishment and medicine. Josie tried to see beyond the neat rows of stitches snaking across her throat and behind her ear, the dressings on her face, and the cast on her arm. Josie looked hard, trying to find a definitive resemblance to Billy. Was it there in her coloring? This girl's hair was light like Billy's but her lashes, roots, and brows were dark. Perhaps if she opened her eyes Josie would see it; maybe if she spoke Josie would hear it in the sound of her voice. But it would be a long time before those eyes opened or that voice sounded.

Her ears were pierced, and her nails were short and ill kept. There were no tattoos or birthmarks that Josie could see. Since there wasn't much skin visible it was impossible to tell if there were any existing scars. That was about to change. The stitches that had sewn this woman's throat closed seemed crude and hastily done but Josie knew better. The surgeon could not waste time on aesthetics when a head had nearly been severed from a body, when arteries and vocal chords and muscle had been butchered.

Josie closed her eyes and pushed against them with her fingertips as she tried to conjure up Billy's face and match it to this woman's. Sadly, Josie couldn't remember what Billy Zuni looked like. In her mind's eye she saw him blue with cold, his skin rubbery from immersion, his blond hair darkened by sand and grit.

Josie's hand dropped, her head fell back as she tried to take hold of other memories; a kid waving at her from the beach, a boy waiting for Hannah's attention as he followed along behind her, a boy surprised that kid stuff he pulled was against the law, a boy who seemed as if he never really belonged where he was -

"What are you doing in here?"

Josie's shoulders slumped; the breath she didn't know she'd been holding pushed out of her. She faced the very unhappy station nurse.

"I just came to find out if . . ." Josie waved a hand in the direction of the bed. She had no name to put with the woman. "How is she? Will she make it?"

"Who are you?" The woman put herself between Josie and the patient. It was obvious the personnel were on high alert. Who was to say that the person who wanted this woman dead wouldn't try to finish the job? Who was to say that person wasn't Josie?

"I found her," Josie explained.

"That's tough." The woman's attitude softened slightly. "It's nice you wanted to check on her, but you can't stay."

"Sure. I'm sorry." Josie bought time as she moved toward the bed. "I couldn't sleep tonight unless I knew something."

"Only the doctor can update. I am sorry."

"Do you know who that would be?"

"I think it's going to be Doctor Stern. The best thing is to check with the hospital advocate. She'll be coordinating with the police."

The nurse tugged the blanket around the woman in the bed and then steered Josie to the door. With one last look over the nurse's shoulder, Josie said:

"Thanks. I feel much better just having seen her."

When Josie left the room, she was satisfied. She had seen the white board above the bed and had a name, height and weight for the woman.

"Let's find out who you really are," Josie mumbled as she put her phone to her ear and waited for Archer to pick up.

***

When Mike Montoya was sixteen and learning to drive his teacher opined that a speeding driver reached his destination only three minutes sooner than a law abiding one, yet a speeder was responsible for seventy percent more vehicular deaths than the good driver. Knowing that this statistic could have been an exaggeration employed to scare the living daylights out of pimply-faced kids, Mike checked it out. He found four statistical references corroborating what his teacher said. The exercise taught Mike two important lessons: first, question everything, and, secondly, more mistakes and little real progress were made when one rushed.

Still, there was more than some urgency to the matter at hand so Mike made it back to the station as quickly as possible, walked through the building, and made his way to his desk. He had barely taken off his jacket and sat down when someone put their hands on his shoulders and tipped his chair back. The scent of Chanel preceded a purr:

"Guess who caught the assist, you lucky dog."

The perfume and the voice took the challenge out of the game. Mike dropped his head back and looked up to see Wendy Sterling's blue eyes sparkling under impossibly long lashes. High cheekbones cut through a heart-shaped face, expressive lips balanced her delicate jaw, and her strawberry blond hair was long enough to fall over her shoulders if she let it loose. She belonged in Hollywood, she lived in Redondo Beach, and she had a thing for Mike Montoya. Mike, though, loved his wife, respected his work place, and was probably the only man in the world who did not lust after Wendy Sterling the second she entered his orbit.

"Got anything good for me?" he asked.

"You know I do." She released his chair. It bounced like a good mattress as she planted herself in the one by his desk and crossed her bare legs.

"Keep it up, and I'll have to report you for sexual harassment." Mike gave no indication whether this was a warning or a joke.

"You can take it. Besides, what kind of settlement could you get off me? I probably make less than you do."

Wendy sent a mega-watt smile his way. As always, he wondered what made some men so darn strong and others so ridiculously weak; some dumb and others too smart for their own good.

"Good point," he muttered.

"Practicality is such a turn on," she clucked, but Mike was done. He looked at his watch. It was time to work, but Wendy liked to finish up on her own terms. "Someday, I'm going to get you to crack. Come on. Give me a smile."

Mike reached for his coffee. "How much time before we're expected at Newton's office?"

Wendy's sigh and disappointment that playtime was over were both exaggerated.

"I told him between three and four."

Mike checked his watch. "That doesn't give us much time. Let's see what you got."

Wendy handed over the first sheet of paper for Mike to follow along.

"The guy in the living room was Jak Duka. Works for Fed Ex, but he's also a daily with local #927. Lives in San Pedro."

Mike put a star on the employment information. Being a daily meant union, and you didn't get to be a full-fledged brother unless you were pretty tight with someone. It wouldn't be hard to track down his friends; getting them to talk would be another matter.

"You take Fed Ex, and I'll follow up on the union," Mike directed. "Anything else?"

"Duka was married. I caught the wife just as she was coming back from the grocery with her two little kids." Wendy paused before adding. "I hate that."

"I'm glad you were the one to break the news."

"My specialty. Telling people that other people are dead."

Wendy grimaced. Mike had seen her impart the news of a murder, an accident, an unexpected natural death and leave the survivor with a sense of peace and direction. Of all Wendy's natural gifts, that was the one Mike most admired. Hers was a unique position. Though she was a senior criminal analyst, the department had recognized she was also valuable in the field as the first contact with victim's families.

"Did the wife have anything to say about why he was in that house?" he asked.

"She figured he was making a delivery."

"In the wee hours of the morning? Using his own car?" Mike's brow beetled. "No one could be that gullible."

"Sometimes you don't see what's in front of your nose. Wives are especially susceptible to that." Wendy handed him another sheet of paper.

"Victim number two is Greg Oi. Quite the Barbie Doll all decked out in a satin dress and heels. I would expect that kind of thing in Los Angeles or San Francisco, but this is the first time I've seen it down in the South Bay."

"Nothing surprises me," Mike noted.

"Wouldn't you like to be surprised just a little?" Wendy's pretty eyes stayed on her report for a millisecond. When she raised them, her lashes threw shadows across the top of her cheeks.

Mike considered her longer than he should. When he couldn't reconcile her professionalism with her audacity, he folded his arms and leaned on the desk.

"You do know what you're saying, don't you?" He was genuinely curious.

"That I do," she answered.

"Then why do you say it?"

"'Cause you are the sweetest, Mike, and there aren't many of you around. Who knows, maybe someday you'll take me up on the offer."

"Jesus, Wendy," Mike sighed. "That's no answer."

"Yes, it is. I'm selfish. I want what I want. Men have been like that forever. Just say I'm a liberated woman." Wendy leaned close to him and he could smell soap.

"There's an office pool on when you're going to cave."

"What are the odds?" he asked, unable to help his amusement.

"Not good," she admitted as she pulled a sad face.

"In whose favor?"

"Not telling."

She laughed and, as she sat back, she knocked a bag off his desk. They both went for it at once. Mike got the bag, and Wendy came up with the contents.

"Books on tape? A little chick-litty for you, aren't they?"

Mike took the CDs back and put them in the bag.

"They're for my wife. Our anniversary is in a few days."

"You charmer," Wendy drawled. "How many years?"

"Twenty-five." Mike opened a desk drawer and put the bag inside.

"I don't think you'll be getting lucky with a gift like that. You want some action? Jewelry. Every woman loves jewelry," Wendy said.

"I think she'll like these," Mike said.

Wendy shrugged. It was clear the conversation was over, but Wendy was not going to give up. Twenty-five years was a long time to be with the same woman and audio books weren't exactly a passionate gift choice. Still, Wendy knew when not to push her luck. She tapped the paper on the desk in front of him.

"Greg Oi, the victim with the platinum wig and the size 12 pumps? In real life, he owns Marshall Fasteners out on Lomita Boulevard."

"Union shop?"

"Funny you should ask that. Local #927 has a lock on the place. They make stuff for airplanes, cars, and motorcycles – nuts and bolts. You'd think he'd be a little more macho, considering." Wendy editorialized but she was back on track a minute later. "Seems Oi's been having labor trouble. The contract is up for renewal and the sticking point is benefits. Oi was standing firm on not upping them and bringing in new hires at much a lower hourly. He also wanted them to contribute a whole lot more to retirement and allow the dye cutters to work on multiple projects. The brotherhood is royally pissed."

"Maybe Duka was sent out to put some pressure on Oi and things got out of hand," Mike suggested. "It can't be coincidence that Oi and Duka were in the same place at the same time."

"It could be anything with this guy. Oi is really rich. I just started checking him out, and already there's a web of subsidiaries, all of them privately held by Mr. Oi. He has some loans but they appear to be for tax purposes. The man could pay them off. Oi lives behind the gates in Rolling Hills."

"Family?"

"I talked to his wife briefly and gave her the news. I have you down to see her tomorrow at nine," Wendy said. "Don't know if there are children in the family, but Oi is involved in a nonprofit that works with needy kids from overseas."

"What kind of needy kids?" Mike asked.

"Don't know yet. I'm getting the public records. All I've got is a website so far and it's pretty lame." Wendy twirled her pencil giving Mike the minute he seemed to want. "What are you thinking? Some connection with the kid in the ocean?"

"I'm not thinking anything. I want to start with why Mr. Oi was on the wrong side of Hermosa. Our surviving victim was young, but she is not a child. Her name is Rosa Zuni, and I don't think Oi was doing charity work in that house."

"He was slumming. Being naughty where he thought no one could see. Everyone does it." Wendy handed him the third page, her suggestiveness more a matter of habit than real flirtation. "More than likely Oi's wife didn't like him prancing around like a Flamenco dancer and for a fee this little lady didn't mind. Our survivor works at Undies, by the way. You know, the strip joint near the airport?"

"I'm liking this," Mike muttered as he made more notes.

"I spoke to the manager. He said he was sorry to hear about what happened. He thought Rosa was a nice girl, but he doesn't know much about her. The club only gets involved if someone's coming on to the girls on the premises. All of them are independent contractors. No insurance, no workman's comp. Smart business."

"Yeah, but he still had to have a social security number for her."

"He did," Wendy said. "It's bogus. As of right now, this woman doesn't exist."

CHAPTER 7

1996

Teuta pulled her six-year-old daughter along as they searched the hospital for Yilli. Room after room it was the same: dirty beds, attendants who seemed to be more wardens than nurses, relatives feeding patients food they had brought from their homes since the hospital provided none. Blood had stained the sheets and had dried where it fell on the floor. Old and young alike languished. They did not look so much sick as starving, lonely, and surprised to find themselves in such a predicament.

On the second floor, Teuta came upon a dark room filled with more beds. Instinct told her to take her children and run. She kept going because it was her father she had to find. A man missing an arm reached his stump toward her. A woman with a burned face watched with one eye, but Teuta didn't think she could really see. There was a boy curled into himself, and he was nothing more than a little ball of bones. Teuta was now glad they had no hospital in her own village. This was a place to die if ever she saw one. She turned away from the little boy and that was when she saw her mother sitting beside a metal-framed bed. She rushed toward her.

"Nënë." Teuta kissed her mother, first one cheek and then the other. "How is he?"

"He will die" The mother shrugged as Teuta took off her shawl. The baby woke and cried. The mother patted the older girl's head and then reached for the baby. Teuta let her go. The mother said:

"This is a good baby." She put her old hand on the older girl's back and then kissed her brow. "This is a good girl."

"Yes. I am fortunate," Teuta answered.

Gingerly, she sat next to her father and tried not to disturb the thin mattress laid over broken springs. He did not open his eyes. He did not know she was there. She took his hand. It was cold; his skin was thin. He was drying up. Soon he would blow away, dead and gone. It would be a blessing for he was a tortured soul. She kept her eyes on his gaunt face to keep from looking at the plastic sheet and the things that came out of a dying body.

"I brought money for medicine." Teuta whispered this as much in deference to her ill father as to secrecy. She did not want anyone in this place to know she had money. Teuta's mother nodded, her head going up and down as was the custom to indicate she did not want the money. Teuta understood. Even she could see that it would be a waste to bribe anyone to give her father medicine. Still, she knew her mother was grateful for the offer.

Then Teuta's attention was caught by a sound. She turned her head to see that it came from her mother. She was crying. Teuta had never seen her mother cry nor had she realized that she loved her husband enough to cry for him. Teuta slid off the bed and knelt by the old woman. She touched the scarf covering her mother's hair. The mother raised her faded eyes and looked at her daughter.

"He came."

"Then all will be well. He sees father dying."

"He asked about you. About your children."

Teuta froze. She opened her mouth, but it was a moment before she was able to ask: "What did you tell him?"

"That you had daughters and a strong husband. I told him you were a good girl."

The baby began to cry just then, and Teuta's father opened his eyes. Mother and daughter watched, sure that this was an omen. But he only stared at the ceiling for what seemed many minutes. Teuta moved toward him while her mother held tight to the children.

"Atë," she whispered. "It is me, Teuta."

He turned his head. His breath was hot and hard to come by, and his eyes were the color of a snow-sky over the mountains, flat and seemingly endless. But he did see one thing: the baby in his wife's arms.

"Boy?" he rasped.

Teuta shook her head. "Vajzë. A girl"

He closed his eyes. A tear seeped out of the corner, but did not fall. It hesitated as if it were looking for a way through the maze of the deep lines and wrinkles on the old man's face. Teuta wiped it away.

She didn't have the heart to tell him she was pregnant again.

2013

Josie tried to think ahead, but it wouldn't be a worthwhile exercise until she had coffee and a few hours of sleep. Still, one thought kept creeping into her mind and it was the worst-case scenario: Billy Zuni could be accused of murder. Josie had already been through that nightmare with Hannah and she didn't want to repeat it. Then again, it could be even worse than Billy being accused of murder; the boy might actually have committed murder. Either way, Billy would be in the mix of suspects until he was crossed off and that was just a fact.

Driving home, Josie called Faye who promised to come over and offer what counsel she could. The next call went out to Mira Costa high school. Josie filled in the horrified principal, asked her to check records for Billy's next of kin, and touch base with the school psychologist to see if there was any recent contact with the boy. Josie also advised that Hannah would be out for the day.

She parked the Jeep just as the news of the murders came on the radio. When she heard the names were being withheld until next of kin were notified, Josie got out of the car. She was dialing Archer as she went up the walk but disconnected when she opened the front door. Max was sitting in the entry beside a puddle of pee.

"Sorry, buddy," she said and ushered him outside. He slunk past her, tail hanging low. Josie let her hand trail over his back as he passed to let him know it was okay. Nobody could hold it forever.

By the time she mopped up the mess and got back to the patio, Max had his front paws on the low brick wall Josie had built. She planted her feet on either side of him, ruffled his ears, and wished she could have slept through that storm like he had.

"What do you say, Max? What in the heck happened last night?" She gave him a hug and took a minute to regroup.

Last night's storm had wreaked havoc on their corner of paradise. Tree branches and palm fronds littered the wide concrete walkway that led to the beach. Patio furniture had been overturned and the wind had blown screens off windows. The damage was small price to pay for the good stuff the storm left behind.

The wind had pushed the smog out to sea, the rain had washed the street clean, and the day had broken sapphire bright. Everything sparkled under a brilliant but weak sun. That brilliance made Josie feel as if she could spread her arms and dip the fingers of one hand in the ocean while touching the snowcapped tops of the San Bernardino Mountains with the other. Life, in that moment, was incredibly simple – except that it wasn't.

Josie gave the dog a quick pat. He lowered himself to the ground and limped back toward the house. In the bright light, the grey hair around his snout glinted silver. The thought that there would be a day when she didn't have Max brought a lump to her throat. Josie couldn't imagine that future. Yet, when someone left your life - mother, friend, beloved pet – someone else moved in to fill the void. Josie's dad filled hers after her mother left and she filled Hannah's and Archer's. Josie wondered who would fill Billy's if Rosa Zuni died? She hoped it wasn't the government. If that was his only option, it might have been better if they left him in the sea.

Shaking off the sense of doom that had dogged her for the last hours, Josie went inside to fill Max's water bowl and food dish. When that was done, she rested her hands on the kitchen sink and hung her head to think what to do next.

"Hey there, Max. Jo?"

Archer's voice lifted her spirits. She walked into the dining room, put her hands against his chest and kissed him.

"I didn't expect to see you so soon."

"Disappointed?"

"Never."

Her arms went around his solid body as she rested her cheek against his chest and listened to the beating of his heart. The chink in her armor – the one her kidnapping had exposed – was still there. Those awful days as a prisoner proved that as much as she wanted to believe that she was mistress of her own fate, she was not. It had been months since that horrible time, and yet her voice still wasn't as strong as it had been, her gaze still not quite as sharp, her decision making not as sure. But good things had come out of that time, too. Josie knew exactly what Archer meant to her now. She wanted to stand beside him, not behind or in front of him and she wanted

Hannah there with both of them. The other good thing was that Archer wanted the same thing.

"You okay?" He pulled her closer. Josie's head dropped back and she grinned at him.

"How come you're so chirpy? I feel like a truck ran over me," she murmured.

"Wait until five. You'll have to scrape me off the pier and pour me into bed." He kissed her forehead, let her loose, and held up a bag. "Breakfast."

"A little late."

"Never too late for this."

"Burt's egg sandwich?" Josie laughed as she went to the kitchen. "I'll put the coffee on."

"Brought it with me. Full service." Archer called, and Josie did an about-face. "I brought some for Hannah, too."

"She's not here. She wanted to walk home."

"You told her what we found in Billy's house?"

"I couldn't avoid it. Montoya showed up and kind of forced the issue. Billy wasn't conscious. I appreciate that he let me tell Hannah in my own time once he saw he wouldn't be questioning Billy."

That was all the explanation Archer needed. Mike Montoya, the sheriff's investigator who had questioned them at the scene was nobody's fool. Billy would be the first one he would want to talk to.

"He seemed like a good guy," Archer noted. "How did Hannah take it?"

"Hard." Josie leaned against the archway as they chatted.

"That doesn't surprise me." Archer tossed a sandwich her way. She caught it.

"Déjà vu all over again," Josie agreed. "She's convinced that the cops won't look at anyone but Billy. I dropped her near the bike path. The fresh air will be good for her."

"I'll feel better when she's home."

Archer dug into the bag again and took out the coffee cups. Josie smiled. How times changed. Nothing like a little near-death experience to pull folks together, even folks as disparate as Archer and Hannah. It was a pity that common ground had come so dearly; it was a blessing it had come at all.

"Can I move this?" Archer asked and pointed to the mess of paper that was on the dining room table.

"I'll get it."

Josie swept swatches and checklists into the huge sample book that had taken up space on the table for the last few months. She was about to close it when Archer took her hand and pulled her into his body, cupping her from behind. He used his free hand to turn the pages of the giant book, flipping one then another and another. Her short dark hair rubbed against his unshaven cheek. Archer turned back to the page that had originally been opened, and put his finger on the white card with the black type.

"That one," he said.

"Funny thing. That's the one I ordered."

"Great minds think alike." He kissed her behind the ear.

"We'll have them in a week."

"Cutting it close if the big event is at the end of the month," Archer noted.

"It's Hermosa Beach. You invite people to a party the night before and they show up," Josie reminded him.

"I wouldn't care if no one came. Just as long as you're there."

"And Hannah."

"And Hannah," he agreed as he turned Josie into him and kissed her again.

Josie put her arms behind his neck and kissed him back. When they parted she closed the book, marking the page with the invitation that simply read:

You are invited to a wedding.

***

It was four in the afternoon when Mike Montoya and Wendy Sterling looked up.

Theirs had been an impressive effort of police work. Not only had their station pulled together, the sheriff himself had been in contact, pledging resources as needed. They didn't need them. In the last twelve hours physical evidence was logged in, packed up, and on its way to the lab for analysis. The coroner had taken possession of two bodies, the surviving victim had not died as had been expected, and the kid – the pivotal kid – was in bad shape but would get better. Once that happened, the dominoes would fall.

Mike had started a white board, dissecting it into thirds, one section dedicated to each of the victims. Their names were printed in Mike's neat hand and encased in near perfect circles. Greg Oi was assigned the red marker, Jak Duka blue, and, lastly, green for Rosa Zuni, aka Billy Zuni's – what? - aka patient in ICU at Torrance Memorial Hospital. Straight lines radiated from each circle and at the end of those radiating lines were short perpendicular ones. What they knew to date had been filled in.

Age:
Greg Oi - 59
Jak Duka – 33
Rosa Zuni – 18-25 (?)
Occupation:
Greg Oi – businessman/philanthropist
Jak Duka – Fed Ex delivery/union daily
Rosa Zuni – Dancer/stripper/prostitute/mistress ???
Residence:
Greg Oi – Rolling Hills
Jak Duka - San Pedro
Rosa Zuni – Hermosa Beach

Addresses, contact numbers, and next of kin were noted where applicable.

Everything about Rosa, save for her name and occupation, was a question mark. No identification had been found in the house or in her purse. There was no car in the garage or on the street registered to her address. There was no computer, but they had found a cell phone. Wendy was on top of getting a subpoena for Rosa Zuni's call records. The tech guys would drill down for any other data. Right now, though, the lack of identification was, in and of itself, a clue that Mike believed to be critical.

Then there was the fourth name in a black circle:
Billy Zuni. Age: 17.
Occupation: Student, kid, screw up, surfer, murderer (?).
Missing: Gun. Knife. Identification for Rosa Zuni. Time charts for each victim: last seen, last heard from. Motive. Connections.

Finished with the board by two, Wendy and Mike spent the next couple of hours making phone calls, and setting up appointments, asking questions when they reached a person who might have immediate information. Mostly they got responses of shock and dismay, exhortations to find the bastard who did this, and prayers that the woman would survive. They were putting the finishing touches on their schedules for the next day when Mike's phone rang. He identified himself, listened and spoke to Wendy who was looking at him expectantly as he hung up.

"Torrance PD was called on a vandalism complaint. They thought we might be interested."

"And why would that be?"

"Someone took a can of spray paint to Greg Oi's private office." Mike sat down again. "And they left an effigy of Oi with a knife through its heart."

"Now that is a bit of acting out by the union boys." Wendy pointed her pencil at Mike. "You've got an appointment over there tomorrow. Bring back pictures."

Wendy gathered her papers, tapped the edge of the pile on the desk to arrange them neatly and stood up.

"Let's go see Carl Newton. Lucky guy. He's going to be prosecuting the biggest murder case the South Bay has ever seen."

Mike stood and put on his jacket.

"Right now, it's an investigation. It's going to be a while before we have anyone he can prosecute."

"Michael, Michael," Wendy said as she breezed past him. "We've got bodies. We've got a whacked out kid. When are you ever going to realize that the glass is half full, not half empty and the one filling this glass up is Billy Zuni?"

CHAPTER 8

1996

Teuta labored, but only briefly. Her labor was so brief in fact that Teuta's husband did not arrive in time to see the baby born. Everyone in attendance at the birth praised God for this good sign. The baby would grow to be a gentle soul who would want no one to suffer.
He would be, they said, a good boy.

2013

"Well, this is interesting," Carl Newton deadpanned.

Mike was thinking that if the man's energy were a color it would be grey. Not dark and ominous, not dove soft, but ill defined like a gathering gloom that could turn into a storm as easily as it could pass by without being noticed. Mike had worked with Carl Newton before and found him extremely competent but unsettling and uninspired. He had once run for District Attorney, but he did not stir the voters' imaginations. If he had ever stirred a woman's, there was no evidence of it. No wedding ring, no personal pictures, not anything that hinted at a relationship.

Mike couldn't tell if the man still harbored political ambitions, nor could he tell if Carl Newton was satisfied with his lot in life. The detective could only hope Newton had the grit to see this one through. A crime of such passion demanded an equally passionate response. Bottom line, it was a surprise the D.A. had assigned Carl Newton.

"Yes. Interesting and complex, Michael. A double homicide." The deputy D.A. said this as if he was having a hard time choosing between the plain or sesame seed bagel.

"Potentially a triple. The female victim is touch and go," Wendy added.

"That will be a first here." Carl voiced the obvious. "I assume you're not ruling out a sex crime or a pact of some sort."

"All scenarios are on the table," Mike said.

"What have the neighbors to say? Were they aware of unusual activity at that house?"

"We haven't had much luck on the canvass yet," Wendy answered. "There's construction on one side of the house. We'll track down the owners and get put onto the contractor to see if he knows anything. An old lady, Mrs. Yount, lives on the other side. She wears a hearing aid, goes to bed by eight, and uses special earphones to hear the television. She has no idea if she was asleep or awake when all this happened."

Mike took up the thread.

"Given the storm, and the closed bathroom window, the female victim's voice wouldn't have carried. Mrs. Yount did indicate she heard booms, but believed it was the thunder."

"And the neighbors across the way?"

Carl Newton did not take notes, but he had a pen cradled in his curled fingers as if it were too heavy to lift. The thought that he was channeling Eeyore crossed Mike Montoya's mind, but only briefly. He tried never to be unprofessional, even within the privacy of his own thoughts so he answered the question.

"Directly across the street is a house in foreclosure and it's empty. There is another one that has been sold but not vacated. The owners went to a movie and came home late. They didn't see anything suspicious."

"What time did they come back?" Carl asked.

"Between ten thirty and eleven. The bodies were discovered at two in the morning, and we're waiting for a time of death from the coroner," Mike answered. "There's also a rental. They have a Westco Security sign, but that address isn't hooked into their system.

"We are covering the most obvious bases: sexual predators within a certain radius of the house, known gang members, drug activity. We'll see if anything pops up in our data bases," Wendy offered. "No drugs or paraphernalia were found in the house. I doubt that's going to be a thread, but we are asking for toxicology on all victims and that includes the boy."

"He's an interesting twist." Newton's lips moved but nothing else. His arms still rested on the arms of his chair, he had not shifted his body, or even inclined his head. Mike's own fingers twitched as if that would inspire Newton. It did not. "What are you thinking about him? He knows the home and the habits of the mother."

"The relationship isn't confirmed yet," Mike reminded him causing Newton's eyes to spark and focus more keenly on the detective.

"What relationship do you think exists?"

"I don't know. I don't want to speculate," Mike answered. Wendy moved, uncomfortable with the passive confrontation.

"Then she is who we believe she is until proven otherwise, detective." Newton countered. "We will at least stipulate that she is guardian to the boy. You said that he asked for her."

"A witness said he called for his mother," Wendy interjected, but Mike edited her.

"The boy didn't call for her. He said the word, mom. The witness couldn't be sure what he was implying, and I agree it was open to interpretation."

"Well, then, that's where we start. Close to home," Newton lectured. "Perhaps he didn't like her line of work. Perhaps the boy didn't like the woman's clients if that is what the men in her house were. Perhaps he was angry because she tried to impose rules he didn't like. Perhaps he is an addict. There are infinite possibilities when it comes to the boy."

"I would say he's at the top of the food chain," Wendy quipped, shrugging when Mike shot her a cautionary look. In the next minute she doubled down but did it deferentially. "Not that it's my call. Statistically, though, you can't ignore the fact that most homicides are committed by a person known to the victim."

"But in this case there are three victims," Mike reminded her. "I would suggest that our universe might be a little broader than Billy Zuni."

"Of course," Wendy agreed, cognizant of the fact that she had overstepped her bounds.

"I have a hearing on another matter," Carl said. "Can you do broad strokes?"

Wendy began, "We confirmed six vehicles on the street at midnight. We have general descriptions, and we've impounded the two belonging to the victims. Of the remaining four, one was directly under the streetlight in front of Mrs. Yount's place. She gets upset when people park in front of her place and walk down to the beach so she took particular note of it when she went to the bathroom. She believed it to be a green Toyota sedan. She didn't get a license plate but noted that the bumper on the back was crumpled and it was missing a hubcap on the right front."

"Did the boy have a car or access to one?" Carl finally moved, raising his right hand and pointing at Wendy.

"No. A vehicle in the driveway is disabled." Wendy checked her notes. "It was last registered in 2001 to Mr. George Lynch. I'm running him down. We found no keys."

"Has the old woman any opinions on the family, Mike?"

"She said they were quiet. They showed no interest in being neighborly. We spoke to the boy's school. He wasn't the best student. He has a juvenile record but all minor offenses," Wendy said. "We've got the hospital on speed dial. Soon as he's awake and able to talk to us, we'll be on it."

"Gut reaction?" Newton asked.

"None regarding motive or perp. Priority is to work on connecting the victims," Mike answered.

"So, you're not keen about putting the boy on the pedestal?" Newton's hand dropped to the arm of his chair. He was twirling his pen, buying into the scenario he was imagining.

"Of course he is prime, but there won't be a direct physical link and juries like their forensics." Mike reminded Newton that he was only working in the best interest of the prosecutor. "The boy was in the ocean for an indeterminate amount of time and was in the hospital by the time the bodies were discovered. His clothes were in shreds; evidence on his person was nonexistent. What we need is for him to talk to us."

"That's very fair, but your experience must tell you he is the one to sit on. Mine certainly does. I'm assuming there is evidence of him at the scene."

Mike took a deep breath. They were wasting time. The deputy had a fascination with Billy when they were a million miles from having anything he could use to file.

"It was Billy's home. There will be evidence of him, but none of it will help your case," Mike reminded Newton.

"In the hands of an exceptional prosecutor anything can be made to be sustainable evidence." Newton winked at no one in particular. "You bring me what you have, and I'll sort it out for you. Don't disappoint by being a bleeding heart or a prude, Michael."

Carl Newton finally moved as if he meant it. His hands went to the edge of the desk and he pushed his chair back as he droned on.

"You've done a fine job in a short time. Don't let the grass grow. I want to fill the press in, not the other way around. Have you spoken to the press yet?"

Wendy shook her head as Mike answered: "The sheriff planned a press conference for tomorrow."

"Is there any need for guards at the hospital?" Carl asked.

"I don't see any overt threat to the woman or the boy at this time," Mike answered.

"That ignores the possibility we've been speaking of. That the boy might be a threat to the woman," Carl reminded him.

"He isn't ambulatory. He suffered head injuries. It will probably be a few days before he's even sitting up," Michael assured the prosecutor.

"The young heal quickly," Newton warned, equally quick to assure Mike that he was wrong.

"Hospital security and staff have been advised of the circumstances. I think we're good," Mike answered, annoyed to be pushed so hard in a direction that was not yet warranted.

"I would hate to see you compromised." Before Mike could point out that it would be the caution of his investigation that would dictate the outcome of Newton's prosecution, the lawyer covered yet another base for the detective. "Have either of you contacted Social Services?"

"I did," Mike said as he was about to leave.

"Billy is lawyered up." Wendy added her two cents.

"Really? Who is it?" Newton asked, fairly licking his lips.

"Josie Bates. She's the one who found him in the ocean. She also discovered the bodies and called it in," Mike said.

"So she knew the mother."

Mike shook his head, "No, they'd never met."

"But she's a friend of the boy. That is interesting."

"Her ward goes to school with him. I think we should take this at face value. Hermosa is a small town. She was on the scene, and she's willing to help."

"Don't be naïve, Michael. She's jockeying for position. Move fast on that boy and watch Bates carefully. She's wily."

"You'll know what we have when we have it." Mike's voice was tight but only Wendy noticed.

"Good. Done." Carl dismissed them. "I'll touch base with the District Attorney himself and see if he'd like me to stand in with the sheriff at the press conference. The citizens will want to be assured that this is an isolated incident. Keep on the boy. That's the way to go. If you need help with Bates, call me."

Carl Newton let them go without a thank you or goodbye. Mike was out the door and gone before Wendy was out of her chair. She caught up with him half way down the hall. She moved in tight and nudged him.

"Lighten up, Mike. He was just throwing his weight around."

Mike walked on with measured steps. Wendy matched his gait. She was happy and energized by the case; Mike Montoya was burdened. She tried again to lighten the mood.

"Come on, Newton's a wet blanket, but his instincts are good and his conviction record is great."

Wendy nudged him once more, but Mike moved away.

"Carl Newton is a mortician," Mike snapped. "He's got a couple of bodies and he wants to dress them up to the nines by painting the kid as a sex crazed psycho or something. For God sake, did you see that glint in his eyes? He wants this to be as simple and salacious as possible. If you think that's okay, you should reassign."

Mike quickened his step, leaving Wendy behind.

"Hey!" she hollered, and her voice echoed down the empty hall until it whacked Mike on the back of the head.

He pivoted slowly. Wendy looked formidable and gorgeous in her outrage. She opened her mouth to let him have it but changed her mind. Mike Montoya wasn't a goody-two-shoes, he was a guy whose sense of fairness was so deeply imbedded it hurt his soul.

Wendy wished he could learn to take things as they came. Sometimes you got what you wanted, sometimes you didn't. She dropped her hands, walked up to him, took a deep breath, and gave him a pat on his shoulder along with the truth:

"This whole thing was friggin' salacious the minute Josie Bates found those bodies and the kid wasn't one of them."

***

Hannah came home an hour after Josie dropped her off. Her shoes dangled from her fingers, and sand clung to her feet. It wasn't long ago that Hannah wouldn't have been caught dead walking alone on the beach. She insisted she felt more comfortable in places where there were nooks and crannies to hide in until she knew where the bad things lived. But time, Josie, and the rhythm of Hermosa changed all that. Now Hannah was a fixture at Burt's by the Beach, her paintings hung in the local gallery, and she walked Max into town. Hannah admired the sunsets and could be found sitting by the water at sunrise when the devils inside her head woke her too early. Josie's house was home, and Josie was glad she was back, but it was Archer who called to her first.

"Hey, brought you a sandwich."

He made room at the table.

"I'll get you something to drink." Josie went into the kitchen. When she returned, Hannah was settled with her elbows planted on top of the table and her sandwich untouched. Josie put a glass of ice tea in front of her. Josie took her own chair. She laced her arms through Archer's and leaned her head on his shoulder.

"You doing okay, Hannah?" Archer asked.

"Tired," Hannah answered.

"I called the school," Josie said.

"Did you tell them everything?"

"The basics," Josie answered.

"I guess it doesn't matter. It's going to be all over the news. That will be bad," Hannah muttered. She looked heartbroken.

"Sometimes it's good. People might rally for Billy," Josie offered even though she knew Hannah wouldn't buy it.

The media got facts wrong, or in the worst case made them up. Gossip started, talk radio turned gossip back to distorted facts, and everyone got caught in the resulting maelstrom. That's exactly where Hannah's mind had gone. Suddenly, she shot straight up.

"Josie, there's a television in Billy's room. He doesn't know about his mom. What if he sees it?"

"The hospital won't let that happen. I promise, he won't find out until he's strong enough and alert enough to understand."

Hannah was about to offer a litany of reasons why the best intentions where Billy was concerned were going to result in disaster, but Faye's arrival stopped her.

"Oh good, everyone is here. How you doing, sweetie?" For Hannah there was a quick hug and a kiss buried in her glorious hair. "Josie. Archer."

"Sorry, I didn't know you were coming." Archer indicated the food.

"Heavens, none for me, but thank you, Archer. I have what you wanted, Josie, but it brings new meaning to the phrase slim to none." Faye opened her purse and pulled out a Xerox. She handed it to Josie as she sat down. "It's so sad that this is all we have of him. Good lord, I've known Billy longer than anyone, and I can't tell you a thing about him."

"I've been beating myself up all night about that," Josie added.

"The first time I can recall seeing Billy he was about eight or nine. I wasn't even sure he lived here. You know how it is around the beach, kids come and visit, people move in and out. You have to see someone ten times before you realize you've seen them once. Billy was different, though. I remembered him every time I laid eyes on him. God, he was such a sweet little kid."

Faye fell silent and then smiled as if suddenly remembering that she wasn't alone.

"The first time I talked to him I was worried because he was out so late for a little one. I asked where he lived and he gave me a piece of paper with his address on it. He never said a word. I think I scared him. Hannah, you didn't think I was scary when you met me, did you?"

"No," she answered, but it went without saying that very little scared Hannah.

"Thank goodness for that," Faye laughed. "Anyway, then he was just everywhere at once. Burt was always feeding him. The poor little thing ate like there was no tomorrow."

"He still does," Josie said. "I met him when he was fifteen. I could kick myself for not following up on that representation agreement. You know, Rosa Zuni looks like she's about twelve herself."

Josie perused the one page, and noted the signature at the bottom of the representation agreement. At least it said Rosa Zuni. Faye watched Josie, and Archer watched Hannah.

"Hannah? Do you know anything about her?" Archer asked, just to engage her in the conversation.

"Mothers aren't something we discussed," she drawled.

The silence that fell was as pregnant a pause as there had ever been. Josie squeezed Archer's knee and bit her tongue. She knew that tone of voice. Hannah was prickly as a pear.

"Well, we'll pray for his mother, no matter who she is," Faye said, smoothing things over. "And we'll pray for Rosa to wake up so she can help Billy. For now, we'll just help out where we can. Burt's setting up a donation box at the restaurant. I doubt Billy or Rosa have insurance."

Josie nodded and crossed her arms on the table. "This feels so wrong."

"Nobody flies under the radar like this unless they make an effort." Archer put words to Josie's thoughts.

"We all assumed neglect and Billy never corrected us. Why would Billy let us think that? Why would Rosa Zuni want us to think that?"

Josie looked at Archer. He raised his palms toward the ceiling, full of questions but out of suggestions.

"Right now we got a flood of information and none of it's good. Let's just plug the leak and then we can figure out what made the dam crack." Archer crumpled the trash. "At least Billy's not going to get some public defender if this doesn't go his way."

"All is well as can be, then." Faye got up. "I'll take care of business at the office, but if there's anything I can help with give me a call."

Josie thanked Faye and saw her out. When she got back, Archer was finishing with the trash and Hannah had her shoes on.

"Well, I guess we've got our work cut out for us," Josie said. She kissed Archer's cheek. "I'll have my phone on. Call me if you find anything. Hannah, make sure Max gets out. I'll be back by seven."

"I'll meet you back here about then, too," Archer said.

They were both headed in opposite directions when Hannah turned in her chair, hugged the back of it, and said:

"Should I start cleaning out my room? I mean, we're going to take care of him, right?"

"That's getting a little ahead of things, Hannah," Archer said as he and Josie exchanged a look.

That didn't escape Hannah's notice. She sat up straighter, her brow furrowing as Josie looked to Archer for help. All he brought to the discussion was a raised eyebrow and a lost expression. Josie widened her eyes, making a mental note to talk to him about having her back where Hannah was concerned. For now, Josie was on her own.

"Why? Why isn't he coming here?" she insisted.

"Hannah, I can't just take Billy," Josie said. "That's not the way things work."

"You took me," Hannah insisted.

"I had your mother's permission, and your trial was over," Josie reminded her. "Circumstances were completely different."

"He doesn't have anyone else, Josie." Hannah dug in. Josie did the same. Archer added the only two cents he could come up with.

"We'll do what's best for Billy. I promise, Hannah."

Hannah turned on him, happy and relieved to have a champion. "He could stay with you. Maybe that would be better."

"That's not what I meant." Cowed in the face of Hannah's hope, Archer backed off but she came right back at him.

"Why not?"

"Hannah, give us a break. We're tired. We haven't sorted anything out yet." Archer tried to appease her but too many women in one room made him nervous. Josie stepped in to end the discussion.

"This is no game."

"No, it isn't," Hannah shot back, impatient with Josie. "That's why we need to figure it out now so Billy doesn't have to wonder if anyone cares about him."

Hannah's unwavering faith in these adults who had protected her was suddenly shaken. She had no idea that Josie and Archer were equally unsure of what they were up against.

"Look, Hannah, we need to take a cue from about a hundred people right now. Decisions about Billy aren't up to us. The hospital, the cops, the district attorney-"

"You can't leave it to them," Hannah pleaded. "You know what will happen if you leave it to them."

"Hannah, stop. Getting hysterical isn't going to help anyone." Josie squared her shoulders, uncomfortable with this confrontation because it was hers alone. "We'll find a relative, but I can't take everyone in."

"Billy isn't everyone."

The snap of those words was like a slap across Josie's face. Hannah stood up so fast her chair toppled. She caught it and grappled with it, but it fell out of her grasp again and hit the hardwood. Max raised his head and whimpered. Archer opened his mouth to speak but decided against it. Instead, he moved to help her but thought better of it when she lunged to right it herself. Grunting in frustration she pushed her hair behind her ear. Her chocolate colored cheeks were a mottle of brick red, and her eyes glistened with tears of frustration.

"If his own mother didn't care, why do you think anyone else in his family will?"

She lifted the chair. It landed on four legs as if to prove her argument was solid.

"Hannah, stop. He's fine. He's safe." Josie reached out, hoping to reassure her but the girl shrugged her off.

"He's not safe like he would be here."

Grabbing her shoes off the floor, Hannah Sheraton turned and walked past the two adults. The next thing they heard was her bedroom door slam.

CHAPTER 9

1996

Teuta lay alone thinking she was glad that her father, Yilli the goat herder, was not alive to see her the way she was: unable to move, to take care of her family, to enjoy the love of her husband. Teuta felt the darkness of her heart but could do nothing to lighten it. She did not know how many days she had watched the sun come up and go down or how many times her husband had spoken to her and she had not answered. She was pondering this when the door of the bedroom opened. Her oldest daughter entered and walked softly across the room with the fussing baby in her arms. Teuta did not stir when she came to the side of the bed. She let a thought cross her mind. She thought: poor little girl, taking care of a house and a family that Teuta, the wife and mother, didn't care about anymore.

"Nënë?"

The girl's eyes were wide with concern. She was only nine, far too young to know about anything bad in this world, and yet she felt its evil. Poor thing, Teuta thought again, and yet she could do nothing more than lie there, look at the girl, and close her ears to the sounds the baby made.

The girl, though, was smarter and braver than her mother knew. When Teuta did not reach for her baby, the girl did not hesitate. She put him under the covers and in the bed with their mother. Teuta kept her eyes fixed on the wall, she did not wrap her arm around the little boy, nor did she breathe in the scent of him, or touch his soft skin, or let his little fingers touch her lips. She didn't pull aside her clothing so he could suckle. It was her daughter who unbuttoned her mother's blouse. Teuta didn't even have the strength to stop her. She should have berated the girl but could not. Teuta tried to ignore the warm bundle that had been put in bed with her, but the baby moved and his downy little head brushed against her lips as if he was asking for a kiss. Teuta's heart softened when his little fingers touched her nipple. He was so helpless and innocent. What was a mother to do?

With great effort, she took her child and pulled him close. She looked at his sweet face. What, she wondered, would become of him? What could his life be in this sad and hopeless place? Perhaps, it would be better than she thought. Perhaps he would grow and be well; perhaps not. Only time would tell.

"Mjaft shpejt. Një dhi e vogël rritet," she whispered.

Yes, soon enough the small goat grows. For now he is only a small goat. She would worry later about when he was big. She pulled aside her clothing and offered the baby her breast.

2013

Mike Montoya parked his car in the driveway of Greg Oi's home, set the brake, opened the door, swung out, and took a minute to admire his surroundings. He didn't often have cause to come to a place like this, on a chore like this.

In Los Angeles violent death came to people on streets that ran past bars and adult bookstores, in houses where too many bodies were packed in spaces too small, or cars, or catch basins, or empty lots, or dry gutters. In the South Bay, car crashes, surfing accidents, and overdoses in pleasant houses or beachfront apartments were the norm. Murder was the exception rather than the rule. But behind the gates of Rolling Hills, a homicide investigation was rare. Then again, everything here was rare.

Down the hill, folks sweltered; up the hill people were warm. Down the hill, folks were assaulted by sounds; up the hill they were blessed with silence. Down the hill the air was heavy; up the hill it was still. Down the hill smelled like a mixture of ocean, sunscreen, fast food and exhaust; up the hill the scent of jasmine, freshly cut grass, and a hint of stables blanketed the terrain. Down the -

Suddenly, the quiet was shattered by a blood-curdling scream. Mike ducked, hunkered down, and pulled his weapon only to find himself positioned and primed to execute a peacock. The damn thing had fallen out of a tree and landed on the hood of his vehicle. It struggled to its feet, craned its neck, and spread its tail feathers as it tried to impress its own reflection in the car's windshield.

"Get off there."

Mike hit the fender. The bird ignored him. He hit it again only to feel like an idiot when the peacock continued to admire itself. Mike tugged on his jacket and turned toward the house. The bird screeched once more as Mike crossed the curved driveway, took the low-rise steps that led to a wide entry, and pressed the doorbell. He didn't hear it ring. When the intercom didn't engage, he reached for the huge brass knocker shaped like a double-headed eagle. Before he could use it, the door opened and a willowy young woman in low-slung jeans and a tight little top that bared a perfect midsection appeared. She gave him a lazy look and held the door like a stripper's pole.

"Mrs. Oi?" The young woman shook her head. Mike held up his credentials. "Mrs. Oi is expecting me."

The woman opened the door wide enough for Mike to step inside. It occurred to him that this might possibly be a diffident daughter, entitled and dissatisfied, but that assessment didn't feel right. If she was the maid, Mrs. Oi was a very understanding woman. If she was a friend, she didn't seem particularly concerned about a cop at the door or the circumstances that brought him there.

"I'm Detective Montoya." He put out his hand.

"She back." Her accent was thick, but her English was decent.

The girl didn't bother to shake his hand before leading him through the house. They went past a tufted ottoman the size of which Mike had only seen in an opera house. It was covered in an animal print, what animal he couldn't say since he knew of none that walked the earth with a purple hide. A chandelier the size of a small planet hung from the domed ceiling. Inside the concave of plaster was a mural depicting snow-capped mountains, rocky hills, and an army of what appeared to be mythical warriors. There was a sweep of stairs to his left and a red and gold dining room to his right. Under his feet was a black and white marble checkerboard.

If the lady of the house was wailing and gnashing her teeth in grief, she was doing it in private. The place was cathedral-quiet and that was not pleasant. It was one thing for a sprawling house like this to be filled with kids, quite another to imagine Mr. Greg Oi sweeping down the stairs in his pink heels and satin halter dress, his bath perhaps drawn by this young lady.

"I'm sorry about your father." Mike took a flier. The girl snorted. He went to the opposite end of the spectrum. "Have you worked for the Oi's a long time?"

The girl sighed heavily as if she were bored silly and moved like every step required super human effort.

"Mr. Oi's death must have been a shock," Mike suggested.

The girl shrugged. Mike gave up trying to engage her and turned his eye to his surroundings. He felt like he was on the jungle ride at Disneyland.

In the cavernous great room the walls were painted shades of beige accented with black. The furniture was upholstered in the hides of things that at one time moved on four legs: zebra, cheetah, leopard. Impressively healthy decorative trees were rooted in pots the size of small bathtubs and crafted out of red mud. Huge abstract paintings hung on the walls. Mike paused in front of one thinking it had all the energy of a feeding frenzy.

In the next room, a mahogany bar stretched the length of one wall. The corners were carved into the heads of elephants, their trunks raised as if to call a thirsty traveler to their watering hole. There was an exquisite pool table, club chairs and a chess table. On the wall was the mounted head of an animal. It had been a beautiful thing: delicate of face, horns fragile, taffy-striped, and spiraling toward the ceiling. The glass eyes were so artistically formed that Mike could see the look of both terror and forgiveness in them. In a Plexiglas case on the bar, a stuffed rodent sat on its haunches, perpetually alert. The house was a museum full of dead, skinned, and mounted animal parts. Mike had imagined Greg Oi a more sensitive soul given his taste in fashion. Unaware that he had stopped to consider the rodent, Mike's thoughts were interrupted by a theatrical sigh from his guide.

"Forgive me," Mike muttered.

The young woman flipped her hair, and their safari began anew.

In the breakfast room a large glass table was set for a party of six, complete with red placemats, bamboo chargers, white bowls and crisp black napkins choked by rings of gold shaped like emerald-eyed snakes. Mike glanced toward the chef's kitchen half expecting to see a wildebeest strung up for the butcher. All he saw was a gleaming kitchen. They went through a laundry room. The girl was holding the back door, but Mike hesitated, retreated a step, and craned his neck.

"Do the Oi's have children?" Mike asked when he joined his reluctant hostess.

"No."

She held the screen door wider.

"A guest then? Relative?"

"No."

Mike smiled. She knew that he knew she was lying. He had seen someone darting around the corner, but it wasn't this woman's place to divulge anything about the household. He tried one more time. "How long did you say you have worked for the Ois again?"

"Long time."

She turned her back on him. Mike caught the screen door before it slammed shut. Outside, a bee buzzed past his ear and he looked after it. It was nice to be in the presence of a living creature. They were on the move again, stalking their prey. Mike knew they were close when he heard the call of a special breed - a rich woman at play. When the girl-relative-maid-whatever stepped aside at the end of the flagstone walk, he was duly impressed by the playground.

In front of him was a nearly Olympic size pool, classically cut into a rectangle. Infinity pools stair-stepped each end and the bottom of the pool sparkled arctic white. The edging tile was robin's egg blue and the concrete was pocked to perfection so that no privileged foot would slip upon it when wet. A queen size float turned lazily in the still, clear water. Curved beds planted with lacy, exotic bushes softened the edges of the decking. Four lounges, a glass table shaded by a huge umbrella and surrounded by six chairs, and an island of an outdoor kitchen made for a space that was bigger than Mike's house and better furnished.

"Damn it! Damn it all to hell!"

He turned toward the screech, catching the young woman's eye as he did so. She raised an arched eyebrow. There was only the slightest twitch at the edge of her lips. She cocked her head. Mike was on his own.

"Thank you."

The woman was headed back to the house by the time he got the words out. She had left him on the rise of a sweeping lawn that rolled right up to the edge of a stunning tennis court.

It was blue-on-blue, lined in white, surrounded on three sides by a tall chain linked fence. Beyond the far fence was a veritable forest of vegetation and above that a hill had been shaved flat to accommodate those who still owned horses. On the court a guy in white shorts and a coolie hat stood next to a basket of balls. One hand rested on the net post the other on his hip. He had good legs but he was watching a woman with great ones. A machine blasted balls at her, and she blasted them right back. Mike was walking down the wide steps when the little blond let loose.

"Damn it! Screw it!"

Her rant was made more interesting when she started wielding her tennis racket like it was a machete instead of executing a precise slice. Her tiny feet minced in circles. Suddenly, she missed a step and tumbled onto the court. The guy in the hat was on her in a second, but she shoved him back.

"Forget it. Forget it, Rob. Leave me alone. I can do it myself."

She got to her knees, found her feet, leaned over, and retrieved her racket. That's when Mike laughed just once. The woman wasn't wearing bike shorts under her tennis skirt. She wasn't even wearing tennis panties with a respectable ruffle. Kat Oi was wearing a thong, and when she bent over Mike got an eyeful of her tight rear end. Attractive as it was, he was beyond embarrassed and grateful that Wendy wasn't with him. The blond stiffened. The pro cringed. Mike composed himself.

"Mrs. Oi?" Mike called. "I'm Detective Montoya."

He took the last two steps quickly, proffered hand, and was rejected yet again. The pro peeled off to pick up the balls as Kat Oi stormed off the court, grabbed a towel, and pushed past the detective.

"I know who you are. I'm not stupid. You said you were coming."

"Of course. Would you rather talk out here?" he asked. "Or maybe you'd like to change."

"Doesn't matter what I'm wearing. Greg's still dead. You're still here. Let's get this over with."

Mike saw the man in the coolie hat look up. Their eyes locked. Mike was thinking the same thing he was: a dead husband might have been a good reason to cancel a tennis lesson. Whatever else the man was thinking was tucked away as he went about his business, collecting balls, and feeding them back into the machine.

"I'll pay you next week, Rob. Same time."

Kat Oi slipped this over her shoulder, and once again Mike Montoya was following a woman who was unimpressed by him. The walk was much brisker on the way back to the house than it had been on the way out and definitely chattier.

"Don't read anything into me playing tennis today. Just don't. People grieve in different ways. I've already called who I need to call. Just don't think everybody sits around wringing their hands in situations like this. Some people need a physical outlet. That's the kind of person I am. I don't fall apart when stuff like this happens."

She ripped open the screen door and Mike wondered how often 'stuff like this' happened to Mrs. Oi. He caught the door and it bounced against his palm.

"I'm not here to make judgments."

"You better damn well not. You try to make me out to have something to do with any of this, and I swear I'll sue your butt."

"I'm just here to get some information that might help us find out who killed your husband and who-"

"And who pulled that little stunt at the office last night?" Kat's voice rose. She had ratcheted it up as she hit the bar before Mike made it through the breakfast room. When he joined her, she was still talking. "I heard about it. I went down to see it myself, but they wouldn't let me in. You tell those guys who won't let me in that I need some personal things."

"If you tell me what it is, I'll find out if it can be released," Mike suggested.

Kat lifted a heavy decanter. She paused. "No, I want to get it myself."

"Did you see the office?"

"No. I just told you the cops wouldn't let me in. Which is just ridiculous. It was just vandals. Those idiots who worked for him did it. That's a no-brainer. It's been nothing but misery since they decided to strike."

"My office is working with the Torrance PD. It may be some time before we'll be able to release anything to you."

Mike moved easily around the room until he could see Kat's profile. She was petite, pretty, and had probably been stunning not too many years earlier. But the Southern California sun had taken its toll. Now that her face was screwed up into a ball of frustration and displeasure, her attractiveness was questionable.

Kat poured two fingers of Scotch into a heavy glass, led Mike out of the game room, and plopped herself on the zebra striped sofa in the living room. She crossed one ankle over the opposite knee. He thanked God for small favors. Kat's skirt was flared and the thong was covered. She took a swig of her drink and then spread her arms over the back of the sofa while he settled in an armchair. Mike crossed his legs, uncrossed them, and then crossed them once more. The chair had looked inviting, but it was stiff and unforgiving. The horsehair upholstery was bizarrely soft and prickly at the same time. It was an ignominious end for a majestic creature.

"I'd like to know about your husband," he began.

"Greg was a good guy. You can put that down on paper. I thought he was a good guy." Sincerity slid across those icy words without gaining traction.

"How long were you married?" Mike poised a pen over his notebook.

"We were together four years." She took another drink and caressed the couch as if indicating that everything in this kingdom did, indeed, belong to her now that the king was dead.

"That's a long time," Mike noted.

"Ho-oh." Kat's foot fell off her knee, the hand holding the drink pointed straight at him. "You think I'm going to give you a woe-is-me shtick? Forget it. I'm not saying I was perfectly fine with things. You take the good and the bad. I know how you found him. You think it's easy living with someone who wants to look like your sister? Look at me. I'm a size two, and Greg was a big man. He kept trying to get into my clothes. I told him to buy his own, but he said he liked being close to me. Like that's why he wanted to wear my clothes. Bullshit. I just had better taste than he did."

She snorted, downed her drink, smacked the glass on the coffee table, and sat back again.

"He liked being close, alright. He would have lived in my skin if he could."

"So it upset you that he was cross dressing?"

"No. Everybody has quirks." She eyed Mike. "Well, maybe not you, but Greg did. I do. I'm picky about stuff. I'm impatient. We all have our little flaws, so I wasn't upset with him. I am surprised he was doing it in public. I thought it was kind of something between us."

Kat Oi reflected for a moment. Mike was always surprised at what people held dear. She shook off the fleeting sentimentality and cut her eyes his way.

"Nobody's going to find out are they? I mean you're not going to tell the papers or anything. I'd be the laughing stock, and I was just finally getting some respect around here. Not to mention what it would do to Greg's reputation. Reputation is very big in his business. He does a lot of work overseas. Those folks aren't as broadminded as we are here."

"We keep some things back to help us in our investigation." Mike saw no point in telling her that if this went to trial the way Greg Oi was dressed at the time of his death would be front and center. "Do you know of anyone who would want your husband dead?"

"Well not me, for God sake," Kat barked.

"Anyone you can think of beside you," he suggested. "Did he socialize with others who enjoyed his lifestyle?"

"I never met any of them if he did," she answered.

"Did he frequent bars? Do you know if he tried to pick up men?"

Kat wrinkled her nose, "You've got to be kidding. He couldn't have fooled anyone that he was a woman."

"He may not have been trying to, but he might have picked up the wrong person."

"He never said anything. I never saw anyone hanging around. Greg was pretty predictable. He didn't go out much. Oh, except to his association."

"Do you know how I can contact this association?"

She shook her head and shrugged her shoulders. "No. They were just guys who came over here from the same country he was from."

"Where was he from, Mrs. Oi?"

"Albania," she answered. "It's like in Eastern Europe."

"How long had he been in the United States?"

"Twenty plus, but you'd think he got here yesterday. It was always 'home this' and 'Albania' that. If Albania was so great, why'd he ever leave? Anyway, I never expected him to explain anything. He was a big boy."

"Was Mr. Oi straight?" Mike probed.

Kat looked directly back. "Exceptionally."

"Do you know anything about his business problems?" Mike went through his checklist.

"There were always problems with the business. If it's not our government, then it's those people he deals with overseas, or someone complaining about a shipment, or some employee going berserk."

"Can you be more specific?"

"Ask his lawyer. Ask Dan Jenkins at Marshall Fasteners," she muttered, only to change her mind when she looked at Mike's impassive expression. "Okay. Look. Sorry. I'm not trying to make this harder. I want to know who killed him, too. The only thing I can tell you is that the new contract negotiations were bad. Greg wasn't used to not getting his own way. He thought the unions should be grateful for the concessions he already made. He dug in and the brothers didn't like it. Greg thought men should be grateful just to work. He said men in this country didn't know how lucky they were."

Kat paused. She put her fist to her mouth and raised her eyes to the high ceiling. She looked back at Mike and it seemed there were tears in her eyes. But it only seemed that way.

"I didn't think anything of it, but two men came here a couple nights ago. I don't even know how they got past the gate. I'll sue the whole damn homeowners association if the guard was drunk or something."

"Do you have a name?"

She scoffed. "The guard? Hell, no."

"I'm sorry," Mike corrected. "The men who came here. Did you know them?"

"No, I've never seen the older one before. There was a younger guy with him. Greg didn't let them in. He seemed really mad." She waved a hand and the huge yellow diamond she wore nearly blinded him. Mike added generous to Greg Oi's resume as his wife collected her thoughts. "No, that's not right. I've seen Greg mad. He had a hell of a temper. When these guys showed up he seemed upset and surprised. Really upset. He even seemed a little scared. I didn't think anything could scare Greg."

"Could you hear what they were saying?"

"No. They weren't here long. Greg hollered something at them and slammed the door. That wasn't like him at all. He played hardball. He was pretty harsh when it came to business. More cold. He didn't yell, he just figured out how to win and did it. But these two upset him. He went in his den when they left. I don't even know where he slept that night or if he did."

Kat Oi's voice had fallen to a whisper. There was a slight tremor in her cheek. It took a minute for Mike to realize she wasn't reacting to a sense of guilt that she hadn't helped her husband. Kat Oi had been afraid, too.

"Where were you when he was talking to these men?" Mike asked.

She indicated a space near the wide doorway. "I was over there. They couldn't see me. We were shooting pool, having a drink, and he told me to stand there to be safe. Where he grew up, someone coming to your door at night could mean a friend or someone ready to blow your head off."

"Was your husband armed?"

Mike saw the word 'no' forming on her lips but then Kat took the high road.

"He has a gun."

"May I see it," Mike asked.

"It won't be here. He had a carry permit. It was legal."

"Would you mind looking? No weapon was inventoried at the scene."

Kat rolled her eyes and got up off the couch like it was a chore. She walked out of the room, was gone longer than he thought she should be, and when she sauntered back in she said:

"It's not here. Maybe it's in his office or did you look in the car?"

"It's not there." Mike answered. "I'll check his office."

"When can I get the car back?" She plopped herself back on the sofa.

"They should be done with it today or tomorrow. My associate will call." Mike smiled. Kat did not. "Perhaps we could get back to the night you had the visitors?"

"There isn't much more to tell. Greg checked the security camera but the men were standing too close so he didn't get a good look. He opened it anyway, and he must have been surprised because he raised his voice right away. By the time I got to a place where I could see, he had kind of dropped back. The other man was yelling."

"Would you recognize those men if you saw them again?"

"Yeah." Kat picked up her glass, raised it, realized it was empty and put it back on the table. "The young one works at Marshall. Big union guy with a big mouth."

Mike took three photographs out of his jacket pocket and showed her a picture of Jak Duka.

"No. Not him," she said. "But he's been here off and on the last couple of months."

Mike made notes and went on smoothly. "When did these other men come here?"

"Day before yesterday." Kat fiddled with her skirt.

"Do you think they came here on union business?"

"I don't know. Greg had his fingers in a zillion pies," she sniffed. She added: "And now it looks like he had 'em in a honey pot, too."

Mike shuffled the photos and showed her a picture of Rosa Zuni taken at the hospital. Mike found it hard to look at; Kat Oi did not. Finally, she shook back her hair.

"The little slut doesn't look so good now, does she?"

CHAPTER 10

1997

Teuta's husband looked to his left and then to his right. He looked ahead and he looked behind. He looked to see if others were afraid as he was, but all he saw were angry people calling out in strong voices, raising their fists. He took courage and raised his fist, too. People wanted to tear down the government and tear apart the politicians and bankers and businessmen who had lied to them.

All these years since freedom the people had worked hard. They made money. The government said to invest the money they worked hard for. Every citizen, they said, would be rich. Money made money. They rejoiced – until now. Now all of the country starved because of the game that had been played. A pyramid. A Ponzi. He knew of no such things! He only knew his money was gone and he was a poor man.

So Teuta's husband marched on the palace with others. He wanted to see the president hang from the balcony of his grand house. Someone must pay and all he had left – all any of the good people had left – were their fists, and their anger, and their fear. Even in the times of their fathers there had been no more desperate times than these.

What was he to do? How would he feed his children?

Teuta's husband raised his fist higher and marched with his countrymen.

2013

When Josie was young, her mother would open the door to her bedroom Sunday morning and say, "Church". Like every other kid on the base, Josie got out of bed without complaint. She dressed in her blouse with the ruffle running down the front, her pleated skirt, and her patent leather shoes. Her mother wore a lace dress and kittened heeled shoes; her father wore his uniform. In the chapel Josie's mother looked at the altar, her father bowed his head, and Josie's eyes were trained on her parents' entwined fingers.

She never knew if they were true believers or simply following protocol. What mattered was that they were all together. After her mother disappeared, Josie's father never went to church again. Instead, Mrs. O'Connor, a well-meaning officer's wife, swept Josie up, determined to save the poor little half-orphan's soul.

Josie didn't resist Mrs. O'Connor's advances, and her father made no protest. Josie was convinced that if she bowed her head lower, and clasped her hands tighter, and prayed harder, her mother would come back. But each time she raised her head, she was sitting next to Mrs. O'Connor who poured her size fourteen body into size ten clothes and was not a natural redhead.

Josie resigned from the O'Connor clan and spent Sundays with her father, watching football and frying burgers. They said more in two sentences than Mrs. O'Connor would in a lifetime of yapping. At the end of the day her father would say:

"Now, that's how God expects man to rest."

Josie would respond: "Yep."

They would fall silent until one of them turned on the TV. It was too hard to sit in the quiet house with the ghost of her mother between them. Josie returned to Torrance Memorial Hospital knowing this visit would be as hard for Billy as Sundays had been for her. There was a mother's ghost hovering in room 217 with Billy Zuni. There was a mother's ghost dodging Hannah.

Josie was getting damned tired of all of them.

***

Hannah walked down the hall holding her books tight so she wouldn't stop and touch every doorway. Her obsessions and compulsions had resurfaced with a vengeance in the last forty-eight hours. Hannah believed nothing could freak her out the way the mountains had, but she was wrong. What happened two nights ago had been beyond nightmarish. Hannah wished she had never followed Josie to the beach. She wished the memory of Billy's near lifeless hand in hers would go away. She was plagued by the image of Josie growing smaller in the distance until she disappeared altogether.

Hannah was shivering, wishing there was some way to stop this sick feeling, wishing Josie hadn't made her go to school, when someone ran into her. Before she got her bearings, it happened again. Her eyes snapped up in time to see two boys in varsity jackets smirking at her. She glared and that only gave them greater satisfaction. They grinned at one another and laughed. Other kids saw what was going on and high-fived the two as they moved on.

"Douches," Hannah muttered and kept going.

School was not easy for Hannah. She had never been in one long enough to make friends, she questioned teachers who didn't want to be challenged, and, in Hermosa, she was hobbled by her notoriety. Teenagers were quick to label one another and Hannah was labeled stuck-up because she didn't fall easily into the culture. They labeled Billy Zuni a retard for his constant good nature and loyalty to her. Everyone thought she hated Billy, but she didn't. He had never treated her like a criminal and she was grateful for that. Still, Hannah couldn't let him get too close just in case something happened and he went away.

Now something had happened, and Hannah almost exploded with the need to comfort herself. A touch at a doorway would help; a razor blade on her arm would be best.

When she got to her locker she fell upon it, rested her head against the cold metal and thrummed her fingers against it. She counted softly, stood upright and twirled the lock.

"Damn." Her hands shook so badly she couldn't get the combination right. Hannah paused and breathed deeply. One finger tapped. She concentrated.

One...
Three...
Five....
Ten...

Hannah's head hurt. She didn't want to be in school. She wanted to be at the hospital. She wanted to tell Billy she was sorry if she had ever hurt him.

"Twelve, thirteen, fourteen. . ."

Hannah froze. Her head clicked up, her eyes narrowed as she stared at the metal locker. She knew that voice.

"Shut up, Tiffany."

Forcing her fingers to quiet, she twirled the lock and tried to ignore the girl behind her. Tiffany sidestepped into Hannah's line of sight, all five-foot six of her clad in her perfect leggings and gladiator sandals. Her hair was long and her make-up heavy. Her mouth twisted cruelly around every word that came out of it.

"Oh, come on. I'll help you count. It will be fun," Tiffany mocked. "Then we can go around touching all the doors."

Hannah yanked open her locker. From the beginning, the coolest of the cool girls had decided it was her job to make Hannah miserable. She executed that charge with relish, especially after she figured out Hannah wouldn't fight back. It wasn't so much that Tiffany disliked Hannah as she did like torturing people.

"Oh, you don't want to play the counting game?" Tiffany cooed. "Maybe you want to go for a swim like your boyfriend did."

She moved again, this time scooting up close to Hannah. Tiffany's little posse hung back, a zygote of bad girls waiting for their cells to split so they could grow into real bitches like Tiffany. Hannah knew that would never happen. Those girls would always be tethered to the blonde by that bizarre umbilical cord of communal self-loathing that passed for friendship. Tiffany's fingers wound around the edge of the locker. She leaned closer to Hannah, tired of not being the center of attention. Hannah slid her eyes toward that hand as she listened to Tiffany's ugly voice.

"I never understood why you let that loser hang out with you. You're pretty in a weird sort of way. You're smarter than Billy Zuni," Tiffany drawled. "Then again, anyone is smarter than Billy Zuni."

Tiffany raised her voice and her pretty kohl encrusted eyes at the same time. Her friends giggled on cue. Satisfied that she had been amusing, she looked back at Hannah and leaned closer still. She was so excited by this little game that her knuckles were white as she grasped the edge of the locker. She licked her lips as if what to come was going to be absolutely delicious.

"I mean only an idiot couldn't kill themselves. Then again, you're not too good at that either. You're supposed to cut your wrist, Hannah, not your arm. Next time you two should try it together. Two heads are better than one. Maybe you'll get it right 'cause nobody would miss two losers like you."

Slowly, Hannah turned and looked the vile girl in the face: the one who had draped herself across the locker, who had decided that it was funny to wish people dead, who had probably wasted countless hours since Billy's ordeal talking about him to anyone who would listen. Hannah touched the locker door.

Once. . .

Twice. . .

Tiffany rolled her eyes.

"Oh God, here we go again. I know, twenty. Want me to help you count. Shall we all help her count, girls?"

Tiffany raised her voice and her friends joined in.

"Six. Seven-"

Tiffany smiled. Hannah didn't want to look at that smile for the count of twenty. In fact, Hannah didn't want to look at Tiffany one second longer.

Without a word, she slammed the locker shut.

***

If Billy were a fish, he would have been a Bonita. In its natural habitat, the Bonita is exquisite: rainbow hued, bright eyed, and swift. Catch one, reel it in, take it out of the water, expose it to the air and that beauty fades instantly: its scales turn to the color of an overcast sky, the light in the eyes fades. Its death throes are pitiful, useless movements that attest to both the strength of the fish's desire to live and the inevitable futility of the fight.

Just when you take pity, just when you realize that something beautiful is about to be snuffed out and you are ready to put it back in the water, someone on the boat clubs the thing over the head and the beautiful Bonita dies.

Here was Billy Zuni, his beach boy brilliance dimmed, his face pale, swollen, and discolored. His eyes were unfocused, and his attempts to make himself comfortable on the narrow hospital bed were pointless. If the club was coming to this little fish, the people wielding it were going to take their sweet time using it. For that, Josie was grateful because it meant they wanted to be sure of the catch before they reeled it in. Poor Billy. There was so much resting on his shoulders and he didn't even know it yet.

"Hey." Josie greeted him quietly as she stood at the foot of the bed. His good eye opened as far as it could. It took a Herculean strength for him to speak.

"Is my mom okay?"

"Rosa's in bad shape." Josie walked around the bed, bringing a chair with her. She set it next to him and sat down.

"She's going to be okay, right?"

"I'm talking about Rosa, Billy."

"I know." He licked his dry, cracked lips. "Rosa's my mom."

"Billy, I've seen her. How can she be your mother?" Josie insisted, but he wasn't engaged.

"I hurt." His head moved side to side on the pillow, his legs pushed at some unseen obstacle, his hands clutched at the sheets.

Josie's eyed the whiteboard. His morphine drip was current. She put a hand on his brow.

"I'll ask them to check your medicine again," she soothed. "Billy, listen to me. Are you listening?"

His eyelids fluttered and then the one eye opened again. Josie took her best shot.

"Two men were murdered in your house. Rosa was almost killed. You were in your house, weren't you? You saw them didn't you?"

Billy's purple-bruised face turned toward her. His lips were swollen and misshapen, his voice ghastly as he whispered:

"I thought she was dead."

"Did you do that to her? Billy? I told the police I am your attorney, so don't be afraid."

He shook his head and she could see it hurt him to do so. Under the eye that was swollen shut, a necklace of tears gathered at his lashes. A sob turned to a moan as the muscles and nerves inside his body rebelled.

"I couldn't do that. I couldn't."

The words came out chopped up like a log. Josie found a tissue and dabbed at his tears. He tried to help her, but his arm was heavy in the cast, the morphine had left him uncoordinated and confused. He mumbled that he couldn't have done that to Rosa. Josie, though, needed facts, not disjointed protestations.

"Did you see it happen?" she persisted.

Again a shake of the head and a stutter of sobs.

"Was there a gun in your house?" Josie pressed.

"No."

Billy's eyelids fluttered, half opening and closing again. His lips moved but no words came out. Josie sat back. She wasn't asking the right questions and even if she did, Billy had a limited capacity to understand and answer. After a moment's thought, she leaned forward again.

"Billy, did you know the men who were with your mom?" He sighed and stayed silent, frustrating Josie. She tried again. "Were there other people in the house?"

Billy nodded. He choked. "I hurt."

She took a deep breath, put her forehead on the metal bed railing, reached through the bars, and took hold of his arm. She shook it gently.

"Archer and I need you to help us. Come on. Just a little more."

Josie tried to temper the urgency she felt. When Billy licked his lips again, she found his water cup and put the straw to his lips. He drank, coughed, and nodded as if giving her permission to continue.

"Where were you earlier that night? The night of the storm?"

"Pier."

"Were you alone?"

He shook his head. "Adam and Cher."

"Good. That's good." Josie said, even though it really wasn't.

Regular dopers, Adam was a surfer who lived in his van and picked up a few bucks working as a handyman; Cher was a self-proclaimed free spirit with too much money and a penchant for communing with nature and young men.

"Cher didn't take you back to her house, did she? You didn't sit in Adam's van?" Josie pressed.

"No. Cher liked. . . waves."

"Did she make you go into the ocean? Were you high?"

Again a negative.

"Why did you go in the ocean?"

"Get away," Billy muttered.

"From what?"

"People. . .the people. . ." he breathed as he moved in and out of consciousness.

Discouraged, Josie put the water glass back on the table. He couldn't have been everywhere at once.

Josie put her hand on his shoulder and squeezed. "Was there anyone else there at the beach?"

"Trey."

"Who is he?"

"Lives next to. . ." He started to mumble and was gone again in the next instant.

"Where does Trey live? Next to who?" Josie pressed, but Billy had only one thought.

"Rosa. . .Please."

"Not now, Billy." Josie pulled the thin blanket up to his chin then held his fingertips in hers. "Is there a relative I can call, Billy?"

Billy nodded as his head fell to the side and his fingers slipped away from hers. They were done for now – or at least Josie thought they were.

"Trey. . . crazy."

"Why is Trey crazy?" Josie leaned close and drew the back of her hand down his smooth cheek. "Why, Billy?"

"Bath salts," he mumbled as he slipped away.

CHAPTER 11

1998

Teuta and her husband sat at the table where they ate their food, and Teuta felt as if she was looking at her father. There were traces of the handsome young man who had wed her, but soon he would disappear forever. The collapse of the economy, the loss of their money, and so little food had caused her husband to grow thin and gaunt in the last few years. Because there was no money to buy things, the factory had closed and he had lost his job. Good men were going to Greece, sneaking in to do work that no Greek wanted to do. They were going into Italy to steal cars and sell them just to feed their families. And Teuta heard worse. She had heard there were other things being sold, precious things.

She looked over at her children just to see their faces. They did not know how desperate times were. Hopefully, they never would. They were but children.

"So we will go?" she asked of her husband. "To Bajram Curri?"

He shook his head to show that they would do just that. He could not bring himself to say the words. His parents were long dead, and he had thought to always live in the family house. Now they would leave.

"My friend's cousin has an apartment. It is a small place, but my friend's cousin has a store. I will work," her husband assured her.

"It will be better for the children." Teuta agreed in the way one must when there is no other choice.

She sat for a while longer then stood up. She kissed her husband who didn't move but only stared at the tabletop. She gathered the children and put them to bed. She told them of the adventure that was coming and answered their questions until she feared she would cry if they asked any more. She tucked each of them under their blankets.

"Nënë," the youngest girl murmured when her mother kissed her.

Teuta kissed her again. She looked at the other two thinking they were good children. She hoped they would like the new place. She hoped they would be safe. Teuta would give anything to keep her children safe.

2013

Mike Montoya was early for his visit with Dan Jenkins, the controller of Marshall Fasteners, and was shown to the conference room to wait. From there Mike could look into Greg Oi's private office and out again through another door that led to the main offices.

Marshall Fasteners manufactured critical widgets: screws that held airplane landing gears in place, switches that deployed a car's airbag, lights that warned a train was on the wrong track. The huge warehouse space was divided into administrative and manufacturing areas. From where Mike stood he could see a labyrinth of hallways and pseudo-offices created by dividers. Inside those cubicles were people who spent their professional lives filling out forms: forms for customs, forms to satisfy government regulators, forms for workman's compensation, benefit forms, union forms, and forms to change forms.

Mike Montoya would not have done well here. His mind would have atrophied and his spirit wilted. The guy who stamped out the screw didn't have it much better than the one in the cubical. Union rules restricted both creativity and motivation. When a man is told he can lift only so much, he lifts less than he is capable of. That was not to say there wasn't drama in such a well-regulated place. In fact, drama was all over Marshall Fasteners right now.

The union demonstrations showed no sign of abating despite Oi's death. Someone had vandalized the man's private office the same night he was brutally murdered. Combine that with the fact that he was in the company of Jak Duka, a man with ties to Local #976, and it was looking like Oi was the corpse to watch if Mike were going to find a motive for these crimes. At least he hoped it was going to be as simple as some union guy going ballistic over benefits.

"Here we go. Okay, now. I have what you need, I think." Mike looked over his shoulder as Dan Jenkins rushed into the conference room, paused, considered Greg Oi's office, and shook his head. "I still can't believe someone did that."

His melancholy was momentary, and he was all business as he settled at the long oval table. Mike took one last look at the mess in Oi's office. The walls were splashed with red paint. Someone had taken time to write 'bloodstucker' and 'death to the man' on the walls. Mike would have thought the misspelling of bloodsucker amusing save for the centerpiece of this mayhem: an effigy of Greg Oi, a knife piercing the outline of a heart, and red paint-blood dripping down the hopsack body. There was a feather boa around the thing's neck. Whoever did this not only hated Greg Oi, they knew a lot about his personal life.

"I hope I have all the information you need." Dan spoke up, politely indicating he was a busy man. Mike appreciated that and sat down next to him.

"Let's take a look."

Dan got up and closed the connecting door to Greg Oi's office. "You don't mind, do you?"

"Not at all."

"I am in total shock. First that," he inclined his head toward the now closed office, "and then to hear Mr. Oi had been murdered. I hope I never hear news like that again, I can tell you."

"I'm sure everyone here was shocked," Mike commiserated.

"That's an understatement. Mr. Oi was fair. This was a pleasant place to work because of him. That's saying a lot these days."

Mike nodded and tucked away that piece of information. "I saw Mrs. Oi this morning. She would like to get some personal things out of his office."

"Kat?" Dan blinked. He seemed confused for a minute. He blushed. There was no mistaking the side note in the man's voice. "Oh, sure. Should I let her in?"

"I'll follow up with the local police," Mike offered.

"Thanks. If there's something in there that Kat wants, she'll expect it sooner than later."

"She's a demanding boss, is she?" Mike asked with a smile.

"She isn't anyone's boss. She just thinks she is."

"So she was more a meddling wife?" Mike inquired.

"A little of both, I guess. She sits on the board. All her expenses went through the company." Dan kept his eyes down as he rifled through the pile of files. "She drew a salary. She's Mr. Oi's widow, so I really shouldn't say she hasn't got an interest in the company. She has an interest in it remaining solvent. Here, this is a list of the board members."

Mike scanned the names without recognizing one. There was no reason he should. His portfolio was nonexistent, so he didn't exactly follow the business news.

"Katherine M. Kudahay? Is that Mrs. Oi?"

"Yes. That's her," Dan said. "I don't think I'd be speaking out of school, detective, if I said she didn't serve this company in any meaningful way. Her appointment was legal, of course. Still, if you want to talk about the business, I wouldn't contact her. Her input was minimal at best. I can suggest others who would be able to help you."

"I'd appreciate the information," Mike said even as he got up and opened the door to Greg Oi's office again. His brow knit.

"It's curious that she's so anxious to get into this office. There doesn't seem to be any personal effects. Not even a picture of Mrs. Oi," Mike mused.

"Who knows what that woman wants?" Mike closed the door and went back to the table. Jenkins' face flushed, embarrassed by his outburst. "Look, she's not my favorite person, but I wouldn't wish this situation on anybody. Even her."

"Were you aware of any tension between her and Mr. Oi? On a professional level, that is."

"The only thing I'm aware of is that Kat wanted him to settle the strike. From what I gathered, she was concerned that if the strike went on the company wouldn't survive."

"Was there any truth to that?"

"We've weathered union problems before," Dan said. "This time it's more vitriolic because the old guard is gone. These young guys, they are a different breed. The thing is, we've been hit like any other manufacturer. We're not doing the volume we did five years ago. The profit margin isn't there, and the guys on the line keep asking for more and more. They should be grateful they have jobs.

Mr. Oi was doing everything he could to keep the line going despite the down tick."

"Sounds like he cared about more than profits."

"Mr. Oi came from nothing. He knew what it was like to have a family to feed and no work. He kept a hundred families fed, and they turned against him. I think he was more outraged by the disloyalty than the union's actual demands. He kept to himself, but I could tell it was eating at him. I think it finally got to him this week. He was just off."

"Could it have been something other than work? Maybe he had personal problems. A girlfriend?"

"You mean the woman that lives with them? I didn't get the feeling he was involved with her."

"Any other women?" Mike pressed.

"I really wouldn't know, detective," Dan said. "He respected me as a businessman, and I respected him. I doubt he knew my wife's name or how many children I have. That's the kind of relationship he had with everyone here. Perhaps it was different in some of his other companies, but I doubt it."

"You weren't cutting checks to women not employed here?" Mike pressed.

"No." Dan was emphatic.

"Were there any men that made you nervous? Money paid out? People who upset Mr. Oi so that his demeanor changed? Trips he took that did not seem to be directly tied to business?"

"If you're talking about some sort of blackmail or a mistress, Mr. Oi would have dealt with it himself. I can account for every cent that goes through this company." Dan sighed. "There was one thing. It's probably nothing, but Mr. Oi wasn't himself when he came in that morning. I mean, the day it all happened."

"What was different?"

"Remember I said he had been preoccupied all week? Well, that morning he was more than agitated. He locked himself in his office. He came out a little past three. That was the last time I saw him." Dan tossed his pen on the table and put his fists to his eyes. He rubbed them hard and when he dropped his hands he looked like a college kid who had pulled an all-nighter. "Boy, I hope I never have to go through anything like this again."

"I hope so, too," Mike commiserated. "So no one saw him that day after three, is that correct?"

"No, sorry, I saw him. Just not in the usual way, you know. Usually his door was open, he'd be up and down all day, going around checking the things, looking in on the line. That day the office door was closed. I went in around noon. He was on the phone and hung up as soon as he saw me. I had a lot of stuff that needed taking care of. Invoices needed to be signed. There was a problem getting a shipment of chrome out of Europe because the Albanians hadn't filled out the environmental impact paperwork properly. And there was a scuffle out front. One of the salaried employees and a temp got hassled trying to get in the building.

"It was a busy day but he didn't even want to know about what was going on outside. He signed what he had to sign and sent me away. I saw him go to the restroom at three. The door closed. I didn't see him again."

"Did you get a sense of what he was doing the rest of the time?"

"The safe was open. I remember that."

"Was that unusual?" Mike asked.

"Kind of, since I didn't know it existed. It was a wall safe behind a picture. I remember thinking it was like an old movie."

"Did you see what was in it? Anything you could identify?"

"There was something in it, but I couldn't tell you what. I just noticed it, did my business with Mr. Oi, and that was it. I never would have mentioned it to anyone if it hadn't been for what happened. The police saw it. Mr. Oi must have been in a hurry because he didn't close it all the way." Dan sat forward and picked up his pen again. "So, you'll let me know if I can let Kat in?"

"We'll leave the office sealed for now. I'll advise her." Mike drummed his fingers on the table, and then asked: "Who takes over in case anything happens to Mr. Oi?"

"The board is going to move someone in temporarily. Everyone is scrambling right now."

Mike made appreciative noises and moved on with his questions.

Do you know the name Rosa Zuni?

Anything about the address where Mr. Oi died?

The name Jak Duka?

Did you ever see Mr. Oi with a gun?

When the answers were no, no, no, and no, Mike made a note, underlined something and said:

"What about disagreements among the board members, employee problems? Anything that comes to mind."

"Got it all here." Dan was happy to be on home turf. Xeroxes flew across the table along with explanations.

We keep a record of anything that might possibly lead to legal action -

Simple customer complaints -

Defective items, quality control issues, missed deadlines -

Mike stacked the papers as quickly as Dan Jenkins handed them over. He glanced at each one, flipped through correspondence from disgruntled customers, Oi's legal team, and reports on manufacturing problems. Wendy would spend hours pouring over these documents, but Mike gave them all a once-over as Dan went on.

"If any of this was a matter of life or death, I would have known about it. Remember, Mr. Oi is — was - full owner of five different businesses that intersect with both the automotive and the airline industry. He also has interests in manufacturing heavy equipment for the port. This would include trucks, forklifts and even the container cranes. These only represent Marshall Fasteners' open complaints. There are others in various stages of completion. Some we're fighting. Some are on appeal. Some will die a natural death. Some we'll settle to save court costs. Mr. Oi wanted to fight every action, but he could be brought around."

"He was a very busy man," Mike commented.

"He was quite hands off, actually. He knew everything that went on, but he only micromanaged one thing."

"And that was?"

"The negotiations with the union." Dan Jenkins jerked a thumb toward the closed door behind which Mr. Oi's effigy sat. "They're the ones that did that. It wouldn't surprise me if one of the security guards let them in. It wouldn't surprise me if one of them killed Mr. Oi. He was a strong man, but they are thugs. You want to look at someone. Look at Mark Wolf. Or how about Sam Lumina? He's a troublemaker. Swaggering bastard. I think he scared some people."

"Even Oi?"

"No," Dan said sadly. "Maybe that was Mr. Oi's mistake."

***

Josie paced back and forth in front of Billy's bed, speaking quickly and quietly into her phone. She didn't want to disturb Billy, but if he woke and had something to say she wanted to be there to hear it. When she walked one way, Josie looked into the hospital hall; when she walked the other way she could see out the window and onto the parking lot. Mike Montoya was on the other end of the line looking through the windshield of his car, waiting for a traffic light to change.

"We should have toxicology in the next two days," he assured her when she told him about Trey and the bath salts.

"I'm not saying Billy did salts, I'm saying that guy who brought them might have flipped out. Maybe that's why Billy was in the water - to get away from this guy."

"Ms. Bates, if he just admitted to you that he was in the house and that bath salts were a factor-"

"He didn't say he was using. He said he was in the house, but he said this guy brought the drugs," Josie insisted. "What happened in that house could only be done by someone who was strung out."

"And the motive would be?"

Traffic was moving forward, but not as fast as Josie Bates was moving. Mike was processing this information, but he couldn't be as excited about it as she seemed to be. One guy strung out might have gone on a rampage, but he would not have come to Rosa Zuni's house armed to the teeth. A hurt kid muttering something in the hospital had to be taken in context.

"Good grief," Josie exclaimed. "Take the information and plug it in. You've got a mystery, Montoya. There's got to be something that ties all this together and drugs is as good as any explanation."

Josie paused. She pushed back her long bangs and rolled her eyes. She sounded like a fishwife. She knew it, but Montoya sloughed it off, and asked for the names of the people at the pier. Josie gave the information to him and added:

"The Hermosa cops will know who they are. I can give you a contact." Josie paused. "Maybe this Trey guy was dealing for someone in that house. At least you can tell the lab what to look for. Oh, and Montoya?"

"Yes, Ms. Bates?"

"Hannah remembered that the man at our door was wearing a cheap blue jacket. The rain made the dye run, and the guy's wrists were blue tinged. Knit cuffs, not elastic. It was zipped up and there was a logo and -"

Josie was about to tell him her impression of the logo but the phone fell away from her ear. She could hear Montoya calling to her. She raised the phone again.

"I'll call you back."

Josie snapped the phone shut and walked into the hall. She looked one way then the other trying to spot the man who had come into Billy's room only to duck out again. He could have been an orderly, he could have been a visitor who made a wrong turn, he could have been a cop, but something told her he was none of the above.

Josie went down the hall, turning her head at every sound, following air that was prickly with something the man had left in his wake: nerves, concern, shame, confusion. She stopped in front of a room at the end of the hall. She could hear a nurse's steady stream of conversation. Josie pushed the door open just far enough to see that this was a private room. Past the curtain, she saw flashes of a nurse tending to her patient.

"Can I help you?"

Startled, unaware that she had been standing and staring long enough to garner attention, Josie stepped back. A bald, clean-shaven man was seriously considering that she might be up to no good.

"No," Josie said. "Thanks."

She went back the way she came, feeling the man's eyes on her. Everyone in this hospital was looking for an assassin. Not that she could blame them for being skittish. Evil recognized no boundaries: movie houses, churches, grade schools, so why not hospitals? She was almost back at Billy's room when her phone rang.

Josie answered it, listened, promised she'd be on her way in minutes, and went back to Billy's room to get her purse. He was asleep so she didn't linger. He probably wouldn't remember she had been there or what he had said to her. Just as well. There was another fire sparking and Josie was going to make sure she stomped it out.

***

The man inside the bathroom heard the nurse wash her hands at the sink in the room. He prayed she wouldn't come into the bathroom, but if she did he was ready. He wouldn't kill her, but he would make sure she didn't remember him. He closed his eyes, leaned his head against the wall, and sweated. He heard the water shut off and the nurse tug on the towel dispenser.

Once again, things went quiet. He strained to hear anything that would let him know if she was still out there, but he heard nothing. He glanced at the toilet. He wanted to pee. No, he wanted to throw up. He was frightened, which was weird. He hadn't been frightened before. Before he'd felt like a goddamn king of the world. Now he felt like a little kid hiding from the Boogie Man. And, like a little kid, all he wanted was to get away and run to someone who would protect him or find somewhere he could hide.

Opening the door a little further, he smashed his cheek against it and rotated to get a better look the other way. He could hear a laugh track on the television. His palms were sweaty. He wiped them on his pants and then again on his blue jacket. He stripped off the jacket and folded it over his arm. Knowing his escape had to be now or never, he chose now.

Half expecting to be confronted, he was relieved to find no one around. On the television the same group of people laughed the same laugh again. He moved swiftly toward the hall door, lay as flat as he could against the wall, and peered out. A second later, he left the room and started to walk. Long and wide, the hall seemed to undulate in front of his eyes as if he were walking on the pitching deck of a ship. He was almost to the end of the hall, hurrying on, head down, thinking of nothing more than getting out of the hospital when he ran into a man.

"Sorry." Instinctively, he looked up as he spun away. Still moving as he held out his hands in apology. "Sorry. Sorry."

"No problem," the bald orderly said.

The man went on. Everything was good. His shoulders pulled back, his chest puffed out. He had not done what he'd come for, but he at least saw the kid. He turned into the lobby and ran for an elevator. He called 'hold it' and a hand shot out, stopping the doors just in time. He squeezed in.

"Thanks," he said.

"No problem."

Josie Bates reached for the button to close the doors, and that was when the man started to sweat again.

CHAPTER 12

1998

Once again Teuta traveled alone to the house where her parents had lived. Yilli was gone many years and now the old woman was dead. She had been dead a long while when she was found and that saddened Teuta. No one should be alone when they died.

Now the mother was buried and Teuta sat in the light of the fading day in the house of her childhood, remembering when there had been goats, and work, and smells of good food cooking. Her father and mother had no understanding of investments, they had no money to give the government, so they had not suffered as the rest of the country did, as she, Teuta, and her family did.

Teuta was sitting, starting to think of her own family - for what good was it to think of her parents now that they were dead? — when she heard the sound of a car bumping over the uneven ground. She looked out the window, curious but not curious enough to get up until the car stopped and a big man got out.

Teuta narrowed her eyes to try to see him better. She touched her headscarf. She arranged her face not so much in a scowl but in an expression that said she was not afraid to be alone and have a visitor she might not want. But then a woman also got out of the car and then a child.

It was only the family who would live in the house, come to see if they liked the rooms. Teuta welcomed this family and wished them happiness. She did not say that it had been a sad house for her father, Yilli.

When they had looked in all the rooms and went away saying they were pleased that they would live there, Teuta slept in her childhood home one last time. In the morning she left the house and did not have a regret. In fact, a great weight was lifted off Teuta. She now lived far, far away. In her new home no one would know hers were the children of Yilli the goat herder's child.

2013

Archer drove down Century Boulevard near LAX. Traffic was moving through a canyon created by the rise of nondescript airport hotels, unmemorable restaurants, and dated office buildings. Archer's destination was somewhere between the legitimate airport businesses and downtown in a no man's land of dollar stores and strip joints.

Before he left Hermosa, he talked with Adam over eggs and bacon at Burt's. Adam confirmed that on the night in question Billy was in a good mood as always; Cher was suggestive and stoned, as always. The third guy, Trey, had come and gone with Billy. He and Cher left soon after Billy and Trey. It was late and Cher's constant chatter got on Adam's nerves. Not to mention it was cold and incredibly wet. The surf, though, was awesome.

Yes, they had all smoked a little weed; no, Adam hadn't seen any bath salts. Adam didn't know anything about Rosa Zuni. Luckily, Archer knew a little bit more than Adam. A quick call to the landlord after Josie gave him the woman's full name landed him the name of her employer, but the management company wasn't going to give some private cop information on the owner of the building. He could look it up in public records. Public real estate records weren't going to tell Archer what he needed to know about Rosa Zuni so he headed to where she worked: Undies. He pulled the Hummer into a parking lot that needed to be repaved and took a look around.

It was ten in the morning, and the joint was open. Actually, the place never closed. The doors opened at 5:30 a.m. and closing time was 2:00 a.m. Archer always wondered what moral parameters three and a half sober hours satisfied. Of course, that assumed patrons were actually sober during those hours and not just drinking in their cars until Undies opened once again.

Archer set the emergency brake and yawned. The last thing he wanted to see in the morning were half-naked women holding onto poles while they pretended to dance. Strike that. He didn't mind seeing Josie half-naked anytime of the morning. Right now all he wanted to see was the back of his eyelids, but there was work to be done. He needed to find a thread that would lead him to a relative of the Zuni's, and if all went well, hook him up with Trey the mystery man.

Archer was considering his two chores when a Chevy drove into the lot. The car was old and on its last legs; not so the woman who got out of it. Archer draped his arm over the steering wheel, lowered his sunglasses and took in all her glory.

She wore purple leggings, a red tank top, a multi-colored scarf, and stiletto-heeled platform sandals. Her hair was long, curly and growing out brown from a magenta dye job. On Rodeo Drive she would have looked like a movie star, a fact that Archer lamented. Hollywood used to do glamor like nobody's business but now it was all about looking like you woke up on the wrong side of the bed, inking every appendage with faux Chinese poetry, and acting like you were pissed off all the time. The woman hefted a giant bag over her shoulder and when she turned around it was clear that the only films she might have starred in were X rated. It was amazing she could even stand given the massive boobs that had taken root on her top half. What made the sight so incredible was that the damn things looked real.

She pushed the door shut with a thrust of her hip, didn't bother to lock the vehicle, pulled her bag close, strode across the lot, and opened the front door to the building. Archer got out of the Hummer, locked it, and followed her into Undies.

***

"Hannah broke two of Tiffany's fingers, Ms. Bates. The girl's mother is talking about suing." Mrs. Crawford's voice remained steady, but it was clear that she was shaken.

"I'll take care of it. We'll cover any medical expenses," Josie said, barely able to contain her annoyance at being called away from the hospital for this. "Hannah will apologize and make amends in any manner Tiffany's mother believes fit."

Beside her, a sullen Hannah cut her eyes to her guardian. Josie ignored her. Her displeasure was nothing compared to Josie's or Mrs. Crawford, Mira Costa High School's principal.

"Tiffany's mother isn't just talking about suing you, Ms. Bates, but the school district and me personally. She claims that we knew Hannah was a danger and that she never should have been registered."

Josie stiffened. Hannah rolled her eyes. In this school, Hannah's arrest for murder translated into an assumption of guilt. It was ridiculous, unfair, and Josie thought they had moved beyond that. Hannah knew better. She dealt with the consequences of her notoriety everyday. Josie and Archer and Faye had made the hassle worth bearing. Now Josie was acting like any other parent - huffy, righteous, unwilling to hear Hannah's side of the story - so Hannah sulked. Josie figured an eruption was about five minutes away, so she decided to use the next four as judiciously as possible.

"I think we can all agree that Hannah is no more dangerous than any other student," Josie said.

"We have a no tolerance policy for bullying," Mrs. Crawford said. "Tiffany has been sent home. She's on probation for three days."

"That's like nothing," Hannah muttered.

"Hannah." Josie admonished her quickly with both a word and a touch. Hannah shook her off. There was no stopping Hannah when she had something to say.

"Give me a break. All Tiffany's going to do is sit home and badmouth me and Billy on the Internet. She said we should both be dead and that we were too stupid to pull it off. That's not teasing. That's not even bullying. That's evil."

"I agree," Mrs. Crawford said, "but there's a difference between bloodletting and cutting words. She didn't threaten you, Hannah."

Hannah pushed herself up straighter, bent an elbow and rested her head against her fisted hand. She sparked with teenage anger, but her argument was all adult logic.

"I wasn't worried about me. Billy hasn't got anyone to stand up for him, so I did. I don't think he'd be better off dead." She dropped her hand and raised her head and asked, "Do you?"

If Hannah had been an archer her arrow couldn't have hit a truer target. In fact, she'd taken out both Mrs. Crawford and Josie with that barb. For Josie the last two days had been spent listening to Hannah's asides, her objectifying of why Josie and Archer needed to step up and take responsibility for Billy. Josie's promise to reach out only so far seemed to Hannah stunning and unfathomable. Why, she wanted to know, was Billy different? It was hard for Josie to explain and almost impossible to put into words.

Josie assumed that Hannah understood the parallels that brought them together: their shared experience of abandonment, their fierce love of a parent who had done them wrong, and their connection as women. What Josie had not counted on was a teenage heart, a teenage mind, a teenage sensibility that dictated that outsiders - like Hannah, Josie, and now Billy - had each other's backs no matter what.

Josie had not counted on Hannah's faith in her, either. Josie was the guardian, the warrior, and the unbreakable lifeline that Hannah clung to. But most of all, Josie's arms were now the mother's arms encircling her. Hannah wanted her friend, Billy, embraced and protected, too.

"Not caring about what happened is the same as wishing he was dead," Hannah pointed out.

"Hannah, nobody wishes Billy dead. Not even Tiffany." Mrs. Crawford was firm. "And it isn't my job to decide what will happen to Billy. I am principal of this school, and I will deal with the problems of this school. I'm not exonerating Tiffany, but I'm not letting you off the hook either. Because you were physically violent, you will be suspended from school for two weeks. I will not see you on these premises for any reason, is that clear?"

"Yes." Hannah accepted her punishment, but wasn't cowed by it.

"Good. Fine." Mrs. Crawford unclasped the hands to check the schedule of Hannah's classes that she had pulled before calling Josie. "You're carrying a full load, Hannah. All of your teachers have the assignments posted online except for art."

"I'm working on a painting for Ms. Trani. She's letting me self-direct," Hannah said.

"Is it due in the next two weeks?" Mrs. Crawford was clearly unimpressed.

Hannah shook her head. "No. End of the month."

"Alright then." She set aside the class schedule. "Ms. Bates, if Hannah needs anything from the school, I'll expect you to come and get it. I'll speak with each of her teachers. I will make it clear that they are to cooperate but not to go out of their way to accommodate her. I do expect Hannah, however, to go out of her way to accommodate them."

"Her assignments will be in on time," Josie agreed. "I'll see that she writes a letter of apology to this girl-"

"I won't." Hannah nearly shot of out her chair, but Josie was fast and her hand clamped down on the girl's arm. Mrs. Crawford didn't miss a beat.

"Then we're done. Hannah, go to your locker and get what you need."

Hannah picked up her satchel and went to the door without so much as an apology to the principal. Josie was about to call her back when Mrs. Crawford beat her to it.

"Hannah? Just so you know, I am in no mood for a confrontation with anyone. You have five minutes. Is that understood?"

"Yes," Hannah answered.

When the door closed, Mrs. Crawford turned her attention to Josie.

"I'm glad you stayed."

"I am sorry. I'll talk to Tiffany's mother. I'll make sure there is no legal action," Josie assured her.

"It's not that. I doubt her mother is going to make good on those threats. Luckily, she isn't blind to her daughter's failings. And if you repeat that, I'll deny it."

"My lips are sealed," Josie promised.

"Great. Look, I just wanted to give you this." Mrs. Crawford handed over a piece of paper. Written on it were a local number and an international number. "I'm embarrassed to say that this is all we have on Billy. When his mother filled out the registration forms she didn't even bother to put down names. We should have caught it, but we have over two thousand students. Registration day is a zoo. We're bound to miss something. I'm just sorry we missed it with Billy. Some kids are just destined to fall through the cracks."

"Hopefully, we can change that." Josie took the paper and glanced at it. "I'll run it down. Thanks."

Josie put the number in her pocket, shook the woman's hand and walked into the hall. Hannah was waiting near the double doors down the hall, her Louis Vuitton satchel bulging with books. There were more in her arms. Before Josie took another step, her phone rang. The caller identified herself, imparted her information, and asked Josie if she understood the instructions.

"Yes. I've got it. Ten o'clock tomorrow. Judge Healy. Chambers? Thank you."

Josie input the information into her phone and said her goodbyes. At the end of the hall, Hannah was waiting and watching as Josie dialed Archer. He was going to have to step things up. The next day at ten in the morning she was going to have to face the judge who would decide what was going to happen to Billy Zuni.

When she passed Hannah, the girl turned precisely and followed her guardian across the campus. It wasn't until Josie pulled the car out of the parking space that Hannah spoke.

"You won't let the county take Billy, will you? He can't survive in the system, Josie. I could, but not Billy."

***

Archer pocketed his phone. The woman in the purple leggings hadn't shown the slightest interest in his conversation. Instead, she filed her very long, very fake, French tipped nails. They looked like spades. It was a look Archer had never understood. Still, he didn't want to hold hands with her, he just wanted her attention.

"So, do you know anything that could help me find this kid's people?"

Carlotta dropped her hands atop a dressing table littered with make-up, gum wrappers and a 32 oz. lidded cup that looked like it had been there for a good long while. They were alone in the dressing room, but there were other people in the place: two guys who looked like they'd lost their best friend, a bartender, and a waitress/dancer. All had taken one look at Archer as he followed Carlotta in and averted their eyes. The smell of cop never quite disappeared no matter how long you'd been off the force. Carlotta didn't seem to mind the stench.

"I told you, I didn't know her very well," Carlotta insisted.

"She must have talked about something," he insisted.

"Honey, I don't have any more to tell you than I told the cops. She worked here for the two years, she didn't really like dancing, but she did what she had to do. You know, to take care of the kid." Carlotta paused and was as close to contemplative as she probably ever got. "It couldn't be worse what happened to her."

"Why do you say that?" Archer moved over and put his shoulder up against the cleanest looking wall. He liked her profile better than the view from above.

"From what I hear, she won't exactly be eye candy if she pulls through. You can't dance all scarred up unless you want to be the freak show on the lineup. You know she's not from here. You know that, right?"

"Yeah? Where's she from?"

"Got me." Carlotta was done with the emery board. She tossed it onto the table.

"Can you guess?"

"Nope."

"Did she ever say Billy was a problem? Was he depressed? Was he acting out? Was she afraid of him?"

Archer pressed forward, but Carlotta was proving a tough nut to crack. She kicked off her shoes, picked up a bottle of white nail polish, and started painting a daisy on her big toe.

"Best I can tell she was fine. He was fine. She didn't say it, but she lived for that kid."

"Did you ever meet him?"

Carlotta shook her head, "Naw. Poor little guy. What's he going to do now?"

Archer took note. Rosa Zuni was so secretive she had led Carlotta to believe Billy was a child.

"We don't know. That's why I'm looking for a relative."

Carlotta shrugged. "Don't look at me. I'm not going to step up."

"I'm looking for a blood relative," Archer confirmed.

"Good." She kept on painting. She was pretty good at it. "Anyway, whatever happened to her, she probably didn't see it coming from here. That day was a wash, no customers. The boss sent her home early. She was okay with that. She said she had a guest coming." Carlotta paused and then shook the polish wand at Archer's reflection. "You know, I'll miss her. She was real polite. Who calls people guests?"

"What would you call it?" Archer asked.

"A guy? I don't know." Carlotta shrugged.

"A john?"

"No, not that one." She dipped her head. "Not any of us."

Archer looked around the room while Carlotta went on with her nail art and stewed a bit. Undies was good to its talent. The dressing room was spacious. At one time it had been pretty spiffy. The wallpaper was originally a burgundy color but it had faded to a sickly grey. The fleur-de-lis patterned flock still sparkled with embedded gold flecks. In the early sixties this place would have been cool, a gentleman's club.

Dressing tables lined each of the long walls. Each space was personalized - a tufted stool in front of one, a vase of fake flowers on another, a blue bridal garter draped over the edge of a standing mirror. Photographs sprouted from the sides of shared wall mirrors – all except for one. Archer went to that station, and ran his finger down the side. Nothing had fallen behind it.

"Is this Rosa's space?" he asked.

Carlotta glanced over her shoulder and drawled. "Aren't you just the Sherlock. Didn't I tell you she was the private type? You see anything there that looks personal?"

"She was here two years and didn't even bring a picture?"

"Nope," Carlotta tossed her hair over her shoulder. It was so long it threatened the artwork on her toes if she left it hanging.

Archer took two steps and stood in front of the woman. He was a big man but the look she shot him said it all: no one was big enough to intimidate her. That was good because he didn't want to bully her, Archer just wanted to be clear that he needed help. He hunkered down and got eye-to-eye with a woman who at one time had been truly beautiful.

"I don't want to put you on the spot, but I need something fast, and I don't know where else to go. Tomorrow there's going to be a hearing to find out who should take custody of Billy. Rosa can't talk. Rosa can barely breathe. Billy's in bad shape and can't help himself. If you've got anything, give it to me. I don't want to see Billy go into the system."

Carlotta looked into Archer's dark eyes. He looked right back into her blue ones. He didn't smile. Carlotta wouldn't have bought it if he did. She was looking for the things she had seen in other men's eyes: smooth lies, a means to an end, insincerity, and cruelty. Archer was looking for something too: the woman she had been, the girl whose dreams had been whittled from an oak into a toothpick. Carlotta flinched first but not because he made her. Something else nudged her along. Archer didn't ask what it was for fear he'd ruin the moment. He stood up and stepped back. She dropped her feet, went to a back cabinet, and rummaged through it. When she returned, she was holding a well-worn picture album.

"This is our shit list." Her chest heaved like a full ocean swell. Archer moved in close to take a look as she flipped open the cardboard cover. "Hold that side, baby, this thing is heavy."

Carlotta turned the pages of the album. Some were torn, others bore the marks of spilled drinks and make-up smudges. Some of the pictures were stapled onto the pages, others taped and some just wedged into the spine. There were Xeroxes, Polaroids, regular photos, and computer printouts. Carlotta was turning one long page when Archer stopped her and pointed to a picture of a gorgeous young woman.

"This you?" Archer asked.

"Yeah." Archer thought he heard her sigh. "I was hot."

"Time's been good to you." Archer told the truth as always. He could see beyond the hair, the lashes, and the purple tights.

"That's a sweet thing to say." She paused, then followed up with: "I'm free for lunch or whatever."

"I'd take you up on it but I'm getting married."

"Figures. The good ones are always taken."

"You're not," Archer said and he meant it. "So what is this?"

"It's like, you know, a rogue's gallery. One of the girls had a creep hitting on her a long time ago and management wasn't doing anything about it. If she got hurt, we wanted to be able to finger the guy, so we took a picture of him. Then somebody else had a problem with a cop. Then Marla had a crush that went bad. We started putting pictures and notes and things so that if anything happened to any of us someone would know who to look at."

"Smart," Archer said.

"Yeah, we thought so."

"Who took the pictures?"

"Everybody. Nobody. Some are stills from the surveillance tape, but it broke a while back. They never fixed it."

Archer took over and turned the long pages slowly, taking in every image. There were pictures of the girls in various stages of undress, of the bartender, of patrons. Most of the clientele looked harmless, all looked like losers, and the notes written beside those doofuses were less than kind. Archer had to admit they showed a heck of a lot of objectivity and wit. Those who didn't look harmless were called out big time: circled in crayon or marker. Giant arrows pointed to them with explicit warnings were called out: toucher, grabber, lurker, curser, strangoid. A few, it was noted, were bad tippers.

"Did you show this to the cops?" Archer asked.

Carlotta shrugged, "I didn't, but maybe someone did."

"What's all this?" Archer pointed to lists beside some of the worst offenders. Carlotta leaned over and took a look.

"Those are the girls the guy was interested in. If one of them came in and we knew he was bothering someone in particular, we switched our sets or did something to keep them apart. See that?" Carlotta pointed to one notation. "That means Charity switched to the midnight to two shift because of this guy. Then see this?" She pointed to a picture of a car. "We put down the license plate because it was dark when someone took a picture of his car. That guy was freaky beyond belief. Nothing behind his eyes, and he'd get really close to you, and talk really loud. But he touched Charity. He would kind of paw at her. Like she could deal with someone grabbing her, but this guy touched her like . . ." Carlotta shivered, unable to find a word to describe the touch. For a woman like her to be afraid the guy must be bad.

"Rosa's not here. Wasn't there anybody interested in her?"

Carlotta reached over and turned the pages until she found what she wanted.

"Him." She put one of those amazing fingernails on the picture. "Rosa wanted us to take it out. I got the feeling she wanted to talk, though, but she was kind of like a whipped puppy. She just said take it out, but we didn't. We didn't want to be responsible."

"Did she say why she wanted you to take it out?"

"No, but I knew why."

"Why?"

"'Cause who in the hell wants to be reminded of an ex?"

"How do you know that guy is her ex?"

Archer took the book and sat down on the little tufted stool. The picture was bad, nothing more than a shadow of a man in a back booth. Carlotta was back at her station, the vial of white polish at the ready, but she hadn't resumed her toenail artwork. Instead, she used the little wand like a conductor.

"Who else would it be? It was like a love/hate thing." Carlotta answered. "You get a sixth sense for this kind of stuff. The couple times he came in, Rosa talked to him for a long time. He was dressed real nice – wore a lot of gold. He put his hand on hers. She took it back. You know, that kind of thing. I saw him shove money at her. She didn't take it."

"So she never told you straight out who he was?"

"No."

"Would you recognize him if you saw a picture?"

Carlotta shook her head, "Nope."

Archer dug into his pocket for his phone and took a picture of the picture in the book. Maybe the sheriff's lab could make heads or tails of it. He wanted a copy just in case this one conveniently disappeared.

"Never really got on her about it. Hey, you know what?" The wand was tapping Archer's way. "It never occurred to me, but what if he was her pimp? I just assumed an ex 'cause she was so sweet. She didn't look like she'd been through the mill, know what I mean?"

"I get you," he assured her.

"Well, maybe that was it. She was running away from a pimp. Tossed out by her parents when she got pregnant maybe? This guy takes her in, but he's bad news. That's why she was talking about guests. Maybe you're right, baby. Maybe that sweet little thing was turning tricks for a private clientele. That opens up a whole world of possibilities, doesn't it?"

Archer closed the book and handed it back to her. "That it does."

Carlotta got up and put it away. Archer sat there thinking. If Rosa was turning tricks and she loved Billy as much as this woman said she did, then maybe she turned him out during working hours. That would make sense. Archer didn't even notice Carlotta watching him, thinking about him, deciding about him. Finally, she set aside her nail polish and opened her drawer.

"I probably shouldn't do this. I've got a number for her. Emergency numbers, but I promised not to let anyone see them unless something really bad happened."

"I'd say this qualifies." Archer noted.

"I suppose."

"You didn't call those numbers when you heard about Rosa?" Archer asked as she handed them over.

"I don't like to get involved in much of anything. I figured someone else would be taking care of things. There's always someone else."

"Not this time." Archer stood up and pocketed the information she gave him. "Thanks. I'll let you know how it comes out."

"Sure you will," Carlotta scoffed.

"I will," Archer reiterated. He took a card out of his shirt pocket. She looked at it. He tossed it on her station. "You want to give me one of yours in case?"

"You are kidding, right?"

Carlotta's lips twitched. She picked up her polish and went back to painting daisies on her toes. Archer thought that was a waste of time. Nobody would be looking at her feet when she danced.

***

Kat Oi's little Louboutin shod foot bounced up and down and down and up again as she waited on the lawyer. She hated that she had to get dressed and go all the way downtown when good old Fred could have just told her what she wanted to know over the phone. What she wanted to know was simple: how did Greg's estate transfer over to her? But Fred needed time to digest the news that his biggest client was dead. He wanted time to review the will, the trusts, all the files that had been generated for Greg personally. The corporate stuff would have to wait for a consultation with Greg's two other lawyers.

Kat moved in the chair and caught sight of her image in the glass that covered a print behind the attorney's desk. Kat turned her head this way and that, sat up straighter, arranged her shoulders. She may not like having to get all gussied up, but she looked darn good when she did. Driving downtown was a pain, too, but at least she did it in style since Greg had given her that cherry convertible. Too bad he wouldn't be around for the ride now. She had plans. Big plans. She would make things happen when she knew what was in the kitty.

Tired of admiring herself, she looked around the office. It was a nice place and it was obvious Fred had some bucks – most of them courtesy of Greg. She noted he also had a homely wife, assuming that wasn't his mother in the picture on the credenza.

"Can you hurry it up, Fred? I've got to beat it before rush hour. I don't want to have to fight the traffic home," she whined.

"Sorry, Kat." Fred took off his glasses, put them on the desk, and offered her a wan smile. "I thought I would have more time to reacquaint myself with Greg's will before I saw you. This all happened so fast. His assets are intertwined, the trusts are complicated."

"I get that, Fred, but you've got to have some idea of how much I'm going to get. I know down to the penny what his monthly draw from Marshall Fasteners is and the payout on his investments. I know what the minimum take is going to be, so don't try anything underhanded. I'm just not clear about the other holdings. Oh, and I want to shut down the nonprofit. Don't try to stop me. I know you got a hefty fee for administering that, so don't try to screw me out of another one for shutting it down."

"Kat, please," Fred snapped. "I'm an attorney, not a grifter."

"I'm just telling you where I stand," Kat answered, unfazed by his attitude. She was the boss now and the sooner he figured that out the better. Or maybe she'd can his ass and get her own lawyer. But Fred wasn't paying any attention. He was looking all serious and those glasses were back on.

"You'll continue to get your salary as a member of the board of course, but-"

"But what?" Kat sat forward. Fred mirrored her, but the desk was too big for them to be nose-to-nose.

"But I'm afraid you may not be the primary beneficiary of Greg's will. It seems there was a child."

Kat shot out of her chair and landed so hard on those Loubitons that the heels nearly punctured the floor. She put her little hands flat on the lawyer's desk.

"You're telling me that Greg had a freakin' kid?"

"It appears to be a possibility."

"Tough," she growled. "Pay him off. I'm his wife."

Fred tried not to smile when he said:

"Actually, Kat, you may not be."

CHAPTER 13

2001

Teuta smoothed the lace her mother had made, arranging it in the center of the table. The beds were in place. The children would share a room that was smaller than the one they used to share, and yet the apartment looked nice and she would make it a fine home.

Her husband had found work with a man who had a store in a real building, not a stall in the street. They sold things for the house and already he had brought home a chair that could not be sold because the fabric was torn. Teuta had fixed it and her husband rested in it. Of course, being a shop man was not the kind of work that would make her husband happy, but he was a good man and soon he would figure out a better way.

The children were in school. She, Teuta, had been to the marketplace to let the townspeople see her. It would be lonely for a while, but soon that would change. Life always changed. Hopefully, this time it would be for the better because it felt like they had been through the worst.

2013

"Ten minutes, Jo. Come on"

Josie looked over her shoulder in time to see Archer raise the sheet and beckon her back to the warm bed.

"Not this time. It's going to be a big day, and I don't want any distractions."

Archer accepted that and took what he could get. What he got was a few more minutes to admire the amazing figure his woman cut. Slim hipped, long legged, a tremendous ridge of spine that was straight and strong and led to one of the finest behinds he had ever seen. Josie leaned over and pulled on a pair of French cut panties, snapped on a matching bra, stepped into her trousers, and pulled a blouse out of the closet. She put it on, letting it hang loose as she went in again for a blazer. She pitched that toward Archer. He caught it and smoothed it.

"If this thing gets ugly, the next time we're going to be lounging in bed won't be until our honeymoon." She buttoned her blouse, tugged on the collar and stepped back, checking herself out in the mirror. Archer didn't see the nod that signaled she was ready for the battle of the day. That was not a good sign.

"Maybe I should just cancel Hawaii," Archer suggested, but Josie was lost in her thoughts and a honeymoon wasn't part of them. She ruffled her hair, decided to open the top button on her blouse, reached out for her blazer, put it on, and shot her cuffs.

"Christ, Jo, you look good," Archer said. "Scary, but good."

She picked up her briefcase, sat on the edge of the bed, and rifled through it. Archer turned on his side and rested his head on his upturned palm.

"Did you get anyone on the phone last night?" she asked.

"No one answered. Their night is our morning. We don't know how old that number is. I didn't even know where Albania was until now."

"At least we both got the same number. That's huge," Josie muttered. "And the other number you got at Undies was Greg Oi's?"

"Yep. I don't think you should share that with Judge Healy."

"Agreed."

Both of them knew this would be the wrong time to suggest any connection between Billy and a dead man, not to mention a more intimate relationship between the dead man and Billy's mother.

Josie paused, closed her briefcase, put it on the floor, and draped her body over Archer's. He enfolded her in his arms without asking any questions. There was something marvelous about a clothed body lying over a naked one. The possibilities were so clear-cut. Either the clothed person would end up naked or the naked person would end up disappointed and dressed. But in this case it wasn't about sex or desire. Archer felt something else radiating off Josie.

"I'm afraid. I'm not the same as I was," she whispered.

"You are where it counts, babe."

His arms tightened and she stayed still in his embrace, listening to the beat of his heart. He cradled her short hair with his big hand and kissed her brow. He couldn't distract her nor could he say anything more. To give her permission to fail or retreat would change who they both were. She had to work this out her way.

"What if I make a mistake? What if I panic, and I don't remember how this is done? Sometimes I think of that hut and the reason why that man wanted to kill me. I think about what I did to him in court. I did it so easily, without thinking. There are consequences to what I do, Archer."

"Apples and oranges, Jo." He touched the bare skin just below the razor cut of her hair and the sharp crease of her collar.

"Maybe," she whispered. "Usually, these things are decisive. You talk the law, manipulate the law, use it to your advantage, and the person who does it better wins. But this is different. I can't really win. There are ten outcomes for every argument I can make and none of them are good for Billy. I don't want to screw up his life."

"You won't."

Josie raised her head. She searched his face, looking for any doubt he had about her and this situation. He lifted his own just far enough to kiss her lightly again.

"If you need a little extra courage, I can help."

Archer put his hands on her jacket and pulled aside the lapels. Josie chuckled. He had broken the spell, called a halt to her self-doubt with a move she was all too familiar with. In another second the jacket would be off and after that naked and hot was a given. She sat up, took his hands, crossed them over his bare chest, and held them down.

"We'll leave it at the pep talk for now." She kissed both his hands. "I appreciate the offer, though."

"When we're married you'll have to make love anytime I say. It's a husband's right."

Josie laughed and stood up. "Someday we'll debate that point."

"How am I ever going to live with you? I'll never win an argument."

"I don't ever intend to argue."

"I might as well get going then." Archer threw aside the covers, reassured by her laugh. Josie swore a contrail of warmth followed him as he headed to the bathroom. She called after.

"I'm thinking the first thing is to find a birth certificate for Billy. If he doesn't have that, we won't have to worry about Child Protective Services because immigration will be after him. I can't help if it comes to that."

"Unless the DA decides he wants to see him in prison," Archer called back.

"Not going to happen," she murmured and then raised her voice, too. "That is not going to happen."

"I believe you." Archer turned on the shower.

"I'm glad you do," she muttered as the bathroom door closed.

Even if Billy wasn't a murderer, the D.A. could charge him as a conspirator, an accessory. Maybe he brought Trey into the house and allowed the attack to happen. *Maybe. Maybe. Perhaps.* Josie shook her head to clear it, and took one last look in the mirror then picked up her briefcase and headed out. In the living room, she petted Max and gave herself a mental pep talk.

"An unforced error, Max, that's all I need them to do," she whispered.

Josie righted herself, smiled at the dog, hesitated, and then opened the door to Hannah's room. It was early but she was already up and painting. The minute the door opened, the sheet came down over her canvas. Josie's eyes flicked toward it. Hannah was stone-faced. For all Josie knew she was painting her as the devil, but that kind of rebellion was preferable to cutting herself or smashing someone's fingers in a locker door.

"You do understand you are here for the day, correct?" Josie said.

"Yes." Hannah's answer was brittle.

"I'll call you later on the land line," Josie warned.

"Okay."

With a last look around the room to see if anything was out of place, she closed the door and resisted the urge to once again engage in debate about Hannah's behavior or attempt to elicit an apology. Then Josie realized she didn't want a discussion at all. Josie Bates wanted what any real parent would: she wanted Hannah to show some remorse for putting her, Josie, in this situation.

***

Hannah listened to the sound of Josie's heels on the wood floor, listened for the bubble of silence that would indicate she was whispering to Max to have a good day, and listened to the front door open and close. She waited a while longer in case Josie came back because she forgot something: a directive, a piece of advice, another lecture.

Finally satisfied she wouldn't be interrupted, Hannah uncovered her canvas and looked at the painting objectively. This was the best thing she had ever done. Mrs. Trani would give it an A, but Hannah knew that this painting could not be graded. There was only one person who needed to be impressed.

Picking up her brush, Hannah began to work on the shading instead of on the eyes. Eyes were the most challenging. They were truly the windows of the soul and right now Hannah's soul was pretty black because no one saw that she had been right to fight back against Tiffany. She would wait to tackle the eyes when her heart was open again. Hannah mixed her colors, she ran the brush in short strokes along the side of the canvas, she cleared her mind, and waited for Archer to leave.

CHAPTER 14

2002

Teuta's husband introduced the men he brought to their home. Teuta was surprised that he had done so without telling her.

"Mirë se vini," she greeted them properly.

And when they sat in the room where there was a television and a couch, she brought them coffee. She brought them food on small plates. She placed a chair just inside the kitchen in case the men might need something more. She sat in such a way that she could see the two men if she looked in just the right way.

One was a relative of her husband. He was not such a good boy, and Teuta was not happy to have him in her home, yet this was what her husband wanted so she said nothing. The other one, the big man, he was dressed in fine clothes that Teuta had never seen in a shop in her town. Nor had she seen such clothing when she had gone to the capitol. She soon found out that this man lived in America.

Teuta's heart almost stopped to hear the word America. Many spoke of the opportunities in that country. Not that she would want to go, learn a new language, leave her country behind, but it was a curiosity to see a person such as this.

The big man spoke of business. Teuta's husband's relative spoke of wanting to work for the big man. He included Teuta's husband in his request.

This made Teuta think he was a good boy after all. The big man seemed used to such requests and he said things that made the other men happy. Teuta, though, heard empty words. He would help who he wanted to help and when he wanted to help them.

Meanwhile, he drank their coffee and ate their food. Soon he would expect to drink their raki. That would be fine since Teuta's husband made the raki himself. Perhaps it would loosen the rich man so that he would offer jobs.

Perhaps not.

While Teuta was thinking this, the door of their small house opened and her children tumbled in. They fell silent the moment they saw the men. Teuta's husband raised his arm and motioned his children forward. He introduced them, each in turn, and to each the rich man said a greeting.

He looked for a long while at Teuta's oldest daughter, and that Teuta did not like.

2013

Judge Healy had a thing for Paris. The walls of his chambers were covered with pictures of the Eiffel Tower, the clock at the Musee d'Orsay, and the Louvre. He had bookends shaped like the Arc de Triomphe and more renditions of the Eiffel Tower on pillows, books, and notepads. He noticed Josie noticing these things as she took a seat at his conference table.

"I've only been to Paris once, Ms. Bates. Mention that you would like to go back and every darn Christmas someone gives you something with the Eiffel Tower on it."

"I promise not to try to get into your good graces that way, Your Honor."

"Smart move." He indicated the young woman sitting to his left. "Do you two know each other?"

"Rita Potter. County Counsel." She introduced herself.

Josie shook her hand before nodding to deputy district attorney.

"Mr. Newton."

"Ms. Bates." He looked over her more than at her as she took her place. She looked back with interest. His presence was unexpected.

Slight and professorish, his salt and pepper hair was worn short but without style. He looked nonthreatening, but Josie had faced off in enough courtrooms to know that you never based your chances of winning on how your opponent looked. But this wasn't a courtroom, the proceedings were not criminal, and his mere presence had put her off the game before it began.

"Shall we begin?" Judge Healy touched a Lucite paperweight in which a miniature Arc de Triomphe floated. "I understand we have a situation before us that is currently the focus of multiple social and law enforcement agencies. I am only concerned with the welfare of the minor, Billy Zuni. Is that clear?"

The three people at the table nodded.

"I have been briefed, and I see that there are still a lot of holes to fill in regarding this young man." Judge Healy pointed the hockey-puck of a paperweight at Rita Potter. "We're starting with you, Ms. Potter."

All eyes turned toward the county counsel, the one person in the room personally charged by the state with making sure Billy Zuni's best interests were served. Thirty if she was a day, Rita Potter was a no-nonsense advocate. Her porcelain skin was unmarred even by make-up. There were no rings on her fingers and only tiny gold dots in her ears. A fine figure was hidden under uninspired clothes. Her doe eyes were pale and her nose a tad short. Her hair was long and lank but naturally blond. The tools of her trade were laid out neatly in front of her, her briefcase set precisely by her side.

Josie looked at Rita Potter and smiled, but the one the county counsel returned was watery and less than inclusive. Okay, so they weren't going to be best friends. That was fine with Josie just as long as she didn't prove to be the enemy. Rita opened a folder, snipped the top page from inside and handed it to the judge.

"We're all fact finding at the moment and the sheriff's department is being very cooperative, advising me as they continue their investigation."

Josie's eyes flicked to Carl Newton. Ms. Potter may think Montoya was fact finding in Billy's best interest, but that was naive. The sheriff's personnel were working with Newton to get a perpetrator locked down fast. The press wanted that, the D.A. wanted that, and the sheriff wanted it off the books. Still, Josie let it go and listened.

"Right now we know that Billy is improving but is still under careful watch at the hospital. His injuries – physical and psychological – make this placement delicate."

"Do we know if he was present in the house at any time during the night?" the judge asked.

"We do not have concrete evidence, Your Honor," Newton chimed in. "We are trying to establish the time frame of his movements."

Josie broke in, not sharing the fact that Billy had admitted to being in the house. "It would take an eyewitness to establish that he was there at the time of the assault. If Mr. Newton doesn't have that, I object to the innuendo. It is beneath him and has no place in these proceedings."

"This isn't a trial, Ms. Bates. No need to be confrontational." Judge Healy reprimanded her. "However, I will not ignore the fact that Billy Zuni is pivotal to Mr. Newton's investigation. Unless and until Mr. Newton tells me that the boy is a suspect in these murders, I will give weight to county counsel's recommendations not the D.A.s insinuations. Ms. Potter?"

Rita Potter's tiny nose twitched, the only sign she was delighted by the import the judge gave her position.

"My office believes a foster family placement is appropriate, but we must inform the parents of the circumstances of the need. So, Mr. Newton is correct to the point that the perception of criminal complicity would raise questions about safety of the foster family. This will limit our choices."

"I can provide any number of character witnesses for Billy," Josie began, but Healy's finger went up again. Josie fell silent knowing she had sounded clumsy, too eager, and off point.

"Other options?" the judge asked.

"We could put him in a halfway house that handles juveniles coming out of Youth Authority," Rita suggested. "Security is higher and that might satisfy Mr. Newton."

"And those are the kids who have served out sentences for murder and assault," Josie objected. "Billy couldn't defend himself physically or psychologically. That placement would be a death sentence."

"That's a bit melodramatic, Ms. Bates," Carl Newton chided.

"It's a sad fact, Mr. Newton," Judge Healy noted. "Even though I wish we could argue the point, Ms. Bates is right. But we may not have a choice if Ms. Potter can't secure a home situation."

"I've identified three group homes, Your Honor." Rita took the opening and made it hers. "One in Westgate, one in East Los Angeles and another-"

Josie interrupted again. "Billy's best interest would be served by keeping him in his home area with access to friends."

"Ms. Bates, please." Healy admonished.

"Your Honor, if I may." Carl Newton slid into the opening. "The District Attorney wants to make sure that Billy Zuni is well discharged, but under very close watch. One of the victims is quite prominent internationally. It would reflect badly on all of us if there was the perception we were not taking his death extremely seriously."

"Dead is dead, Mr. Newton. This court cannot be swayed by who the victims were in life. If you have evidence, we will then talk about keep away in county jail, but not until you bring me something solid."

Josie's heart stopped. It never occurred to her that anyone would consider such a radical move. In keep away, Billy would be isolated in a setting where there was no concern for his age or temperament. Jail was jail and isolation would make it even more gruesome.

"Mr. Newton has no such evidence," Josie objected again, unnerved by how much latitude the judge was giving the deputy D.A..

"And Ms. Bates is ignoring the fact that this boy might be a danger to himself. Consider the reason he is in the hospital. It was sheer madness to go into the ocean in a storm. That action could be construed as suicidal. I would have to ask why he wanted to kill himself? One answer might be that he had just killed two people and assaulted a third and did not want to be brought to justice."

"Billy has no history of violence, depression, or suicide attempts. His record shows only minor infractions that plague half the juveniles in California," Rita interjected and Josie was grateful. Newton, though, was not to be put off.

"This is a complicated situation," Carl Newton agreed. "However, we cannot ignore statistics, and statistics favor someone close to the victims. The person with access to the scene and a personal connection at least to Rosa Zuni is Billy Zuni."

"Fine. Alright," Healy intervened. "Ms. Bates, in your perfect world, where do you see this boy?"

"ILP. Independent living supervised by Child Protective Services is the appropriate decision."

"Do you really think putting that boy back in a house where people were murdered would be beneficial to his physical or mental state?" Rita scoffed.

Josie turned her head, locking down this woman's attention. They were supposed to be on the same side, but it didn't appear that was the way this was going to go.

"No, I do not," Josie said. "But if the court grants him that status, I will personally see that he is settled somewhere that is both safe for him and meets the requirements of the district attorney's office as they continue their investigation."

She appealed to Judge Healy, the only person in that room who really mattered.

"Your Honor, Billy has no means, physical ability, or stomach for flight. He is devoted to his mother, and his only concern has been for her. Also consider that Billy is part of the fabric of Hermosa Beach. I can provide affidavits from citizens willing to transition Billy back into the community until either the District Attorney no longer finds him a person of interest – which he has not stipulated at this point - or his mother is well enough to exert parental rights. That would seem to be in the best interest of this child."

"In this case it doesn't take a village, Ms. Bates," Healy sighed. Her solution was not going to be considered. "I cannot turn Billy over to a town. It's hard to believe no one has come forward. No relative, not even a friend of the mother."

"That is precisely the point," Carl Newton concurred. "Billy has never had any supervision, and I can document that. The mother's youth might be a factor, but if she was neglectful of Billy while she was well, her judgment now that she is so desperately injured must be questioned. It is the court's responsibility to act in his best interest, certainly, but you give weight to the broader criminal issues. You truly cannot separate the two at this point."

"But, I believe that the court should err in consideration of Billy Zuni as a victim," Rita insisted.

"And little Billy can skip off to the beach Scott free," Newton muttered, surprising everyone with this cut, but only Josie took exception.

"Why is the District Attorney even at this meeting?" she demanded. "He undermines the seriousness of this problem. He would only be happy with a keep-away placement in county jail. If that happened, Billy could never go back to the community. I've seen it happen to a teenager before. The consequences are devastating and the dangers incalculable. I won't let it happen again."

"Ms. Bates," Judge Healy warned, "I am the one who says what will and will not happen to this boy. Is that clear?"

Josie detected a note of empathy under the judge's reprimand, but he had no idea how deeply personal this was. She had been wrong to let it show.

"My apologies," she murmured.

The judge cut his eyes to Carl Newton. The reprimand sent to the deputy D.A. was equally sharp.

"Mr. Newton. You are here as a courtesy because you requested it. If you are planning to charge this boy tell me now, and we'll have a different conversation."

Newton shook his head.

"Then we are all agreed," Healy turned back to Josie. "Ms. Potter notes that Billy was regularly turned out of his house."

"This is true, but beach culture is unique, Your Honor. "

"I would suggest that cultural parameters are not your strongest argument," Healy warned. "There are laws against vagrancy and curfews. It sounds as if Billy was as good as homeless, so arguing that I release him to independent living in a community that had no care for him before this incident isn't appropriate. I will not consider it."

Rita Potter jumped in again.

"Judge, we really only have one choice and that is foster care. Given that, all we have to do is decide on the venue. I am concerned about a halfway house because of his injuries, but I also am aware that we don't want to put any citizen at risk. Foster parents without minors in the home would be the first choice."

"Mr. Newton? Last go-round. Speak now," Healy passed the ball.

"Billy Zuni is a seventeen year old boy with raging hormones," Carl Newton noted. "What a young man does and what he says are often two different things at that age. We must be extraordinarily vigilant."

"Okay, then. I've got a full calendar this afternoon and I'd like to at least get a sandwich before I address it. So, listen up. Here's the deal. Ms. Potter. I am ordering a full psychological work-up."

"In anticipation, Your Honor, I've already been in contact with Doctor Hardy. He's set aside time tomorrow."

"I'd like to have a doctor of my choosing also examine Billy," Josie stated.

"Do as you wish, Ms. Bates, but I will rely on county counsel," the judge said. "Ms. Potter, interface with the hospital doctors also. Find out if there are going to be any physical limitations or special needs that might affect his placement. I want that along with the psychological work-up. I want a list of approved options and that means specific families willing to accept him. Ms. Potter, you will also communicate appropriately with Ms. Bates, Mr. Newton, and all other interested parties."

"Yes, Judge," she answered.

"Mr. Newton, your office will coordinate with Ms. Potter on an hourly basis if that's what it takes. I do not want a public fight about this boy's situation just to satisfy your egos. Is that clear?"

Everyone nodded.

"If there is nothing urgent in the next forty-eight hours, we will be back here. . ."

He consulted his calendar, picked up a pen, and made a notation while he spoke.

"Day after tomorrow at three o'clock. We will entertain witness, but stay on topic. I will make a ruling based on the information we have that day. Mr. Newton, you are excused from that hearing unless you bring something concrete to the table. That's it."

Everyone made motions to move on but Josie had one last card she wanted to play even though she knew the game was over.

"Judge? We didn't discuss the KSSP."

"It's a moot point, Ms. Bates. There is no relative to whom I can release him." Judge Healy dismissed her out of hand.

From the corner of her eye she thought she saw Rita Potter and Carl Newton exchange a look. Rita stepped forward to add her two cents even though the judge had been clear. It was the failing of lawyers to want to always have the last word for the record.

"Ms. Bates has a private investigator looking for a relative. Even if he identifies someone, let's see what kind of attention he or she gives Billy after the county places him. That way we can determine the true level of interest."

Josie pleaded with the judge. "If I find a responsible relative in the next forty-eight hours, will you at least consider kinship placement? Or release him to independent living. I will personally vouch for Billy remaining in the jurisdiction."

"Will he be living under your roof, Ms. Bates?" Carl interjected.

The last-word bug bit them all much to Judge Healy's dismay. He tossed his pen onto the table.

"Ms. Bates is his legal advocate not his guardian. That would be a conflict of interest I would not allow. That's it, if you weren't clear before. I'm done. You've all got your marching orders. See you in two days."

They pushed their chairs back from the table, but the judge had one more word for Josie.

"Ms. Bates, I expected more from you. From now on, let's keep it real."

Josie couldn't argue with him. She had expected more from herself.

CHAPTER 15

2004

Teuta ducked behind a street stall that sold leeks and potatoes and little else. It was late afternoon and the men were xhiroing, walking round and round the streets of the town before stopping to talk, take coffee, smoke, and drink raki as was their custom. Sometimes it was hard to gyro, for there were many more cars these days, most taken from other countries.

Teuta was happy that her husband did not take a car that he did not know where it came from even though his distant relative often tried to give him one. Teuta and her husband were cautious people. They did not like receiving a gift for no reason, and Teuta did not like strangers driving through her town. She did not like the foreigners who walked across the mountain for fun. Those people acted like the villagers were children who didn't understand pity when they heard voices filled with it. Pity was pity, no matter what the language. Pity made Teuta angry, as did the poverty, and her children not having warm clothes.

But what was one to do?

Since the answer was nothing, Teuta thought instead of the goodness in her life. Her husband had found work in the chrome mine thanks to the American who had come to their home. It was hard work and did not pay much, but her husband was proud again. They were blessed. So many of the men sold vegetables on the street corner like the man who owned this stand in which she hid *herself. He used to be a foreman at the factory where they made glass. Now he was nothing.*

"Can I help you?"

Startled, Teuta whirled around, holding her bag to her breast. She laughed a little, thinking how silly it was when the panic came upon her. She shouldn't be hiding among the vegetables without knowing what she was hiding from. It was a feeling, nothing more. It was fright because she did not know the people in the cars and on the street.

Because she did not want this man to know she was fearful, Teuta pointed to a very big leek. He was pleased. It was the most expensive leek he had so he spoke of it while he wrapped it: how it came from soft earth, how it had suddenly one day been perfect, how he knew she would cook it just so. She paid no attention, only handed over her money knowing she could ill-afford to be buying this vegetable when she grew the same in her own garden. Ah well, better that than explain that she was afraid and hiding from nothing.

Teuta left the stall deciding it was the heat that made her heart beat faster, and her sweat making her headscarf moist. Perhaps it was that the man from America was back. He was coming to dinner, and Teuta wished to make him a fine meal to thank him for helping her husband. She would make byrek with this leek and they would talk about the byrek and the children would stand quietly.

Teuta was smiling when she joined the gyro, made her way up the street and turned toward the school. She arrived just as the old man whose job it was to ring the hand bell did so. Children poured out of the building and she shook her head at the girls. There was no work for men, what would there be for girls who were educated? But her husband insisted that all his children go to school. Teuta didn't like the little one to be out of her sight to go to school, and yet she sent him as her husband wished.

Standing at the top of the crumbling stairs that led to the building, Teuta craned her neck and saw her beautiful daughters. They waved at her and then looked back at the English teacher who had come from America. He worked for no money. He was a volunteer and that meant he did what his government told him even if he didn't want to. Now her daughters giggled behind their hands at him, thinking they were in love. He would be gone soon, and another would come. These girls would not get to America by marrying a handsome foreign teacher. Teuta would not like it if her girls married a man who did not have brains enough to get paid for his labor. Her girls laced their arms as they veered off toward the far end of town. Young girls walking alone together without their father or brother was something new. Then she saw her son.

"Besnik! Besnik!" she called.

The other mothers looked at her, then they looked at her son. Who could not look at him? This beautiful boy whose eyes were so bright, whose smile was more glorious than the sun, whose heart was bigger than any in the entire village.

"Nënë!" Even his voice rang with beauty.

Her boy came alongside her and they began to walk together. Already he was talking to her, taking her hand even though he was old for such a thing. That was when she heard a car behind them. She nudged her son aside to let it go by, but it slowed. It stopped. She was called.

"Teuta? That is you, is it not?"

A little breeze fluttered the end of her scarf. She was still smiling at something her son had said, but that smile faded when she saw who was speaking to her.

"Gjergy. I thought you had gone to Shkodra." She said this even though she could see he had no interest in her. He was looking at her son who smiled his glorious smile back at the man.

"So, this is your son. He is a fine boy." Gjergy slid his eyes back to her. "He is seven, now. Seven years old. And Yilli. Is he well?"

"My father is dead." Teuta was sure he knew this full well, but she could not help herself and answered him anyway. It was cruel of him to ask.

"Ah." Gjergy's eyes went back to the little tow-headed boy. "And your boy goes to school, does he?"

"He walks with me, Gjergy. He is a child."

"You are a man, are you not?" Gjergy teased and the child smiled wider.

"He is a child," Teuta reiterated.

"And your daughters? I see you let them walk without a man."

"They walk together. It is modern times." Teuta's gaze followed the man as he considered the girls standing next to the store that sold clothing. Gjergy's eyes lingered on them and then came back to her.

"It is a shame Yilli is dead. Your oldest daughter, she is beautiful. All your children are beautiful, Teuta."

"They are a blessing," Teuta said.

"Or a curse," Gjergy countered. "Only God knows which."

He drove off. Teuta could see that he did not look at the road. Gjergy did not have a care for the men walking or the women shopping for their vegetables. She saw that he looked into the mirror. She saw that he looked at her and the boy who still held her hand, who still smiled, and the daughters who still giggled, probably speaking of the American who came to teach them a language they had no need of.

2013

"Here. Take this."

Sam Lumina handed his wife, Mary, a glass of wine and then stood beside her to watch the people milling around the small house. In one corner there was a group of men, tightly circled around Mark Wolf who was taking being pissed off at Marshall Fasteners to new heights. Sam would have to talk to him. A funeral wasn't the place to get on a soapbox about work. There were people here who weren't brothers. You never knew who might not share your opinion, you never knew who might think you were more than just talk. People misinterpreted stuff all the time. Just look at Jak Duka. He was an idiot. It was because he was an idiot that he was dead.

Sam took a drink. It wasn't Mark's rant that was making him nervous; it was the icy anger shooting off his wife. He followed her gaze to the group of ashen-faced women huddled around Jak's widow. They offered spoken words of condolence and silent prayers of thanks that they were not in that woman's shoes. Children ran through the living room, reached up to the table laden with food, grabbed a cookie or a cold cut, and went on their way again, trailing little bubbles of laughter. Even Jak's own kids didn't really get it, and Sam's son was right there with the big boys, shoving and pushing.

By the window, the old man spoke to two others even older than he. Their heads shook back and forth as they agreed with what he was saying. One of them raised a fist and shook it. Sam's wife's attention had moved from the women to the old men.

"Good grief. You'd think those guys had lived here long enough to figure out that we nod to agree and shake our head to disagree. And why is your uncle still here? I hate that old man. Why is he still here?" Sam's wife groused. "That's all I want to know."

"Because he's my uncle," Sam snapped.

"He's your uncle that you haven't seen in thirty-years, for God sake," Mary sniped. "He didn't know Jak, and still you trot him out like he's something special. Those old guys act like they've known him forever."

"You're so damn American." Sam took a drink of his beer thinking that was a funny thing for her to say. The old man said the same thing about Sam. That was the only thing the old man had been wrong about. Sam knew where his loyalties lay.

"I don't mind you having a relative in, but he's just weird." She waved her wine glass his way. "He doesn't talk to me. He doesn't say please or thank you."

"What was I going to do, leave him at home?"

"Sure, why not? We haven't had one second alone. Your own son hasn't seen you for more than two seconds," she muttered. "And I thought he was going to leave tomorrow. He hasn't packed or anything."

"Just a few more days until we get some things sorted out. He knows all about what's coming through the mines at home. He can help us with the negotiations with the new management."

"Really?" she drawled. "You're telling me that this guy is somehow going to make things right and you all will get back to work? That's dumb. And what's this home stuff you started talking? This is home."

"You don't know what you're talking about. A couple more days." Sam took a drink and added: "Men don't talk to women about business where he comes from."

"Well, this isn't where he comes from," she groused.

"Okay, I got it," Sam snapped. Then he realized that attitude might do more harm than good. "I'm sorry. I know it's tough. Just trust me."

He put his arm around Mary and pulled her close. He would never admit it, but he would be happy when the old man was gone, too. Much as he thought he had the stomach for all this, he really didn't. Much as he thought he had the conviction that justice was on their side, he wasn't so sure. The strike, the old man, his unhappy wife, Oi and Jak's death, were all taking their toll.

"Why don't you see if Sharon needs anything before we go."

"She needs her husband back. I can't even imagine what he was doing in that house?" the young man's wife clucked. "A stripper? I can't believe he was doing a stripper and Sharon so gorgeous and all."

Sam looked at Sharon and thought that beauty was in the eye of the beholder. He said: "You don't know why he was there."

His wife only made a sound like women make when a husband says something particularly stupid. Sam had to get her under control.

"Okay, he was there to talk to Mr. Oi," Sam said under his breath. "Don't you talk about that, you hear me? Don't mention it to anyone but that's what it was. Wrong place, wrong time."

"Sharon should know. She thinks he was cheating," Mary hissed.

"Believe me, she doesn't want to know what business Jak had with Oi," Sam assured her.

"Any business with that man was bad. I'm glad he's dead." Sam took his wife's arm and squeezed hard. She turned an angry face his way. "That hurts, Sam. Jesus, what are you doing?"

"You can think anything you want, just keep your trap shut. Do you understand me?"

"Around here?" she snorted. "All these people think the same thing. Heck, maybe one of them did it just to clear the way."

"Jesus, what's wrong with you?" Sam's accent got in the way as it always did when he was excited.

"Sharon thinks it might have happened because you guys didn't want Jak. She's terrified that Jak had something to do with killing Oi just to prove to you guys that he was tough enough to be one of you. She thinks he couldn't take it so he shot himself. That's what Sharon thinks."

"And she thinks he was doing a stripper. Sharon is going to say a lot of things. Give me a break." He shook her a little and the wine spilled out of her glass.

"Okay. Okay. All you wanted to do was work." She looked over at the women huddling around the widow. "I'm just saying, I'd understand if one of you guys got Oi, and maybe Jak got caught in the crossfire."

"You don't know anything about what happened in that house or why."

"Do you?"

She turned toward her husband and looked at him with her big black eyes. She wasn't a pretty woman but she did the best with what she had. Her make-up was nice, her dress decent, her ass was outstanding and her boobs beyond compare, but she was always poking her nose in where it didn't belong.

"Jesus, Sam. Do you know?"

"I don't know nothing. Nobody here does. If Sharon knows what's good for her she'll let it all be. Maybe you should encourage her to do that."

He buttoned his jacket. His eyes darted around the room. He was worried someone was watching. No one was. Mark was getting all in a lather again. The guys around him were getting drunk and buying into it. The women were still being women.

"No one's going to forget Sharon. We'll take care of her and the kids. We're all going back to work without a contract on Monday 'till they can figure it out. Oi's estate doesn't want a cash cow shut down anymore than we do. You tell her. We won't forget."

"Everybody forgets," his wife complained.

Unsure of what they were talking about anymore, she peeled away and joined the women, leaving her husband staring at the floor. He was thinking about family, thinking about honor, thinking about his union brothers and a dead guy who ran a company where they used to all work pretty happily together. He was thinking about history and determination. Sam was thinking harder than he had ever thought in his whole life. Then Sam looked up.

Mark was pointing his finger at the group of men around him like he was giving orders. Big talker. He never actually did anything. Sam clicked his eyes an inch and saw his wife take Sharon Duka in her arms. He saw the utter terror and grief etched on the widow's face. Then Sam realized he was looking at the old man. He thought he saw the old guy smile, but it was really just the way the light hit his eyes that made him look like that. The old man cocked his head.

Sam nodded. It was getting late. It was time to go.

***

"Get it! Get it! Don't let it go in the water!"

The woman in the pedal pushers and sunhat danced around on the sand, waving her arms, calling to her daughter. The girl — overweight and uncoordinated - was trying to track the trajectory of the Frisbee her mother had thrown. It didn't help that her mother wasn't the best Frisbee thrower; she always made it sound like her daughter wasn't a good catcher. And there were people around to hear her mother yell at her. The girl hated that. She was probably the only fat kid in Hermosa Beach and her mother made her chase a Frisbee in front of kids who looked like they never ate anything in their whole life.

The plastic disc wobbled and then hovered as if it were trying to decide whether to lead her into the pier pilings or back to the beach. Finally, it shot off toward the water. The girl lumbered after it, head up, arms up, fingers stretching as she prayed, just this once, to catch it. She jumped as high as she could, hoping to at least bat it out of the air. The water was lapping water at her feet as she made one more valiant effort before losing her footing. She crumpled, falling on the wet sand. In the next second, she let out a howl of pain. Her mother's high shriek of panic came next.

"Oh no! Oh my God! Honey, are you okay?" She ran awkwardly over the sand toward her daughter.

"No!" The girl called back. Then she realized that she hadn't just stepped on a shell or a rock, she hadn't just twisted her ankle. She raised her head and screamed for real. "Mom! Mom! I'm bleeding!"

***

Kat had poured herself a scotch and soda an hour earlier even though it was well before the cocktail hour. In fact, it was so far from the cocktail hour it wasn't even lunchtime. Now she was nursing the last of it. God knew why she bothered since there was plenty to be had. She reached for the bottle on the desk and refilled her glass sans soda or ice. As she did so, Kat saw that she had company. She sat back in the big chair that had been Greg's and looked at the gorgeous young woman standing in the doorway.

"What?" Kat snapped.

"What happen now?" The young woman walked into the room, picking at her fingernails, her eyes at a lazy half-mast.

"I'm figuring it out. I'll know soon," Kat snapped. "Where's the other one?"

"Doing lesson," the girl said.

"Go help her." Kat took a drink and sat forward in the chair as if she was about to work, but the girl didn't leave. Kat demanded: "What?"

"Did you kill him?" she asked. "He was weird, so maybe you kill him."

"You are so stupid. Why would I kill him?"

The young woman shrugged as if to say why not?

"Do we go home now?" she asked.

"Probably. Leave me alone. Get out of here. Keep the kid busy," Kat directed.

The girl retreated, gracefully melting into the shadowy hall. She wore no shoes, so Kat couldn't hear her steps across the marbled foyer. Kat drank. She tried to ignore the giant question mark that had replaced the girl in the doorway. What in the hell was she going to do with them now? What in the hell did Greg do with them?

Kat took another drink and pulled more papers out of the desk drawers. She relegated the catalogues from Joan's Closet, feminine apparel for men, to the same pile as the receipts Greg had kept for everything he bought for his charming little habit: special shoes, clothes, wigs, jewelry.

"Fool," she muttered as she rifled through them all.

The man had spent a small fortune on dressing up. All cash. He was fanatical about that. Even the house was paid off. When it was appropriate, she would sell this big place and find herself a fancy condo on the Miracle Mile or in Century City. Something with a city view.

She found one of Greg's cards with a woman's name and number written on it. She called. It was a seamstress. Greg still owed her six hundred bucks for letting out a gown. Kat told her to take it up with Greg's wife and hung up. She had a good little ugly chuckle over that but it was short-lived and small comfort. The wife thing good old lawyer Fred had dropped was a gruesome surprise, indeed. If that woman Rosa Zuni survived, if she chose to lay claim to Greg's estate, then Kat was screwed big time.

Kat's fingers drummed on the desk as she eyed the passports she had found. They were Greg's and the two girls. Kat's own was there, too. She had hoped to find something else. She wanted proof that the other woman was legally Greg's wife since even Fred couldn't tell if the marriage certificate he had shown her was authentic or legal. Not that it mattered. That woman could drag things out so long that Kat would have to pay her off.

But if the broad kicked off, that would help a lot. Then Kat would take the next step and deal with the kid. DNA and all that. Good old Fred-the-attorney was clear. Kat didn't have to worry as much about the woman as she did about the boy. If Greg was the kid's father, or if Greg had adopted him, then he could lay claim to all that Greg Oi owned.

Kat grabbed her tumbler. It was so heavy it felt like a weapon. She took a drink. She was working herself up. She pushed back her hair with her free hand, drained the glass, and put it on the side of the desk. She missed and it fell to the floor. The crystal was so dense and the rug so thick the glass didn't break when it hit the ground. Kat left it where it was and pushed aside the passports. She cleared a space for Greg's ledger that accounted for all of his personal expenses down to the last dime. One side of her lips pulled up in an expression of admiration. Despite everything she found out since his death, Kat admired Greg.

He wasn't an engineer, he wasn't a chemist, he wasn't a metallurgist, he was just a man with a sharp eye for opportunity and the guts to take it on. She flipped through the book. There was nothing new in those pages.

"Oh Greg," she sobbed suddenly.

Tears just kind of spilled right out of her eyes. Kat's head fell forehead onto the ledger and rested there. She listened to the silence in the big house that was supposed to be hers. Knowing it might not be made Kat sad. Then it just started to make her angry again.

She sat up, unwound the string from the grommet on an old envelope, and dumped the contents onto the desk. She fanned the contents. There were pictures of Greg when he was much younger: tall, slim-waisted, dark haired. No wonder she cottoned to him. In this picture he stood in one of those Albanian villages he loved so much. If Kat had come from a place like that she would never admit it. She picked up a picture, cocked her head.

"The Addams family looks better than you guys."

The people in the photograph didn't smile or touch one another. They looked beaten until you looked really close and saw their eyes. There was something spooky about those eyes staring straight at the camera as if they were ready to fight. The littlest kid looked sweet, though. She snapped it down and picked up another one that showed Greg in front of a truck. Another picture of Greg with a group of men sitting at a table in a café, coffee and a bottle of liquor in front of them. She put those back in the envelope.

There was a pile of neatly folded letters. She scanned them to her computer to translate later. By the time she was done looking through his stuff, she had pocketed three hundred bucks and change, made a file for follow-ups, and tried the two phone numbers that had been hastily written on the back of Greg's cards. She reached for the receiver. Dialed the first one. It rang and rang. She dialed the second one. It rang and rang, too, but finally a machine picked up.

Hi everybody you've reached the Lumina family. Press 2 for Mary and 3 if you want to leave a message for Sam.

CHAPTER 16

2005

The boys looked for treasure in the rubble of a building that had fallen down during the last big snow. They threw stones and moved the chunks of concrete and crunched broken glass under their feet. They hollered at one another and laughed and posed atop the mess as if they had taken a fort. Their Shqiptare faces were on, jaw's taut, eyes narrowed and hard. They were little conquerors of nothing.

They stopped now and again to clean one another's shoes using the water that had puddled here and there on the cracked foundation. Teuta's son played with them. His shoes were dusty, so he knelt and used his fingers to put water on them. He did not notice the man who watched. He did not notice when the man sent the other boys away and that they went quietly because this was the kind of man who was to be obeyed. He did not notice the man until he was right behind him.

When Teuta's son looked up, and he smiled as was his way. The man smiled back but it was not a nice smile. The boy did not know that. To him, all smiles were good.

"Do you remember me?" the man asked.

"Yes, I remember," he finally answered, just to be polite.

The man nodded.

"You are almost nine years old, are you not?

"Yes." The boy forgot about his dirty shoes and stood up.

The man did not move. He only kept looking at Teuta's son as if he was afraid he might forget what the child looked like. Even when a cloud passed over the sky and made everything grey, when the boy thought it might rain, the man still did not move. When the rain finally began, the man did not seem to care that he got wet. Then when the boy was cold and said he must go, the man shook away whatever thoughts he was having.

"You will tell your mother I am coming."

"Yes."

The boy ran to do as he was told because he was a good boy, and because he was a little frightened even though he didn't know why.

2013

Mike and Wendy each had a copy of the toxicology reports. Wendy had already read them but she went over them again for his benefit.

"Rosa was clean. Oi was positive for cocaine. He tested for alcohol. Jak Duka's level was negligible. Billy was clean."

"Any word on the guy he says was with him? Trey?" Mike asked.

"Nope. The two people at the beach only knew that he came and went with Billy about five minutes before they took off. Hermosa PD is looking."

"Remind me of the house inventory?"

Wendy rifled through her file for more information.

"Half a bottle of raki. It's the traditional drink in Albania and Turkey, lots of places in Eastern Europe. There were a couple of beers in the fridge but mostly it was stocked with regular groceries. No drugs in the house. The boy's room was clean. It hardly looked lived in. Rosa's room was a mess, but nothing unusual."

"Did you find any prescribed medications?" Mike looked at Wendy thinking she was at her most beautiful when she was concentrating like she was now.

"No. None."

"No birth control?" Mike asked.

Wendy shook her head, "None listed."

"Ask the hospital if they checked for an IUD or found a cervical cap."

"What are you thinking?" Wendy asked.

"Given where she worked, I'm thinking she might have had a few boyfriends."

"The women there say no," Wendy assured him.

"There might be some guy who doesn't even know he's in the mix," Mike suggested. "A boyfriend who has nothing to do with Undies. It just seems strange to me that a good looking young woman wouldn't be concerned about pregnancy."

"She wasn't the first time," Wendy reminded him.

"Put that thought on hold until we find a birth certificate for Billy," Mike warned. "Was there anything on her phone?"

"Yep." Wendy reached for the phone records. "Normal things you'd expect. Lots of calls to Billy's number. Same back from the kid to her number."

"I wish we had Billy's phone to see who else he was calling," Mike mused.

"That thing is at the bottom of the ocean. We'll get his records."

"Great." Mike shook his head slightly. "Still, given the number of calls it's hard for me to believe this is a mom who didn't care about her child. There were three calls from Greg Oi in the days leading to the murders. Nothing from Jak Duka. She made a call to Oi two nights before the attack. There were three the day of the murders. I suppose he was telling her he was going to see her that night. Oh, and here's something interesting. Oi called Lumina's number two nights before the attack."

"That's interesting. It was the same night he showed up at Oi's house uninvited," Mike mused as he rolled his pen over his desk. "From what we know Rosa talked about the kid, liked him, and was protective of him. The boy is concerned about Rosa. He asks about her before his own injuries. She gets a call from Oi in the morning and immediately makes one call to Billy. When was the last one that night to Billy?"

"Just one at eleven," Wendy said

"Well before the fireworks started. Note that one of Oi's corporations owned the house where he died. The manager says he put Rosa in personally, but she paid the rent. Oi wasn't keeping her, but he was helping her out." Mike checked his watch. "Billy is scheduled for his psyche evaluation today. We can talk to him tomorrow."

"You should have had first crack at him. Why do they treat kids like they're something special?" Wendy gathered her work.

"Because they are," Mike reminded her.

"Oh, come on," she rolled her eyes. "Harbor General's emergency room is filled with minors on the wrong end of some other angry kid's gun or knife. It's a zoo, Mike. Billy Zuni isn't any different because he lives in that idyllic little patch of sunshine and likes to swim in the sea."

"Tell me how you really feel." Mike raised a brow and Wendy laughed.

"I'm just saying that we lose our edge down here, we look the other way and chalk up drugs and drinking to the way things are at the beach. I've never liked the wink and the nod. We don't see the bad stuff that often in the South Bay, but that's no excuse for getting lazy. You know why?"

"I'll bite," Mike said.

"Because when something really bad goes down, we get all courteous. We don't think bad enough. We don't think big enough. We're provincial."

"Billy offers some special challenges, but the midnight swim isn't evidence of anything."

"My money's on him," Wendy said. "Always has been."

"Then prove it," Mike challenged.

"I will, my friend. Just give me another ten hours, and I'll have a surprise for you." Wendy stood up and hugged her files like schoolbooks. "I haven't been sitting on my gorgeous behind while you're out doing detective stuff, you know."

"Do you want to fill me in now?"

"A few hours, Montoya. That's all I need. If what I got pans out, I'll hand you this case on a silver platter – or at least Carl Newton will have enough to file."

Mike eyed her, but didn't push. He was no fan of counting his chickens before they hatched.

"I can't wait," he said. "Have you heard anything from Torrance cops on the cameras at the factory?"

"They have a couple of frames. They think it's three guys inside just before three a.m. No one is identifiable. They knew where they were going and how to avoid security. The cops are working on fingerprints, checking out the stuff they used for the effigy. The paint on the walls came from the factory. We need one of the brothers to rat out whoever vandalized Oi's office."

"Are they still demonstrating down there?"

Wendy shook her head, "Nope. I checked in with Jenkins. The board has called a special session and the union agreed to arbitration. Oi was a known quantity. Now the local is getting nervous. They're backing down. The vandals were nothing but pranksters."

"Don't discount the incident at Marshalls. You're focusing on Billy because he's the only one who fits with Rosa and that gives you tunnel vision." Mike pointed a finger at her, less in accusation then in challenge to make her case. "Wrap up Rosa's assault, but do it in context where Billy is concerned. Where is the gun, and why were there two weapons? How did he overcome three adults?"

Wendy shrugged. "You're the detective, and I'm a lowly analyst. I give you the pieces and you put them together."

Mike wondered if he noted a touch of bitterness in her tone, but before he could pursue it, Wendy was paying no attention to him. She was gracing a desk officer with her glorious smile.

"Hey there, Deputy Daniels."

"Torrance sent this over for you to take a look." Daniels grinned back.

Wendy thanked him, but Mike took the package and opened it. Wendy leaned close, her perfume had weathered the day well but wisps of hair escaped her bun and curled at the nape of her neck. Mike gave her the routing slip.

"From Butterworth. They picked these up in the search they did of Oi's office. This stuff was in Oi's safe."

"Want to go to the movies?" Mike held up the clear plastic bags. Inside were tapes and DVDs.

"A date," she purred. "I thought you'd never ask."

***

"Hey Sterling." The tech guy pushed his glasses up to get a better look at her.

"Hello, Peter. Working a double shift? I thought I saw you here last night, too." She whipped two chairs in front of a monitor and patted the seat for Mike.

"Cutbacks. You know how it is." He grinned at Mike. "Detective Montoya. How are the girls? What are they up to?"

"Both in college." Mike handed over the bags.

"Ouch," Peter pulled a face. "You can't even afford to breathe."

"You're telling me," Mike laughed and nodded to the evidence bag. "Can we take a look at those or are you headed home?"

"Naw, I can hang out a while." He shook out the bag and grinned. "I haven't seen these things in a while."

Peter pulled out two cassettes. He reached in the bag again and came back up with five jewel cases.

"Start with the DVDs," Mike directed as he took up a position behind Wendy.

"You don't want to sit?" She looked up at him. He shook his head. She cut her losses. "Suit yourself."

They heard a little whoosh and Peter's monitor swallowed one of the DVDs. He pushed a button, rolled his chair back, and put his feet up on the table.

"Show time."

It took less than a second for the action to kick in. First the screen filled with a blush of color. Then the color wobbled and moved aside to reveal a bedroom. Wendy said:

"Nanny cam."

"Probably." Peter leaned forward, grabbed a mug, and settled back again.

"Nice room," Mike mumbled.

"Not very interesting," Wendy noted.

There was a large window to the left of a queen size bed that was on a platform. There was no headboard. The window covered two thirds of the wall. Beige curtains hung at either end, but the foliage outside was so thick the curtains were unnecessary to keep prying eyes at bay. The walls were painted blue. There were no pictures. There was a chair and a small table near the bed. On the table was a clock but no phone. It was a place where someone slept but didn't claim ownership. A second and a half into the video, they heard the sound of a toilet flushing. The screen filled with the blush color once more. This time it was easy to identify what they were looking at: a body mass.

"Bellybutton." Peter called out.

"Boobs." Wendy's comment kicked the men's eyes up a notch.

"Peter," Mike said. "Can you tell what kind of camera took this?"

He shook his head, "The resolution isn't that great. The angle isn't anything to crow about. It's small and cheap."

Wherever the camera was situated, the woman had paused in front of it before turning casually and walking away. If she knew the camera was there, she didn't care.

"Nice ass," Peter said.

Wendy clucked in mock dismay. "All this time I thought nothing impressed you guys down here. I figured you'd seen it all."

"You kidding? This is a treat compared to what I usually see. You two working porn? I thought the valley had a lock on that," Peter asked.

"Something a little closer to home," Mike muttered as Wendy looked closer. "It's not Kat Oi. This one's too tall, too curvy."

"Look who's noticing curves," Wendy tossed off. "This chick's young. Look at her skin."

The woman turned again, proving Wendy's assessment correct. She was young and her breasts were beautiful, big and natural. Her waist was tiny and her hips in perfect proportion to the rest of her. Her arms were up so she could shimmy into a t-shirt. She hadn't bothered with panties and it was clear she didn't buy into the Brazilian waxing craze. She turned just as the t-shirt fell onto her shoulders. They still couldn't see a face. She pulled back the sheets on the bed, offering another great moon shot just before she climbed in.

Still no face.

The woman in the bed pulled up the sheets and slid down until her head was on the pillow. She was restless. She turned and then turned once again. Finally, Mike confirmed what he had guessed the minute he saw the woman's abs.

"She lives at the Oi house. Mr. Oi is getting more interesting by the minute."

"Did you ever think it could have been the wife who set this up? Maybe she wanted to make sure he wasn't getting anything on the side in his own house. Take that one out and put in the next one." Wendy wiggled her fingers and Pete obliged. This time a younger girl appeared.

"I think that's the girl I saw at the back of the Oi house. I just got a glimpse of her. Slow it down. Pull in tight on her face," Mike ordered.

"What are you thinking? Sixteen?" Peter posed the question but got no answer.

"Pull it back," Mike directed.

"Maybe younger," Wendy suggested.

The girl was trying on lingerie that had been laid out on the bed. She was delighted, thrilled to be playing dress up.

"Maybe we should get Mrs. Oi in here for a chat." Wendy said.

"No. Call Judge Jorgensen. Get a search warrant. Let's not give her a chance to clean up the house."

"You got it." Wendy got up and they started for the door. Mike followed her. "What do you want it to cover?"

"The entire property. I want the garage, too, and access to all drawers, closets, everything including behind the walls. Oi had a wall safe at the office, so he might have the same at home."

Mike and Wendy conferred as they made their way to the door.

"Hey! You guys want to take a look at the oldies but goodies?"

Wendy and Mike stopped. Peter held up the cassettes. Wendy shrugged. It was Mike's call.

"Might as well," he said.

The first was a video of Greg Oi talking to a group of men.

"That's the factory," Mike said. "Can you turn it up?"

Peter made some adjustments. He couldn't get the sound up, but they could hear Greg Oi's voice. It was a deep, manly baritone and he spoke forcefully. It surprised Mike considering how the man was dressed when he died.

"See if you can clean it up and get it translated, Peter," Mike asked. "Anything will help."

"You got it. Any idea what language that was?" Peter asked.

"Albanian," Wendy answered.

"Like near Iraq?"

"Like near Serbia," Wendy said.

The tech guy shrugged and Mike assumed that hadn't enlightened him much, but he'd figure it out. He took out that cassette and put in the next one.

"Man, this is old," Peter muttered. "Don't know if we'll get much. Look at the static. The tape's really worn."

"Keep it running," Mike directed.

"It's not going to do any good. Give me a while. Let me work with it. Maybe I can do some magic." Just then the door opened. Peter looked over his shoulder. "Man, grand central tonight."

The deputy at the door acknowledged Peter even while he spoke to Wendy. "Sterling, here's the lab report you were waiting for."

"See you later Peter." She forgot about the tape as she walked into the hallway and turned to Mike. She gave him a playful poke in the chest with the report. "You are so going to owe me dinner, Mike."

Mike took it. Read it. Read it again and took a deep breath. "Damn."

***

Hannah walked fast down Lomita Boulevard as she headed toward the hospital, cursing herself for taking the bus and not her car. It had been a while since she'd driven her Volkswagen and since she didn't know if it was insured anymore she decided against driving. The last thing she needed was to get pulled over and have some cop hassle her. But the bus from Hermosa to Torrance had taken forever. It would take another forever to get back home before Josie got home. There was nothing to do about it now so Hannah hurried on.

She was almost at the edge of the hospital grounds when a car swerved toward the curb. Hannah kept walking; the car kept rolling. When it was ahead of her it stopped, and the passenger door was flung open. That's when Hannah paused and really looked at it. She considered her options, realized she had none, and walked up to the Jeep. Josie sat behind the wheel, her eyes on the road but her command clearly directed at Hannah.

"Get in."

Busted.

CHAPTER 17

2005

Teuta's husband listened as his wife told him what had happened in the building where their son played.

"He will stay home. He will not go to school," her husband said.

Teuta remained silent. It was what she expected but not what she wanted. Her son should not have to live like that.

"But surely," Teuta said, "there is a way. He has done nothing. Reconciliation. We must ask for intervention."

"There is no money," her husband snapped.

"But you work. Certainly there is money for this," she pleaded.

Teuta's husband did not argue with her though he was angry. He didn't argue because he was afraid. Instead, he left the house. He went to have coffee. He would drink alone in the café. Who would he talk to about this shameful thing? Who would help them? What was there to be done but to close up the house? Left behind, Teuta sat at the table with her chin cradled in her upturned hand. She looked out the window of her apartment. There was nothing to see, nothing to be done.

"Nënë?"

Teuta looked up. Her oldest daughter was there as if by magic. Teuta had not even heard the door open and yet here she was. So beautiful. So lovely. So smart.

Teuta sat back in her chair. A thought was coming to her. It was not a good one. It made her mother's heart heavy. Yet, was it not the mother's job to keep her children safe? Yes, Teuta thought as she looked at her daughter. That was a mother's job.

"Sit with me," she said, and the girl did.

Teuta began to talk and, as she talked, she saw through the girl's eyes that she understood what she was being told. Teuta saw that her daughter was not fearful, and that was a good thing. So Teuta continued to talk until her husband returned. The family sat and ate their evening meal. Neither Teuta nor her older daughter spoke of what had passed between them.

2013

The silence inside the Jeep was deep and thick as Josie drove the short distance to the hospital. It exhausted her because it was bloated with bad feelings: anger, displeasure, and frustration. With all the trials that had tested her and Hannah, the saving grace was that none of the bad things had been a result of their own doing.

All that had changed when she saw the girl hoofing it down Lomita Boulevard. That kick in the gut Josie felt was a baptism of disappointment any parent would have had a hundred times over by the time their kid was sixteen. But Josie wasn't a parent. What should have been a teachable moment instead felt decisive and not in a good way.

Josie pulled into the long drive that led toward the hospital garage and handed her keys to the valet. Hannah hesitated, but there was no getting around the situation. She had to follow. It wasn't until they were waiting for the elevator that Josie looked at the girl. Hannah's chin trembled, but there was no telling whether it was with the effort of keeping her own anger in line or because she was sorry she had disappointed the woman who had done so much for her. Josie stepped forward and pushed the button again.

What in the heck was she supposed to do? Put her arms around Hannah? Forgive her for disobeying? Chat her up, as if nothing had happened? She rejected the last option. Something had happened and it was big and important.

The elevator came. They stepped inside, turned in lockstep, and the door closed. Hannah didn't even have the decency to stand behind Josie in shame. When they reached the second floor, Josie pointed to a sofa in the waiting room.

"Wait here. I don't know how long this is going to take."

"I want to go with you." When Hannah made a move to follow, Josie turned on her. Hannah fell back but only half a step.

"Is there something you don't understand about the word wait?" Josie growled.

"It was the first word I learned," Hannah shot back.

"Good. Then it won't be hard."

Cruel as that sounded, Josie was tired of the board game Hannah pulled out when she didn't like the roll of the dice. Josie got it. Hannah's young life had been a tortured one, but it wasn't anymore; Hannah had been neglected and abused, but she wasn't now. Josie was her champion, Archer and Faye were her family. Burt and half the people in Hermosa were her friends. Josie was done pretending Hannah was an outsider. She pointed to the sofa and turned her back. She wasn't more than half a dozen steps away when she pivoted and walked back to Hannah who still stood defiantly in the middle of the waiting room.

"Look, I'm not happy right now," Josie said. "You blatantly disregarded the instructions I gave you this morning. I get why you did. I get why you did what you did to that girl in school. I understand that you want to do something to help Billy. You are afraid for him and feel impotent, but you're not helping and there are consequences to your actions."

A couple entered the room. They looked worried and tired. Josie took Hannah's arm and moved her away as she lowered her voice.

"Do you want the school to expel you? Do you want the court asking whether or not I am fit to be your guardian? Do you want to get arrested for truancy? Is that what you want?"

Josie's voice began to shake. Never, not even when she realized her mother was gone forever, had she given in to this kind of emotion. It embarrassed her. It was frightening to care so much about Hannah. Josie put up her hand. She did not want to tangle with her now, not in the state she was in.

"Don't answer that. You know it was wrong to leave the house, so don't act like you're the aggrieved party."

"But-"

"Stop. Don't argue. Don't debate. I wasn't looking for a playmate when I became your guardian. I thought I had something to give you. If you don't want it, then we can rethink this whole thing. Right now I would appreciate it if you could step up to the plate. Think before you act. Now sit down and wait. Right now this is about Billy, not you."

Josie went through the double doors and past the one nurse at the desk. The woman looked as Josie passed and looked at her even longer than that.

***

Nothing had changed in Billy's room. The bed nearest the door was still empty, the curtain still drawn around Billy's bed, and yet Josie was overwhelmed with a sudden sense of foreboding. She touched the curtain but hesitated before drawing it back. Her shoulders slumped in relief when Billy looked her way and tried to smile.

"Hey, Ms. B."

Billy Zuni was propped up in bed, the food on his tray picked at. She was at his side giving him a cautious hug a second later.

"I was so worried. We all were."

"Thanks, Ms. B," he whispered, hugging her with his good arm. Josie held him back and then let him go.

"How you doing?"

He shrugged. "Better than I was, I guess."

"Has the doctor been in to talk to you? Do you know how long they're going to have you here?"

"I'm not sure. They said my head was still bad. Pretty much everything hurts. They didn't tell me much."

"I'll see what I can find out. Are you done with this?" she indicated the tray.

"I'm not real hungry."

"That's a good lunch. It looks like they want you to eat." Billy's eyes went to the window. Josie tried again as she moved the table away. "You know what? I'll sneak you in a burger. Burt will fix one with all the trimmings."

Billy nodded. That half smile was there again, but it was barely a shadow of the real thing.

"There were a whole lot of important people talking about you this morning, Billy." Josie sat down, put her hand on his arm, and shook him a little. "Billy, you've got to pay attention to me. You need to know what's going on. Please, Billy. Look at me."

"I don't want to know," he whispered.

***

Archer never liked standing in the middle of a crime scene, but he hated standing in the middle of an abandoned crime scene even more. The yellow tape was gone, dusting residue was everywhere, furniture was left as it had been found, blood had dried, discoloring and cracking depending on the surface where it landed. Like the scent of a burned and ill-seasoned stew, you couldn't specifically identify the mix of smells in a place like this, but when you breathed in you knew it wasn't good.

To make matters worse, once the cops were done they were done. The victim, their family or friends, would have to clean up the mess. That wasn't an easy task for someone left shell-shocked in the wake of a violent crime. There were services that would clean, scrub and steam a place as clean as it could get but that didn't really change anything. Indoor crime scenes were always left scarred by the violence and the Zuni house was no exception.

He walked over to the front window and took a look at the flag that had been thumbtacked over the front window. At one time it had been bright red but the sun had faded it to an ombre of pink and coral. A frame of the original red could be seen where the wall blocked out the sun. In the middle, a black double-headed eagle was stamped onto the cheap fabric. One eagle head was missing a beak where the paint had flaked off. Archer took out his phone, snapped a picture and did a search although he didn't need to. It was the flag of Albania and now he had two pieces of information about a country that meant nothing to anyone in Hermosa Beach until a few days ago.

Pocketing his phone, he worked the thumbtacks out of the right side of the flag, took the free corner and tucked it crosswise at the top of the window. The day was pretty, but not as brilliantly sunny as it had been the day before. The news said another storm was brewing down south, but Archer took that forecast with a grain of salt. Weather reports were nothing more than educated guesses based on flawed data, observations, old wives' tales, and the pain in someone's knees. He pushed open the ancient louvered panes that flanked the window. The house was just far enough from the beach and the louvers just narrow enough that airflow was almost nonexistent. Still, it was better than nothing.

Across the street a kid shot out of the driveway on a bike and disappeared down the street. Another house had the front door open but the screen door closed. Way down to the left a woman walked a dog. Life went on. The louvers were dusty, so Archer wiped his fingers on his pants as he looked at the sofa. The bloodstain looked like Australia now that it dried. The only thing new was the mail on the floor by the front door.

Archer ambled over and picked it up: mailers, flyers, an electric bill. He was about to toss it back onto the floor when a postcard caught his eye. It was a notice from Go Postal, the printer down on Hermosa Boulevard. Normally, he wouldn't have given it a second thought except that it was addressed specifically to R. Zuni. Drop shipping went to resident not a specific person. He turned it over and saw a note scribbled on the back.

P.O. Box fee is due R.

Archer pocketed it. He would bring it to the hospital where Rosa Zuni lay in a coma. Technically, he wasn't tampering with the mail if he did that. On his way, he might just swing by the place, pay what was due, and take a look at the contents of Rosa's P.O. Box.

He walked back to the kitchen. There was nothing in it now. Greg Oi's pink pump was packed away with his dress and stockings and held as evidence. Greg Oi was naked as a jaybird on a slab waiting for the coroner to get to him. The room looked bigger without Oi's body sprawled on the floor.

Archer went up the stairs that still creaked. The spindle was still missing. The railing had been broken clear through when the paramedics hustled the stretcher to the ambulance. At the top of the stairs, Farrah was still smiling that toothy smile of hers, and her nipple was still erect and inviting. In the light of day, though, she looked a little world-weary.

On the landing, Archer poked into the boxes. They were filled with kitchen utensils, hardback books that smelled of mold, and clothes that even the Salvation Army wouldn't want.

In Rosa's room, the clothes on the floor and bed looked like they belonged to a doll they were so small. This time Archer got a good look at the blow-up of the naked people. It was just a big, cheap poster. In the background was a picture of a castle, in the foreground vines and flowers formed a frame. It wasn't his idea of a romantic picture, but it sure wasn't pornography. Rosa Zuni was starting to feel a lot less a monster.

Archer knew there was nothing good to see in the bathroom but he looked anyway. The blood had dried to a deep dark brown and the smears told the story of that night: Rosa fleeing her attackers, Archer cradling her, the paramedics trying to save her. He noted the marks on the wall but saw none on the doorjamb. She had been cornered in there. Hunkering down, Archer took a closer look at a shoe print. Billy had admitted to being in the house and seeing Rosa. Montoya said they had a shoe print, but if this was what he was talking about Archer couldn't see it. Standing up, he checked the door. There was no lock but there were security bars on all the windows including the small one high up on the bathroom wall. Rosa Zuni was doomed from the start.

Except. . .

Archer narrowed his eyes as people do when they are trying to grab something flitting through their memory. It was gone as quickly as it had come and was replaced by a wish that he could see Montoya's reports. It would be good to know if Rosa's blood was on either of the corpses or theirs on her body.

In the bedroom, Archer paused at the desk and picked up the Albanian magazine. It was five years old. He'd like to know when Rosa Zuni landed in the U.S. He'd like to know when Greg Oi got here. He'd like to know about Billy's birth. There was so much Archer would like to know about a country and people half a world away and it was time to get some answers.

He got his phone and punched in the number for his friend at the DEA, spent no time on pleasantries, and gave him the phone number Carlotta had given him. He asked for help running it down overseas along with any other information he might have on Rosa or Billy. Archer threw Oi and Duka in for good measure and hung up. He had no idea if what the agent found out would hurt or help Josie in the next hearing, but it could go a long way to satisfying his own curiosity.

In Billy's room Archer grabbed some clothes: jeans, t-shirts, and a button down just in case they couldn't get a t-shirt over Billy's cast. He found Billy's backpack in the corner of the room, swung it on the bed. Whether Billy actually studied was questionable but he brought the books home.

English literature.

Biology.

History.

Archer tossed them on the bed and then put the clothes inside. When he was finished, he slung it over his shoulder only to find that he missed one. Archer pulled out another book. This one was worn, soft with age and written in Albanian. Archer flipped the pages. There were two markers. One a picture of a man and a woman and a girl, the other was a letter that had been folded and unfolded so many times it was falling apart, the ink was faded and illegible.

Archer put it back. Billy would probably want it, and Archer wanted him to explain it.

***

Billy Zuni's smile faltered, wilted, and finally vanished as he took in all the information Josie had given him about the meeting in Judge Healy's chambers. She had done her best to be upbeat, but Billy wasn't stupid.

"Do you understand the choices, Billy?"

His shoulders rose half-heartedly. "I don't get to choose anything."

"You can choose what you want me to ask for," Josie said

"Will the judge let me go home?"

She shook her head. "No, Billy. I promise you don't want that."

His head bobbed. Tears came easily to him now. Words got lost in the lump in his throat but he managed to say:

"Just no jail. I didn't do anything to go to jail for. Not even juvie."

"I'll do my best." She squeezed his hand, hoping he didn't take that gesture as a promise. "Are you sure there aren't any relatives who would step up?"

"I don't know any," he mumbled.

Josie knew he was telling the truth. Thousands of people couldn't name one person in the world who cared about them. Either there literally weren't any, they had lost touch with the ones they did have, or multiple marriages and ill will had diluted the connections. Old people died alone, run away kids ended up in the system only to be cut loose when they were eighteen with no place to go, and people wandered the streets, homeless. How sad, how outrageous that Billy was one of them. And if Josie failed to win the least restrictive placement, then Billy Zuni would fade into memory. He'd never come back to the beach the way he left it.

"Then we're going to have to give the judge reason to put you in a home setting. Are you ready? You have to tell me the truth even if you think it sounds bad. This is just between you and me."

When he nodded again, Josie began.

Josie: You came from Albania, is that correct?

Billy: Yes.

Josie: Why did you come here?

Billy: I don't know. I was little.

Josie: Didn't Rosa say?

Billy: Rosa said it was dangerous to talk about it.

Josie: And she never gave you any reason?

Billy: No.

Josie: Did you know those men in your house?

Billy: I knew the man who dressed like a girl. Mr. Oi.

Josie: Was he a friend?

Billy: We lived in his house for a while, but we left. Then I heard Rosa talking to him on the phone. I don't remember the language much, but I knew she was talking to him.

Josie: Do you know why she was talking to him?

Billy shook his head again. Josie let go of his hand and sat back. Rosa hadn't told Billy that she kept in touch with Oi. That was her secret and she went to great lengths to keep the relationship from Billy. Perhaps Billy was Oi's child. Women kept their children from the biological father for all sorts of reasons. Carl Newton would argue that Billy was enraged to be kept apart from his father – a wealthy one at that. Josie could argue exactly the opposite and say that Billy would never hurt the man who was his father. She began again.

Josie: Can you make a guess why he called her?

Billy: No. I didn't like it, but I didn't ask what it was about. I didn't want to know.

Josie: Did you kill Mr. Oi and the other man?

The change in Billy was so sudden and fleeting, Josie almost wasn't sure it had happened. Billy's eyes narrowed, his shoulders broadened and tensed, the muscles on his exposed arm corded. Josie saw what Carl Newton only imagined: a young, strong, man, angered, hair-triggered and ready for a fight. Not a boy at all. Perhaps, the rose colored glasses were hers.

Billy: Jesus, Josie. Why would I want to kill anybody?

Josie: Because one of them hurt Rosa.

Billy: When have you even seen me do anything mean?

The tears came again as Billy wilted. Whatever she had seen disappeared as quickly as it had come.

Josie: Never, Billy. I have never seen you hurt anyone.

Billy: And where would I get a gun?

Josie: I don't know.

She paused but only briefly. She could not – would not – be fooled. Billy may be remorseful, he may be angry, he may be despairing, or he might be faking. It was up to her to figure it out.

Josie: What time did you leave the beach with Trey?

Billy: It was late. My mom said I could come back after midnight. She didn't want me too early. I was having a good time anyway.

Josie: Why did Trey go with you?

Billy: He was hungry, and he was messed up.

Josie: Did he go in the house?

Billy: After me. I went in first.

Josie: Did he hurt anyone?

Billy: Mr. Oi was hurt when I went in. I just ran upstairs to find Rosa. It was awful. The knife was in her back. I pulled it out and I was crying.

Josie: What about the man in the living room?

Billy: I didn't see anyone.

Josie: The man on the couch?

Billy: There were no lights. I wanted to find help for Rosa. That's all I wanted when I went down the stairs. Then I saw someone. I thought it was Trey. I really thought it was Trey.

Josie: Who was it?

Billy: I don't know. I ran away. I just ran and ran. I don't know what I was running from. I never knew what we were running from."

"Okay. I'm sorry." She ducked her head, she looked into his face but he averted his eyes. "Whatever your problems were, they're nothing compared to what's coming down the road, Billy. I know there are things you're not telling me. You'll have to if I'm going to help. Tell me right now who Rosa is. She's not your mother, is she?"

Bill's shoulders fell, his eyes closed as if he was finally going to rest after a long journey. Finally, he looked at Josie Bates.

"Rosa's my sister."

"Where are your parents?"

"In Albania. They gave me to Rosa." Billy leaned forward so that his lips were close to her ear. "She saved me. She kept me safe. They wanted to kill me, Ms. B."

"Who wanted to kill you?" she whispered back.

"Rosa knows." His voice got smaller. "I'm so afraid."

A chill ran through Josie Bates. His confession implied that she could protect him. The truth was that she could only try to protect him. Her arms went around him awkwardly. The plastic of the IV cold against her arm, the much worn hospital gown soft under her fingers, and Billy's body convulsed as he started to cry in earnest.

"Who wants to kill you? Your parents?"

He shook his head against her shoulder. "I thought it was Mr. Oi. Rosa hated him."

"Then why was he in your house?"

Billy's head moved back and forth against her shoulder.

"I don't know. She always said they would come in the night."

He pulled back as if to look at her. Instead, he gazed through the window, tears washing down his poor, beaten face.

"She didn't like me going in the storm, but she said I had to. I thought it was just me they wanted to kill, but they tried to kill her, Josie. I should have been there. I should have. . ."

That was as far as he got. The weeping was deep, the shivering uncontrollable, and the fear real. His head fell back onto Josie's shoulder.

"Shhh. We'll figure it out."

Josie murmured words that meant nothing. Her brain turned furiously, spinning from one end of the spectrum to the other, from a conspiracy, to Rosa's madness, to the possibility that the madness was Billy's.

This was how Mike Montoya found the lawyer and her client. He could not afford to think of them any other way. Josie saw him and pushed the crying boy away, buying time as she covered him with the blanket.

"This is a privileged conversation."

"I am here to question your client," Mike said evenly.

"When I'm done," Josie shot back. "When he's composed."

"I'm sorry. You're done now," Mike ordered.

"Josie?" Billy struggled to sit up.

"Don't say anything Billy," she directed. Then to Montoya: "Give us five minutes. Let him pull himself together. She looked past him to the door where a uniformed deputy stood. She looked back at the detective. "Montoya?"

"Ms. B. What's going on?" Billy called.

"Billy, as your lawyer I am advising you not to answer this man's questions."

Montoya had the right to try to question Billy, but she had the obligation to make it darn hard if not impossible to do so. Mike's shoulders swiveled to indicate the man behind him.

"This is Deputy Sheriff Price. He will be stationed outside this door."

"Are you arresting my client?" Josie put herself between the detective and the boy.

"Deputy Price will be insuring that Billy does not pose a danger to himself or to anyone else in this hospital."

"Montoya, a moment," she pleaded. "Outside, Montoya. In the hall. Please."

"Ms. Bates, let me do my job."

Josie backed toward the window, hands up. She wouldn't interfere, but she didn't want to be removed. Mike stepped to the foot of Billy's bed.

"William Zuni, you are going to be questioned in regard to the assault and attempted murder of Rosa Zuni-"

Billy shot forward. "I didn't do anything!"

Josie tried to restrain him, but the strong man had resurfaced and he pushed back as Mike Montoya advised him of his rights.

"You are under arrest for the assault with intent to kill Rosa Zuni. You have the right to remain silent-"

"Oh, no. Oh, my God," Billy cried.

"This is ridiculous." Josie raised her voice, objecting, attempting to distract and deter. "What proof? What proof do you have?"

"You have the right to an attorney. If you cannot afford an attorney, one will be appointed –" Mike went on.

"We have the right to know, Montoya. What evidence is there?"

Mike answered her question, but locked eyes with Billy Zuni.

"A knife was found at the beach near the pier. This afternoon, our lab confirmed your client's fingerprints and blood consistent with that of Rosa Zuni on it."

"I took it. Josie! Josie, tell them what I said." Billy grabbed her arm and pulled at her. "I told you. I took it away."

"Quiet, Billy," Josie snapped. "Don't say anything."

But Billy couldn't hear her. Blind with terror, he clutched at her with his good arm, spitting out his denials.

"I swear, Josie. I could never hurt her. I just took it away."

"Deputy Price," Montoya called. "We need assistance!"

"No, I've got it." Josie pivoted, determined to get control of the situation, but Billy was hysterical. The IV stand tilted, tipped and crashed to the floor behind her, ripping the tubing out of Billy's arm as it went. Josie lunged for it instinctively. At the same moment Billy threw his arm out. His cast hit Josie's face. She reeled, falling into the chair behind her.

The next moments were nothing more than a blink of an eye, and yet they crawled painfully by as Josie watched Deputy Price and Detective Montoya subdue Billy but not quiet him. The room filled up. A nurse with beautiful hands rushed in, bending like an athlete, discarding the IV tubing even as she sterilized Billy's arm. Billy threw her back. An orderly slapped restraints on the boy's arms, tying him to the bed frame. The nurse injected him, and Josie's stomach turned.

Her hands went to her ears, her eyes shut. She was back in that mountain hut, restrained, drugged, and terrified. She not only understood Billy's fear, she had lived it. But the other part of her psyche leapt forward to a stronger place where survival mode took precedents. Josie Bates was fashioning her argument for a judge, a jury, the press, anyone who would listen.

Billy Zuni could not have understood his rights, Your Honor.

His injuries precluded understanding.

Billy Zuni could not have understood his rights because he was medicated, Your Honor.

That was how she would raise her voice in his defense, but all she could do now was listen as Billy's cries became whimpers.

Josie hung her head. Her jaw throbbed. She tasted blood at the corner of her lip. Raising her head, she shook back her long bangs. Montoya was finished; Billy was exhausted. The nurse stood back. If she was rattled she didn't show it.

"Anything else?" she asked the cops.

Mike shook his head. Josie's eyes followed the nurse and the orderly as they left. That was when she saw the last person who had rushed to Billy Zuni's room. Hannah stood in the doorway, accusation in her eyes. This, she seemed to say, was all Josie's fault.

A second later she bolted.

CHAPTER 18

2006

Teuta waited by the door where the men who ran the mine worked. These were the head offices and no one but bosses went in. Certainly, no woman went in. That was why Teuta waited to speak to the man she knew was inside: the man who lived in America, the man who came often now to see to business. This was the man who, when he accepted coffee at Teuta's home, watched her daughter and was kind to her son.

Just when she thought her courage would not last, the door of the important offices opened. One man came out. He did not see her as he left to walk home. Another man came out. She thought, perhaps, she had missed the boss of all of them, but she had not. He walked out the door and paused to look over the village as if he owned it. As if he were king. Like a king, he held many lives in his hands.

"Sir," Teuta called as she stepped from the shadow of the building. Greg Oi turned.

"It is Teuta, is it not?" he said and then he smiled. He was not as much Shqiptare as he was American now. As she began to speak, she could only hope that was so.

"I have come to ask you a favor," she began.

2013

"Hannah!"

Josie was after her, but the girl was fast and nowhere to be seen by the time Josie pushed past Montoya and got to the hall. A nurse gave Hannah away, looking toward the emergency exit as she picked up her receiver to call security. Josie threw herself at the door, hit the bar hard, and ran into the well. The door closed slowly behind her, allowing Montoya's voice to leak through the opening. Josie couldn't hear what he was saying, but she knew he was giving orders to secure Billy and his room. Then all she heard were her own feet pounding on the concrete stairs, heading to the place Hannah would be. She pushed through the exit door, dashed onto the third floor waiting room, and ran into the ICU. Montoya was already there, coming from the lobby area.

"Come on."

He touched her arm without breaking stride, and they were off again. Josie itched to run. The ICU wasn't big, but she couldn't see Hannah. Unable to restrain herself, Josie sprinted ahead, drawing her fingertips across the window to Rosa's room. The blinds were drawn and they shouldn't have been. The doctors couldn't monitor Rosa if they couldn't see her. When she was close enough, Josie grabbed the jamb, swung herself into the doorway and stopped dead. Montoya came up behind her.

"Damn." Montoya muttered.

The room was empty, the bed freshly made, and the monitors silent. Josie turned so suddenly she caught Mike's shoulder as she pushed past him and confronted a nurse.

"Where's the woman who was in there?"

"Hey." The woman pulled back more angry than scared. Behind Josie, Mike pulled his badge and held it up.

"Where is the patient who was in there? Is she alive?" he asked.

"She's been moved. Fourth floor. 460," she answered.

Josie was already headed for the stairwell, but the nurse stopped Mike.

"She's still serious. That woman won't do the patient any good."

"I'll take care of it." Hoping he hadn't lied, he followed Josie. He was still thirty-seconds behind her, but this time he went up the stairs, too.

"Bates!" The sound of his voice startled her. She paused and looked down on him. "Take it down a notch."

"When I know Hannah's okay."

She took the last steps two at a time and exited to the fourth floor. Montoya caught up with her easily. They threaded around visitors, patients and nurses. Montoya took her arm. His grip was tight enough that Josie only had two choices: slow down or deck him. He must have known that she was considering the second option because he gripped harder and pulled her back.

"Hannah might not even be here."

"She'll be there. She'll want Rosa to tell you the truth to save Billy. She'll try to make her do that, Montoya."

No sooner had those words come out of her mouth than she caught site of Hannah ducking from the waiting room into the ward.

"There she is." Josie started to walk faster. "I'm good, Montoya. Let me go."

Before he could decide if he would do that, Hannah Sheraton screamed.

"What in the hell are you doing?"

***

"Samuel Lumina, Jr. give me that! Give me that right now!"

Mary Lumina had just about had it. The old man was still living in their house, still treating her as if she didn't exist, Sam was getting more unbearable everyday, strutting around like some foreign cock-of-the walk spouting off in Albanian. He didn't even speak the language that well. He sounded like an idiot. And now Sammy was turning into a five-year-old chauvinist, running wild, not listening to his mother. He had grabbed her good perfume and ran with it like a football. She thought she'd been chasing him, but when she got to the living room he was nowhere to be seen.

"If you break that bottle, so help me I'm going to take it out of your hide. I swear, Sammy! Where are you?"

She swung her head left then right and finally got on her knees to see if he might have gotten under the sofa. Just then she heard a whack and thunk. Mary shot up and ran to the laundry room. Sure enough, there he was, grinning from ear to ear, standing next to the closet where the water heater was housed. The only saving grace was that she was not overwhelmed by the scent of Jasmine Lace perfume, and that pretty much meant the bottle didn't break when he threw it in.

Pushing up her sleeves, she stuck her hand into the closet where the water heater was. It smelled moldy. She would have to talk to Sam about that. Her fingers spread, she strained and finally she touched the bottom of the cabinet. She cursed as her kid careened around the house. God knew what he was going to get into. Soon as she retrieved the perfume, she was going to give him the biggest time out ever.

Just as she was planning how to take the kid down a notch, her fingers brushed against something. It didn't feel like her perfume bottle. What else had that boy put down there? She wiggled her fingers and finally caught hold of the fabric and pulled out the small bag. Sitting on the floor with her back against the wall and the bag in her lap, Mary hollered.

"Sam Lumina, junior. I'm coming to get you. I swear! I'm coming!"

But she wasn't going to get him. She was opening the bag.

***

People's reactions to a threat are as individual as a fingerprint and it was no different with the three people who ran to Rosa Zuni's room.

Hannah threw herself into the fray without thinking of the consequences.

Josie analyzed the situation quickly, determined where the danger might be coming from, and moved to block it.

Mike Montoya locked everyone down and would investigate when the situation was secure.

When Mike and Josie arrived, Hannah had already reacted in character. She was sprawled on the floor as if she had been pushed aside. That meant she had attacked before assessing the danger. While Josie put herself in front of the girl she stayed true to character and catalogued what she saw in case she was called to witness. Mike

Montoya pulled his weapon. He ordered the two men leaning over Rosa Zuni's bed to:

"Step back. Step back. Put your hands up."

"They were trying to kill her," Hannah cried as she scrambled up off the floor. She made another run at them but Josie blocked her.

"Are you hurt?" Josie muttered.

"No, but he had his hands on her." Hannah pushed against Josie who pushed right back.

"Stay quiet," Josie ordered.

Hannah stopped struggling. She took one step and then another until she had her back against the wall. In the hall there were the sounds of people panicking, running, and calling to one another. Mike Montoya didn't bother to look behind him. He knew they were there. He knew they were alarmed. He knew they had to go.

"Ms. Bates, if you would please see that the doorway is kept clear."

Josie turned. She took Hannah's hand and handed her off to a woman outside the door.

"Could you make sure she gets to room 217?"

To Hannah she said:

"This time, I mean it." Josie put her hand on her cheek. "I'll find you as soon as I can. You stay with Billy. He needs you now."

When they were gone, Josie closed the door part way. She could see Rosa Zuni. The woman didn't seem to be in distress and nothing seemed to be disturbed. More interesting were the two men standing on either side of her bed.

The younger one on the far side of the room had complied with Montoya's order. His hands were up, his eyes darting between Montoya and Josie. The big man, the one with his back to them, the one who hovered over Rosa Zuni, did not move. He had not thrown up his hands, and hidden hands were not a good thing.

Seconds ticked by. The big man sucked them all into his orbit. He was a powerful presence. Josie amended her thought. Something powerful radiated from him as if whatever had brought him here was so insistent, so urgent, neither Mike Montoya nor his gun would stop him from what he intended to do.

Montoya, though, wasn't feeling it. He was all business. "You."

Mike moved as he looked for an angle to get a bead on the man's face. There was a lot to be learned from the set of a person's jaw, the pull of his lips, and the look in his eyes. Given the way the man was poised, though, it was impossible to see. The disadvantage did not concern Mike. His hand and his resolve were both steady. He moved another inch, paused where he felt solid footing, breathed steadily, and spoke authoritatively even as his finger tightened on the trigger.

"I will only ask you once more. Stand straight. Show your hands. Move away from the bed. If you make any threatening move, sir, I will shoot you."

The man against the wall opened his mouth. The big man must have made some movement because the younger one never spoke.

Seconds ticked by. The silence was only broken by the sound of air inflating the wrappings around Rosa Zuni's legs: first one, then the other; whooshing and shooshing, moving the blood through her system so she didn't throw a clot. It was as if that machine breathed for them all as they waited for the big man to make his decision: turn and face Mike Montoya, or go for the unconscious woman in the bed.

Finally the big man unfurled, revealing himself as he wished to be revealed. His neck was thick, and his white hair was dense and shaved like a soldier's with a fringe at the top and short on the sides. The skin on his neck was leathered as if he had spent his whole life bent over a failing field trying to coax something - anything – to grow. His arms were long, and his clothing nondescript but neat. He could have been anyone, but he wasn't. He was the man who found Rosa Zuni irresistible. It seemed almost painful for him to drop his hands and hold them away from her. He splayed his fingers as if he knew the drill and was unimpressed by it, perhaps even contemptuous of it.

"There is no need for a gun." His voice was low, quiet, unconcerned and foreign.

"Turn around, please. Keep your hands where we can see them."

The air stirred as if the man had shrugged it away. In the shadowed room, nerves were rubbed raw by the odd whooshing of the machines and the deathly silence of Rosa Zuni. Whoever this man was, nothing frightened him. Not even Mike Montoya's gun.

Deliberately, he did as he was told until he stood in front of them: shadowed, ancient looking, and yet so of this time. Wrinkles were chiseled deeply at the corner of his sharp, narrow eyes but they radiated into a smooth brow. The furrows from nose to mouth were cut deep yet only served to add parenthetical emphasis to his strength rather than draw his expression down to defeat. A face that had once been handsome was now proudly set in age. His presence was made more dramatic by the sunlight slashing through the half-opened blinds. It banded his hair in shades of silver and pewter, his jacket in dark and light. Against the wall, the young man moved. The old man lifted a finger his way.

"Do not do that."

The old man's voice was smooth as sea glass, warm as August sand, and heavy with an accent that was thick as a marine fog. The right side of his lips tipped up as he addressed Mike Montoya.

"He is a boy. Only a boy."

"And who are you?"

The man's lips tipped disdainfully as if the question was beneath him. The sun shifted and the bands of light gave way to a sash of grey that covered his eyes like a blindfold. He said:

"I am Gjergy. This woman and the boy belong to me."

CHAPTER 19

2006

Teuta tied her daughter's dress with a blue bow. She turned the girl and smoothed her hair. The girl let her mother do what mothers always did at such a time.

"You will be a good girl," Teuta said.

"Yes, nënë," the girl answered.

"Perhaps you should stay here. Stay with me. Perhaps this will not help."

The girl reached out and touched her mother's face. She was young but she knew more than her mother.

"No, nënë. I will go, and then you will all come, too, someday."

Teuta nodded. The girl had always been wise. Teuta only wished it could be done more properly. The village would talk when they knew of this. They would say that her daughter was in trouble, but they would be wrong.

"It's fine, nënë," she said again.

Teuta nodded. She put a flower in her daughter's hair and opened the door of the bedroom. Her daughter walked straight through. No hesitating. Why should there be? She was doing what must be done.

Teuta followed her daughter out of the room and went to stand by her husband. He was a strong man, but Teuta could see that there were tears behind his bold eyes. The daughter stood next to the man from America. The other daughter watched with her parents. The little boy, happy with this excitement, went to stand by the older girl. Teuta put her hand on his shoulder while she said her vows.

It was done. Whatever was to come would be in the hands of God. She only hoped her husband would never find out it was she, not God, who had put her children in the hands of this man.

2013

Mike Montoya kicked aside a chair.

To the big man: "Step away from the bed. Please face the wall."

To Josie: "Ms. Bates, if you could please move so those men can assist."

Montoya had broken the spell the old man cast and Josie did as she was told.

To the security officers he said: "If one of you would check that man for weapons." Mike indicated the younger of the two men. "And the other watch me."

To the older man: "Put your hands against the wall. Open palmed. Spread your legs."

The men secured the scene and Josie went to Rosa Zuni. The woman looked serene, and peacefully unaware of what was going on around her. While she was still heavily sedated, there was no doubt she was healing. Wounds that had been as radiant and red as if she had been branded had cooled to a rosier pink. Her flesh was knitting itself over the jabs and stabs and slices. Her gown was fresh, her IVs were intact, the stitches encircling her neck showed no indication that they had been disturbed. Someone had combed her hair. If anything was done to her, if these men had meant her harm, there was no evidence that they had accomplished what they set out to do.

"We didn't touch her." The young man threw that over his shoulder. His voice shook, but only a little. He, too, had an accent, but it was tamped down. Enough years in the U.S. erased all but traces of it. Unlike the older man, he had an attitude.

"Ms. Bates, could you ask a doctor in please? I'd like to confirm that Ms. Zuni is alright."

Josie ducked out of the room just as Mike Montoya was finished with his task. He kept a hand on the big man's shoulder as he queried the security cop dealing with the younger man.

"Officer?"

"Nothing." The officer backed up and let the young man turn around.

"Excellent. Thank you." Mike tapped the older one and he also turned just as Josie returned with the doctor.

Montoya spoke to her briefly. Josie heard her say:

"There's a consultation room down the hall. They'll show you."

Without much ado, the men in the room regrouped. The two persons who had caused the ruckus were flanked with one security guard ahead, Mike to the side and the second guard pulling up the rear. Montoya paused as he came abreast of Josie:

"You might want to come."

"I'll be there in a minute." Josie smiled her thanks before going back to the bedside. The doctor was just finishing up.

"She's fine. I can't see that anything was disturbed. I'll be glad when she's gone. This is a hospital, not a safe house."

The doctor tugged on her stethoscope and left shaking her head. Josie was about to follow but hesitated and looked back at Rosa Zuni. Everyone seemed to want that poor woman gone. Everyone except Billy who loved her ferociously and fiercely protected her with his evasions and cryptic explanations of their situation.

Josie went back to the bedside and took one more minute with this woman who would have saved everyone a hell of a lot of trouble if she had died. But the only eyewitness to what happened in that house was Rosa Zuni, and she lingered between life and death.

Josie touched Rosa's hair, thinking it a gentle, wonderful thing that Hannah who didn't believe in miracles thought this woman would open her eyes and exonerate Billy just because Hannah wished it so. Poor Hannah. Disappointed again.

Josie picked up Rosa Zuni's hand and held it in both of hers. She doubled over to rest on the cold metal of the bedside restraints. If this woman was not a monster then what was she?

A protector?

A martyr?

A mistake?

Josie's mind was a fog of vague questions that she didn't even know how to begin to ask. She was tired. She was lost. She whispered:

"Who did this to you?"

There was no answer. She hadn't expected one. The monitors glowed. The air pumped. Josie opened her fingers. There was business to be done with Montoya and the men who had been in this room, yet before she could leave Rosa Zuni's small fingers twitched and closed around Josie's. Her clasp was weak, sliding away even as she tried to make the connection. Josie raised her eyes, frozen as she watched the woman's eyelids flutter. Afraid that a sudden movement might stop whatever was happening, Josie leaned forward cautiously and put her lips close to Rosa Zuni's ear.

"Who did this to you?"

Josie turned her head and put her own ear next to Rosa's mouth. She waited. Finally, on the back of the tortuous breath that came from Rosa Zuni rode one word:

"Billy."

***

Archer had been inside the Zuni house longer than he realized. When he stepped out onto the porch, the sun was just starting its decent. Billy's backpack was slung over one shoulder. He would stop at one of the shops in town and pick up a pair of tennis shoes because it was a sure bet that flip-flops weren't going to cut it where Billy was going. Archer had the magazine, the book, and the box reminder from Go Postal.

He was already in the Hummer, key in the ignition, phone in hand to check in with Josie, when a man came out of the place next door. Young and strong, he was also clearly ticked off as he dragged a packing blanket to the dumpster on the street and tossed it in. He wiped his hands on his jeans and headed back into the construction. Archer gave up on the call, opened the car door, and followed.

The place had been framed out into big rooms, tall ceilings, and wide doorways. He breathed in. There was nothing like the smell of bare wood and plaster to get a man excited and Archer was no exception. It looked like the electrical was done and most of the plumbing put in place. To his right was a stack of top-of-the-line hardwood for tongue and groove flooring. Some of it had been knocked down and lay spread out over the foundation. To his left was a huge kitchen. He would have liked to explore the second story but followed the sounds coming from the back of the house instead. Back there the drywall was up on most of the walls but Archer could see through the studs to the fence shared with Billy's place. The man he had seen was bent over the toilet, cursing and muttering.

"Hey. Hello!" Archer called.

The guy twirled fast, straightened, and shot into the room where Archer stood. He was armed with a plunger, but the look on his face said he could use it to kill if he had to.

"Hold on, man." Archer put out his hands. "I just want to talk to you."

The man narrowed his eyes, checked Archer out, was satisfied with what he saw, and lowered the plunger.

"Sorry. I thought you were the other guy." He turned around and walked back through the framed doorway.

"I wouldn't want to be the other guy."

"Damn straight." He bent over the toilet and started in with the plunger again. Archer arced around a sink and vanity that was left in the main room and stood between two studs so he could talk to the guy.

"I've got this all hooked up. The owners are running out of dough and they want to live in this back area while I finish the rest of the place. Now I've got me a squatter and he's squatting in all the wrong places. Goddamn mess. Disgusting."

Archer didn't have to see what he was complaining about, he could smell it. The guy was right. Someone hadn't been feeling too well. It would have been a whole lot better if he'd just tossed his cookies on the slab. At least that way it could have been washed off.

"Why don't you just get a hose and run it down?"

"It's not just the barf," the man muttered. "There's something else stuck down there. I've got to dig it out. I think there's a pry bar out there."

Archer looked around, saw the pry bar, retrieved it, and handed it to the man.

"This place has been nothing but trouble," the man groused. "If I scratch this it's going to come out of my nut."

"Sorry to hear that," Archer commiserated. He had to pick up a few tabs in his time and it was no fun. He admired the guy for being on the up and up.

"So what can I do for you?" The contractor kept at his work, but he seemed to have calmed down. Maybe it was just having someone to complain to that did it.

"Name's Archer. I'm a friend of the kid who lives next door. Guess you heard what happened."

"Damn. I scratched it. I'm going to have to replace it." The man grunted and went at his chore with a vengeance since there was nothing to lose. "No, what happened?"

Archer filled him in. He turned briefly resting an elbow on the porcelain seat and putting one hand on his hip.

"No shit?"

Archer raised a brow. The man took a moment to think about what he'd been told. He took a deep breath.

"Randy," he said. "I'd shake your hand but you should probably pass."

"I appreciate it," Archer answered.

"You're not a cop." Randy went back to his work but this time with more finesse than brute force.

"Private off and on. Do you know the kid? His name's Billy."

"Yeah, I've seen him."

"And?" Archer pressed.

"And nothing. I've seen him." Randy was offhanded.

"How often?"

"Man, I don't know. When I'm here. I come early in the morning. My crew is in and out. I was gone a few days on another job, then with the rain nobody was working. Sorry, can't remember the last time I saw him. I never talked to him."

"What about the woman who lived there?"

"Yeah, she was a cutie." Randy paused. He turned his head. "Hey, sorry. I forgot. I hope she makes it."

"Do you remember anyone else in particular?"

Randy grunted as he shook his head and maneuvered the pry bar. "Almost had it. Sorry, no. I don't really pay attention. You know how it is. You work, you run from job to job."

Archer shifted his weight, tapped a hand on one of the studs. There wasn't much more to say. He knew exactly how it was with most people. Memory was unreliable. Unless there was a steady flow of men into Rosa's house, nobody would have given her a second thought.

"Thanks. I appreciate the time. Is it okay if I come back later and talk to your crew?"

"Sure, just don't sit down to tea if you know what I mean."

"I promise. Short and sweet." Archer took a second to really look at the room he was in. Two of the walls already had board up. The one facing Billy's house was open. In the corner he saw what happened to the flooring. Someone had dragged a few pieces from the front of the house and used them to make a tee-pee of sorts. "Your guy made himself right at home."

Randy glanced up.

"Can you believe it? He built himself a tent like a goddamn boy scout. He even made a fire. I'm lucky he didn't burn the place down."

Archer wandered to the campsite and poked at the burned spot on the concrete. There were a couple of empty cans, half a piece of bread and some chicken bones. No wrappers. Whoever had been in here was probably dumpster diving.

"How long did you say you've been away from this place?" Archer asked.

"Five days. Maybe six."

"You didn't come yesterday at all, or the day before?"

Randy shook his head but he was concentrating on the task of unplugging the toilet. He tossed the bar and it landed on the foundation with a clatter.

"Aw hell, I give up." He left and came back with his tools. "Can you stick around long enough to help me move this?"

"No problem." Archer went over and waited for him to undo the nuts. "You probably don't have any idea who's been camping out here, do you?"

"If I did, there wouldn't be much left of him," Randy laughed.

Archer squeezed into the room and together they lifted the toilet. It was a nice piece of porcelain. They put it inside the bedroom. Randy looked in. "Maybe I can fix where I scratched it. I hope so. Not much margin on this job."

Archer stepped out of the bathroom and Randy stepped back in, picked up the pry bar again, and dug into the pipe.

"Got it!" He pulled out the metal probe and with it came the thing he'd been fishing for. Grinning, he turned toward Archer to show off his prize. Archer was duly impressed. In fact, Archer couldn't take his eyes off the cheap blue jacket dangling from the pry bar.

***

One of the security guards stood upright near the door of the conference room. The two men were on the sofa: the older man sat comfortably, the younger man was still wired. Montoya had drawn a chair up in front of the sofa, but he got up when Josie came in and huddled with her briefly.

"Did you get Hannah settled?" he asked.

She nodded. "She'll stay in Billy's room. They took off the restraints."

"That's fine," he said, not quite satisfied. "Anything else I should know?"

Josie shook her head and fell back. Thankfully, Montoya had no more time to waste on her. He sat down again and gave his full attention to the men on the couch.

"My name is Mike Montoya. I am a sheriff's detective. Do you understand what that means?"

"Police. You are police," Gjergy answered.

"And you?" Mike looked at the younger man.

"Yeah. I'm okay. I live here. I'm a citizen," he said.

"That's very good. You are not in any trouble, but we are concerned about the woman in that room and why you were there."

"Who is that woman?" The older man cut his eyes toward Josie.

"That is Josie Bates. She is representing Rosa Zuni's son, Billy."

"She is not his family," Gjergy stated.

"No. I'm a friend and his attorney," Josie answered. "I watch out for his well being since his mother can't."

The young man leaned toward the older one and whispered. He chose his words carefully and they came haltingly. Life in America had almost wiped out the language he once spoke.

"Gentlemen. We would be grateful if you spoke English." Mike directed his comment to the younger man. "I need to get some basic information from both of you. What's your name and where do you live?"

"I live in San Pedro," he mumbled.

"Your address?" Mike asked.

"200 Rose Avenue."

"And your name?"

Mike raised his eyes. His pencil was poised. He appeared to wait patiently for the answer. In reality he was looking at the young man and wondering why he didn't lead with his name.

"Sam Lumina." Mike gave no indication that he had heard that name before from Kat Oi, from Dan Jenkins, from Torrance police department's reports on the union behavior outside Marshall Fasteners. "My name's Sam Lumina and this is my uncle, Gjergy Isai. He's visiting. Look, we weren't doing anything wrong. We don't need guards or nothing. We were just-"

"Stop." Gjergy's hand came up. "This man will ask in his own time."

The only indication that Mike Montoya was a little perturbed that this man seemed to be giving him permission to do his job was a smooth, small smile.

"And your name is Gjergy? Could you spell that?" The old man did. "And your last name?"

"Isai. I am Gjergy Isai. I am from-"

"Thank you. The name is good for now. Let's start with Mr. Lumina. I'll try to be expedient."

Mike purposefully went to the younger man, curious to see if the older would take exception. He didn't. He sat straight and tall and seemingly disengaged. Everyone in the room knew he wasn't.

"Mr. Lumina, where do you work?"

"I'm a machinist." Again, Mike noted, he did not answer the question.

"Are you employed?"

"Yeah. I work at Marshall Fasteners. Look, I don't know why you made us come in here. I just don't understand this at all." He wiped his forehead. His eyes never quite connected with Mike's as his frustration grew.

"You've been having some kind of excitement over there at Marshall," Mike noted conversationally. "Mr. Oi, the owner is dead. Did you know that?"

"I heard," Sam said.

"I understand there was a lock out. I also understand there was some trouble inside the building. Do you know anything about that?"

"Sometimes the boys get excited," Sam answered. "Someone wanted to make a point, maybe. I don't know who."

"It was an interesting point that was made in Mr. Oi's office."

"Yeah, well, like I said, I heard about it. Somebody puts a knife in a dummy, but that's not how Oi was killed so what does it matter? I don't see any connection," Sam snapped.

"The woman in the room where we found you was attacked in the same house where Mr. Oi was killed. Did you know that?" Mike eyes were still on his notebook. When there was no answer, he glanced up. "Did you?"

Sam Lumina shrugged. "Yeah. I know. That's how I know she was hurt."

"What is your connection to Ms. Zuni, Sam?"

"I don't know her. She's related sort of, but I can't remember how. Everyone is related in the old country." He sniffed and moved and postured like a school bully. Before he went on Gjergy interrupted.

"You must forgive my nephew. He has had no dealings with police, so he is afraid."

Mike smiled with well-practiced sympathy. A door had opened and he had walked through.

"And you aren't?"

"No. I am not afraid. In my own country, I have been known by the police," the old man said. "But here it is different. Here the police hope to help, I believe. This is what happens in America, is it not?"

"Yes, it is. We do hope to help people who deserve our help. We take great care in determining who is a victim but also to find out who is not."

Josie moved and so did Montoya. There was a warning in the subtle shifting of his shoulders and it was for her. This wasn't a courtroom; this was his arena. She fell back and remained silent.

"We know that Rosa Zuni needs our help," Mike went on. "We don't know why she was hurt or why Mr. Oi and another man were killed. We don't know who might have done these things, and that's why everyone is suspect. Including you."

"That is wise." Gjergy's eyes hooded, his lips moved with the right words but twisted themselves into an expression of disdain. "In America many things go slowly, but sometimes you are not cautious. I appreciate, sir, that you are cautious."

"That way we make fewer mistakes. We also like to know who we are talking to. Where are you from?" Mike switched back, trying to take the old man off track a bit but he turned just smoothly.

"Albania," Gjergy answered. "Our country has been invaded many times but never by America. Perhaps that is why you may not know about my country."

"How long have you been here?" Mike went on, unwilling to be drawn into the conversation Gjergy seemed determined to have. He didn't care what went on in Gjergy's country; they were in Montoya's country now.

"Too long," he answered. "I should have been going home now."

"He came last Wednesday," the young man interrupted. The old man's shoulders drew back and his displeasure flooded the room. Sam took a stand. "You did. He came last Wednesday, and he's been living in my house. My wife can vouch for that."

"Thank you," Mike said. "Mr. Isai, this will be quicker if you simply answer my questions."

"I understand," Gjergy answered.

"Did you arrive in this country last Wednesday?"

"I did."

"Do you know anyone else in this country other than Mr. Lumina's family?"

"Yes. I know Albanians who have come here. There is a community."

"May I have your passport, please?" He asked this of Gjergy and then asked Sam, "And your driver license, please?"

The young man fumbled with his wallet and handed the license to Mike who made notations and handed it back. Mike flipped through the passport, made more notes, and gave it back. "Are you here on business or did you come just to see family?"

"I have family business. The girl, she is my business. I have come to find her and the boy." Gjergy lowered his chin and looked at Mike from under lowered lashes.

"That's an interesting way to put it. You didn't come to visit her?"

"No, not a visit," he admitted.

"Why would you come all the way from Albania to find Rosa?"

Mike's eyes went cold. Gjergy responded in kind. He looked at Mike and no one else.

"Rosafa has been missing from us a long time."

"Rosafa is her given name? And what is her surname?"

"Zogaj," Gjergy answered.

"And what is her relationship to you?"

"She is from my village. Our village is of the same clan."

"But she is not a blood relation?"

"She is blood," Gjergy answered. "We are of the same clan."

"Over there, people are related by clans and then some. It's different." Sam Lumina spoke up. Mike acknowledged the information and then asked Gjergy:

"But Rosa's immediate family? They asked you to come find her?"

"Her grandfather, he is dead, so I came to find her."

"And Billy?" Mike pressed. "He's her son?"

"No, he is her brother. She took her brother away with her," Gjergy explained. "She went with a man who promised a better life, but it was not better. The man she went with promised her she would be safe." Gjergy's inflection went flat, his voice darkened, and he seemed to be looking through Montoya. "Rosafa should have known she would never be safe. She was a stupid girl for believing that. He did not keep her safe, did he?"

"How did you find her?"

"We hear things from those who live in this country. They send back news to Albania. This man took many young women away. This man, this Mr. Oi, he is known in our villages, but I only came for Rosafa and the boy. That is all."

"Sir," Mike Montoya asked. "Are you telling me that Mr. Oi was involved in human trafficking? Are you implying that Rosa Zuni was brought here as a sex slave?"

***

Mike Montoya, Josie Bates, Gjergy Isai, Sam Lumina and one member of the hospital security team made their way back to Billy Zuni's room. Whatever the nurse had given Billy had calmed him but hadn't knocked him out. He and Hannah were conversing quietly when Mike and Josie entered. Hannah was alert and suspicious, her green eyes first checking out Montoya and then questioning Josie who responded with a steady gaze. Hannah understood she was to remain quiet. She took Billy's hand. The boy looked at her and then at the adults.

"Josie?"

"It's okay, Billy," she assured him. "Detective Montoya wants you to meet someone."

Drained from everything he had already gone through, Billy made no objection. Montoya stepped forward.

"Billy, I'll have a lot of questions for you, but right now I only have one. Do you understand me?"

"Yes."

"Good."

Mike raised his arm and flipped his wrist. Billy and Hannah looked toward the doorway, but Mike and Josie looked at Billy as Sam came into the room. "Billy, this is Sam Lumina. He lives in San Pedro. Do you know him?"

"No," Billy answered.

Mike looked over his shoulder to see Gjergy was still half hidden by the curtain.

"Sir?"

Gjergy changed places with Sam and the room was smaller for it.

"This is Mr. Isai. He says he is related to you, Billy. Do you recognize him?"

Billy narrowed his eyes. He looked longer than Josie thought he should, but finally he shook his head. He was still shaking it when he said: "No, I don't think so."

"I know you, Besnik." Gjergy Isai smiled at the boy in the bed.

CHAPTER 20

2006

The car drove down the street of Bajram Curri. The man behind the wheel slowed as he approached the school. His narrow eyes watched the children as they came out of the building then slid to the mothers who waited at the top of the crumbling steps. He did not see Teuta and this surprised him.

He stopped the car and turned off the ignition. Children were streaming out of the building now. He caught one, a young man too old to be in school. The boy pulled away, he was ready to fight. Then he looked in the big man's eyes and thought better of it.

"I am looking for the Zogaj children."

"They are gone."

The big man's head tipped. "Where have they gone to? The mountains?"

"To America."

The man let the tough boy go just as he caught sight of Teuta, her arms held out to the youngest of her daughters.

There was no need to speak with her. She had done what a mother could do. It was not enough, of course. It only made things more difficult.

But life was always difficult, was it not?

2013

"This changes everything, Montoya."

Josie picked up her coffee. It was hot and bitter, but this was a hospital cafeteria so she had not expected anything more than a passable cup.

"No, it doesn't."

"Of course it does," she scoffed. "Those two men handed us something you can dig your teeth into. If Oi was trafficking, maybe he crossed someone, they came after him, found him at Rosa's, and that was that. Thank goodness Billy wasn't in that house. Thank goodness there's someone who knows his history."

Mike Montoya rhythmically dipped his tea bag into his cup of hot water as he listened. A wisp of steam twirled above it. He understood all too well how new information in a dire situation could make one's hopes rise. It was better, though, to temper those hopes. In Mike's experience, they were dashed more often than not. Still, Eastern European organized crime was something he had not considered and it certainly wasn't an idea he could dismiss. He set aside his tea bag while he considered Josie Bates.

When they met, she had been squared off and fearful of losing her hold on the great weight she carried. Now she looked off into some distance, imagining life was normal again: Billy was out from under the cloud of suspicion, the sun would shine on the beach, and the biggest professional challenge she would face would be representing a drunk driver. He would not have thought it, but Josie Bates was a romantic. Gjergy Isai was a fairy godfather who had come to save the boy prince.

"I'm surprised you're willing to accept all that at face value." Mike sipped his tea.

"Don't tell me you're one of those people who think defense attorneys have no soul?" she quipped.

"I would never presume."

Josie laughed and then scooted forward, crossing her arms on the table, lowering her voice.

"I'm just pointing out that this is a far better theory than Billy Zuni suddenly deciding to murder two men and assault his sister."

"His sister," Mike mused. "I have to say, I'm at least happy to have that cleared up."

"I'm happy to have it corroborated. I always hated the thought that his mother turned him out."

"It's better if a sister does it?" Mike asked.

"No, but it explains a lot of things. She was younger than Billy when she came here with Oi. Whatever made her leave their home, whatever led her to that house and that job, was probably pretty bad. I think it is amazing that she kept body and soul together for both of them. Can you imagine what would happen if you'd been dropped in Albania and told to survive when you were that age?"

"I'll grant you that," Mike agreed. "But if Mr. Oi is the bad guy, what was he doing at Rosa's house dressed the way he was?"

"Who knows what their relationships was?" Josie shrugged.

"What would you think if I told you that Rosa thought she had married Oi?"

"I would say Billy thinks the same thing. Is it true?"

"We've got something that appears to be a marriage certificate. I'm trying to authenticate it. It could be a ruse; it could be the way Oi got the girls over here. It would be hard to resist a pitch from a successful man who tells you he's going to take you to America and that he wants to marry you."

"See! There you go." Josie pushed her agenda. "Rosa thought she was married. He gets her over here and sells her to some guy. Or maybe she was indentured, working off what she owed him at the club. You've got to find out if Undies has any connection to the Albanian community." Josie was off again, extrapolating, anticipating, and eager to be done with this. She looked almost girlish when she widened her eyes and asked: "So?"

"So?" Mike responded.

"So you have enough to put Billy way down on the ladder in your investigation. Get rid of the officer. That kid is stressed enough."

"I'm surprised you'd want me to do that. Mr. Isai suggested that whoever attacked Rosa Zuni also wanted to harm Billy. You should be pleased that I am going to keep that deputy outside his room. Don't forget, we still have the knife."

"We'll stipulate to the knife. It's worthless to Carl Newton. You know that." Josie deflated. Her shoulders slumped, and she wrapped her fingers around the Styrofoam cup. "Billy's not your guy, and you know it. And we have relatives now who will watch out for him."

"Ms. Bates, do you mind if I talk to you as a friend?" When she didn't object, Mike set aside his tea and laced his fingers. "I know you want to think that you can walk into Healy's courtroom, he'll wave a magic wand, and release Billy to Mr. Isai, but he won't.

"The wheels of justice turn slowly. We'll have to verify Isai's claims. Even if we do that, you'll be dealing with immigration for Billy and extensions for Isai. Lumina isn't exactly all warm and fuzzy, so he's not going to embrace Billy. Not to mention Lumina's involvement in the union activities. Those guys aren't off our list for these murders. Judge Healy won't go for any of this. While these two are interesting, they aren't the solution to your problem."

"Lumina will do what the old man says if I can convince Healy this is a viable option," Josie insisted.

"Fine then," Mike answered, "Let me play devil's advocate. Judge Healy releases Billy to Mr. Isai's custody and they all hang with Lumina until Rosa is well. Then what? They go back to Albania one big happy family? Ms. Bates, Billy and Rosa don't have passports. They don't even have driver licenses or birth certificates that we can find. Do you really think Billy would want to be deported? Isn't this his home?"

"You're right. You're right."

Josie put her fingers on her temple and rubbed away the headache that was starting. She hated clutching at straws. She dropped her hands, gave him a reluctant smile.

"I don't want to do your job, I just want to keep Billy out of the system. If Gjergy Isai makes that happen, I'm all for it. He's the only one I've got, Montoya, and I'm grateful."

"No one wants to take Billy out of the mix more than I do, believe me," Mike said. "If trafficking is involved, then the attack on Rosa might have been meant as a message to other girls. That would explain the viciousness of it."

"You mean whoever is behind this knew Rosa was going to the cops?"

"It's a scenario I could live with," Mike said.

"And I can think of ten more. I just don't have the time to explore them all." Josie was played out. "I'm getting married at the end of the month."

"Congratulations."

She blushed and Mike thought the handsome woman he had met days before became a beautiful woman as she thought about her wedding. Young, happy, and beautiful. Weddings could do that to a person.

"You've probably got a few family things that are going to the backburner, too," she suggested.

"A few," Mike admitted.

"Then we both need this to go away," Josie said.

"It will, but we can't cut corners even for a wedding."

He was right and, since there was nothing to say, she let her eyes wander. Her gaze fell on an older man who was helping a little boy with his milk. Mike saw so much in her expression, but mostly he saw sadness. He could relate to that. He knew what it was like to want to desperately make something right that could never be made so.

"I'll take the guard off," Mike said.

"Thank you."

"My pleasure." He stood up and indicated her cup. "Are you done with that?"

When she nodded he took the cups and napkins and threw them in the trash. Mike picked up where he left off when she joined him.

"Why would such a rich man be involved in trafficking?"

"Men do a lot of things because they can," Josie suggested.

"So do women." The detective raised a brow but Josie countered.

"Women usually do what they have to. Maybe this was Jak Duka's deal and Oi was helping him. Have you checked to see if they're related?"

"They are not," Mike answered. "Duka was a snitch, selling out the brothers."

"That's not smart. I wonder what the payoff was? If it were just the two men I'd lay odds on a union hit. But it wasn't the two of them. But they are all Albanian." Josie ambled toward the elevator with Mike Montoya. "Eventually you'll figure it all out, the media will have a field day, and we'll all probably be shocked at how simple it all was. But I don't have the luxury of time. The hearing is tomorrow."

"I'll see if I can run something down on Isai." They reached the wide hall. "I'm not promising."

"Understood."

"I'll see you tomorrow."

Mike Montoya put his hand out. Josie Bates took it before he walked into the elevator. When it closed, she thought she saw his demeanor slip just a little. He looked tired. Not that she could blame him.

She felt exactly the same way.

CHAPTER 21

Josie sat on the wall that separated The Strand from the sand. She balanced herself with the palms of her hands and stretched her legs out in front of her. Hannah sat in the sand at her feet. Max had been left at home. Her eyes were closed, her lips tasted of salt, and her short hair spiked with the breeze. Southern California would get more rain soon, but not that evening. It was perfect, this silence. It was even more perfect when it was broken.

"I'm sorry, Josie." Hannah looked up when Josie didn't respond. "Josie?"

Josie opened her eyes. It seemed like days had passed since she had found Hannah disobeying her. Given everything that happened, that transgression seemed trivial. The apology, however, was epic.

"I heard you." Josie opened her eyes. "I appreciate it."

"I was going to wait like you told me, but when I saw the cops going to Billy's room I just couldn't sit there."

Josie slid off the wall and put her back up against it so that she and Hannah were shoulder to shoulder. Again she was struck by Hannah's unique beauty. Today her eye shadow was a sparkling mink color mixed with pink and her lipstick was magenta. Huge gold hoops hung from her ears. She was going to be so much her own woman in a few years.

Her fears would never be replaced with peace, but there would be no need to cut away pain with a razor blade, to touch things to make sure they existed, to watch doors in the hopes that those who walked through them would walk back in again. Someday Hannah would conquer her devils and reach down to help someone struggling with their own. She would love Josie, but she wouldn't need her. Her apology proved that time was close.

"I doubt I would have stayed in that waiting room either. In fact, I probably would have shut the locker on Tiffany, too." Josie draped her arms over her knees.

"If we were related then I could blame it on genetics," Hannah suggested.

"We'll put it down to osmosis," Josie answered, keeping her eyes straight on toward the ocean. She couldn't see the shore, but she knew it was there in the same way she knew all would be well with her and Hannah. "We butt heads because we're so much alike. You've been a good friend to Billy, but you can't help him right now."

"Can you?" Hannah slid her eyes toward Josie, but Josie didn't look back.

"I don't know, Hannah. Everyone has some skin in this game. The District Attorney wants someone to prosecute, and the county counsel wants to be Joan of Arc, and now we've got Gjergy Isai. I've got a shot at navigating it all, but if you go off half cocked it will make it harder."

"I was hoping Rosa would just say something to stop what was happening to Billy," Hannah said. "That's all she needed to do. I thought she could find the strength."

"One word can make all the difference," Josie muttered, thinking of the one Rosa Zuni had managed. "Are you sure Billy never told you anything about his life before he came here? Really, Hannah, if he did you have to tell me now."

"No, nothing. I swear," Hannah insisted. "You know how he was with me."

"Like a puppy dog." Josie chuckled, but Hannah was shamed.

"I should have been nicer. I just didn't want to get close in case all this didn't last." Hannah picked up a handful of sand and let it run out like an hourglass. When it was finished she asked: "Do you believe that man?"

"Gjergy?" Josie inclined her head toward her left shoulder and shrugged with her right. "I don't know. I don't think the trafficking implication holds water."

"Why not?" Hannah picked up another handful of sand, seemingly distracted by it. Josie knew better. Hannah was hanging on every word, so Josie ticked off her laundry list.

"Rosa lived alone with Billy. She had possessions. She paid their bills. She came and went as she pleased at her job. The women she worked with never saw anyone threaten her. In fact, at least one of them saw Greg Oi try to give her money. If he was into trafficking, he'd be taking money from her not trying to give it to her."

"She worked in a strip joint," Hannah objected.

"But not a brothel. She could have talked to anyone. She could have gone to the police," Josie reminded her.

"Unless someone threatened to hurt Billy. Isn't that what she told him? That someone wanted to kill him?" Hannah asked. "Maybe they came to get Billy, he wasn't there, and they took it out on her."

"Then where does Billy fit in? There are enough young girls to traffic. Why choose one who has a little kid?" Josie pointed out. "Rosa took care of Billy. They both let everyone believe she was his mother. There was clear intent to what she was doing."

"Billy has the Stockholm syndrome," Hannah announced and picked up more sand. She looked up to see Josie's confusion. "Is that so strange? I was willing to take the fall for my mom and she was a murderer. I still love her because I understand her. I was never afraid of things the way she was. And you still love your mom even though she left you. You don't even know why and you love her."

Josie hung her head and pulled her lips tight.

"It isn't strange at all that he would feel so strongly about Rosa. It doesn't feel right. It doesn't make sense," Josie mumbled, wanting to be done with any thought of either of their mothers.

"What would make sense?" Hannah asked.

"I have no idea," Josie answered.

Hannah scooped up more sand. Two, three, four times she did this. The fingers of her other hand stretched until they were barely touching Josie's hip. They were not women who held onto one another, but they wanted to stay within reach; they were not given to lamentation, but they did need to give voice to their fears; they didn't entertain flights of fancy, but they did harbor reasonable hope. Hannah withdrew her fingers leaving Josie grateful for the small show of solidarity and the instant of affection.

"That's what makes this all so scary," Hannah said offhandedly.

"What? That I don't know?" Josie asked.

"That no one does," she answered. "It's scary that everyone is trying to figure out this puzzle and so far the only piece you have is Billy."

"And?"

"And you're trying to fit all the pieces around him and the more you press and poke and try to make the pieces fit around him, the more you damage him. Everything that makes him Billy is going to get bent and squished and broken until he doesn't fit in anywhere in the puzzle, but you're all still going to insist he's the middle piece. Maybe someone else is the middle piece."

"But Billy is the one who makes sense," Josie said. "You can't deny that."

"What about the Fed Ex guy? It's like he's forgotten. And no one has even thought that it might just be some crazy who went into the house and did 'em all. It's like when people paint. They think they want to paint a face, but they don't think beyond a nose and eyes and mouth. There are a lot of things that go into painting a face, like catching the look in someone's eyes that you wouldn't notice right away, like how the shadow or light make a difference in someone's expression. Or the way someone moves their lips just a little and instead of looking angry they look sad. It's the same with this. I think there are a lot more possibilities about what happened in that house."

Hannah let her hand rest on the hill of sand she had created.

"Billy's not like me, Josie. He doesn't have places in his head where he can put the bad stuff and lock it up. Billy's like the ocean, everything swirls together and he gets confused."

With her open palm, Hannah erased the hill and made the sand flat again.

"Maybe somebody needs to take Billy out of the mix and see what's left. Why doesn't someone do that?"

Josie raised one eyebrow but her eyes never left the beach. The sun was low and there was a sparkle on the water. She could hear the gentle waves rolling to the shore. They were the kind you could walk in and your troubles would be washed away. She rested her head on the wall behind her.

"That's not the way the system works, Hannah."

"I know."

Hannah gazed into the distance at something only she could see. It was close and it was important, but it wasn't to be shared with Josie so she went back to funneling sand. She wasn't counting out loud, but Josie had the oddest feeling that Hannah knew exactly how many grains had passed through her fingers.

***

Mary Lumina tried not to think of anything but the dishes she was doing. There were three more plates and two glasses. Oh, and the roasting pan. The old man had seemed to like the roast. The old man had seemed to like just about everything that night, but that still didn't make her feel any better about him. In fact, it scared the beejeebies out of her to think that he could sit at her table, talk to her husband, pick up her child, and put him on his knee given what he had done. She was thinking about it all when suddenly there were arms around her. The dish she was washing flew out of her hand and hit the floor as she twirled out of the man's grasp. It didn't make her feel any better to see it was Sam who had grabbed her.

"Jesus, what's the matter with you, Mary?"

She put her hand to her heart. "You scared me. That's all."

"That's all? I do that all the time, and you don't go throwing dishes at me."

"I wasn't throwing it. I dropped it." She pushed her husband out of the way and got down on her knees to clean it up. He did the same. She pushed him aside again. "I can do it."

"Okay. Okay," Sam stood up. There was no pleasing her these days. "Look we're just going to go out and see some of the guys. You need anything?"

She shook her head. She didn't want to look at her husband. He'd see something was seriously wrong. Then he'd start asking question. Then he'd want answers, and she didn't want him talking her out of anything.

"Sure. That's good. I might take Sammy and go on over to Sharon's and see how she's doing and all."

"Okay. But don't be out too late. You know how wound up Sammy gets," her husband warned.

"Yeah, I know," Mary muttered.

She finished sweeping the shards into the dustpan, got up and put the broken dish in the trash. When she turned around, Sam was there again. Before she could slip away, he grabbed her and pulled her close.

"I just wanted you to know it's all going to be good. Really."

She stopped fidgeting and looked up into her husband's eyes. He nodded and winked at her, and it was almost like having the old Sam back.

"Okay. If you say so."

"Where's your purse? I need a few bucks."

She wiggled out of his grasp, "I'll get it."

"Just tell me where it is-"

He never finished his sentence. She was already in the bedroom, digging her purse out from the back of the closet, fumbling for money in her wallet, before rushing back to give him all she had.

"Here. Have fun."

She shoved the money at him and he kissed her cheek while he pocketed it.

"Thanks, honey. And no worries. Uncle Gjergy is going to be gone soon, and I'll be back to work. Yep, everything's going to be fine."

She nodded and he left, taking the old man with him. She started to shake the minute the door closed. Suddenly, Sammy came tearing through the kitchen with the television remote. He pointed it right at her.

"Bang! Bang!" he cried and then leered at her. "You're dead."

***

Archer took the lawn chair that had been in Rosa Zuni's living room and one from the kitchen and carried them both to the backyard. Off the back door there was a three-by-three patch of brick that served as a patio and beyond that, the ground was rock hard. In the middle of the dirt, a huge avocado tree thrived while every other bit of greenery around it had shriveled and died. On the far side of the house was a gas bar-b-que, its metal lid eaten through by rust.

Carving out this little personal patch of parched land was a grape stake fence that had weathered its share of summers. To the rear and the right, the fence was in decent shape but to the left – the side that separated the Zuni house from the construction next door – there were a couple of slats missing.

Randy the contractor was long gone. He had taken Archer's card but neither he nor his crew would be around for the next few days, so Archer wouldn't be hearing from him. Archer assured him that was no problem and then set up the campground again. He dug the packing blanket out of the dumpster and draped it over the ill-constructed teepee frame so that it would appear nothing had been disturbed. He ran down to the convenience store, picked up a six-pack of bottled water and some nuts and put them outside. The only thing missing was Josie – and Trey.

***

Mike Montoya sat at his desk with his feet up on an open drawer. It was a slow night and the two other deputies on duty were talking quietly, creating background music that helped Mike concentrate. Halfway around the world the sun was breaking over Albania. He had spent the last hour trying to get a handle on the country, the man named Gjergy, and information on Rosafa and Besnik Zogaj.

Albania's history was fascinating. The darn place had been invaded by just about everyone on earth starting around the beginning of time. There was a fifty-year span where the Albanian people suffered under a dictatorship that made the Soviet set up look like Disneyland. It had no industry except for a brisk trade in chrome mining and human beings. Albania, it seemed, had quietly become the human trafficking capitol of the world. That added another note to Greg Oi's white board listing and credence to Gjergy's claim.

After a quick check with Dan Jenkins, Marshall Fastener's controller, it was found that two mines in northern Albania supplied one hundred percent of the chrome used in the Torrance factory. Mike liked that connection and passed it along to his contacts at the feds. If the Eastern European mafia were at play, the Feds would know about it quicker than he would.

Gjergy proved a bit more of a problem. The feds were following up, but they hadn't offered Mike much hope that they would come back to him any time soon with information on the man. Albania was a country without records of birth, death, marriage, or property ownership. Add to that, the clan system still took precedents over legal relationships, and it was an almost impossible nut to crack when it came to deciding who was who and what claim they laid to anything.

Sam Lumina was an easier target. Local and vocal, there was enough information on him to keep Mike engaged for a while. Sadly, he was predictable and boring and there was nothing in Mike's gut that told him he had done anything more than maybe decorated Greg Oi's office with some of his buddies. Sam was a bully, but he appeared to be bullied by Gjergy. Yet he had been at the Oi house with Gjergy Isai. That much Mike knew.

The detective tossed the report he was reading, put his head back, and closed his eyes. Behind him the men laughed, before their voices fell quiet as they talked of serious things. Mike smiled, suddenly reminded of Christmases past when he would be in his chair, almost asleep in front of the television, and the voices of his wife and girls would drift from the kitchen. Those were the days. They weren't coming again no matter how he longed for them so he dropped his feet, regrouped, reordered, and started to rethink. He pulled a pad of paper closer, picked up a pen and made two columns. In one he listed what he knew and in the other he would list what he needed to know in order to forward the investigation. He never got to the second column.

"I brought you some pizza."

Wendy Sterling's lips were so close he could feel her warm breath on his neck. Before he could turn his head, she pulled a chair up to his desk and made herself at home. She wiggled her fingers, motioning for him to clear a space.

"I thought you'd gone home to that wife of yours."

She put her files on the end of the desk and the pizza box in the middle. She opened it with a flourish and graced Mike with a smile. It didn't escape his notice that her lipstick was fresh, her hair newly brushed and some musky perfume had been recently applied. He continued to look at her as if seeing her for the first time.

"Mike? Hey, Mike?"

She touched his hands, her fingertips were warm and small and soft. He looked at them. Her skin was milky white against the olive color of his. He slid his hand back.

"Are you okay?" she asked.

"Fine. Sorry. I was just thinking of something." He moved his hands and opened the pizza box. "Cheese?"

"And cold. But beggars can't be choosers." She wrinkled her nose. "I took it out of the fridge. I don't think it's all that fresh."

Mike took a piece. Wendy handed him a napkin. He said: "Someone was probably saving it."

"It's not marked. Fair game." Wendy grabbed a piece and sat back. Gorgeous as she was, even Wendy was fraying a little around the edges on this one. He could see it in her eyes, or rather under them. Lavender circles of worry and exhaustion had appeared. They finished their pizza. Wendy indicated the box. Mike shook his head.

"Me either. I should have taken the chicken," she said. "Sorry."

"It's the thought that counts." Mike set the box aside.

"Did you talk to anyone at the strike force?"

"I did," Mike answered. "The agent I spoke to actually laughed when I told him what we've got. He said when it came to anything out of Albania our guess was as good as theirs, but he promised to do what he could."

"Did you tell them about Oi?"

Mike nodded. "Sure. Of course. The big Albanian community is New York, Greg Oi didn't spend much time there, so I'm not sure there's a connection. Unless they're were testing the waters with Oi. You know, he brings the girls back and ships them east. I'd really like to get my hands on the records for that nonprofit."

"Kat Oi already shut it down, but I'll get the information."

Wendy drew a hand through her hair and rested her eyes on the stack of papers she had brought with her. She flipped her shoes off.

"You know that knife? The thing is custom made and old. It's not going to do Deputy D.A. Newton any good. Josie Bates wouldn't have to blink to discredit that."

Wendy rifled through her folder and withdrew some photos and put one on the desk.

"Pictures of the victim's wounds. The two guys were taken out by a guy who knew how to use a gun but was no marksman. Oi took two to the torso. He would have survived this one."

Wendy pointed to the black and white sketch and the X marking the wound under the arm.

"But the second nicked the aorta and tore it. Done deal."

Wendy snapped three more black and white photos in front of Mike that, while lurid, did nothing to capture the true horror of what happened to Rosa Zuni.

"The knife caught Rosa on the wrists, hands and forearms. She was deflecting as best she could but not fighting back. She was probably on her back initially. You can see she had her wrists crossed. The right one crossed over the left. It appears to be a purely reflexive move." Wendy held up her arms to demonstrate. She dropped them a minute later and used her pen to point to the other wounds.

"So the attack was a surprise, or she was surprised by who was attacking her and was literally paralyzed," Mike suggested. "Either way, she would have seen his face."

"It might be a she," Wendy countered.

"Mrs. Oi?" Mike suggested.

"Possibly. Or what about the woman who lives with them? If the trafficking thing holds any weight, maybe she wanted to be higher on the totem pole and perceived that Rosa was in favor."

"We haven't talked to Duka's wife," Mike suggested. "In fact, we really don't have much on him."

Wendy made a note, but said: "I don't think there's anything there. We know he and Oi had union business they didn't want to advertise."

"But if he's meeting Oi on the sly at Rosa's house and the wife misunderstands, it could have meant trouble."

"Mrs. Duka thinks her husband's fooling around and wants to pop Rosa?" Wendy inclined her head and pulled up her lower lip. "Could be. She sees Oi in his little get up and gets even crazier?"

Mike and Wendy chewed on that. Wendy had met Jak Duka's wife and seen those two little kids. The woman would have to be a magician to pull it off.

"I don't think so, Mike."

"Me either. Did you get anything on the pocket litter?" Mike asked.

"No pockets in Oi's gown," Wendy said. "They found his suit in a small bathroom downstairs. A wallet, a driver license, eight-hundred-fifty-eight dollars and twenty-three cents in cash. No credit cards."

"All of it still in his wallet?"

Wendy nodded. "If he was paying Rosa Zuni for anything, she hadn't provided it yet or he hadn't ponied up. There was twenty bucks in her wallet and almost a hundred stashed in a bureau drawer."

"His phone." Wendy took another report and handed it to Mike. "We have three calls to Rosa Zuni's phone the day of the murders. No texting."

"What time were those calls made?" Mike got up wrote on the white board as she spoke.

"8:32 a.m., 2:47 p.m., and 8:30 p.m. They talked for twelve minutes at 8:30."

"Rosa called Billy right after the night call." Mike drew lines connecting phone times.

"The guard saw Oi drive out at 3:14. Protesters were still outside."

"Did he see Sam Lumina?"

"He couldn't remember anyone specific. Just said the same old crowd."

"Did he notice anyone following Oi?" Mike asked.

"He noticed a car stopping to let Oi get out of the lot. The only reason he kept watching was because somebody had pelted the boss's car with eggs a couple days before. The street was busy, so it was unusual for a car to stop on Lomita. He said usually you just had to wait it out for an opening."

"Did he see what kind it was?"

"Old," Wendy laughed. "Back end had some damage. What are you thinking? Someone followed Oi to Hermosa? Maybe it was the car Mrs. Yount saw in front of her house."

"Possibly. Keep it in the back of your mind." Mike went on from there. "And what day did Gjergy arrive?"

She gave him the date. It was three days before the murder.

"And the day two men we believe are Isai and Lumina showed up at the Oi house and upset Greg Oi?"

Wendy looked at the date he was pointing to and the light dawned.

"Two days before the murder." His smile was slow and satisfied. "And a phone call to Lumina's house after the visit."

"That's good. We need to get them in here and ask about that. When we get to Oi's house with the search warrant I want the security camera files. I'm thinking it wasn't union business that took them there, or Lumina would have been the one talking to Oi. But Kat Oi says the old man talked. The old guy found out where the girl was, Lumina is Gjergy's contact in the U.S., he's a relative, and he works at Marshall." Mike snapped his fingers. "There's your three legged stool. This has never been about the union."

"Nice, Mike."

Wendy said as she rifled through her papers and came up with the copy of the Albanian marriage certificate.

"There's a signature at the bottom and the name of a town. It's almost ten years old. Seems like the time Rosa and Billy showed up in Hermosa. Rosa had to be, what, fourteen-years-old? Maybe they can marry 'em that young in Albania, but it would land Oi in the slammer here. It's not legal so Kat Oi has nothing to worry about."

"It doesn't matter. If she thought it was valid and that Rosa and Billy pose a threat to her inheritance, she could have acted. Who's to say that she didn't call Sam Lumina over that night? She's a member of the board, she knows what goes on and that means she knew Lumina was one of the tough guys. Maybe he alerted her to Gjergy and she figured it was a way out if Gjergy took the girl away. Kat might have thought sending those two to Rosa would simply get the girl gone," Mike mused

"That's good. We can look into it," Wendy agreed. "Oh, and the lab thinks it's a shoe print in the kitchen, but no treads. They probably won't be able to match it to anything. What was the old guy wearing today in the hospital?"

"Loafers. Hard soles. I don't remember what Lumina had on," Mike answered. Wendy shrugged. It was just another snippet of information to paste into the collage.

"I already gave you Lumina's record, but I went back and ran Kat Oi. She had three moving violations in the last year, four parking tickets, and a disorderly conduct complaint at a local restaurant. Two were in Hermosa, one on Manhattan Beach Boulevard, and one on the 2700 block of Century Boulevard. The last one is about three blocks from Undies."

"Jak Duka had a juvenile record. I'm working with the DA to try and get it unsealed. He had a fender bender on Torrance Boulevard and Hawthorne last December. The insurance companies settled. He had also been held briefly for defacing Marshall Fasteners building during a lockout, which I find totally weird. Why would a guy hanging with the picket line end up dying with the guy they're fighting?"

"Was anyone else arrested in that incident?" Mike asked.

"Yep, Mark Wolf and Sam Lumina. The three of them were together. Thick as thieves according to some we interviewed."

"It's all good, Wendy." Mike tossed his pen on the desk as if they had just solved the mystery rather than put a few pieces of the puzzle together. He looked at his watch.

"So, are you going to pull the guard off Billy's room?" Wendy asked.

Mike shook his head. "Already did. I can't justify the expense, and I can't really say I'm thinking Billy's good for any of this."

"Be that as it may, we are making something out of all this clay. We're a good team, Montoya."

"That we are," he answered.

"We should celebrate," Wendy suggested. "What do you say? A cocktail? We can do a little more brainstorming and-"

Just then the phone rang. Mike raised a finger and Wendy fell silent, happy he hadn't said no outright.

"Detective Montoya." A slow and even lovelier smile crossed his face. He turned away. "Hey, honey. I'm sorry. Yeah. Yes. Just a little while." He listened. "You go on to bed. I love you, too."

He put the receiver down but didn't let go of it. Wendy took a deep breath and put on a brave face.

"This was the anniversary night, wasn't it?" she asked.

"Kay understands." Mike said absently. "I'm sorry, you were saying?"

Wendy's smile turned brittle. "It wasn't anything. Go on. Get home. I haven't got anything to do tonight. I'll keep at it a while longer."

Wendy Sterling, slipped her feet into her shoes, got up, patted Mike Montoya's shoulder, and left it at that. There was something about a guy who really loved his wife that took all the fun out of it.

CHAPTER 22

Josie parked behind Archer's Hummer, grabbed the bag out of the back of the Jeep, and walked the block to Billy's house. The yellow tape had been removed, but other than that nothing had changed. The broken down car was still in the driveway. No doubt the VIN number had been run and found to be of no interest or it would have been impounded. The plant on the porch was still dead, the pot still broken. She tried the front door. This time it opened and once inside Josie called:

"Archer?"

There was no answer. The living room was the same except someone had thrown a sheet over the couch where Jak Duka died and Jak Duka's body was gone.

Josie went through the kitchen. The memory of Greg Oi dead and dressed like a jolly big hooker was not as chilling to her as the image of Duka. Josie had seen Duka's face in real time, and Oi had been face down in a dark room. The only real image she had of him was from a professional headshot run in the newspaper. He was a handsome man: full face, fleshy at the jaw, his nose was short and his eyes were steely. He did not appear to be a man you crossed. It must have been an epic battle between him and the union. Too bad he wasn't going to be around to see how it all played out.

Josie opened the back door, checked out the chairs and the broken fence and then went back through the living room and up the stairs. It wasn't until she was on the landing that Archer called back to her. She found him on his hands and knees scrubbing the bathroom floor just off Rosa's room. He tossed his brush in the pail and sat back on his heels. She sank down and sat facing him.

"Looks good," she said, although she knew blood never washed out of grout no matter what you did.

"Not bad," he said. "Just in case Billy ever comes back here. I wouldn't want him seeing this."

"He won't come back," she answered. "You know that."

Archer nodded as he contemplated the bathroom.

"Someone will."

"I guess you're right. Someone will." Josie looked around, taking a moment because Archer was. Finally, she asked: "Did you find anything interesting?"

"Maybe." He told her about the Albanian book Billy carried. "I have a friend in San Pedro. He's a retired union guy. He's Croatian, but he might know something that will help us. What's up with Hannah tonight?"

"I sent her and Max over to Faye's."

"Letting her off the leash are you, Jo?"

"One of these days you'll crack yourself up, Archer, and I'm going to be there to see it," Josie teased and still she didn't get a smile. That man guarded the few he had with a vengeance. "I decided two weeks is too long for house arrest."

"Good job." Archer waited a beat. "She's a helluva kid because of you, Jo."

"No thanks to me the way she turned out. No thanks to Linda for sure. Maybe she got her fatal flaw from her father." She chuckled softly. "I hope she outgrows it, or she'll have nothing but heartache."

"What flaw would that be?" He got up and emptied the bucket into the sink.

"The justice gene. Fight for what's right at all costs."

"That's the pot calling the kettle black," Archer muttered.

"Yeah, but I believe in the law. Hannah's like Hammurabi. She has her own code. One of these days I'm going to ask her to write it up."

"Can you have her do that before we get hitched? I'd hate to cross her." He offered his hand. When she took it, he pulled her up, pulled her toward him, and gave her a quick kiss and a proactive apology. "I hope this isn't a waste of time, sitting out there in the dark."

"The midnight picnic will make it worthwhile no matter what," she murmured.

"You're easy to please, woman."

Archer passed her on ahead when they got to the stairs. The scent of pine cleaner and soap and old blood was left behind. Outside, they settled down, adjusting the chair until they could see the construction clearly. The cover of the avocado tree threw them into deep darkness so she doubted anyone on the other side could see them unless they were looking. Josie shook out a blanket she had taken out of the back of her car and draped it over her knees. She tossed Archer a jacket, a sandwich from the bag, and offered a thermos of coffee. The night wore on. The air was cold and the moisture made for a deep chill and that pleased Archer. Whoever was camping out next door would positively be back if it rained or got too cold. He'd bet his P.I. license that person was going to be Trey.

**

Wendy Sterling could have waited until the morning to show Mike Montoya what had been waiting for her when she got back to her desk. She also could have called him and told him about it. But what was on the DVD was really something he should see.

That's what she told herself when she left the office, drove to a modest neighborhood in Torrance, found his house, and got out of her car. She was half way up the walk when her step slowed and her hands started to sweat. She almost turned back. She should turn back. This wasn't a game anymore. What surprised her was the sudden knowledge it never had been. For the first time in her life Wendy wanted to know what kind of woman could hold a man she wanted.

Once she was honest with herself, Wendy did what she'd come to do. It was eleven o'clock when she rang Mike Montoya's doorbell. She licked her lips, stood straight as an arrow so that her impressive chest was on full display, and put a smile on her face. She was prepared to greet the lady of the house, but it was the master who opened the door.

Mike didn't look surprised, nor did he look upset, and that left Wendy feeling like a schoolgirl with a crush on her teacher. In the office it was easy to imagine so many things. Here, it was hard to imagine anything other than Mike comfortable in his slippers and his wife asleep in their bed.

Wendy held up the DVD. "I'm sorry. I really am."

Mike took the DVD. It did not escape his notice that her hand was shaking. He stepped aside.

"Come in."

Wendy stepped over the threshold and into Mike Montoya's world.

***

A breeze moved the leaves of the avocado tree above Josie and Archer and picked up the tarp covering the roof of the house next door. There hadn't been a sound from the street since ten. It was a weeknight, traffic was intermittent, and Josie was slumped in the lawn chair, her head cradled on her upturned hand as she slept and Archer kept watch. It was just after eleven when Archer touched her. She opened her eyes to see him holding a finger to his lips. He pointed to the hole in the fence, reached for his flashlight but didn't turn it on. Eventually, they heard sounds: metal falling, a scuffling, a laugh, one voice talking and no other answering.

A pinpoint of light moved like a firefly, unsteady and darting. A stronger breeze blew through the yard and the waxy leaves of the huge avocado scratched against one another again. Josie set aside her blanket. She looked toward Archer just as the low clouds folded in on themselves and opened a bit of sky for the moonshine to slide through.

The beats went on. Josie channeled Hannah as she counted the seconds. Finally, Archer gave her forearm a squeeze. He was on the move. Tall and broad, he cut out a piece of the night in a silhouette she would recognize anywhere. Before he left, he bent toward her, put one hand on her shoulder and gave her the flashlight with the other.

"Light it up if he comes this way."

He disappeared down the side yard. There was no gate so he didn't have to worry about the sound of a latch or the creak of a hinge. Josie uncoiled, moved to the broken fence, narrowed her eyes, and peered toward the framing. Suddenly, a match flared inside the tent. Josie smelled the unmistakable scent of dope just before she heard Archer's voice.

"Trey, my man. We've been looking for you."

***

"I thought you'd still be celebrating the big anniversary," Wendy said.

"Kay was tired."

"Oh. Well, I'm still sorry to bother you."

They were in a neat little room: sofa, television, an armchair and pictures of the family. Wendy looked at the family photos while Mike turned on the television.

"Beautiful girls."

Wendy picked up a picture frame that had been made in some grade school classroom. Mike's daughters were tall. Both had long, black hair and exquisite smiles. They were happy girls. Mike was handsome, but back then he had been devastatingly so. He had his arms around the girls on one side and a woman Wendy took to be his wife on the other. Kay Montoya was a pretty woman but no beauty queen.

"Your whole family is lovely. I-"

Wendy had picked up another picture, but this one shut her down before she could finish her sentence. The girls were older. One of them wore a graduation gown. The smiles were still in place, but the family dynamic had changed. Mike's arm was no longer around his wife. His hand rested on her shoulders because she was sitting in a wheelchair. Mike pressed a button on the television as he glanced at Wendy, and then the picture in her hand.

"Parkinsons. That's why we're not out dancing on our anniversary." Mike took the picture but Wendy held onto it as she met his gaze.

"I'm sorry for being such a witch."

"You aren't." Mike took the picture and put it back on the table. "I was flattered, Wendy. All that attention gave me cred with the rest of the guys. I just figured you were practicing for when the real thing came along."

Mike sat on the sofa. He held the remote in both hands. Wendy still stood.

"Why didn't you say something?"

"Because my wife deserves her dignity, and because no one wants pity, and because I'm afraid to talk about it. If I did, I'd never be able to work."

"You're a good man." Wendy sat down in the armchair and let her gaze rest on the television.

"Kay is an exceptional woman." Mike pointed the remote. "Let's see what we've got."

Wendy cleared her throat. She couldn't look at Mike and had to force herself to sound as if she wasn't ashamed.

"Peter got that tape working enough to see what was going on. He put it on the disk. I was going to wait until tomorrow, but I didn't think I could sleep if you didn't know about it."

Mike's arms rested on his knees as the screen filled with the image of the blue room, the queen bed without a headboard, and the window with the curtains. There were no bushes outside the window.

A man could be heard talking. He was getting excited and then angry. He moved into the camera's view. It was Greg Oi. He was not speaking English and from what they could make out, he was dressed in women's clothes. They heard a girl's angry voice, speaking the same language. Greg Oi's rage grew as he veered out of the picture.

Suddenly, there was the sound of flesh on flesh and a woman twirled into the scene. She hit the bed and fell to the floor as Greg Oi roared. At the same time a young boy ran to the woman's side. He threw his arms around her. He buried his face against her back.

Slowly, she pushed back her hair, lifted her eyes, and Mike Montoya saw what Wendy Sterling had: Rosa Zuni looking at the man off screen and the child, Billy, crying into her shoulder.

But it was what happened the next second that made Mike sit up and back. Without warning, Billy flew toward the man off screen, fists raised, a blood-curdling cry coming from him.

The last image the camera took was Billy Zuni looking like he could kill.

CHAPTER 23

"This is bullshit. I mean really. Total bullshit man. Let's go back to my place. It's freaky in here."

"Give me a break." Archer kicked at the couch. "Sit down."

"I'm not sitting there. I know what happened there."

Trey shivered and worked his long jaw as if trying to find some other words that would get him out of this place. There weren't any. The guy who grabbed him was big and the woman was tall and buff, so he was pretty sure he was screwed. And the woman was even creepier, looking hard at him like she would turn him to stone.

Josie, on the other hand, wasn't thinking about him that way at all. She was trying to connect this guy – the one who needed a shower and a haircut – with the man who had fallen through her door. He was probably the right guy but she was proving what all law enforcement knew: eyewitnesses weren't all that reliable. She couldn't have picked him out of a line-up.

"You've got two choices. Sit down and tell us about it." Archer kicked the couch again.

"What's the other choice?" Trey asked.

"We call the cops right now." Josie found her voice. It sounded like she didn't care one way or the other but she did. More than anything, Josie Bates wanted first crack at this guy.

"You're going to call 'em anyway," Trey complained, still giving the couch the stink eye.

"But if you talk to us, we can help you fill in the blank spots. It will go smoother that way when you finally get to the cops." Archer pulled a thumb toward Josie. "She's an attorney. She'll sort of give you pro bono counsel."

Josie slid her eyes Archer's way, surprised at his audacity. It wasn't good to mess with a witness, but Archer was paying her no mind. Trey, on the other hand, liked this situation a little better now. He shuffled over to the couch and sat in the middle on the edge of the cushion.

"Okay. Okay. I'm ready. What do you want to know?"

"How about everything that happened the night of the storm starting with when you hooked up with Billy," Archer suggested, but Josie amended.

"How about you start with before you hooked up with Billy the night all this went down?"

She sat in the dilapidated armchair while Archer stood. Though he doubted this guy would run, he didn't want to take a chance. Archer almost lost him in the tangle of wood slats and packing blanket as it collapsed around them. He didn't want to chase him down in the open.

"I don't know, man, the day was kind of a fuzzy. Know what I mean?"

"Make it unfuzzy," Archer prodded. "Where'd you eat?"

"Caught some breakfast over at the church. Dumpster dived some behind Scotty's. Burt gave me some fries."

Archer exchanged a look with Josie. That would be easy to corroborate.

"Did you know Billy from Burt's?"

"Naw, I met him here," Trey said.

"How long have you been crashing over there?" Josie nodded toward the house next door.

"A couple days. A week. I'd had my eye on the place because the back room was mostly walled, and the john was working. When the storm started rolling in I knew there wasn't going to be anybody coming back to work. Then when it hit it was so humongous that there was no way it was going to dry out soon. I figured I had another good five days, maybe more. Someone came by once, and I just knocked down the tee-pee and went through the fence same way you did."

"So what was the deal with you and Billy?" Josie asked.

"Oh yeah, about that." Trey's hands gestured with no particular meaning. "I ran into him when I was coming through the fence. Bam!" Trey smacked his hands together and grinned at them both. He needed to see a dentist. "Like a frickin' cartoon, man. So he's like, hey. I'm like, hey. So I ask if he's got like some food or a jay or matches. Hell, I take anything. Never know when it will come in handy."

"And did he?" Josie asked.

"No." Trey looked crestfallen. "He said he couldn't go in the house to get any food."

"Did you ask why?"

"He said his mom didn't like him in the house at night."

"Did he say why?" Archer asked.

"Nope."

"You weren't curious?" Josie asked.

"Nope. My old lady didn't let me in the house ever after I was like fourteen. I figured he had it pretty good if he just couldn't go in sometimes." Trey looked at Josie and Archer as if they were a little crazy, but he was into his narrative. "So we took off to see what we could find. You know, it ain't like Hermosa Beach is friggin' New York City. We walked all around. He showed me your house, but I already knew who you were. I'd seen you playing volleyball. I knew where you lived and that girl that lives with you."

"Great." Josie wasn't happy with her house being on anyone's tour.

"We came back here. I asked Billy if he could sneak me in, you know, like so I could sleep on the couch. Sometimes it's nice to sleep on something soft. But he said no, and it sounded like he was really sorry he couldn't let me."

"But that wasn't the night of the storm, right?" Archer asked. Trey shook his head.

"I was kind of surprised to see him that night. I figured his mom would keep him inside 'cause it was pretty blastin' out. But he comes out all weird and spooked. He was just charging through the rain. He saw me and yells at me to come with like we're off on some adventure. So I grabbed my stuff, and we ended up at the beach. It was damn cool. I'm telling you, those waves were like – like I don't know what - and it was kind of dry under the pier. Cold, but dry. Windy, but kind of dry."

"You had a jacket though," Josie prompted before he could debate how cold or dry it had been that night under the pier.

"Wasn't much of one," Trey sniffed. "I took it off the hook at Burt's. I shoulda gone for the one with all the pockets."

Josie wished she could blink Trey away and put a normal person in his place. If this were the best she could give Judge Healy, Billy would be sent away for sure.

"Why did you stuff it down the drain?" Archer asked.

"I saw the cops and I thought, you know, like they might be over there 'cause they knew I took the jacket." He looked sheepishly from Josie to Archer. "Stupid, huh?"

Both Archer and Josie knew it wasn't a stupid move for someone as high as Trey had been that night. Drugs can make even the most ridiculous things seem sane, the ugly sublime, and violence seem amusing.

"Did Billy say why he was anxious?" Archer asked.

Trey shook his head, "I don't think so, or I don't remember. I was high. I scored good a couple weeks ago, so I had a nice stash. You have to be careful 'cause you never know when times are gonna be lean." He looked from Josie to Archer. "What else do you want before we get to the big show?"

"Anything you can think of that went on at the pier that was odd?" Josie asked.

Trey shook his head hard, "Nothing. I swear. We were hanging and having a good time with the two other people who were there. Billy kept asking what time it was. He wanted to go home but he couldn't go 'till a certain time."

"And you went with him when it was time to go home?" Josie asked while Archer paced behind her.

"Yeah." Trey's eyes darted around the room, resting in one corner before snapping toward another as if he were trying to reconstruct that night. He swallowed hard, craned his neck exposing a prominent Adam's apple and a homemade tattoo just behind his ear.

"Holy shit. I was wasted. I admit it, but even if you're doing some fine shit, there's some stuff that just shoots you right out of a high."

"Billy says you were doing bath salts. White Lightning. That's heavy. It can make you go crazy. Do stuff you won't normally do."

Trey shot Archer a disdainful glance. "I handle it."

He turned back to Josie, but then he looked slyly back at Archer. The minute their eyes met, Trey knew exactly what the big man was thinking. Trey shot off the couch and went for the kitchen and the back door. Archer's reactions were good and his trajectory gave him the advantage. He caught Trey on the angle and body slammed him from the side. Trey skidded into the wall, bounced off it, and crumpled to the ground. His arms went over his head as his knees came up to his chin. Archer was on him in a second, putting the guy in a headlock.

"I didn't do it. You're gonna pin that crap on me! Let me go!" Trey screamed and wiggled and shuffled his butt and pushed at the floor with his heels.

"Stop. Calm down!" Archer pulled up on him. "I'm not going to hurt you."

"Ow! Ow! You're killin' me! Help!"

Archer rolled his eyes at Josie. He picked Trey up by the shoulders, stood him up, dusted him off, and took him by the scruff of the neck back to the couch.

"We don't want to pin anything on anyone, but if you jerk us around it's going to be a long time before you are partying at the beach again. Got it?"

"I won't lie," he whimpered. "I swear, I won't. I hardly took one step in here and that's the truth. Okay, maybe two. I just wanted to see what I could score."

"Jo. Let's get to it." Archer took a chair close enough to get Trey if he had to give chase.

Josie: What time did you come back to the house?

Trey: Late. I don't know. I was messed up.

Josie: Did you walk with Billy?

Trey: I followed him. A little behind.

Josie: How was he?

Trey: Tired. Wet. Cold. I guess we both were soaked, but I thought the rain was more like warm slime on my head. I remember thinking that. Billy wanted to get home.

Josie: Did he do the salts?

Trey: (shaking his head)

Josie: Did Billy go into his house?

Trey: (nodding)

Josie: Did you go with him?

Trey: I waited for him then figured he wasn't coming back. I thought he went to bed, and the door was open.

Josie: Then what?

Trey: I figured to grab some food, like I told you. I opened the door and came in and man – it was awful.

Josie: The body on the floor?

Trey: (Shakes his head and shakes it and shakes it). No, man. I hear a scream. I mean even with the salts and shit, that scream scared me sober.

Josie: Where did it come from?

Trey: Upstairs. I was paralyzed sort of like, you know, a zombie. Then I think to myself, 'run to the tent. Run'. But I don't move 'cause I'm wasted and everything went quiet, so I figure maybe I was imagining it.

Josie: Who screamed? A woman? A man?

Trey: I don't know.

Josie: Then?

Trey: Then everything happens at once. I see the chick on the floor. Big girl. I hear someone pounding down the stairs. Then Billy comes racing past me and out the door.

Josie: And what? What? We're tired. Come on.

"Billy comes running through the kitchen, man. He had a knife. A big, friggin' knife. He goes out the door, and he's screaming, and I start to run, too. And we go all those blocks to the beach, and he turns around, and you know those lights at the pier? Well, all I see is that knife, and it's bloody, and I think, "Shit, he's nuts. He's going to kill me." But he doesn't come at me. He yells at me to go get you, and it's raining, and lightning, and the thunder, man, makes it all kind of surreal. I'm looking at the knife and he's screaming to get you and lightning's going on and I'm hysterical and so is he. It was like some damn horror movie.

"Then Billy comes at me, and I think he'll stab me, but he shoves me and says it again and I take off running. Then I think – I don't know what I think – but I look over my shoulder and Billy's heading down to the water."

Trey's eyes got so big they looked like they were going to pop out of his head.

"I stop for a minute because I'm thinking, "Why is he going down to the water?" Then I see this guy 'cause the lightning is going nuts. He's standing looking down at us and I take off. Then I look back and Billy's running into the water."

His head flips from Josie to Archer.

"I yell at the guy, but he just turns around and next I see he's gone. Poof."

Trey's fingertips came together and then went apart like he was releasing something.

"I'm freaked out. I'm thinking, shit, man, this dude is no good. Or maybe he just couldn't hear me. Or maybe he's scared as me. Or maybe I'm imagining him. I mean, I don't even know what was going on except I couldn't see Billy, I couldn't see the guy, and the world was ending, man. You got that? It was like the world was freakin' ending. The end of the freakin' world."

A trembling breath sucked in through Trey's teeth but didn't come out again. His shoulders shuddered. He hung his head in shame.

"I'm a turd. A turd! I should have stayed with him. I should have, like, gone and done a man-to-man kind of thing with that guy up on the avenue, but I didn't. At least I told you. Man, that's gotta be worth something. I told you, right?"

"Do you think you could have told someone a little earlier? Like the next day?" Archer asked.

Trey raised his head. His self-recrimination hadn't lasted long. He put a finger to his chin.

"I thought about it, man. I mean, I'm living right next door and all. Yeah, I should a said something."

"Where were you when the cops came?" Josie tapped his knee to get his attention.

"I wasn't over there. When I left your place I just kept running. I woke up over on 22nd about ten in the morning. I started thinking it was a bad dream but then I see the yellow tape and I just kinda kept my distance. I mean, what was I going to tell them? That Billy had a knife with blood on it? That wouldn't be cool."

"Could you identify the man you saw?" Archer asked.

"It was dark. He was like a shadow."

"And you're sure there was only one guy?"

"That's what I saw." Trey shook his head again and then looked sadly at the two of them. "This sucks. I mean about the knife. Billy seemed so normal, you know?"

**

Josie went home alone and satisfied. Trey's timetable from the beach to the house and back again didn't leave Billy time for an assault or to kill two men. That information would be enough to keep Carl Newton at bay during the hearing in Healy's court.

Archer went home too, but he wasn't alone. Trey was going to be his houseguest, sleeping on the deck lounge until Archer could get him to Montoya. If Archer locked the connecting door he could get some sleep and the only way Trey could get away would be to scale down three stories to The Strand. Trey was down with the arrangement since they convinced him nobody would care about the bath salts, and no one would think he had a hand in the killings. The promise of a full breakfast at Burt's sealed the deal.

Letting herself into the dark house, Josie didn't think anymore about the two men while she made the rounds of her home. The kitchen was clean, and the coffee ready to be brewed when the sun came up. Max slept on his bed but he opened his eyes when Josie touched him. She got on her knees and put her cheek close to his snout. He kissed her with one lazy lick and was asleep again.

She picked up the mail Hannah had put on the entry table: bills, fliers, a catalogue from a cruise line. To the side of the table, a large box rested against the wall. Josie carried it to the dining room table. The packing tape came away. She opened the box, broke the gold seal, and pushed back the white tissue paper. She had no idea how long she looked at the neatly folded dress inside. In the end she refolded the tissue paper, closed the box, and set it back against the wall. The first time she touched her wedding dress, Josie didn't want to have anything on her mind except Archer and her vows.

Finally, she looked in on Hannah. No matter how long they were together, this ritual felt surreal. There was a moment between putting her hand on the doorknob and the door opening when Josie wondered if she had dreamed Hannah. But when the sliver of light from the kitchen was wide enough to illuminate the room and the bed, Josie was as reassured. Her charge, this child, was there.

The girl slept deeply. Her arm was thrown over the pillow she hugged to her body, and her hair spread across the pillow under her head. Josie smiled at the fairytale tableau. Princess Hannah rested, but there was a pea under her mattress that kept her dreams from being sweet. There had been one since the moment she was born and this time that pea was Billy Zuni.

Josie took one last look around the room. The little red lacquer stool Hannah had brought with her from the Malibu house and the box where she kept the reminders of those fateful days were in their place. Thankfully, the days of cutting away her pain seemed to be behind her.

Josie went in and picked up the cell phone that had dropped beside the table. She put it back where Hannah could reach it and resisted the urge to touch the sleeping girl. On her way out, Josie glanced at the easel. For a second she was tempted to raise the sheet that covered the canvas Hannah guarded so zealously. Instead, she passed it by. Hannah would show it to Josie when she was ready. In her own room, Josie fell on the bed fully dressed and slept.

Everyone was safe: Billy and Rosa in the hospital, Hannah and her in the house and Archer in his.

For now, the world was right.

CHAPTER 24

2006

Greg Oi glanced at the sleeping girl beside him and the little boy beside her. They looked like the children they were with their hands clasped together. They had never been in an airplane, never seen an airport, never had new clothes such as he bought them, and they were exhausted. He reached over and checked their seat belts. He pushed the button so the back of the airplane seats no longer reclined. The stewardess passed and smiled at him as if to say he was a good father. Just as well. No one in America would understand that the girl was his wife and the boy was now his son. But no one would ask. This was a strange country. People saw only what they wanted to see and were outraged only when it was the fashion to be.

He looked forward as the landing gear went down and the big plane started its descent into Los Angeles. What, he wondered, would these two make of their new home? He turned his head to look out the window and wondered what either of them would make of him when they saw him for what he really was. Then he smiled. They would make nothing of the way he lived his life because they had no choice. It was the bargain Teuta made.

It was done.

2013

Morning found Mike Montoya and Wendy Sterling behind the gates in Rolling Hills and parked in Kat Oi's driveway. Wendy eyed the house while Mike fielded a call from Archer. When he was done, he said:

"Josie Bates' investigator is bringing in the guy who was with Billy."

"Great," she mumbled.

Mike slid his eyes her way. "Don't you want to know what his story is?"

"Sure. What's his story?" Wendy fidgeted with her seat belt, reached down to pick up her purse, lowered the visor, and looked in the mirror. Still she didn't look at him. Mike reached over and flipped the visor back up. "It was fine you came last night. I needed to see that DVD."

"It could have waited until this morning. I had no right to intrude." Wendy spoke as if she was exhausted by the conversation before it took place, but it hadn't and she wanted to get it over with. "I'm sorry about your wife. I'm sorry for making you uncomfortable. I feel like a fool."

She turned on him. Shame and anger sparked in her eyes.

"Am I the only one who didn't know? Was everyone laughing at me and the way I was carrying on with you?"

"No. Nobody else knows. Or if they do, they don't say anything about it. And nobody was laughing at you. I don't think there's a man in the place who wouldn't be flattered by your attention."

"You weren't," Wendy pointed out.

"Yes, I was. I just didn't know how to respond."

"You could have said that your wife was damn sick, and you didn't have an ounce of energy for games, and that I was being slutty."

"But you weren't, so let's forget it. We've got work to do."

"Yeah. Okay. Forget it." Wendy pushed her door but didn't get out. There was something she needed to know. "How bad is it? I mean, how long?"

"God knows and maybe Kay. Neither of them are saying." Mike put away the phone and checked his inside pocket for his paperwork. He opened his door but before he got out of the car, he said: "I bought her a necklace for our anniversary. She loved it. Thank you."

Wendy swallowed the lump in her throat and got out, too. They met in the middle of the wide driveway. When they reached the porch, Mike pressed the bell. Kat Oi opened the door and scowled at the pair. Mike handed her the warrant.

"It's duly executed, Ms. Oi."

Beneath her expert make-up, her face was pinched and pale. The last few days had taken their toll, and Mike was not without sympathy.

"Who's she?" Kat Oi glared at Wendy.

"I'm Wendy Sterling, Detective Montoya's criminal analyst. I'm assigned to your husband's case."

"Did you bring her along 'cause you're going to have to frisk me or something?" Kat demanded.

"No, Mrs. Oi. We're here to search the premises."

"For what? What are you looking for?" She threw out her hip and planted one hand on it as if her posturing was enough to keep them out of her house.

"We can refer you to the warrant," Wendy answered, but still Kat Oi didn't take the paper. Wendy stepped forward. Kat dropped her hand and side-stepped to block her.

"You can both wait outside until I get my attorney over here. I'm not just going to let you tear up my house without someone here to make sure that I'm getting a square deal." Kat put her hand on the door to close it. Mike put his hand on the other side and the door remained open.

"It would be wise to call your attorney, but we don't have to wait for your lawyer, Mrs. Oi."

Mike inclined his head toward Wendy. She took her cue and pushed politely past Kat.

"Detective Montoya tells me you have a young woman in your employee and another girl in the house who is not related to you." Wendy slowly pirouetted, taking note of everything there was to see. Finally, she smiled at Kat. "If you could tell them we're here, we'd appreciate it."

"Nobody's here but me." Kat shot her a withering look.

"When do you expect them back?" Mike herded Kat away and shut the door.

"I don't." Kat crossed her arms and rubbed them through her pretty blouse. "They're gone. They were my husband's relatives."

"He has a lot of relatives," Mike noted.

"And if he were here he wouldn't put up with this bull. I don't have to tell you what goes on in my house. You can look all you want. You can do what you have to do, but you better hurry because when my lawyer gets here he's going to kick some ass. I'm a widow. My husband was murdered. You can't push me around, and you can't say I had anything to do with his murder. I have an alibi."

She stormed toward the living room, muttering, railing, and flailing her arms. Mike winced when she wobbled on her very high heels.

"Well, if she just isn't a piece of work," Wendy muttered, and then smiled. "Shall we?"

From the living room they could hear Kat Oi's voice rising to a shriek. Mike was happy he had not become a lawyer as his mother wanted. Even five hundred dollars couldn't buy an hour of his time to be at Kat Oi's beck and call.

"Good hunting," Mike said.

They went their separate ways. Wendy to a physical search and Mike to Kat Oi who was in the living room.

"Red Riding Hood better not mess anything up," Kat said when he joined her.

"She's very conscientious and careful," Mike assured her.

"Maybe you should help her. It would make things go faster. That way you'd see there's nothing for you to find out here."

"I'm sure she'll be good on her own. Do you mind if we sit down?"

Kat tossed the phone onto a table cut from a huge burl. She crossed her arms then uncrossed them. "I don't have to answer your questions. I know that. Even if you read me my rights, I don't have to answer anything. I could take the fifth."

Mike unbuttoned his jacket and tugged at the knees on his pants as he sat down. He wished people wouldn't watch so much television.

"Mrs. Oi. We aren't here to accuse you of anything. We're looking for any information or physical evidence that might point us to the person who killed your husband. You want that, don't you?"

"Yes," she pouted.

"And you would rather I talk to you here and not at my office, is that correct?"

"Yes," she grumbled.

"Good."

"Fine. Okay. Don't expect any coffee or anything," she complained.

"I already had mine, thanks," Mike said.

"Oh, now you're a comedian." She plopped herself on the zebra sofa.

"I want to ask you about Rosafa Zogaj." Mike opened a small envelope he had been holding, took out three photographs and laid them on the table in front of Kat Oi. Her lashes lowered. She looked at them. She thought about them.

"We know she lived in this house. We know her brother was with her," Mike stated.

Finally, Kat picked up the photograph of Rosa Zuni. A shadow passed over her face, and then she tossed the photo back on the table.

"I can't believe she's alive."

"You know who she is, don't you, Mrs. Oi?"

"I didn't know her name until Fred showed me that marriage license. I couldn't make heads or tails out of it. I don't think he could either, but I knew it had to be her." She sighed miserably as she crossed and uncrossed her legs. "I don't know what made her so special."

"How long have you been aware of her?"

"A year maybe a little less. I followed Greg to that club she works at. I saw them together, but it didn't seem like she wanted him around. So I figured it was some kind of obsession thing for him. When you showed me the picture of her all cut up, the first thing I thought was that Greg did that to her. I thought maybe he went nuts or something because she didn't like him. Then I realized it couldn't have been him. He's dead, too."

"Did you ask him about her?"

"Once," she admitted.

"And?"

"And he. . ." Kat hugged herself. She looked out the window. Mike looked at her. Her chin trembled. She confessed: "He cried."

"I beg your pardon?"

Her head snapped back. "He cried, dammit. He went on and on about trying to do the right thing and honor and family. I think he loved that girl. I didn't know what their relationship was. I don't know anything about it, but it meant a lot to Greg."

"Did you know about the boy?" Mike nudged Billy's photograph across the table. She glanced at it.

"I never saw him before. Fred thinks Greg had a kid, so it might be him." Kat took a deep breath and for the first time spoke the truth. "This hasn't been the best week of my life. No matter what he did, or who that woman was, it doesn't matter. I was happy with Greg. I always thought he was happy with me."

"Mrs. Oi, is it possible your husband was involved in human trafficking?" Mike asked.

"Who said that? Who?" Kat shot straight up and pointed her finger at Mike. "You tell me because I'll knock their block off. Greg helped people. Young people who needed jobs and couldn't scratch out a living in Albania. And those girls were happy to be here. They could come here and work, or stay there and get married when they were twelve. You should see those places those girls came from. He was doing a good thing bringing them over here."

"Did you ever see him hurt any of them?"

She slumped back again, "No. I never did."

"Did he ever hurt you?"

"He slapped me once or twice," Kat admitted. "But it wasn't like he beat me."

"The two women who were here a few days ago, were they part of his charitable efforts?"

"Yeah." She mumbled. When Mike didn't respond, when it was clear he expected more, Kat gave him what she had. She was tired and wanted someone to talk to. "Maybe I was dumb. I just accepted these girls coming and going. I didn't ask. It wasn't my business. They arrived. They lived here for a while, learned the language, and they went to work somewhere. All except Era. She lived here all the time."

"How long was she here?" Mike asked.

"Two years about."

"So she's not a maid?" he confirmed.

"No. She helped out the new girls the foundation brought over. They can't get a job if they don't speak English or know the basics about America. That makes sense, right? Greg paid their expenses, but some of the guys in his association helped get them jobs. All the Albanians helped."

"Do you know a man who goes by the name of Gjergy Isai?"

Kat shook her head. "No. Never heard of him, but it sounds like one of those guys from the old country."

"The man who came to your door the night before your husband died. The one who came with Sam Lumina? Can you describe him again?"

She bit the corner of her bottom lip. "Old, big. Greg was big and so was this guy. They kind of looked alike. Like bears. This one had short grey hair. Buzz cut. I only saw him for a minute maybe."

Mike nodded. The lady of the house had not been introduced to Gjergy Isai. At least now Mike had corroboration that Isai, Oi, and Lumina were connected as he and Wendy thought.

"Let's talk about Rosa again."

"Look, there's no explaining Greg. I went back with him once to the place he came from. It was harsh. I mean really, really harsh. People wore the same clothes everyday because that's all they had. There was no work. There were no rules, no regulations. Every house had a steel door. Do you want to know why?"

Mike's silence gave her permission to go on.

"Because a bunch of years ago people from one village came in and shot up the village Greg came from. They killed a whole bunch of people over God knew what. Now every apartment has a steel door, every person – even the kids – have guns and weapons. We went to one of his relative's houses and they had a whole room with nothing but guns. I saw little kids coming out of school playing with brass knuckles. What kind of people let kids have that kind of stuff? What kind of people shoot each other up for no reason?"

The eyes that looked at Mike Montoya were big and round and, for the first time, honest. She turned away and gazed out the French doors, seeming to look beyond her beautiful yard, the pool, and the tennis court. She was seeing a village overseas in a place that she couldn't even imagine existed until Greg Oi took her there.

"It made me sick, and I felt selfish. I couldn't even guess at how it affected Greg. Men from there are so different. There were secrets in that country and they weren't good. I could never understand even if I spoke their language. I was happy to come back here. Greg? He never left it behind. He thought he was the Godfather. He had a big heart and he brought young people to

America so they could make a better life." She turned her eyes back to Mike. "That's what he did, didn't he? They did have a better life, right?"

Mike didn't want to point out that Rosa's could have been better.

"What do you think happened to your husband?"

Kat blinked. A tear rolled out of one eye. She wasn't tough. She wasn't even a bitch. She was scared and the big man who had stood between her and the world was gone.

"I don't know," she whispered. "And I don't want to know about these girls. If they ended up dancing in some strip joint, then Greg still did a good thing. It was better than where they'd been. I believe that. I know that."

Kat Oi ran out of steam. She collapsed on the sofa, and put her hands on her knees. Her head hung low, her jewelry sparkled in the light coming through the windows. When she sat up, her face had changed. She pushed herself up, and went into the next room. She came back with a picture.

"I found this when I was going through his things." She handed the picture to Mike. "I found a picture of Greg standing outside of a farmhouse, and I found that. That's a picture of the old man who came here with Sam Lumina that night. I'd swear it. I know he's a lot younger, but I'd swear it's him. I think they were friends then."

Mike kept his eyes lowered. There was no doubt. This was a picture of Gjergy Isai as a much younger man. Greg Oi stood by his side, both looking like poor imitations of superman with their chests thrown out and their fists planted on their hips. Kat was back on the sofa.

"And the way you found Greg dressed?" Kat went on. "Those were his comfort clothes. When he was upset, he got all dolled up. I guess the fact that he dressed like that with me meant he really trusted me. I thought it meant he loved me. But if he was dressed like a girl in that woman's house, maybe that meant he loved her, too? Do you think that's what it meant? That he loved her, and I was second choice?"

Mike took the photograph and left Kat to her thoughts. Wendy stood in the doorway. She gave him a nod and held up two plastic bags. He excused himself and went to her.

"A ledger." She held up the large bag. "Looks like he indentured them for a couple years and then knocked 'em off the books. He got a nice chunk of change up front from the families. The girls end up nannies, housemaids, bar maids that kind of thing. Looks like there are some men who bought off the women's det. Maybe this was kind of like a mail order bride set-up."

"Anyone of interest in there?" Mike asked.

"Actually, there's a name that is missing. Rosa isn't there. But I've got this." She held up the smaller bag. "I found them in a trick drawer in the desk."

"Wall safes, trick drawers. Oi wasn't a trusting man."

Wendy held out passports for Rosafa Zogaj and Besnik Zogaj. "If Rosa was emancipated from his little scheme, he was still holding her hostage."

Wendy opened the bag, retrieved the two documents. She opened the first. Mike looked at a picture of a lovely, childlike Rosa Zuni. Wendy opened the second one and showed him a picture of a little boy, tow headed, bright-eyed boy they knew as Billy Zuni.

CHAPTER 25

Sam Lumina's wife thought she was going to throw up. Or faint. Or throw up and then faint which would be the worst. What would have made it totally worse would be that she did it in front of the lady across the desk. She was gorgeous, but she also had a way about her that made Mary feel that everything was going to be okay. It was like she really wanted to help.

"Are you sure you don't want a cup of coffee or a glass of water?"

"No. That's okay. Thanks."

Wendy Sterling smiled and waited. And waited while the woman across from her fidgeted and held onto her purse like it was going to explode if she let it go.

"Look," Mary said, "I don't even know if I'm doing the right thing, but I think I am."

"Then you probably are. Maybe we could just start at the beginning. Is there something specific that brought you here?"

"It's the thing that happened in Hermosa. You know, the two guys who died?" Mary whispered.

"Yes. And the woman," Wendy said.

"She died, too?"

"She's critical," Wendy answered. "Did you know her?"

Mary shook her head," No, I don't know her."

"Did you know the men?" Wendy asked.

"I knew Jac Duka. I'm good friends with his wife, Sharon. My boy plays with hers."

"I'm so sorry," Wendy commiserated.

"And, well, Mr. Oi. My husband works at Marshall Fasteners, but I don't know him personally. I mean I didn't know him. I never spoke to him, that is." The woman fidgeted. That was a good sign. Wendy could work with nervous; belligerent was a different matter.

"Okay." Wendy smiled her woman smile, which was quite different from the klieg light smile she used on men sitting across the desk from her.

"So would you like to talk about Jak Duka? I mean, since you knew him."

"Oh, God!" she finally broke down. "I don't know what I want to talk about. You see there's this guy who's been staying with us. This old man. He's like really weird, and he's some relative of my husband's, and I think he had something to do with all this. No, I know he did. He is so scary, and he hated Greg Oi. I heard him talking about him."

"What exactly did he say?" Wendy leaned closer, lowering her voice, signaling she was ready for any confidence this woman had to share. If she decided to play hardball, Wendy would deal with that later.

"Well, I don't really know. I just know I would hear him talking about Mr. Oi. It was the way he talked about him. He didn't speak English when he was talking about him, so I don't know exactly what he was saying but believe me, it wasn't good."

"What about the night of the murders?" Wendy prodded.

"He was out. He came in late and then all these old guys came into my house. It was like the movies, you know?" Mary's eyes widened and her words got breathy.

"Was your husband with his uncle?"

Mary's brow pulled together as if surprised by the stupidity of that question.

"Well, sure, he had to drive him around. But it's the old guy, he's the one. I have proof."

Wendy's pulse quickened. She had two quick thoughts. First, she was amazed that this woman didn't put two and two together. If she had proof that Gjergy Isai was responsible for the deaths of Oi and Duka, and she admitted her husband was with the old man, then that made her husband complicit. The second thought was much simpler. She was thinking about what Mary Lumina might possibly have brought her.

"I'll be happy to look at whatever you have, naturally," she said.

It was like the heavens opened up and gave Mary permission to unburden herself. She plopped her purse on Wendy's desk. Clearly there was more in that purse than lip gloss by the hollow sound it made when it hit. Mary Lumina opened it up and withdrew a cloth bag. She put it on the desk and slid it toward Wendy.

"I found this in our house. It was hidden," she whispered. "You test it. I know what you're going to find. You're going to find that old man's fingerprints on it."

Wendy slid the bag across the desk. Her pulse was beating so fast she was almost sure her watch was going to jump right off her wrist. The bag was old and soft and she didn't have to open it to know what was inside. She looked anyway.

"You've brought me a gun, Mrs. Lumina."

Mary lowered her voice even further. "We don't own a gun. It belongs to the old man. You test it. It's the gun that killed Jac and Mr. Oi. I'm telling you, it's the old man who did it."

"You're very brave to bring it here," Wendy assured her.

"I just want him out of my house," she insisted, emboldened by Wendy's praise. "I want him out of my life. I'm afraid for my husband and my child. I don't mind telling you, I'm afraid of him. He doesn't like women. I don't know what his beef was with any of those people, but he is scary."

"I'll get this to the lab right away. We'll check ballistics. We'll look for a serial number, but, Mrs. Lumina, we're not going to be able to tell if he pulled the trigger. We can't finger print him without cause."

"I thought of that. He has no idea who he's dealing with. That old goat never cleans up anything. I brought you this." She dug into her purse and came up with a shot glass. "Test that. I can swear in court that was the glass he used. And I guarantee you, those are the fingerprints you're going to find on that gun."

***

Rita Potter had her papers, pens, and briefcase set out precisely on the table in front of her. A woman Josie presumed to be a CPS caseworker sat with her, portfolio in her lap, staring straight ahead, lost in thoughts that did not seem to be unpleasant. A gentleman sporting a ponytail and a jacket a size too big for him blinked behind rimless glasses as he reviewed notes that appeared to befuddle him. Mike Montoya was behind county counsel and to the right. Judge Healy's clerk answered a telephone call, laughed and hung up. A court reporter was set and ready for testimony. The two people Josie most hoped to see – Sam Lumina and Gjergy Isai - were there, also.

Sam pulled a thread on his jacket, and the button popped off. The courtroom was so quiet everyone heard the curse he muttered and the clatter as his button fell. He went after it. Gjergy watched with little interest. Then Josie saw a slight tic in the older man's jaw. He knew she was there, but when he faced forward without acknowledging her, Josie walked down the aisle and took a seat on the bench in front of them. Sam was up, noticed her, and scowled. She spoke to Gjergy.

"Thank you for coming," she said.

"Will the judge give me Besnik?" Gjergy asked.

"Not today. I'm hoping he'll allow you to speak. Anything you can offer as proof of your relationship with Rosa and Billy will be helpful."

"I have my word," Gjergy answered and Josie resisted the urge to point out that no court of law took anyone at their word.

"Until we can get proof, then, I'll just ask you to speak to the association we are trying to establish." Josie took a deep breath. "But you understand, the judge might now allow this."

"What's going to happen to the kid if you can't get him to see it our way?" Sam asked.

Josie held her tongue. She disliked this man so much she wished she only had to deal with Gjergy. At least he was focused on Billy.

"He could go to foster parents - people who will look after him until the criminal matter is resolved," she explained for Gjergy's benefit. Josie had no doubt Sam Lumina knew the options. "A lot will depend on Rosa."

"Rosafa," Gjergy corrected.

"Yes. Rosafa. Hopefully, she'll be able to identify you soon. Then the judge might allow temporary custody to transfer to you. At that point, you and Rosafa will deal with immigration and social services."

"It's complicated." Gjergy sounded like he was mocking her.

"We'll take one step at a time. I'll help as much as I can," Josie assured him.

"In my country the law is clear."

Josie smiled. What was there to say? He came from a country where the law was whatever the top guy said it was. Josie stood up, but Gjergy had one more question.

"The policeman. He wishes to talk to me again. Is it your law that I must speak with him?"

Josie glanced at Montoya. He was watching them. She turned back to Gjergy.

"You don't have to, but I would advise it. I can be with you when you talk to Detective Montoya."

"We shall see what the judge says," Gjergy decided.

Josie sidestepped back to the center aisle, pushed through the bar, handed a sheaf of papers to the clerk. He immediately rose and disappeared into the judge's chamber while Josie took her place at the defense table. Unable to help herself, she stole a glance at Montoya. She cocked her head. He nodded politely. She turned away just as the judge entered the courtroom. Everyone rose and the clerk called:

"Department 10 is now in session. The honorable M. Jason Healey presiding. Please be seated."

"Morning everyone," Judge Healy said.

The greeting of those in attendance was a hash of morning and judge and Your Honor spoken in various tones and inflections. It was a harmony that Josie loved and had since the first time she entered a courtroom. When they were once again seated, Healy opened Billy's case file, and laid it out.

"You are all here, and, I am assuming, ready to proceed with the fitness hearing of the minor, Billy Zuni." The judge sat back. His chair bounced a little as he settled in. "I understand Mr. Zuni will be released from the hospital day after tomorrow. That means a decision today is imperative. If anyone has additional information regarding Mr. Zuni's physical condition, speak up now or forever hold your peace."

"Your Honor." Josie stood. "I would like to bring to the court's attention that a relative has been located. I would like to read his name into the record and call him as a witness if it please the court."

"Why was he not made available sooner?"

"He is in the United States as a visitor. It is a complicated situation which might better be discussed in chambers."

"In its own good time, Ms. Bates. Let's start where we left off, and then we'll consider new information. Ms. Potter, it's your show. Let's get to it."

Doctor Hardy was called to the stand. As he passed, Josie noticed that his pants were a size too big, yet he seemed perfectly comfortable in his clothes. He raised his hand, blinked in cadence with the swearing in, and was seated. Rita Potter dispensed with the pleasantries quickly and got to it.

Rita Potter: How did you find Billy Zuni during your examination?

Dr. Hardy: He was lucid, fully aware of who I was and why I was there. He could walk albeit with some pain and unsteadiness. He is no longer on morphine and is clear-headed.

Rita Potter: What were your initial impressions?

Dr. Hardy: Billy is a mentally healthy seventeen-year-old boy who was able to answer my questions, at times reluctantly. He was inordinately gratuitous and pleasant, almost childlike at times. I do not believe that he is mentally deficient or suffering any mental illness, but he was evasive regarding his family.

Rita Potter: Did Billy confirm that Rosa Zuni was his mother?

Dr. Hardy: His answers were always an affirmation of a close mother/son relationship. He easily slipped between calling her his mother and using her given name.

Rita Potter: Did this concern you?

Dr. Hardy: Not particularly. If a child has been put in a confusing position regarding family affiliations, he or she will default to the easiest, simplest relationship.

Rita Potter: Examples?

Doctor Hardy: Children who, through no fault of their own, find themselves in an ever-changing familial landscape exhibit this behavior. If there are multiple marriages, the child might default to calling a stepparent mother or father because it is embarrassing or difficult to explain what happened to the biological parent. Consider also children of abuse who are forced to refer to a person – family member or not – in a certain way. An abducted child might use a family reference to ease the horror of his or her situation or be instructed to do so in order that the abductor not be found out. In the latter case, such behavior may protect the biological family that has also been threatened.

Rita Potter: Where might Billy fall into this spectrum?

Doctor Potter: It is impossible to say. Two things stand out in my mind. He is overly cautious about not rocking the boat he perceives himself to be in, and he is a very intelligent young man who does not wear that intelligence on his sleeve.

Rita Potter: Do you believe him capable of committing violence upon a person?

Doctor Hardy: I can't answer that. I had limited time with Billy. He appears good-natured and talkative, yet says very little of a personal nature. He continually apologized for causing problems. He is well scripted. It appears to me that Billy Zuni has created extreme parameters for himself.

Rita Potter: Is that an unusual thing for a teenager to do?

Doctor Hardy: No. A seventeen-year-old boy is very adept at this. He might be swaggering on the campus of his high school, and yet be solicitous as he sits at a table with his grandparents. Billy expertly negotiated the conversation especially where Rosa Zuni was involved. This does raise a red flag if it is behavior considered along with other circumstances."

Rita Potter: What are parameters?

Doctor Hardy: He has severe separation anxiety. Rosa's safety is equated with his safety. He would do anything to keep that status quo.

Rita Potter: Could something have disturbed this delicate balance enough for him to become violent? Say, the attention of men that Billy perceived might change the relationship between Rosa and himself?

Doctor Hardy: Speaking in the abstract, yes. Drug use could bring on the type of violence that was visited on Rosa Zuni. We might even consider something like parasomnias. That could explain-"

"Your Honor," Josie interrupted without rising, throwing off the rhythm of Rita Potter and her witness.

"Ms. Bates?" Judge Healy recognized her.

"Doctor Hardy is talking about sleepwalking as a possible explanation for criminal behavior that hasn't been established. I don't understand why we are taking that tangent?"

"I only wanted to cover all bases, judge," Rita said. "The choices before you range from incarceration to family placement. State of mind, and possibly disposition to violence, should be taken into consideration."

"Agreed," Josie countered. "However, I have reported to both the investigating officer and the court that we now have a witness who clearly documents the timeline on the night in question. Billy was at the beach during the time of the assault, he did not test positive for drugs, and he has no known problem with parasomnias"

"Can we move on from this testimony, Ms. Potter?"

"Your Honor, I do think Doctor Hardy's testimony needs to be considered. No reasonable person walks into a raging ocean, nor does a reasonable person assault another so viciously."

"Your Honor, please," Josie objected. "Two grown men were killed and Rosa Zuni's attack took time that Billy could not possibly have had."

"But, judge," Rita pleaded. "I am not including the two murder victims in the scope. We are only concerned with facts in evidence including Billy's behavior. Even if we disregard the knife, he admits to leaving the scene where the woman was near death. If he does have these sleep problems, this is something the people who will eventually be charged with his care need to know. Further testing is imperative before he is released from the hospital."

"Point taken, Ms. Potter." Healy made some notes. "Doctor Hardy, how long would these tests take?"

"A day. Possibly two," he answered. "I believe Billy's history is well documented. I would like to explore not only the psychology but the physiological aspects of sleep deprivation, erratic eating, familial rejection, etc."

"The court appreciates your thoroughness, Doctor Hardy."

He was dismissed and Mike Montoya was called and dutifully sworn. "Detective Montoya," Ms. Potter began. "Your investigation is ongoing, but in the matter at hand, the disposition of Billy Zuni, I would like to ask you directly if you are going to be charging him with the murder of Greg Oi or Jac Duka."

"No, we are not at this time."

"Will you be charging him with the assault on Rosa Zuni."

"The District Attorney has not filed charges, but Billy Zuni has been read his rights as a precaution."

"Detective," Rita asked, "What do you know about the relationship between Billy and Rosa Zuni?"

"We believe that Rosa is Billy Zuni's older sister. They are not U.S. citizens and may have been held here illegally by one of the murder victims, Greg Oi."

"In what capacity would he have held them?"

"We are still trying to sort that out," Mike began and then proceeded to fill the court in on, Kat Oi's story, the passports, the DVD, and his discussions with the federal strike force and immigration.

Judge Healy stopped bouncing in his high backed chair. Placement of Billy Zuni was no longer standard operating procedure, yet he looked concerned as he asked:

"Detective, are your federal contacts sufficiently motivated to fast-track their investigation?"

"Yes, Your Honor, but Albania does not have the information infrastructure we enjoy over here. I'm sure Mr. Isai could speak to this matter."

Judge Healy looked into the courtroom and then spoke to Josie.

"Ms. Bates, is that your witness?"

"It is, Your Honor."

The judge crooked a finger. Gjergy stood up.

"I will consider you sworn to tell the truth to this court. Is that understood?"

Gjergy nodded.

"Do you have any proof of the relationship between you and either Rosafa or Besnik Zogaj, also known as Rosa and Billy Zuni?"

"I do not, Honorable Judge," Gjergy answered. "I can say her mother is Teuta and her father is Flori. Her grandfather, my wife's cousin, was Yilli the goat herder. To this I swear."

"But you have no papers?" Healy insisted.

"No, Honorable."

"Thank you, sir. You may sit."

Gjergy did as he was told, but something in the judge's demeanor bothered Josie and she stood up.

"Your Honor, I would like to point out that the Albanian community in the South Bay is small and close knit. There is every possibility that they will open their arms to Billy."

"Do you have specific housing possibilities for Billy?"

"No," Josie admitted.

"Judge," Rita spoke up, annoyed with the turn this was taking. "We are off message. Someone foreign to the American culture is not a viable alternative to state placement. There is enough confusion as is."

"Agreed. Is Detective Montoya needed any longer?"

"Only one more question," Rita said.

"You posted a guard at Billy's hospital room. Are you concerned that Billy is a threat to himself or to Rosa Zuni?"

"No," Mike answered, "but I remain cautious."

"I'm done with this witness."

"Ms. Bates? Your turn."

Josie stood.

"This morning my investigator brought you a man who was with Billy Zuni on the night of the murders."

"My criminal analyst is working with him, but there are serious questions about his reliability."

"I am sure you'll find everything in order," Josie said. "His story can be corroborated by two other witnesses who saw Billy that night."

"Ms. Potter?" Judge Healey called on the county counsel and motioned Josie down.

"One last witness, Your Honor. If Mrs. Anderson would take the stand."

The woman who had been waiting took the stand and offered testimony on available placements for Billy: two private homes in the far reaches of the county, one group placement home for probationers from California Youth Authority and, naturally, space in juvenile lock-up in county jail.

"Ms. Bates? Do you have alternatives?"

"Outside of the possible association with Mr. Isai, I have a confirmed placement in Hermosa Beach with a local restaurant owner, Burt Hunter. He has firsthand knowledge of aftercare and is a friend of Billy's. I've outlined this offer in the papers provided to you."

"Anything else?"

Judge Healy looked from one counsel to the other. When they didn't respond he said:

"Thank you, both. This is a complicated matter that this court will attempt to uncomplicate. Detective Montoya? Do you have the DVD you spoke of?"

"I do have a copy, Your Honor."

He handed it to the clerk who had come to the bar, he in turn handed it to the judge, who then called a recess. Mike Montoya left the courtroom as did Mrs. Anderson. Doctor Hardy remained at Rita Potter's request. While they talked quietly, Josie stared at the great seal above the bench and the relief of Minerva, the goddess of wisdom, hewn into it. Hopefully Minerva was sitting on Healy's shoulder because she had sure deserted Josie. If Josie Bates was the judge, she had no idea what she would do with Billy Zuni.

CHAPTER 26

Seven days a week, seemingly twenty-four hours a day, Ante Fistonich could be found in his restaurant aptly named Ante's. The place had been in San Pedro almost fifty years serving up grilled meat and cabbage soup. Somehow the man had convinced the city of San Pedro to name the street outside the restaurant Ante Avenue. More than once Archer had sought him out during an investigation that called for someone who knew something about everyone within a twenty-mile radius of his place. Archer gave the man a 7.5 on the scale of ten for trustworthy information. In his book, that was pretty darn good for a guy who didn't want to burn bridges and who didn't owe Archer anything.

Archer opened the heavy wooden door and walked from the gloom outside into the cave that was Ante's place. Though he couldn't see the man's eyes, he could feel them as he made his way past the ox-blood upholstered booths and cracked veneered tables. Photographs of Ante with various people who grinned like celebrities lined the walls, but all were unrecognizable as such. The ceiling was covered in popcorn plaster. Archer found the man himself in the back booth, the one that had a great view of the front door but was set an angle that kept him out of sight until you were almost in his lap.

"Ante. When are you going to remodel this place?" Archer hailed him and waited for a response.

Archer waited. Seconds of silence passed. Ante was convinced this affectation put the fear of God into people. Archer thought he had just seen too many Humphrey Bogart movies when he was learning how to speak English. Finally, the man's hand rose and a finger pointed heavenward.

"See that? See that?" Archer raised his eyes even though he knew the conversation they were about to have by heart. "That ceiling. The city will tell me it is asbestos. They will make me pay their corrupt inspectors because they will say the ceiling is poison and that I must have more inspectors just to tell me what I already know. It is not asbestos. Do you see anyone sick? I sit here every day and all night, and I am not sick. You see any of my customers sick?"

Archer looked around. Two booths out of twenty had someone in them. Three waitresses who had been there since the day the place opened lounged by the front door. Somewhere in the back there was a cook who probably smoked while he stirred his pots and roasted his meat.

"How would you know if they were sick or not, Ante? If they don't come back they might be sick? Maybe they died because of that ceiling."

Ante dropped his hand and chuckled. The ceiling was of no consequence. He would never pay anybody money when he did not have to, and he liked the place the way it was.

"My customers always come back, and if they don't it is because of the food. That stinking cook sometimes makes bad food. I miss the old cook. He was good, but he didn't like America." Ante picked up his demitasse cup and lowered his head to put his lips on the rim. Before he did, he said: "Sit. Sit. At least look like you are here to eat and not torture me."

Archer slid into the booth across from Ante. It was the same conversation they had each time they saw one another. The old cook had been gone for twenty-five years. Archer couldn't tell the difference between the old cook's skill and the new. Cabbage was cabbage, the grilled meat exceptional, and the salad never tasted the same way twice even though it was nothing more than iceberg lettuce and bottled dressing.

"I don't think your brother would like to hear you say that. He's been cooking for you since the last one took off."

"Bah," Ante waved that away. "He does his best. He is my brother. He's okay. So, why are you here? It has been too long, my friend. We used to see you more often."

"I used to work for the police. I'm retired now. I'm getting married."

The old man lifted his heavy head. His brow was as wide as his jaw, his jaw as wide as his neck. If you didn't know Ante Fistonich, you would think he looked fearsome. Then again, most old men looked fearsome. It was because all the terror they had known in their life slowly bubbled up from inside and settled in the wrinkles and lines of their face like sediment. Archer understood. That was why he was not afraid of Ante Fistonich. Now the old man looked Archer up and down to see what could be told by the younger man's expression.

"You are happy. It's good to find a woman when you have years on you. Tell me, is she young?"

"She's a woman," Archer answered.

"Ah, she's old," Ante chuckled. "You should find a young girl. They will take care of you in your old age."

"When I'm old I'll get rid of this one and find a young one," Archer assured him, and Ante laughed all the harder.

He lowered his head again, hanging it between fleshy shoulders, resting his chin on a barrel chest. His cotton shirt was so thin Archer could see the ribbed wife-beater beneath it and the edge of a tattoo peeking out from under the short sleeves. Around his fleshy neck was a gold chain. On the man's left wrist was a gold bracelet and on his finger a gold ring. Like an Indian bride, he wore his wealth, not trusting anyone with his money. Word on the street was that Ante had been some kind of hero when the Croats and Serbs went at it. It was a story Archer didn't doubt. Ante never spoke of it, so Archer didn't either.

"You look worried, my friend," Ante said though Archer would be hard pressed to know how he came to that conclusion.

"I am curious, Ante. I have a friend with a problem."

"I know your problem." Ante raised his eyes again. "You have coffee while we sort it out."

Before Archer could say no, Ante motioned to one of the waitresses. A moment later a demitasse cup was in front of him. Turkish coffee wasn't his thing, it was like trying to drink mud out of a thimble, but he took a drink nonetheless.

"It's the blood in Hermosa Beach. That's bad business. Very bad."

"You're psychic, Ante."

"I am smart, Archer." Ante tapped the side of his nose. "I hear from the workers. Business is off because of the strike on Oi's place. So many of our good boys work for him. He should have given them what they asked. It wasn't much."

"Is it one of the good boys who killed him?" Archer turned the tiny cup a quarter turn but kept his eyes on his host.

Ante shook his head. "I don't think so. They come in. They drink. Some say it's a good thing Oi is dead. That is all talk."

"Who says that?"

"Sam says that. He's got a big mouth. Most are worried one of them killed the man. They don't like not knowing. They say every brother should know everything the other one does. I say that's bull. The smart man keeps his mouth shut." Ante raised his cup, sipped his coffee. "You want to eat?"

"No, not this time. Thanks."

"Is that your woman? The one in the house with you when you found Oi? Is that who speaks for this boy?"

"Yes. She'll be my wife," Archer said.

Ante sat back, "I don't know nothing about the boy. No one talks about him."

"What about the name Duca? Jac Duka?"

"Him, I don't know." The big, heavy head shook again.

"Can you put me on to any of the guys who come in here? Vouch for me so they'll talk?"

Ante barked a laugh and fingered the heavy gold at his neck.

"Do you think I'm God himself?" Ante smiled broadly as he spread his arms over the back of the booth. "They come here and drink and I hear talk, but they don't make no mistake. Those boys are Albanian. I'm Croatian. We got no problem with the Albanians, but they think they gotta fight everybody. Maybe they do. They got nothing to sell except themselves. They do anything for money and pride."

Archer nodded, understanding completely what Ante was alluding to. When his work brought him to Wilmington or San Pedro or anywhere the unions had hold, Archer ran into cultural clashes and always it was old country culture that won out. Even third generation men didn't leave it behind. They may like America and the opportunities it provided, but it was the motherland or the fatherland that held their hearts. Croats were the good guys, Serbs the devil and now he heard the Albanians were the backward stepchildren. It all depended on whom you spoke to.

"Albanians are the worst, you know what I mean? Croats, we move on. We take care of business. We don't hold nothing against nobody. Serbs, Albanians. All hard headed."

"That's why I came to you. You're a fair man, Ante. You're a respected businessman. You know everyone, Ante. I've got two big problems."

"Only two? You are blessed, Archer."

One of the waitresses came and brought fresh cups of coffee. Archer held up his hand. She shrugged and left only one cup for Ante.

"I am, Ante, but still these problems need to be solved. I've called a friend at the state department, but I believe that your influence will help me find the answers more quickly."

Ante pulled up his shoulders. His eyes closed. The palms of his hands rose slightly as if to say what Archer said was true thanks to God.

"First, what do you know about trafficking girls? Have you heard anything about that?"

"It happens," Ante shrugged. "Albanians have nothing to sell so they sell their people: men to Greece and Italy to do work no one else will do. Women and girls for sex and who knows what else."

"Does it happen here? Did you hear about Greg Oi trafficking?"

"I don't know about Oi, but I know I don't want to hear about the ones who do these things. That is bad business, and I don't want it down on my head. I can't help you, Archer."

"Can't or you won't?"

"Same difference." Ante blew him off. "Even if you were my no-good brother and it was his daughter I wouldn't stick my neck out."

"Can you at least give me a name, someone I can talk to in the Albanian community?"

"Why would I want you to do that? I like you. You gotta watch your back every second with them." Ante pulled his bottom lip up and shook his head so that his jowls quivered. "They don't care if your woman is Mother Theresa. They can make a buck with her, they will. These girls are nothing. What else got you worried?"

"I've got a guy who showed up claiming he's related to the victim and the boy. His name is Gjergy Isai. I also have something that looks like a marriage certificate between Oi and the girl that got stabbed."

"Why doesn't she tell you all this?" Ante raised a bushy brow. His reluctance to get involved was starting to make Archer nervous. He had thought they were chasing ghosts, but now he wondered if they had a tiger by the tail.

"Nobody knows if she'll live, Ante. Her name's Rosafa Zogaj, but she goes by Rosa Zuni. She works at a strip joint called Undies." Ante raised a brow. "We're thinking that maybe Oi put her there, sold her. What we can't figure out is why he would let her bring a kid along and why the marriage certificate?"

Archer took a deep breath. Saying this all out loud made him realize just how crazy it all sounded, yet one look at Ante and he realized it wasn't crazy at all. The man listened, his brow beetled, taking in every word as if it were a story that didn't surprise him.

"I'm sorry," Archer went on. "It's all complicated. All I really want to do is keep the boy close to home. My woman thinks the judge is going to put him in a group home, and we all know it's better to be with family. If I had some proof that this guy, Gjergy, is related to Rosa then we might have options with the court."

"Is this a good boy?"

"Billy is a very good boy," Archer assured him.

"The cops want this information, too, heh?" Ante asked.

"They do. I won't lie."

"If I get it to you that's it. I don't want the cops coming at me." Ante wagged a thick finger at Archer.

"You got my word," Archer promised.

"Where are you looking to find out about Gjergy Isai? What town? North or South Albania?" Ante pressed.

"North. A place called Bajram Curri. Do you know it?"

Ante nodded. "Yes, my friend, but do not ever try to say it that way if you are in Albania. I know someone who drives a furgon from Kosovo. Bajram Curri is hardly of any consequence except that the President of all Albania is from Tropojë District. That is where Bajram Curri is."

Ante faded into the corner of the booth, picked up his phone, and punched in a lot of numbers. The man spoke low despite the fact he wasn't speaking English and Archer wouldn't understand a word. There was a glint of gold when he leaned forward to ask Archer for the phone number he was given at Undies as well as Archer's own cell number. Archer gave them; Ante repeated them. Archer heard the name Gjergy Isai, Greg Oi, and Rosafa Zogaj passed off before Ante offered profuse thanks and prayers to God. He reiterated the name Zogaj. The phone was back on the table, and Ante was talking to Archer again.

"My friend will call you. He will ask in Barjam Curri to see if that's where Oi was from, and if that's where this girl comes from. He will find what you need if he can."

"Thanks, Ante. I need the information sooner than later. "Archer put the contact's name into his phone and reached across the table to shake Ante's hand.

"Sometimes God wills what is best for us and we do not appreciate that."

"I'll just have to hope that God's on top of this one, then."

Ante was laughing as Archer left the restaurant and stepped out onto the street. Though the day was gloomy, he was nearly blinded by the light. That's how dark Ante's place had been.

He dialed Faye.

"Hey, it's me. Have you heard from Josie?"

Faye told him she hadn't then asked, "We're still on for tonight, right?"

"We are," Archer said, hoping he and Faye weren't making the right call. "See you tonight."

He pocketed his phone when he opened the car door and saw the book he had taken from Billy's backpack. He grabbed it and went back to Ante.

"One last thing," Archer said. "Do you know what this is? Or someone who can translate it?"

Ante put his hand out and touched the worn book reverently.

"No need to translate, my friend. That is the Kunan. That is the holy book. The book of rules. That is the law."

***

Judge Gayle Lynds, presiding judge of family court, had a penchant for chocolate covered almonds. Knowing that she could not be trusted to be moderate, she never kept a bowl on her desk. Instead, she put a bowl in the clerk's office down the hall which forced her to get up, think about what she was doing, and decide if she really should have a handful of chocolate covered almonds. The answer, after minimal consideration, was always yes. That meant at a specific time each morning and afternoon she would head to the clerk's office for a candy fix.

To get there, she passed three chambers, one of which was that of Judge Christopher Healy. Although he had not specifically thought to corral her on her quest for candy, he was happy to see her and motioned her in. Actually, happy was the wrong word. Grateful might have been a more appropriate adjective.

"Come here. I want you to take a look at this."

Judge Healy replayed the Montoya's DVD of Rosa and Billy. He did so twice. Gayle raised a shoulder.

"I've seen worse. We both have." She pulled up a chair. "What's got your judicial panties in a knot?"

Healy tossed the remote onto his desk. "That's the kid involved in the Hermosa Beach thing. I'm trying to decide what to do with him. Newton wants him in county jail even though he hasn't been charged, county counsel wants him with a family even though we're not sure if he's violent."

"Did you have a workup done?" Gayle asked.

"Yeah. Inconclusive."

"If you're thinking that tape is reason to incarcerate him, I'd think again. That's a little boy going after someone with little boy fists. Get a current tape that shows the big boy in all his teenage glory doing the same thing and you might have cause to put him away."

Gayle waited. She wanted her chocolate covered almonds, but she was presiding judge. If one of her judge's had a problem it was her problem. Finally, Christopher Healy told her what was really bothering him.

"We've got the feds, we've got the D.A., we've got an immigrant community, immigration and naturalization services. Christ, every damn agency's kitchen sink is thrown in to this thing. If I make the wrong call and that kid is violent, I'm going to take it on the chin if I place him in a low security situation; if he's not and something happens to him in lock-up, I'm in trouble with the watchdog groups. I'm too close to retirement to have any controversy now."

Gayle nodded. She bit her lower lip. Healy was right. He was between a rock and a hard place.

"We all know we try to do what's best for each case, but sometimes circumstances narrow our options. Look," she said, adjusting her expression into one of sincere regret that her counsel had to be of the practical sort. "I know you're a good guy. We're all good guys, but let's get real. It's just one kid and he's old enough to watch his butt. We can't save 'em all, Chris. That's just the goal, not the reality. I wouldn't agonize over this."

"I guess," he agreed.

"So, if we concur on that point, then we have to ask ourselves, what is the prime objective?"

Chris looked at her, waiting to be told what the prime objective was.

"The prime objective is not to end up with any more dead bodies, right? And, to mitigate the circumstances under which a dead body might appear. Concurrently, one must protect an excellent judicial career. If something goes wrong, the public must see that you have given weight to all options in terms of protecting both the kid and the public, erring on the side of protecting the public. Greater good and all that." She waved a well-manicured hand. "If there is one chance in hell that kid is a killer, you've got to put him where there's the least chance he can cause anymore problems while keeping him safe until the cops and the D.A. get their act together."

"That's the point, Gayle. Where?"

"Oh Chris. Chris," she chuckled. "It's so obvious?"

Healy was feeling like a dolt. He looked at her again. Looked hard. It took about thirty seconds for the light to dawn. When it did, Chris Healy knew what he had to do. On top of that, it was a decision he could live with.

When she left, Gayle Lynds figured she had earned her chocolate covered almonds: Chris Healy was pleased, county counsel would be pleased, the public would be pleased. The only one who might not be so happy was the kid, but that's why judges got the big bucks. They had to make the tough calls.

***

Just as Judge Healy was walking back into the courtroom, Wendy Sterling was tooling toward Mike Montoya's desk. Just as Judge Healy was about to deliver a ruling that would surprise everyone in the courtroom, Wendy Sterling was about to deliver news that really surprised no one once they thought about it.

"Mike. I've got the registration on the gun."

Mike stood up and went to the white board. He wouldn't choose the color of marker to use until she gave him the news.

"It belonged to Oi."

Mike picked up the green marker and wrote GUN with an arrow back to Oi's name.

"He couldn't shoot himself in the back." Mike turned toward Wendy. Her grin broadened. "I've got the lab on it. Stand by."

She turned on her heel but before she was more than a few steps away, Mike called after her.

"Good work, Wendy."

"Thanks, Montoya."

CHAPTER 27

"Are you about ready?"

Josie knocked on Hannah's bedroom door, heard an affirmative, and figured that meant five more minutes. Josie waited on the patio with Max, arms crossed, as much for warmth as reassurance. She was still shaken by Judge Healy's ruling. The only saving grace was that Rita Potter had agreed Josie could tell Billy in the morning – which meant she'd have to tell Hannah tonight.

"I'm ready."

Josie turned. Hannah was standing on the patio looking like she belonged on Fifth Avenue instead of in Hermosa Beach. The front of her hair was braided and wrapped turban-like over the crown of her head while the rest of it fell almost to her waist in a cascade of curls and kinks. Chandelier earrings with stones the color of her eyes skimmed her shoulders. An oversized turtleneck framed her face and the winter white wool offset her dark skin. Her leggings and boots were tar black and shiny.

"I should have dressed up." Josie looked down at her jeans, her cowboy boots, and her purple sweater that covered her to the fingertips

"Archer won't kick you out of bed for eating crackers," Hannah said as she walked to the gate while Josie put the dog inside and locked the door.

"Sometimes you could just pretend to be a kid," Josie said.

"Compared to what most say, that was pretty mild," Hannah answered as they started to walk.

Heavy clouds hung over the shore and the surf was kicking up. Josie's hair ruffled in the wind and Hannah's swirled over her shoulders and back again.

"It feels like a storm is coming again. But it won't be as bad as the last one." Josie stuck her hands into her pockets while she made small talk.

"Nothing could be as bad as the last one."

Hannah made small talk, too, knowing that what happened in court wasn't good. Josie had come home and immediately taken Max off without bothering to check on her. When she didn't come back right away, Hannah ventured out and saw Josie standing at the end of the street, keeping watch as if hoping something good would sail in from the horizon. Now, walking with Josie, Hannah knew there was no ship coming in.

"Billy's going to be placed, isn't he?" Hannah asked.

"I was going to tell you over dinner."

"Is he at least going with a family?"

"No," Josie answered.

Hannah stopped walking. Josie turned to face her. They were in front of one of the original beach houses. It was painted green, and a fisherman's net full of dried starfish was hung from the patio wall. Three surfboards were propped in one corner. Inside, a man was fixing dinner while a big screen TV flickered and flashed. He had long ago stopped worrying about who might be looking in. A handful of people ran and biked on the path. In the distance they could hear music from Hennessy's. Billy should have been with them on a night like this. That's what Josie was thinking when she faced Hannah.

"He's going to jail," Hannah whispered.

Josie shook her head. "The judge ordered him held on psychiatric watch."

Hannah whispered: "Where?"

"County."

"That's a criminal psyche hold."

"I'm sorry." Josie turned and started to walk. Hannah came along side of her and touched her arm.

One...

Three...

Five....

Then she took Josie's sweater in her fingertips and drew close.

"He's not crazy, Josie."

"I know." Josie's hand covered Hannah's. "The judge didn't want to take any chances."

"It's because he thinks Billy hurt Rosa. That's it, isn't it? The judge doesn't want to be the one to let him free, just in case."

"That's part of it. But it's not jail, Hannah. It could have been jail."

"It's worse," she muttered, letting go of Josie. "So what happens now?"

"We wait. We see. It's a safe place."

"Safe for who?" Hannah snapped.

"Everyone. Even Billy," Josie assured her.

"Does he know yet?"

Josie shook her head. "I'm going to tell him in the morning. I don't think you should see him. It will just make things harder."

"How could it be any harder?" she demanded.

"It couldn't," Josie admitted. "I am so sorry. This ruling came out of left field. But he's a minor. All the records will be sealed. This isn't going to affect his future."

"He'll know someone thought he was crazy," Hannah muttered.

"He'll get over it."

"The way I got over people thinking I'm a murderer?" Hannah challenged.

"I can't help what people think, and I can only do my best."

Josie blessed the dark. She didn't want Hannah to see that she was ashamed she had failed Billy. She walked on, wishing she hadn't promised to meet Archer for dinner. Then again, a down hour or two might be the best for all of them.

Josie hadn't gone more than three feet when she felt Hannah's hand again. This time she wasn't touching or pulling; this time her arm laced through Josie's.

"It will be okay," Hannah assured her. Josie nodded, reached for the door, and opened it.

"We won't stay long. We can talk when we get ho-"

"Surprise!"

Josie stopped so suddenly that Hannah ran into her. Fifty people grinned at them, laughed, and waved at Josie. The ceiling was strung with white crepe paper and gold colored cardboard stars and wedding rings. Faye was clapping hardest of all, calling out her congratulations. Archer stood beside her but broke away to take Josie in his arms.

"We thought you'd never get here, babe." He held her close and whispered in her ear. "Faye's been planning this forever. You okay with it?"

Cheek to cheek, he felt her nod and when he held her away he saw that her eyes glistened. The last few days had been hard on her, but this minute the hardship was forgotten.

"A bridal shower? Really?"

Archer nodded. It was so un-Josie and yet ...

And yet it wasn't.

She pulled him with her as she waded into the crowd, accepting congratulations, leaning down to hug the old lady who ran the hat store, giving a kiss to the mayor who was the worst volleyball player on the beach. She exclaimed over the table filled with gifts wrapped every which way from fancy gold paper to plastic shopping bags. On top of the pile was a volleyball inscribed with a Hawaiian wish for happiness and Josie and Archer's names. She picked it up, twirled it on one finger while the bartender worked furiously and servers laid a spread on the banquet table.

Billy was forgotten. Even Hannah was forgotten. This time belonged to Josie and Archer and that was just the way of the world. No human being could live forever in the shadowy land of worry or carry the burden of righteousness every waking moment – not even Josie.

"Hey, Hannah!" Burt limped her way with a glass in his hand. "You need to have something to toast with."

"Thanks." She took the plastic wine glass filled with pomegranate juice and sat on a stool near the bar. He swung up and sat beside her.

"You're not mad we didn't tell you, are you?"

"No."

"You are," Burt teased. "Don't be. Archer didn't know until yesterday because we had to ask him if he thought it was okay to go ahead without Billy."

"It's okay, really. Billy would have wanted you to. He was pretty excited about Archer and Josie getting married," Hannah said as her eyes followed Josie.

"How about you?" Burt gave her a nudge.

"Yeah, I'm happy."

Hannah meant it because she was in awe of what she was witnessing: soul mates, a true partnership, love, and respect. Despite all the people in it, the world really did revolve around those two people.

"Everyone needs someone who's there just for them." Burt put his elbows back on the bar and beamed. "Yep, that's what everyone needs. Know what I mean?"

"I do, Burt."

Hannah barely heard him wax poetic about love while she waited for Josie to look her way. When that finally happened, Josie's eyes sparked brighter, her smile widened, her chin lifted, and Hannah was warmed by the attention. She made a move to get off the barstool, but in the next second the tall woman bent down to hear yet another well-wisher's story. Josie threw her head back and laughed. She looked at Archer who was the center of his own group. Josie mouthed a 'thank you' to Faye, and the older woman mouthed back 'your welcome'. Then Josie Bates raised her hand to motion Hannah over to celebrate with them only to see that the barstool was empty.

Hannah was gone.

CHAPTER 28

2013

The *furgon* got a late start from Kosovo. Not that there was a schedule to meet since each small bus waited until it was filled before leaving. That morning there had only been three people wanting to make the journey into Albania, and the driver was not going to waste time on three people. But then, God be praised, so many rushed to his *furgon* that an hour later he had to find boxes to set in the aisle to make extra seats. The last to come was a young man. His hair was too long and his shoes too dirty, so the driver knew he was no *Shqiptare*. Praise God again, he could make this boy pay the foreign rate. It would be a good day.

But the boy spoke the old language. He was, he said, from the United States and he worked to bring peace to Albania - which was where he needed to go. The *furgon* driver was surprised. He had heard of these Americans who came and went. There was as much peace as there ever had been in Albania, so what more peace could a boy bring? But foreigners had strange ideas that mostly made no difference one way or another.

The boy sat on the box at the driver's feet for the long ride into Bajram Curri and they talked of many things because the boy was curious, and he spoke the language, and he understood the ways, and the driver was pleased to pass the time pleasantly. He asked the boy if he knew a man in America named Archer.

The boy said, no, America was a very large country. There might be millions of men with such a name.

"Me të vërtetë? Miliona?"

The boy shook his head, a sign that he agreed with the furgon driver's statement. He said again:

"Yes, millions."

The furgon driver considered this. Suddenly, he swerved, and the boy sitting on the box was thrown back into the old woman who held a chicken on the box behind him. There, in the middle of the road, a little car had stopped to let out a passenger. The furgon skidded on the stones that littered the road. The driver righted the little bus, the boy said soothing words to the woman and her chicken, and they began to speak again. The furgon driver said that in Albania there were many people with the same names also but not millions. The boy shook his head again, agreeing with this wisdom. Then the furgon driver asked if he knew of Gjergy Isai who, the driver believed, was from Bajram Curri, or a family named Zogaj who, perhaps, did not live there he believed. The boy did not, but he was bright and full of energy. He offered to ask around for such a man and for such a family.

The furgon driver smiled at this good boy. While he drove, he told him the story of how all the way in America, a high judge was waiting to hear about Gjergy Isai and the Zogaj family and the history of their clans. It was a most important thing, and all of the whole United States needed to know this information. When he stopped the furgon and the people got off to go to their homes and businesses, the sky already looked threatening and the furgon driver knew that much snow was coming. The boy was the last to leave the little bus, and the driver imparted the information of the phone number of the man named Archer should the boy come across news of Gjergy Isai or the Zogaj family. If the boy were to find such information, he would be a hero in his homeland. The furgon driver did not say that he, himself, preferred not to get out in the cold to inquire after these people even though he had promised to do so. Since the boy seemed not to be suspicious of this strange request, he said he would do what he could, and that he would tell the driver when next he saw him, and he would call the man named Archer and speak in English to him.

They said their goodbyes. The boy who was to bring peace threw his backpack over his shoulder and walked off, happy with whatever brought him to this place. In his cell phone was the number in America. The furgon driver called blessings to the good boy. He had done what had been asked of him as best he could. It was out of his hands. He would have coffee. He might have raki to warm himself, and he would wait until people came to fill up his furgon so he could drive back once more to Kosovo.

***

The old men sat in a circle in Sam Lumina's house. Mary had gone to see Jac Duka's widow. Sam wasn't happy that his wife spent so much time at Sharon's house because those visits were starting to make her jittery. Tonight, though, it was probably good that she had gone and taken Sammy with her. Sam poured drinks. His Albanian was good, but the language came so fast from the old men that sometimes it was hard to follow. Gjergy stayed mostly silent, listening to advice, to the thoughts of these old men who still understood the old ways but who also knew how America worked.

"I had a call from Ante," said a man so old his skin looked like parchment. "They have sent home to ask about you, Gjergy."

"And what will they find? That Gjergy is who he says he is?" another scoffed. "It is nothing. What is needed is a decision. The judge has made things very difficult. It is your honor, Gjergy, and that of your family. But you will not get the boy if there are jailers. You will not even be able to see him."

Gjergy nodded. He drank coffee from a small cup. Sam had made the thick coffee hoping for praise. Praise enough, he supposed, that Gjergy did not dislike it.

A man with a broad face said: "This is complicated Gjergy. Perhaps, you should go home. Perhaps, you should-"

"*Ndaluar. Ju flisni si një grua.*"

Gjergy's head swung toward the man. His small eyes glittered. He insulted the man by saying he talked like a woman, advising that Gjergy should go back home, runaway. That Gjergy whispered this insult was all the more injurious and the man colored, but he was right. Gjergy did not understand that this was America. Some things could not be accomplished in the way in which they should be accomplished.

"The girl will wake, and she will tell them about you and the boy and her. She will tell them about Oi," parchment man said.

Gjergy agreed. Indeed, she would tell them, and the judge would have to think on what to do, and that would take a long time. Gjergy would do his business and be gone before the judge decided what to do. Everyone in that room should have known that Gjergy was not afraid. These men had lived too long in this country where things came easily.

"Unë do të merrni djalë."

The decision was made. He, Gjergy, told them he would not return home this way. The girl was too sick and of no consequence any longer. He would take the boy. He almost laughed when he saw the look in the eyes of these old men. He, Gjergy, had never needed their counsel and asked for it only out of respect. He needed only Sam.

"We will go tomorrow. Sam and me. Then I will leave."

He saw Sam waver, but knew the younger man did not have the courage to defy him. Sam showed the others out and Gjergy went to his room, closed the door, packed his things, lay on his bed, and waited for the morning. Since he did not sleep, he thought about this country and tried to think what was wrong with it. Then it came to him.

These men had forgotten how to walk on stone.

***

Hannah sat on the little red stool, looking at the lacquer box. She had brought both these things from Fritz Rayburn's Malibu house and they reminded her of two things: the last place she had lived with her mother and the last time she had been afraid. Hannah unwound the braids and let her hair fall free. She gathered it up and pulled it over one shoulder and then buried her hands in her face. She was not despairing; she was simply exhausted by the ever-changing landscape of her life. Her heart was a hundred years old, and she knew what she had seen at Burt's. It was life moving on. How could she celebrate a beginning while Billy's life was ending?

It was wrong.

It was cruel.

It was undeserved.

The judge's ruling wasn't justice; it was ass covering at Billy's expense. Hannah put her hands on her knees and looked around her room: the closet with the louvered doors, the big bed covered with a purple cloth shot with gold threads from India, the dressing table that she had painted in the colors of the earth and sky and sea, the chair in the corner, the windows looking toward Hermosa Boulevard, and her easel.

She stood up and turned back the sheet that covered the canvas. It was time to finish. Hannah mixed the blues, laid the color, added white accents, the black outline, and was satisfied. The eyes were pools not to drown in but to float in and therein lay their magic. Peaceful eyes. Perfect eyes. The phone rang. She picked it up.

"We missed you," Josie said.

"I didn't feel like partying. It was a good surprise," Hannah answered.

Josie laughed, "Yes, it was. Faye says she's sorry she kept it a secret from you."

"That's alright. I'm used to-"

Hannah caught herself. Josie had been right at the hospital. The past wasn't an arsenal to be used against someone who had never attacked her. She said:

"It's cool."

"Hannah, I'm going to Archer's. Will you take Max out? Is that okay?"

"Yes," the girl said quietly.

"I'll be back early. I promise. We'll have breakfast before I go to the hospital."

"Don't worry, Josie. I'm fine. Really."

"Okay. I'll see you in the morning."

"Josie!" Hannah called her back, relieved when she was still there. Hannah said: "You won't worry, will you? I don't want you to worry."

"No, Hannah. I won't. Sleep well."

The line went dead. Hannah held her cell to her heart for a moment. She pulled in a deep breath, sat down at the dressing table, and wrote a note that she put on the easel. When she was done, Hannah went to the entry where Max was curled up on his rug. She hunkered down and drew her fingers through his fur. Once, twice, three and four times, and then he woke as old creatures do: slow and blurry eyed, surprised by nothing, accepting of whatever was in front of their nose. She thought it strange that the dog chose to sleep so that he could watch the front door and the comings and goings of those he had grown to love. He waited better than she did; he accepted with more grace than she did.

"Come on, Max." Hannah didn't bother to put the leash on him. Max would not run away even if he could, and it was wrong to tether him to anything.

They walked out into the night, the old dog and the beautiful girl. She held the gate and saw that his hip hurt. They ambled down the walk street, Max sniffing at the walls that separated small gardens or squares of concrete patios. Lights shined from most of the houses, and inside everything was safe and warm. Few people drew their curtains, something Hannah never understood. Someone standing in the dark, like she was, could see everything. From the clock on the kitchen wall to salt and pepper shakers on the dining room table where Mr. Harrigan hovered over his computer. She could see the bunnies and stars on the Glaskow children's pajamas as they sat together in one big chair watching television.

Hannah's nose twitched when a raindrop fell on the tip of it. She wiped it away. More fell, but she paid them no mind. There were hours before the real storm hit and hours before Josie came home; precious time that Hannah needed.

Throwing her head back, Hannah let Hermosa sweep over her: the wind, the scent of wet sand and briny ocean, the sense of contentment from the houses where families gathered, the sounds of music muffled by closed patio doors, the rush of water and the peace. Tears came to Hannah's eyes and she shook them away. She did not love Hermosa Beach, she did not love Josie or Archer, and she did not love these people. She would not love them. This had been a dream and she was waking up.

"Come on Max." Hannah spoke more sharply than she intended. Ignoring the underlying quiver in her voice, she hurried him back to Josie's house. If she didn't get there soon, she would not be as brave as she knew she must be.

She walked quickly and the old dog kept up as best he could but still Hannah had to wait at the gate. Inside, she bedded him down but did not hunker by his side to pet him to sleep. Mechanically, Hannah went about doing what she must: lights were turned on, the few dishes were done, and the mail was stacked. She made her bed, put away her paints, dealt with her clothes and, finally, sat at her dressing table and opened her lacquer box.

Hannah had an overwhelming desire to run to the shore and throw the thing into the sea. Instead, she stared at the contents and thought of her mother, of Miggy who had disappeared into the streets again, of her father who she had never known and didn't care to know. Hannah always knew she would have to save herself, but she never knew she would have to do it with a heart so full of pain. She needed to make it stop.

Hannah took out a set of keys and a pair of gold handled scissors. Finally, she peeled back the red velvet lining and uncovered three razor blades. In the low light, the finely honed edges glinted. They were the most beautiful things Hannah had ever seen: simply constructed, pedestrian in their purpose, and yet so full of promise. She chose one and pushed up the long sleeves of her hoodie.

In this light, the map of raised scars on her forearm looked like a relief map of pink and white and brown hills and valleys. She was a pitiful sight, and that thought almost made her put the razor away, but she was cutting before she knew that she had begun. There was a long, thin slice in the flesh that bled enough for Hannah to be satisfied. She switched hands and this time she drew the blade down her left arm.

Once . . .

Twice . . .

Three times she used the blade. Turning her arms out, she watched the blood seep from the wounds. It was warm and it dripped onto the glass top that covered the table. She felt better. The anger wasn't there. The fear was gone. The pain was nonexistent. All that was left was the resolve to do what she must.

Hannah tossed the razor blades back in the box and picked up the scissors. She raised her hands and looked at the blood staining her wrist. It was time to be done with this.

***

Josie woke in Archer's arms: warm, blessed, and damn scared. Her eyes darted around the room, but there was nothing there. Gently, she moved Archer's hand and slid out of bed. He turned, murmuring something in his sleep as she left. In the living room Josie looked around, half expecting something to materialize. There was nothing in the apartment but familiar things. Josie ran her fingers down the rosary beads that hung around a beer bottle Archer had put on the bookshelf. The light from the coffee maker in the kitchen glowed. She opened the door to the deck and walked to the railing. Hermosa slept, so there was no one to see the tall, naked woman on the deck of the old apartment building.

Josie raised her face. Raindrops fell on her shoulders, and lips, and chest. Her breasts pricked with the cold, her muscles tightened, but she paid no mind. She was trying to grasp that elusive, insistent feeling that had disturbed her. It was so familiar.

What was it? What?

Then she knew what it was and the knowledge was more terrifying than she could have imagined. Backing away, wrapping her arms around her nakedness, Josie Bates sank to the floor of the deck and faced the thing square on.

This was the same feeling that had awakened her long ago in Texas when she was just a girl. It made her leave her bed and go to her mother's bedroom door. That feeling caused such fear that Josie could not, would not, open that door.

Huddled on the deck, Josie was suddenly no older and no wiser. She was thirteen again. Her head fell back. Tears fell from her eyes and mixed with the raindrops. All alone, she cried in the black night.

Someone was leaving her again, and she couldn't open the door to stop them.

CHAPTER 29

2013

The *American boy had been with the Peace Corps for one year and seven months. There were still five more months before he went home. As much as he had come to love Albania, he would never be Shqiptare. No Shqiptare would run for the sheer pleasure of running, climb the pill boxes that littered the countryside willy-nilly, jump across streams when he could step over them, or chase cows that were perfectly happy not to be chased. Old women waved their fingers at him as he passed, old men looked at him with faded eyes, children stopped playing, mothers stopped hanging their wash to watch him go by, and always he called out to ask if they were well, waving his hand, giving them a great big American smile.*

He stopped to speak to the old woman who knit while she watched her sheep, the one who said she had seven daughters, and two were not married, and one would be happy to go to America to marry to him. He laughed and said he did not need a wife. The toothless woman laughed back and assured him he would change his mind when he saw her daughters. Then the American volunteer asked after Gjergy Isai, but the woman did not know him. So he asked after the Zogaj family and the woman smiled her toothless smile. She pointed him toward the mountain and a trail he knew a little. She warned him to be careful where he stepped because he was a good boy, and her daughter needed a husband. She did not want him to walk on the mines that were still buried under the earth.

He went off, calling his thanks for her warning, and wishing her the blessings of God. Then he did as he had been told. He stepped carefully across the rock and stones so that he didn't get blown to smithereens before he found the Zogaj family.

2013

Hannah parked the VW in the small lot on the west side of Torrance Memorial Hospital. There were only six spaces because this was used only to discharge patients. It was raining pretty hard, so she put up the hood on her slicker, got out, and dashed toward the wide awning. The automatic doors opened. The guard had taken shelter inside. She smiled at him.

"Back in a minute. Late discharge."

He mumbled something and made no move to stop her. She took the elevator to the second floor. It felt like the twilight zone in the hospital. Patients had been fed, bathed, medicated, wounds redressed, charts noted. The shift had changed. The lights were low. There was silence, as if everyone had bedded down by a campfire and dozed off. Hannah measured her steps, not wanting to bring too much attention to herself. The young nurse behind the desk smiled at her. Hannah smiled back but kept her hood in place.

"It's raining again, huh?"

"Yep," Hannah answered.

She walked on. At the far end of the hall, a man was mopping the floor. To her left were a couple of shower rooms. There was a wheelchair outside one of them. Hannah didn't hesitate. She wheeled the chair into room 217 where Billy slept.

"Billy?" she put her hand on his shoulder. "Billy. You've got to wake up."

His eyes opened. He smiled at her. She slipped the hood off her head and, as she did so, a look of awe crossed his face.

"Hannah, what did you do to yourself?"

Hannah put her hand to her head and felt the prickly stubble. It was all that was left of her hair. She had taken out her nose ring and washed her face clean. She wore shapeless scrubs and tennis shoes. Anyone in that hospital could look at her and swear she was not the same girl who had been sitting by Billy Zuni's bedside all these days.

"It doesn't matter. You've got to get up."

"But why did you cut off all your hair?"

Billy struggled to sit up and Hannah helped him.

"Are you on any drugs?" she asked.

He shook his head, "I don't think so. Why?"

"Because I'm going to get you out of here and if you need meds I'd have to figure out how to get them." She looked around the room. "Archer said he left clothes here."

"In the closet," Billy directed. "Does Josie know you're here?"

"No. We can't call Josie. You've got to get dressed now. We don't have much time."

Hannah found a pair of jeans and started to shimmy him into them, but he pushed her away.

"No. Stop. This isn't right. I want to call Josie," he hissed.

Hannah glared at him. She wasn't angry with Billy as much as she was afraid for him. She thought he would just go with her. She never thought she would have to tell him why.

"Just do what I say, please. We'll work it all out, I promise."

"I wouldn't go without Rosa. I won't go without talking to Josie."

"Well, you're going to have to," Hannah snapped. "And if Josie knew about this, she'd get in trouble because she's your attorney."

Billy grabbed hold of her shoulders so fast Hannah lost her balance and fell back onto her heels.

"Hannah. I'm not doing anything just because you tell me to. That's what I did with Rosa. I did what she told me, too, and look what happened. I wasn't there to protect her. I don't want anything to happen to you."

Hannah blinked at this strange person, a man so unlike the boy who dogged her footsteps, who smiled even when the kids at school made fun of him, who took in stride his mother's orders to stay out of his own house. Here, in this room, he looked as if he had aged. He was not going to weather the storm, he wanted to face it. But Hannah knew better. It was a trick of the light that made him seem as if he could stand on his own. They had to do this together.

"You can't help Rosa where you're going," Hannah got on her knees again. "Josie's coming tomorrow to tell you they're going to put you into the psyche ward. They can keep you as long as they want, Billy. They think you're crazy."

"I'm not crazy, Hannah."

"I know," she whispered.

She put her hands on Billy's legs once more and pushed his jeans up, nudging his hips right and then left until they were on. She stood up and eased the button-front shirt over his cast and around his shoulders. She spoke quietly, quickly.

"Get in the wheelchair. We have to hurry."

"Where are we going?"

"Somewhere safe. No one will think to look where I'm taking you."

Billy made a move. Hannah helped him off the bed.

"Okay, but first there's something I have to do."

"There's no time."

"Then I don't go."

"Okay." She put his backpack in his lap and covered him with the blanket from the bed. Hannah got behind the chair, grasped the handles and asked: "Where to?"

"You know where," Billy answered.

****

"Oh God, Hannah."

Billy's knees buckled but he stayed upright and put his hand on his sister's hair. He touched her swollen face and lifted her bandaged hands. He cried silently, his sorrow so deep he could not give voice to it. Hannah lowered her eyes for a moment. When she looked again she saw a miracle. Rosa Zuni's eyelids fluttered. Like a blind person, she moved her hand but missed the connection with Billy. He grasped it and guided it to his chest. That's when Rosa Zuni opened her eyes.

"Besnik," Rosa whispered. *"A jeni mirë?"*

Billy sobbed. His gut pulled together so that he could hardly speak. Finally, he managed.

"I'm good, Rosafa."

Her eyes closed to show she understood and they stayed closed as she drew on the last of her strength.

"Unë të dua, Besnik," she whispered. *"Drejtuar."*

"No, Rosa. No," Billy sobbed.

Hannah drew along side.

"What does she say?"

"She said she loves me." His gaze lingered on his sister and then he swung his head toward Hannah. "She said to run."

CHAPTER 30

2013

The American who had come to Albania to make peace found the house in which the Zogaj family lived. The father had gone off to work, and the mother was tending to a garden in front of her house. There was a girl who saw the young man first. The mother came to the front of the property near the fence and watched him come. He hailed her with all the polite greetings of a respectful person. She greeted him back, asking how he felt and whether things were good.

He replied that he was good. Yes, indeed, he was very good. So he asked after her and when they finally agreed that all was well with them, the young man who came to teach the children English but now was on a mission for the furgon driver asked the woman:

"A e dini Besnik Zogaj? A e dini Gergy Isai apo zotin Oi?"

"Do you know Besnik Zogaj. And do you know Gergy Isai and Mr. Oi?"

The color drained from the woman's face and she fell at the young man's feet. The girl screamed and ran to her mother. And the young man did not know what was happening and, when the mother was revived, he wished that she had never told him.

2013

"Okay. Yes. You're sure? Yeah. Okay. I'll meet you there. Half an hour?"

Josie was starting to dress before the call from Montoya was even disconnected. Archer was out of bed, buttoning his shirt even though it was still early.

"What's up?"

"Billy's gone. The nurse went in to check on him when the shift changed, and he wasn't there. His backpack is gone, his gown was there."

"Let me guess. Hannah's not answering her phone," Archer said.

"I'm going home to see if I can find anything there, then I'll meet Montoya at the hospital."

Josie zipped her jeans and pulled on her sweater and stepped into her boots. When she looked up, she saw Archer staring at her. He knew she hadn't told him everything. There was no sense keeping it from him.

"Rosa Zuni died last night."

Archer pulled his lips together. "Anybody see Billy or Hannah around her room?"

"We didn't get that far." Josie strode across the room and pulled her jacket from under the bed. "I think we can probably assume that's where Carl Newton is going to go with this. He'll argue that Billy finished the job with his sister and took off."

Archer grabbed his keys. "How is he going to explain Hannah?"

"I doubt there's any explanation needed given the way she's been acting. Love sick teenager, doing anything for Billy," Josie took her purse off the hall table.

"That's easy to discount." Archer opened the front door.

"Not in front of a jury," Josie said. "No need to worry about it now."

"You go on to the hospital," Archer said. "I'll get to your place and see what I can put together."

Josie kissed him. There was nothing more to say. Both of them knew Billy Zuni was in very big trouble.

Mike Montoya kissed his wife good-bye. She murmured to be careful but the warning came out scattered with pops and clicks as she tried desperately to get her vocal chords to work properly. Beneath his lips her head shook on a neck that could barely hold it up any longer.

"You wait for Sarah before you try to get out of bed," Mike said and then whispered, "I love you."

Even with the dark, even though the rest of her being trembled uncontrollably, her smile was steady and beautiful.

"Get the bad guys," she said.

"Always."

Mike smoothed her hair and left the house wondering if he was ever going to find out who the bad guys were.

***

The sky had opened up and Archer dashed through a sheet of rain to unlock the door to Josie's house. He held it wide so Max could go out, but one look outside and the old dog decided to stay where he was. Archer didn't push it. Above him, the tarp billowed and he made a mental note to finish the skylight before the wedding. He wanted a picture there with Josie in her wedding dress, Hannah, and Max. The light would be beautiful – if it ever stopped raining.

Pocketing his key, he gave the living room a once over, poked his head into the kitchen, and then headed to Hannah's room. The door was closed. He walked in and flipped open the plantation shutters. The bed was made perfectly and that was unusual for Hannah. Her paints were still there. That was worrisome.

Archer opened the closet. One section of the hanging garments had been pushed aside. Hannah had left what Archer considered her 'fancy' clothes: diaphanous, embellished, and embroidered blouses and dresses. On the floor, her high heels, extreme wedges, and thigh-high boots were still there. Gone were her jeans, sweaters, hoodies, t-shirts. Not all of them, but enough for Archer to know that Hannah wasn't planning on going clubbing.

The question was what had she planned? More than likely, she hadn't planned at all. Archer hoped she had been impulsive because people would remember a girl without a plan. They would especially remember a girl like Hannah.

At the dressing table, Archer sat on the small chair and planted his feet solidly on the floor with his hands on his knees. He didn't like what he saw. Blood had dropped on the glass top. Hannah had tried to clean it up but she had been in a hurry because Archer could still see a telltale trail. Then he saw something else: a scattering of hair. They were just little bits but they had clung to the glass. He pushed back the chair and bent down to follow the trail of hair to the trashcan. He picked out paper: homework assignments, drawings that had been discarded, receipts. At the bottom of the can Archer found a nest of beautiful, black hair.

"Damn, Hannah," Archer breathed.

He was about to dial Josie when he saw the little lacquer box, the gold handled scissors and the bloodied razor blades. And there was one thing Archer didn't see. He dialed Josie. She answered. He said:

"She took the keys, babe."

***

Mike Montoya parked in a red zone outside the hospital, got out of the car and buttoned his coat as he passed through the big doors, and then something made him turn around and pause. Sam Lumina and Gjergy Isai were coming toward him. Lumina's head was down but it kept swinging left and right. Isai walked straight on, his step quick.

"Hello." Mike greeted them. Gjergy Isai registered no surprise, but Sam Lumina stopped dead in his tracks.

"Good morning," Gjergy said.

"I'm surprised to see you here? Who called you?"

"Nobody called us. We just came to see Billy," Sam said. "We just, you know, wanted to see him. My uncle insisted."

"Then you don't know what happened?"

The two men shook their heads. "Come on then, I'll tell you on our way upstairs. Ms. Bates should be waiting for us."

***

Wendy Sterling got into work just before the rain started and just after the morning mail was distributed. She ran through it before she took her coat off. Still standing at her desk, she found what she had hoped for but hadn't really expected.

She sat down, opened the envelope, read through the contents and then read through them again.

"My, my," she whispered as she dialed Mike. She waited and when he answered Wendy Sterling said: "Mike, it's me. I just got the prints back on the gun."

***

Mike Montoya noted the placement of everyone on the second floor. Josie Bates was standing in the doorway of what had been Billy Zuni's room. She was talking to a nurse. There were three people behind the long desk. A patient was being wheeled out of a room at the far end of the hall and one of the hospital's religious volunteers was going into another room. Gjergy Isai and Sam Lumina stood with their backs to the wall, waiting.

Mike Montoya walked past Josie Bates. She must have sensed something, because she looked up and then stepped into the hallway to watch him. He walked past the nursing station and up to the two men. Gjergy Isai met his gaze but Mike ignored him. It was Sam he wanted to talk to.

"Sam Lumina? You are under arrest for the murders of Jac Duka and Greg Oi. You have the right to remain silent. . ."

CHAPTER 31

2013

It had taken the young English teacher two hours to get back to Bajram Curri from the mountains. It wasn't very late in Albania, but by his calculations it was very early in America; too early to call the man whose number he had been given by the furgon driver. So the young man crawled into his bed fully dressed because there was no heat in his apartment and the steel door made the whole place as cold as a freezer. He would sleep for a few hours and then call the number. But an hour passed, and then two, and he could not sleep because of what he knew.

He crawled out of his bed and saw that it would be a respectable hour in the states. He dialed his phone. Thousands of miles away, the phone that belonged to the man named Archer rang. Before they connected, though, the signal went out and the call was cut off.

The young man tried again and again. Each time the connection was missed, his heart beat faster. This was not good. What he knew was not good at all. Finally, he was talking to a man named Archer. He told him what he had found out from Teuta Zogaj.

***

Hannah and Billy sat inside the little Volkswagen. Rain drummed on the roof. Outside was gray and cold; inside the car was warm and close. They had never sat this way before, side-by-side, silent, equally frightened, neither wanting to admit it.

"How are you feeling?" Hannah asked.

"I'm okay," Billy mumbled, but she could see he was pale and trembling. Their flight and the sight of Rosa had shaken him. He didn't look at her when he asked: "What do we do now?"

"We'll figure it out," Hannah said.

"Do you think we should call Josie?"

Hannah shook her head, "Not yet."

"What about Archer? Maybe we should call him, just to let him know we're okay."

Hannah shook her head. "I don't think so. Maybe in a few days. Maybe in a few days they will have figured out who killed those people and who hurt Rosa. Then we can go back. If they put you in the psyche ward, you'll never get back to normal."

"Okay," Billy said but it wasn't clear if he agreed with her or if he was just tired. He blinked and looked around. "Where are we?"

"I used to live here."

Hannah took a deep breath. The big house was still impressive. It was a seemingly simple construct, but closer inspection revealed a marvelous origami box of a home: glass butted stucco, stucco melted into copper, copper ran into tile, and that tile surrounded a pool of water that welcomed visitors with a serenity that masked the sickness of the people inside. Only now there weren't any people inside. A discrete For Sale sign was stuck into what had once been a bed of extravagantly exotic plants. The sign was weathered, the words faded, as forgotten as what had gone on behind the walls. Hannah reached into the back. She pulled her duffle and Billy's backpack over the seat.

"Can you handle this?"

She held up the backpack. He nodded and she gave it to him. She reached back and grabbed another bag. She had enough food to last them a few days. If they needed more, she knew where there was a little store where only the locals went. Right now they just needed some rest.

"You ready?"

Billy nodded. For a minute Hannah wasn't sure if she was. Then she swallowed her fear. There was no one in that place who could hurt her any more.

"Let's go."

Hannah had parked deep into the long drive so that the car couldn't be seen from the highway. Together they dashed around to the front of the house and stopped in front of a gate that was as tall as the ten-foot wall that surrounded the house. It had oxidized to the strangely pleasing blue-green of exposed copper. A relief of angles as sharp as a maze of thorns was etched onto its surface.

"We'll never get in."

Billy raised his voice so he could be heard above the rain. Hannah ignored him. She touched the gate. It opened as it always had. Another touch and it revolved. She led Billy through and touched it from behind. The gate closed. It was a brilliant collaboration of art and engineering.

"Come on."

Together they hurried through a courtyard paved in buff colored tile surrounded by walls of smooth stucco. Cut through the middle of this outdoor room was an endless pool. The water flowed under a glass wall that bared the heart of the house. The glass used to sparkle; now it was muddied, streaked with dirt and dust.

In front of it, in the middle of the pool, stood the bronze statue of a nude woman. She was contorted into a position of perpetual pain - or ecstasy - depending on one's point of view. Hannah had once asked Josie what she saw when she looked at it. Josie saw pain of the most humiliating and personal sort. So had Hannah.

She tore her eyes away from the statue and touched Billy's arm as she went by.

"Come on."

He followed her to the entrance. Hannah had the key to the house, but the realtor had secured it with a lock box.

"Now what?" Billy asked.

"Wait here."

Hannah dashed through the rain, through the courtyard, and back out the gate. She came back a minute later carrying a baseball bat.

"I use this to hold up the hood on my car when I put oil in."
Hannah held the bat in one hand. Water ran down her face and
sluiced off the little hair she had left.

"Let's go, Hannah. Let's go somewhere else," Billy pleaded.

"Let's not," Hannah answered.

With that, she walked into the shallow pool and under the
gaze of the tortured nude, drew back, and hit the glass wall with the
bat. It shattered but didn't break. Hannah didn't back away from the
shards or flinch at the sound. She hit the glass again and again until a
sheet broke away, leaving a jagged gaping hole in the wall. She felt the
shards floating through the shallow pool and bouncing off her shoes.
It was then, when the glass didn't cut her, when she had broken into
the house that used to be her prison, that Hannah Sheraton became
truly strong and free. She put her hand out to Billy as she threw the
bat into the pool.

"Come on. I'll help you."

Together they walked through the broken window and into
Fritz Rayburn's Malibu house.

***

It was a well-documented fact that when rain fell, Southern
Californians lost their ability to drive. When a storm hit, Southern
California drivers lost their ability to think. It was raining and that's
why traffic was a snarl from the South Bay all the way to Lincoln
Boulevard and beyond.

As Josie drove in fits and starts, she waffled between
believing that Hannah and Billy were safe at Fritz's house or that she
was headed in the wrong direction entirely. She didn't bother voicing
either her concern or her hopes to Gjergy Isai. He sat beside her in
the car, eyes forward, wanting to get to Billy.

She had promised Mike Montoya to take the old man back to
Lumina's house, but she didn't say when she would get him there.
First she wanted him to help her convince Billy to come back. He
promised to talk to the boy about his parents and the country he had
been taken from, Josie would talk to Hannah about coming home,
and Archer would keep tabs on Mike Montoya and Sam Lumina. If
what Montoya believed – that Sam Lumina was responsible for the
deaths because of the union troubles – Archer would let Josie know

it was safe for everyone to come back. It was a flimsy plan, but a plan nonetheless.

"There."

Josie pointed to the house in the distance. Gjergy kept his eyes on the structure as they drew closer. When Josie pulled into the drive, he cut his gaze to the Volkswagen and then back to the house.

"They are here," he said.

"I knew they would be."

Josie pulled on the emergency break just as the first roll of thunder sounded.

***

Wendy slipped into the room where Mike Montoya was talking to Sam Lumina. More correctly, Mike was talking and Sam Lumina was acting like he could care less. Wendy gave Mike the information he was waiting for. Mike glanced at it.

"I see a green Toyota is registered to you, Sam," he said.

"What of it?"

"A green Toyota was seen parked on Rosa Zuni's street the night of the murders."

"Like there aren't a thousand green Toyota's all over the place?"

"Not many with the specific body damage yours has." Mike set aside the DMV report. "But what really concerns me, is the gun, Sam. The gun that killed Jac Duka and Greg Oi was registered to Greg Oi. Ballistics confirmed that. And, they also confirmed that your fingerprints were all over it. We just find that a little odd."

"I've seen the gun before," Sam drawled. "Yeah, I saw it at the plant. Mr. Oi let me hold it. That's how my fingerprints got there."

"And could you tell me how this gun got into your home? That is the real curiosity here. Your wife found it in the heater closet in your home. It seems as if someone was trying to hide it."

"Stupid bitch," Sam muttered.

"Concerned wife and mother," Mike answered. Wendy took a step back and leaned against the wall next to the door. It never ceased to amaze her how easily people blamed others when the truth of their crime was staring them right in the face. "Your wife thought Mr. Isai had something to do with the murders, but his fingerprints aren't on the gun. Only yours are. And your prints aren't just on the butt. We have a partial on the trigger. I just don't see how you can explain that away."

"How do you know his aren't on that gun?" Sam challenged.

"Because your wife provided us with a glass he used so that we could match them. There was no match. But we had your prints from your previous arrest." Mike leaned forward. "Yours and Mr. Oi's Sam. Come on, we know that Jac Duka was playing both sides of the fence, feeding information to Oi about you guys and votes on the upcoming contract. The whole thing has been heated. We won't press for murder one if you level with us now. Manslaughter? You could get off with-"

Mike stopped talking, interrupted by a knock on the door. He looked over his shoulder, catching a glimpse of a deputy and Archer as Wendy opened the door and stepped into the hall. She came back a minute later, went up to Mike and leaned down to whisper in his ear.

Mike cocked his head. He raised an eyebrow.

"When did the call come in?"

"Just now," she said. "He's trying to call Josie Bates. He thought you should know. I called the Lumina's house. The wife says Isai isn't there and she doesn't know where he is."

Mike stood up and turned his back on Sam Lumina.

"Did you corroborate?"

"You're kidding, right? Archer said the conversation was sketchy. He got the basics." Wendy looked at Sam. "It makes as much sense as anything else. Ask him."

Mike pivoted. Sam looked away, bored with the whole thing until Mike asked:

"Mr. Lumina, what do you know about blood feuds?"

CHAPTER 32

Josie Bates had not forgotten anything about Fritz Rayburn's house: not how impressed she'd been the first time she'd seen it, not the lavish furnishings, not the lengths Linda, Hannah's mother, would go to protect her claim to it. This time all Josie felt was sad because this was where Hannah thought she would be safe.

The hood of Josie's parka was raised and she kept her head down as she walked quickly toward the gate. Beyond the house was the stormy sea, behind her Gjergy waited in the Jeep. He would come when she called him in. Josie gave no more than a passing glance at the For Sale sign. She didn't hesitate when she reached the gate. She touched it, it swung open, she walked through, but she didn't bother to close it. Hopefully, they would all be walking back through it sooner than later.

She saw the padlock on the front door, the jagged hole in the towering glass wall and the baseball bat lying at the bottom of the shallow pool. Her eyes played over the statue. Raindrops pockmarked the water in the pool. Broken glass sparkled against the sand that had blown into the water and settled on the bottom tile. She stepped into the cold water, waded through it, and went into Fritz Rayburn's house.

She climbed out of the water into the foyer and listened. She heard nothing and no one would have heard her. The living room was empty and the walls were bare. She started for the staircase, but hadn't taken more than a step when she saw Hannah emerge from the dining room. Josie opened her mouth to speak, but all she heard was Hannah scream her name. She turned just as Gjergy Isai swung the wet baseball bat at her head.

***

The silence was epic. The ceilings were so high Hannah couldn't hear the sound of rain on the roof, or the sound of the waves at the beach, or Josie breathing. The afternoon gloom was liquid, seeping into every corner of the empty huge room. Hannah's shock was palpable and Gjergy's indifference to her and Josie lying on the floor was chilling.

"Where is Besnik?"

Hannah shook her head. Her eyes darted to Josie who hadn't moved.

"Do not look at that woman," Gjergy ordered. "Look at me."

Hannah did as she was told. Her heart pounded, her body shuddered, and her brave heart felt small.

"There is no reason for you to be fearful," he said.

"I'm not afraid of you. I'm not afraid of anyone," Hannah answered.

Gjergy understood. She was afraid for her friend and afraid for the woman who had spoken for her friend. Love gave her courage. He understood that all too well. It was the same for him.

"Why did you do that? Why did you hurt Josie?" Hannah took one step forward, but when he raised the bat she stopped.

"She would try to stop me and I have come a very long way and waited a very long time to find Besnik," Gjergy said.

"You won't find him ever."

"Do not lie to me," Gjergy roared. "I can kill you. I can kill her. It makes no difference as long as Besnik dies."

"Why? He doesn't even know you," Hannah screamed back.

From the corner of her eye she saw Josie move and Hannah prayed she could hear what they were saying. If she could, Josie could tell someone what insanity had happened here if Hannah couldn't.

"It is our law," Gjergy answered.

"What kind of freakin' law says you have to kill a kid?"

"The Kunan is our law." Gjergy moved but did not take his eyes off Hannah for longer than a second. Facing down a girl, he felt no urgency and his curiosity had got the best of him. "This is one persons house?"

"It was," Hannah answered. "He's dead."

"He was a president?" Gjergy asked.

"No. He was a freak. A freaky old man like you."

Gjergy snorted. He tapped the baseball bat against his leg.

"He is not like me. I am a man who only wants justice. Rosafa knew that and she would not tell me where Besnik was. That was all she would have to do and she refused." He turned back to Hannah and smiled. "Rosafa was well named. She was brave." He turned toward Hannah. "Rosafa was like you, I think. You protect him out of love. I hunt him out of respect for the law."

"Tell me what law you're talking about," Hannah demanded. "Tell me what Billy did."

Instead of answering, Gjergy leaned against the stairwell wall and asked.

"Do you know what it is like to starve?"

"I know what it is to be hungry," Hannah said.

"That is different. Starving, it makes women old and men useless and children cry. When I was younger than Besnik, my country suffered under a president who enslaved us. For fifty years there was but one car in our country, and it belonged to the president. He said God did not exist. He took our work. He told us what we could eat and where we could go. The people had nothing left but family and honor.

"That is how we lived. And the president put mines around our country to keep people out, but we knew it was to keep us in. He made our countrymen his soldiers to make sure we did not leave. Yes," the big man mused, "I was twelve. I was a boy."

Gjergy seemed to have lost himself in his tale, but Hannah didn't kid herself. He knew where he was, he knew who she was, he knew what he wanted to do and he didn't care if it was wrong.

"Billy wasn't even born when you were twelve," Hannah ventured.

The old man blinked. The light was growing dimmer with the storm and the passing of the day. This man was a shadow, a silhouette, a deadly presence that Rosa Zuni tried to guard Billy against in the only way she knew how – by keeping Billy away from their house. Escape would have been impossible when Gjergy found them. Rosa was proof of that.

"What did he do to you?" Hannah balled her fist, stepped forward, and demanded an answer. Her efforts were futile. She might as well have been a gnat nipping at the ear of a plow horse.

"I will tell you." Gjergy spat the words at her. "My brother was taking me across the border. We went at night, and it was Yilli who guarded the border. Yilli's rifle fired and killed my brother. I saw it. I witnessed his death. With my eyes, I saw him die."

"Then talk to the Yilli guy." Hannah moved a bit, trying to position herself in front of the sliding door that led to the wide patio and the steps down to the beach.

"The Kunan says I could kill Yilli to revenge my brother, but the president outlawed the justice, the blood feud. So I waited for the revolution and freedom. When it came, Yilli stayed in his house and I could not enter to take his life. The Kunan says I could kill his son, but Yilli only has a daughter, Teuta, who I was not allowed to kill."

"Holy shit," Hannah breathed. "You're going to kill Billy because his grandfather shot your brother?"

"It is the law," Gjergy stated.

"It's screwed."

With that, Hannah threw herself at the glass door and screamed.

"Billy! Run! Run! Josie! Help! Josie!"

The old man started. With a great roar born of centuries of culture, a half a century of fear and anger, and an instant of surprise when he saw this moment slipping away, Gjergy lunged across the room determined to silence Hannah. As he did, Billy ran down the stairs as best he could, letting out a blood-curdling scream as he dashed for the front door. Hannah's head twisted and she saw that Billy was going the wrong way. Gjergy turned, too, but his hard shoes skidded on the wood floor.

"It's locked, Billy! It's locked!" Hannah screamed and just then the lock on the sliding door gave way. "This way! This way!"

Billy twirled and he dashed toward Hannah but Gergy had almost righted himself and grabbed for Billy. The teenager used his cast like a weapon, deflecting the old man. Gjergy roared, found his footing, and went after Hannah and Billy who had already escaped into the gathering gloom.

***

Mike Montoya drove and Archer rode shotgun. It had taken mere minutes for Archer to relay the basics of the story to Mike, Mike to repeat it to Sam Lumina, and Sam Lumina to give up Gjergy Isai. Bottom line, Sam said, the old man would have killed him if he didn't help him finish up the blood feud.

Yeah, a blood feud.

That was ancient law and Sam couldn't say no. Gjergy was supposed to take care of the kid and been out of the country before anyone was the wiser. All Sam had to do was drive him around.

Sam drove him to Oi's house, but Oi wouldn't tell where the kid was.

They followed him to Hermosa.

They found Oi dressed like a woman.

Which was totally weird.

They found Jac Duka giving Oi the skinny on who was going to vote which way in the contract talks.

Traitor.

Gjergy found Rosafa. Gjergy wasn't supposed to hurt her. That was against the Kunan, but she wouldn't give up the kid.

Gjergy went crazy. They could hear everything downstairs.

It was sickening.

Oi couldn't take it. The idiot went for his gun, and Sam went for Oi, and it all happened so fast, and Jac just sat there like a lump.

What was I supposed to do? Oi knew the score, but when he heard that girl screaming it was too much for him. He was going to shoot my uncle. I grabbed the gun, like just to get it away from him. He ran. I shot him. God, that was weird. Like I was shooting a woman. That's when Jac started to get up. I shot him. I just turned and pulled the trigger. I didn't even think. Self defense. Pure and simple. It was self-defense. That's what it was. I didn't know what my uncle did to that chick. It sounded bad, but I didn't know and I didn't know the two guys were dead. I just ran to the car with the gun. I saw the kid and the other guy go in. I saw everyone running back out. I hid. I hid in the car with the gun. . .

Mike had heard enough. He left Sam Lumina to Wendy Sterling. The story was one for the books, but they would have plenty of time to sort it out. Right now, though, they didn't have a lot of time; they had to get to Josie who was more than a half an hour ahead of them and not answering her phone.

***

Josie struggled onto her hands and knees. Her stomach heaved. She opened her mouth to throw up but nothing came out. Her ears rang, her brain was jangled, her eyes unfocused. She put her head against the floor, raising it again in time to see Gjergy Isai run out the door toward the beach.

Calling on every ounce of strength she possessed, Josie got to her feet. She stumbled, she walked, and weaved, and fell. She got up again, and again, and the last time she tripped over the bat. Pain shot up her shoulder, and the back of her head felt like it was caved in.

Picking up the bat, she leveraged herself. Single-mindedly, Josie put one foot in front of the other, gaining speed only to fall back a step when her head began to spin. Sweating, she tore off her hooded jacket and tossed it aside before falling against the open glass door.

She squinted at the figures on the beach. The old man was faster than she had imagined he could be. He was gaining on the teenagers, but they were still ahead of him, headed for the old wooden pier and the dinghy tied to it. Suddenly, Billy collapsed. Hannah ran back for him. Josie could hear the old man bellowing. It didn't matter what he was saying; she knew what he meant.

Gjergy wanted blood.

***

"Jesus." Archer cursed in frustration when he saw what was coming.

The rains had soaked the Malibu Mountains loosening the earth. A rock slide had closed Pacific Coast Highway going north.

"I see it. I got it."

Montoya reached for a light and put it on top of his unmarked unit, stepped on the gas, and turned the wheel until the car was riding on the shoulder – a shoulder that actually didn't exist.

Archer raised a brow. He didn't think Montoya had it in him. Montoya raised one right back as if to say he wasn't surprised to be underestimated.

They flew past a mile and a half of stopped cars, past the rocks, and swerved back onto PCH. It was wide open all the way to Fritz Rayburn's house.

***

The sky had opened up. Josie ran toward the shore. The waves rolled in, but not with the rage of a week ago. The wind was not gale force, but she still struggled against it. Sunset was covered over with dark clouds. Ahead, Gjergy, Billy and Hannah stumbled across the wet sand.

Billy was up and for a moment he and Hannah were one person. His arm was around her shoulders and they started forward again. But Hannah was slight, and even her heroic spirit was not enough to move them any faster. Then they were apart, Hannah clutching his good arm as they made it to the pier.

Gjergy was moments behind them and Josie seconds behind him, but even as she gained on him, the old man didn't look back. He got to the old pier and lumbered toward the two kids. Hannah abandoned the rope that tied the skiff, jumped up, and threw herself in front of Billy Zuni.

"Leave us alone. Go away. He didn't do anything to you."

Gjergy ignored her. He had eyes only for Billy. Winded, Gjergy's chest heaved as he tried to catch his breath.

"Move the girl away. Move her, Besnik. I have no care for her."

"I do," Billy called back.

"And so do I," Josie cried as she came up behind the old man.

The bat was poised at her shoulder. Josie waited for him to make a move toward Billy. Instead, Gjergy stood as he had in the hospital room: still as a statue, turning only when he decided to turn. This time, though, hidden hands were a worry. This time, when Gjergy faced Josie there was a knife in his hand.

"Put it down," she said.

"What difference will it make if I take one more life?" he growled.

"In our courts, it will make a difference."

From the corner of her eye Josie saw Hannah put her arm around Billy's waist. The rain fell and the ocean swelled. Beneath their feet, the old pier undulated. There was no good way for this to end, but Josie had to mitigate the outcome.

"Listen to me. Listen to me. Our courts will take your culture in to consideration. But if you hurt Billy, if you try to take his life purposefully, our judges won't have any mercy. Do you understand that?"

"Consideration?" Gjergy scoffed. "That is weakness. A crime is committed and someone must pay. That is law."

"But not someone who had nothing to do with the crime," Josie insisted. "Your brother died fifty years ago."

"And his killer's blood flows in that boy. Besnik owes his life for the life of my brother. I saw my brother die on a mountain and all he wanted was for us to be free as Besnik has been free."

Gjergy stood his ground, raising the knife, and pointing it at Billy. Josie steeled herself to attack, but Gjergy made no move for the boy.

"Oi was my friend when we were young. He knew of my brother. He knew of the blood fued, but he married Rosafa. He took the boy so that Besnik could escape justice. That was foolish. Distance and money could not save him. No man can save Besnik." His arm shook, his voice rose above the surf with a roar. "The Kunan says I am justice." Gjergy advanced on Josie. "You will not keep me from what I must do. No woman can do that."

Gauging the distance, Josie held her breath, aware that the teenagers' eyes were on her but hers were on Gjergy. His rage was beyond reason, his devotion to the ancient Albanian law unshakable. Josie could no more understand his justice than he could submit to hers, so she defaulted to a law they both understood: survival of the fittest.

Josie Bates swung the bat at the knife and screamed at Hannah and Billy.

"Get out of here. Run. Go! Go!"

Hannah and Billy ran: past the man who was on the defensive. They ran past Josie who prayed she had enough strength to keep the old man at bay long enough for them to escape. They were on the beach when Hannah turned back.

"Josie!"

"Go. Get as far away as you can."

Hannah and Billy did as they were told and Josie had to trust that they would find their way. In front of her Gjergy Isai was rising, the knife still in his hand, the rain streaming down his face, the waves drumming their furious score to this drama.

"I will find him. He cannot run far enough," Gjergy called.

"Our law won't let you," Josie promised. "I won't let you."

"My country does not judge me. Yours cannot either." He pulled himself to his great height. "I am Albanian. I have walked on stone."

"Yeah?" Josie spit the rainwater out of her mouth and narrowed her eyes. "Well, you're not on stone now, you bastard."

Josie Bates fell to the pier and swung the bat at his knees. It hit its mark with a sickening crunch. The old man's hard soled shoes slipped, his weight threw him backward, and Gjergy Isai fell into the angry sea.

CHAPTER 33

Mike Montoya reluctantly turned away from the view of Hermosa Beach when Archer opened the door to Josie's house.

"It's Saturday, Montoya. Don't you ever take a day off?"

"Now and again," Mike answered, as he took Archer's hand. "Is Ms. Bates here?"

Archer drew the detective inside and called: "Jo? We've got company."

She came from the back of the house and, even though she smiled, Mike Montoya thought she looked tired. It could have been that she was still recuperating from the injuries she sustained in Malibu, but he thought it was simpler than that. He thought Josie Bates was sad. She didn't bother to say hello, and that didn't surprise Mike. Instead, she asked:

"Did you find Hannah?"

"No, I'm sorry. That truck stop where they abandoned the car is pretty busy. They could be anywhere by now. We've been in contact with state agencies but . . ." Mike shrugged and Josie interpreted as she led the way to the living room.

"But Hannah isn't going to make a peep until she believes Billy is safe."

"That's what I came to talk to you about. I think we can discount a continued threat from Gjergy Isai. His body washed up in Manhattan Beach."

"Really?" Josie said this as she took the couch. She seemed only politely interested in his news, but Mike knew she couldn't wait to hear what he had to say.

"He drowned." Mike opted for the leather chair and stated the obvious.

"No surprise there." Archer sat next to Josie. "I doubt he had a lot of experience with the ocean given where he came from. Josie said she lost sight of him pretty quickly."

"Yes, it's a pity you couldn't have just held put out a hand. Maybe dragged him to a place where he could latch onto the pier."

"I was still out of it, Montoya. Remember, he attacked me. I was lucky I made it to the pier at all," Josie answered.

"Of course, you're right. No one could accuse you of depraved indifference." Mike looked square at Josie and raised a brow. She didn't flinch so he pushed on. "And the surf was bad. You could have jeopardized yourself if you tried to help. And he couldn't help himself at all given that he was probably in shock. It seems that his knee-caps were broken."

"That old pier wood can be slippery, detective. Especially when it rains," Josie noted.

"I suppose he could have broken them when he slipped. It's just odd that the bones on both legs were broken in exactly the same place – shattered actually. It was almost as if he'd been deliberately struck with something very heavy."

"I can't imagine what." Josie leaned into Archer as she held Montoya's gaze.

"Perhaps it was the same thing that he used to hit you," Mike suggested.

"Gjergy hit me. He was a strong man."

"Did he break that window with his fist?" Mike probed.

"I don't know," Josie answered. "I don't remember much."

Mike nodded and drummed his fingers on his knee just once. He knew Josie was lying and so did Archer, but there would never be any proof that anyone had assaulted Gjergy Isai. Montoya had no doubt that whatever weapon was used against him was now on the ocean floor, deep in the water off a private beach in Malibu. He tried once more. All he wanted was the truth; all he wanted was for everything to be tidy.

"You didn't see Hannah or Billy attack him with anything, did you? If they did, I doubt even Carl Newton would file against them. Clearly, there's an argument to be made for self-defense on their part."

Josie shook her head, "No. They were long gone. I sent them away like I told you. Look, Montoya, they didn't do anything that would interest you or the courts."

"You mean other than Hannah interfering with an open investigation?" Mike chuckled.

"She's a kid helping another kid. Teenagers run away all the time. At most that's a misdemeanor under these circumstances. There's no money in the budget to prosecute them," she answered.

"Hannah and Billy wouldn't know that. And you're forgetting Billy's immigration status," Mike countered. "He's in this country illegally."

"That's a federal concern." Josie waved him off.

"It boils down to what those two believe, doesn't it?" Mike challenged her. "Right now they probably think we're hunting them and not in a good way. In fact, unless they were around to see Mr. Isai slip on that pier, they may think they have to hide from him, too. I'd like them to know Isai is dead and I'd like to know what they saw in that house or on that pier."

Josie's heart beat a little faster, but her expression remained composed. All she had thought about since that afternoon was finding Hannah and Billy, but now she was thinking it might not be bad if they laid low until something bigger came along to distract Mike Montoya and Carl Newton. Eventually, Gjergy Isai would be a footnote on a crime log and the teenagers' return to Hermosa would not be worth mentioning. Now, though, the condition of Isai's body made the circumstances of his death suspicious.

"Jo?" Archer gave her shoulders a squeeze. "You zoning out on us?"

"No, I'm good," she answered. "You were saying, Montoya?"

"I was just saying that the DEA checked out the story the American volunteer told Archer. The blood feud was confirmed. It's hard to imagine this kind of thing still goes on."

"Italy has vendetta," Archer pointed out. "Gangs keep scorecards. The cartels just take out two for every one of theirs. This one was pretty radical, though, given that Isai was avenging a killing that took place almost fifty years ago. What I don't get is why he didn't go after Billy when he lived overseas?"

"The feud rules are pretty specific. The male relative has to be at least nine years old. Billy's mother made the deal with Oi when Billy was eight. Arranged marriage was normal, Rosa was a beautiful young girl and there wasn't much time to get Billy out of the country. It seemed a win/win."

"So what happened? Why didn't everyone live happily ever after?" Josie curled her legs under her and leaned against Archer.

"Albania culture is steeped in a tradition where men are warriors. Oi's cross-dressing was too much for Rosa. She used her P.O. box like a safe deposit box. We found years of letters between her and her mother. It was pretty clear that the girl would rather die than live with Oi. It was also Rosa's job to protect her brother from everything. She couldn't allow him to live in Oi's house under those circumstances.

"Oi probably never expected her to raise a fuss, but when Rosa ran away he felt guilty. He had failed family and in his culture that was not acceptable. His wife has receipts from a firm he hired to find Rosa and Billy. They found them, but they couldn't force her to go back to Oi. He let her live in one of the houses he owned, but she insisted on paying rent. He found her a couple of jobs, but finally she found her own job at Undies. There wasn't much more she could do without an education."

"But how come Oi was in that house dressed up if Rosa didn't want anything to do with him?" Archer asked.

"We can only speculate, but I assume Rosa was smart enough to know she needed a lifeline. When Oi told her Gjergy was here, he probably didn't know what to do. Kat Oi told us the dressing up was a comfort thing for him. Maybe Rosa was willing to let him act out because he was the only one who stood between Billy and Gjergy. If Oi hadn't been dressed the way he was, maybe things would have been different. Maybe he would have reached his gun and been able to fend off Lumina."

"And Jac Duka?" Josie asked.

"Ah, Duka." Mike was happy to tie up loose ends for his audience. "He told a friend that he thought Oi was going to make the shop non-union. He wanted to insure himself a place in the new organization. He and Oi had a meeting scheduled to talk about the contract vote, but plan's changed when Isai and Lumina came in. All we know is that Oi told Duka to meet him at Rosa's. He had no skin in the feud but he was Albanian. He probably wouldn't have tried to stop Isai, but Lumina says that Duka got nervous when he heard what was going on upstairs. Lumina couldn't believe he'd killed Oi, and when he thought Duka was coming after him he just reacted. That left the two men downstairs dead and a woman being slaughtered upstairs. Lumina couldn't take it, so he ran to his car. He saw Billy and Trey go in and was trying to decide what to do when they came running out with Gjergy Isai on their heels." Mike shook his head. "Crazier and crazier."

"Rosa must have thought the inmates were running the asylum in this country when she saw Oi for what he really was," Josie mused. "Add to that having to be on your guard every second of every day. It's incredible she could put one foot in front of the other."

Mike nodded. "Can you imagine people in this country taking on a life and death commitment for a relative?"

"I'm not sure I could do it," Josie admitted, and then she asked the question no one had thought of. "Montoya, does Isai have family? I mean, we're thinking this is the end because Isai is dead, but what if one of that old man's relatives believes Billy killed him? Will someone else come to finish the job? Does this thing go on forever?"

"I don't know. If it happened once, maybe it could happen again."

"Then Billy's living under a death sentence," she said.

"What about family court? Do they still want him?" Archer asked.

"It's not for me to say, but there's a good chance they will if he turns up tomorrow. After he's eighteen the court won't pursue placement." Mike answered. "It's funny when you think about it. Our system is relentless when it comes making rules for minors. Then some artificial deadline is met and we wash our hands of them. It's as if they never existed."

"And halfway around the world there might be people who won't ever let Billy off the hook. He has no choice but to live under the radar. What kind of life is that?" Josie muttered.

A silence fell over the room as the three adults considered the unthinkable: Billy Zuni's young life balanced between an ancient, emotional death code and a cold, controlling, modern justice system.

At least he had Hannah with him. Archer put his arm around Josie and said the words that needed to be said; the ones everyone wanted to believe.

"Hannah and Billy will be fine. Right, Montoya?"

"I have no doubt. Those two have proven to be impressively capable." Mike buttoned his jacket. "I guess that's about it."

"What did you do with Sam Lumina?" Archer asked as they all got up.

"He's charged with two counts of second-degree murder. Carl Newton would have preferred to prosecute someone for Rosa, but he can't stretch it to her."

Archer and Josie walked him to the door, but before they got there Montoya's eyes were drawn to the painting over the fireplace.

"That's beautiful."

"It was a gift from Hannah. She painted it," Josie said.

"She's very talented."

Josie couldn't argue that. The picture had taken her breath away. She knew who the woman in the painting was the minute she lifted the sheet covering the canvas; she was a composite of Josie and Hannah. The note found on the easel was as beautiful as the painting. *Never worry. I love you. I know you love me.*

"She's an amazing person, and so is Billy," Josie murmured.

Mike cleared his throat. "I'll assume that you'll be available if my office has any more questions."

"Always," Josie assured him as she opened the door.

Mike stooped, picked up a box that had been left on the porch, and handed it to her. Josie's wedding invitations had arrived, and she held them close while the detective walked toward the gate. Josie called to him:

"Montoya? Thanks for keeping an ear out for news about Hannah."

"My pleasure. And I assume you'll let me know if you hear anything." Mike smiled. He saluted her and then added: "Oh, and congratulations on the wedding. Getting married was the best thing I ever did."

With that he was gone. The day was ending and the house was too quiet. Archer took the box and put it on the hall table. He was about to close the door when he changed his mind, grabbed Max's leash, and said to Josie:

"Come on. Let's take a walk."

She didn't need to be asked twice. Josie put her arm around Archer's waist. He wrapped his around her shoulders, careful of the bruising at her neck. Max ambled along beside them as they walked to the beach.

The rain was gone, and the sea was calm. The sun hung low on the horizon in a sling of purple, pink, and gold. Archer helped Josie over the low wall and then climbed over himself. They sat on the edge as Max rested his paws on the wall between them. Archer petted his head; Josie buried her hand in his fur. The minutes moved on. Josie cut her eyes toward Archer. He was staring straight on, thinking hard. She could feel those thoughts, and they were troubled. She had no idea how uneasy he was until he spoke.

"I don't want to get married, Jo."

Josie went cold. She was as blindsided by that statement as she had been by Gjergy Isai's attack. The only difference was that this hurt more. She didn't look at Archer; she couldn't look at him. He was not obligated to her and never had been. That didn't mean Josie wanted this to be happening.

"Okay," was the only word she could manage.

"Don't you want to know why?" he asked.

Tears came to her eyes. It was not like her to cry and it was not like her to beg. It was also not like Archer to be cruel, so she asked why knowing his answer would be reasonable. More the pity. She could debate a flawed premise.

"Look at me, Jo. Please."

Archer pushed Max down and put one big hand around the back of Josie's neck. The other one he rested on her cheek. She resisted, but finally she turned toward him. Archer's eyes roamed over her amazing face. There were tears beneath her lowered lashes; there were unspoken words on her trembling lips.

"I have to find Hannah first," he said softly. "We can't get married without a witness."

Archer kissed her brow and each of her eyes. When Josie's arms came around him, when she whispered 'thank you', and when her tears began to fall in earnest, Archer pulled her close and smiled even though no one could see.

READ ANOTHER THRILLER NOW!

KEEPING COUNSEL
USA TODAY BEST SELLER

It is the duty of an attorney to do all of the following: To maintain inviolate the confidence, and at every peril to himself or herself, to preserve the secrets of his or her client--
Business & Professional Code

Prologue

He hung his head out the window like a dog on a Sunday drive. The whipping wind roared in his ears and slicked back his long hair, baring a wide high forehead. His eyes narrowed, squinting against the force of hot air hitting his face at 75 miles an hour.

Sinister. That's how he looked. Like he could take anyone down.

Women could fall at his feet and he wouldn't give two cents even if they were naked. That's the kind of man he was. But if they were naked, he'd give 'em a grin for sure.

"Hah!" he laughed once, but it was more of a shout, just to make sure he was still alive and kickin'.

He was feeling neither here nor there. He had a woman. She didn't make him happy. Thinking about her, he stepped on the gas and the ribbon of road blurred, turning molten under his wheels. The asphalt was hot as hell; still steaming though the day had been done for hours.

Hot! Hot! Good when you're with a woman, bad when you're in the desert.

Lord, that was funny. True things were the biggest kick of all.

But damn if this wasn't the most lonesome strip of land in all New Mexico and him a lonesome cowboy ridin' it on the back of some hunkin' old steed. Cowboys were the good guys. Had a code to live by guns to carry. And cows and horses, they just needed a stick in the ribs, a kick in the rear to get 'em going. No need to talk. No questions. No answers.

Do you feel happy? Sad? What are you feeling now? Good. Good. You'll be going home soon. Do you feel anxious? You're so quiet. Do you feel? Good. Good.

He was hot like a stovetop. Hot like a pot about to boil and damn if he wasn't sitting right on the burner, all these thoughts in his head making his lid start to dance. He'd blow the top of his head right off and out would tumble all those good jokes, and lines that would make women weep. Hot damn. Make 'em weep.

He shook his head hard and wrapped one hand tighter around the steering wheel while he pushed farther out the window, head and shoulders now. The old car swerved but he got it back on track, straight on that dotted line.

He loved those dotted lines. Man perforating the world. Tear here. Send the part with him on it back for a refund.

He shook his head like the dog he was pretending to be. His lips went slack and he heard them flapping, even over the noise of the wind. What an ugly sound and he wasn't an ugly guy. So he turned into the wind and it blew his head empty. When he turned it back, the hot air ran straight at him and made his eyes tear.

Life was wonderful again. Television was a blessing. Doctors cured themselves of cancer with a thought. Smart and fancy women could be had with a smile and a wink.

Damn, life was good.

It had taken a while but he was cookin'. He was the most scrumptious thing on the menu.

"Whoeee!" he hollered, and the wind lashed that sound around and threw it right back at him as he hung his head out the window. He pulled it back inside just a snail's trail before the semi whizzed by.

He thought about that close call and making love and a cigarette all at the same time. The close call was past so he tossed aside the image of his head rolling around on the asphalt. His lady was a pain in the ass; thinking about her was idiotic. The cigarette, though, he could do something about that.

Two fingers burrowed into his shirt pocket. He was already tasting that first good drag and swore he could feel that swirly smoke deep in his lungs. But the pack was empty and crinkled under his fingers. His smile was gone. He didn't feel like hollerin' anymore.

Two hands slapped atop the steering wheel and he drove with his eyes straightforward on the lonely road. He just wanted one lousy cigarette.

But anger wasn't right. He plastered a grin on his face. The new him. New and improved. He accelerated down the four-lane, singing at the top of his lungs in a voice that he was almost sure didn't belong to him. It was too smooth.

Smooth like the turn of the wheel, the slide of the stop he made four miles down. He was still singing when he palmed the keys and unwound his long legs, and stood like a rock 'n' roll god in a pool of fluorescent light at the Circle K convenience store.

He took a minute to admire himself in the side mirror. He didn't like the way his dirty ice eyes looked, so he admired the night sky. Nothing like these black New Mexico nights. Stars as plentiful as rice at a weddin'. He tucked in his shirt so he looked really good. Handsome.

Damn, life was fine.

Whistling softly, he moved on. Pushing open the glass door, he stepped inside, surprised at how vibrant everything seemed now that he was straight. Michelle Pfeiffer looked like she could just walk right off the cover of People and give him a little hug. The Slurpee machine's neon blue and pink letters quivered as if overjoyed to be colored pink and blue.

He ambled over to the register. Little Fourth of July flags were taped all over the place: flags next to the Smokey Joe Hot Salami Sticks, flags wavin' over the stale donuts under the Plexiglas counter box, flags pokin' out of the almost-hidden condom place on the shelf behind the counter.

Hot damn! Independence Day. He almost forgot. Good day for him. He did what he liked, when he liked. There weren't nobody around to tell him anything. Only his cowboy conscience, only his roamin' man code, to keep him in line.

The smokes were neatly stacked on a metal thing above the counter. He looked for the Camels. Left, third row down. Filters one row lower than that. It was the same at every Circle K. What a mind! He could remember everything.

He wandered toward the counter, laid his hands atop it, and peered over; half expecting a pimply-faced clerk to pop up like a stupid kid's toy. Nobody. Just worn linoleum, a wad of gum stuck to it turning black. Great. He could take a pack. Just reach up and be on his way.

But he knew right from wrong. He wanted to follow the rules and felt bad when he didn't. It took a while sometimes for that feeling to happen, but it always did.

Then he saw her.

She was fixing coffee at the big urn right next to the two-for-ninety-nine-cent burgers in those shiny gold and silver wrappers behind the glass, under the red lights that never kept the damn things hot. Whooeee, he loved those burgers.

The woman was another matter. He could tell what kind of woman she was right off: fat and fussy. She was wearing a stupid little Uncle Sam hat that didn't fit. The store manager probably made her wear it, but he still hated it. She should have some pride. He hated her. She didn't even care he'd come in. She was supposed to care.

Hop to it. A little service here.

With that thought, the heat caught up with him. Just exploded his head like a potato too long in the fire. This time it wasn't funny. This time he felt sick. The lights were too bright. Too much pain inside his head. Hand out, he found the door and pushed it hard, his other hand held tight to his temple.

The heat smacked him good when he walked out of the white light and frigid air of the store and back into the desert night. He pressed his temple harder as he walked to the car and got in.

He checked himself in the rearview mirror. His hair was a mess. He'd feel better if he looked better. Get the comb. He leaned over to the glove compartment thinking his head would split wide open, and laced his hands around the first thing he found. It was cool and it was metal and he held it to his head.

No comb. He needed a comb. Maybe that damn clerk would notice the second time he walked into her store and sell him some smokes and a comb. Then he'd feel better.

He looked through the window of that Circle K again. She was still making coffee. Ignoring him. He needed a cigarette bad, he needed a comb, and now he needed some aspirin. He hurt so bad he could cry, and she was just standing there making coffee.

Inside again he turned right, and walked up to the woman who was putting the big lid on top of the huge steel urn that would brew coffee for whoever it was that might come to a godforsaken place like this in the middle of the night. He walked right up to her, and she felt him coming because she turned around. Her eyes were hazel and real clear and he saw himself in those eyes, reflected back the way people saw him.

Hot damn, he was a good lookin' cowboy.

And when he smiled at his reflection, she smiled right back. She didn't have a clue. They never did.

ABOUT THE AUTHOR

Rebecca Forster began writing on a crazy dare and now has penned 25 novels including the acclaimed Witness Series and the USA Today bestseller, *Keeping Counsel.* She holds an MBA in marketing, loves to travel, sew and play tennis. She is married to a superior court judge and is the mother of two sons.

Write Rebecca at:

http://www.rebeccaforster.com

CPSIA information can be obtained at www.ICGtesting.com
Printed in the USA
LVOW05s1712111213

364858LV00003B/223/P